Command The Moon

Kathryn Moon

 Created with Vellum

The unauthorized reproduction or distribution of a copyrighted work is illegal. Criminal copyright infringement, including infringement without monetary gain, is investigated by the FBI and is punishable by fines and federal imprisonment.
Please purchase only authorized electronic editions and do not participate in, or encourage, the electronic piracy of copyrighted materials. Your support of the author's rights is appreciated.
This book is a work of fiction. Names, characters, places, brands, and incidents are the products of the author's imagination or used fictitiously. Any resemblance to actual events, locales or persons, living or dead, is entirely coincidental.

This is a Magical Ménage Romance and is not suited for those under the age of 18.

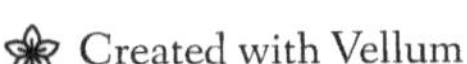 Created with Vellum

Lana. This one is thanks to you. So suck it.
Also, I love you. You are the best!

If I command the moon, it will come down; and if I wish to withhold the day, night will linger over my head; and again, if I wish to embark on the sea, I need no ship, and if I wish to fly through the air, I am free from my weight.

-Magic, Witchcraft, and Ghosts in the Greek and Roman Worlds: A Sourcebook By Daniel Ogden

Chapter 1

Gifts and Curses

October 8th 2000

"**W**hy did my mother die?" Zee asked.

She'd found Aunt Noddy in the kitchen after midnight. Or Aunt Noddy had anticipated Zee's late night visit to the kitchen. Four years into life on Swans Island and Zee had yet to know if her Aunt—Great Aunt, really—didn't sleep at all, or simply had (another) supernatural ability to tell when a young girl might need to talk. Over a plate of muffins. Which she and Aunt Noddy would surely pay for eating early by the wrath of a teenage Sam in the morning.

Zee watched her aunt's careful hands break off the top of the muffin, revealing the soft, still melty, chocolate chips inside.

"Because we are cursed, ved'mitchka," she said, 'little witch' in her old tongue, and she then added, "with a gift."

Zee's eyes stretched wide and her mouth hung open as she thought this through. "Gifts can't be curses," she said.

"Gifts are curses," Aunt Nadia said gently. "Curses

make you special, and gifts set you apart. They are cut from the same cloth."

Nadia patted the counter and waited as Zee lifted herself up to sit there, passing her a muffin.

"Believe it or not, ved'mitchka, but when I was little, Nikolaev girls were treated even worse on this island than they are now," Nadia said before taking a large bite. Her elbows rested on the counter next to where Zee sat, heel tapping against the cabinet doors.

Zee wrinkled her nose. Earlier that day she'd been chased across the playground by awful Chris Murphy and his pack of rabid classmates as they shook handfuls of stones and flicked them at the back of her ankles as she ran. She found a hiding spot behind a utility door and chanted an invisibility charm to herself. *I am small, I am quiet, I am forgotten, I am invisible.* While she hid she thought of what her aunt might have done, imagined turning around on the playground stones and stirring up a wind to blow all her terrorizers to the ground. Imagined casting them to sleep so she could have *one* afternoon of peace.

"My sisters left the island—lived lives that didn't belong to them. Normal lives. They came back, eventually, after their husbands had died and my nieces were born and grown, but it was late and they were already sick. Zoya, your mother and Samara's mother, came back too when they got sick, but it's not this house that keeps us well. It is our gift," Aunt Nadia said, waving a pale hand in front of the small candle in its holder. Flame flared to life and then died out again as her hand drew back to her muffin.

"Our curse," Zee echoed.

"You leave a gift untouched, it spoils, turns to rot," Nadia said. "And that rot will spread."

"Our mothers died because they were not witches," Zee

said. "I *have* to be a witch." The muffin turned to glue in her mouth. She thought occasionally - and only sometimes, because Aunt Nadia and her cousin, Sam, were *everything* to her, but sometimes - of *not* being a 'Nikolaev' girl. But this was out of the question. Her last name was Lane—her grandfather's name—but it didn't matter. She was Nikolaev. There was no erasing her blood.

"No, my little darling," Aunt Nadia said, smoothing her fingers through Zoya's thick coffee brown curls. "It's not about 'have to.' You *are* a witch. Your mother was a witch. Witches must make *magic.*"

June 9ᵗʰ 2017

Zee came in through the greenhouse after closing the shop that evening, canvas straps of grocery bags digging into her shoulders. She plucked a jasmine blossom off her favorite plant and cupped it to her face to sniff. Sam was in the kitchen, white blonde hair frizzing out of her ponytail as the black pot on the stove steamed in her face. She was standing on the same old brick Nadia had used. There were two traits that ran strong in the Nikolaev family, magic and a diminutive stature. Sometimes Zee thought Sam looked a little like Nadia, fair and slender. Her own resemblance had been washed away by whoever her father was, making her a shadow version of her cousin, dark hair and eyes and skin that tanned at the first blink of the sun.

Joni Mitchell was crying on the stereo. *She's gotten into tarot cards and potions, she's laying her religion on her friends.*

"I don't like this song," Zee said.

Sam startled over the stove, and Zee couldn't tell if she

was surprised to see her back from the market, or surprised to hear the music.

"The wood sorrel outside needs looked at," Zee added.

Sam wrinkled her nose. "Fussy plants. That one never liked me. Noddy was better with the wild ones."

"Like us," Zee agreed and Sam smiled.

"Did you hear the news?" They said at the same time.

Zee huffed and hefted her bags onto the counter. "Damn. I thought I got that one first."

"Maria James called."

"What? Why?"

"Some people here like me," Sam quipped, glancing at her cousin.

"What?! Why?!" Zee teased, arranging the grapefruits and lemons together into a bowl.

"I think it has to do with Cam actually," Sam said drily. Cameron Cleeves, Sam's hunky, marine meteorologist, nearly-fiancé *was* popular on the island. "I think she was calling to see if he was back. She asked if you were home too."

Zee snorted. "She probably wanted to strike the blow first. Unfortunately for her, absolutely everyone at the market took special care to tell me You-Know-Who was back in town."

Sam hummed sympathetically and then lifted a sodden sack of herbs up out of the pot. Zee took a sniff. Rosemary, Rose, Rose Geranium...power, peace, protection.

"You have a theme going there. Are you worried about us?"

"Just stocking up," Sam said. She glanced at Zee over her shoulder and Zee could feel the stare on her back. After a pause Sam added, "It'll be good for the island."

Zee snorted. "What good has Johnny Sharpe ever done for anyone?"

"People will come to see his studio, to see him work."

"Swans Island is fine," Zee said. "We have...lobsters. And, you know, scenery and hiking and stuff."

"And a locally renowned fortune teller," Sam said.

Zee bit her lip to stifle her annoyance. But it was true. While the locals might not *like* Zee and Sam, they loved referring tourists to the island witches on the cliff. And Zee made good money on those tourists. Something she would be sure to forget to thank the townie assholes for later.

"I'm sorry," Sam said after Zee's silence. "He was awful to you."

"Mrs. Humphrey wants another baby," Zee said, hoping to steer the conversation away from her old heartaches. It probably didn't even matter now. She'd dreamt of someone new the night before. Maybe fate would give her a new soulmate to break her heart. She glanced at Sam and added, "Let's have some of those carrot muffins ready."

"So she can show up tonight and you can do that thing where you have it ready at the door and just take the money, and make them think you can read their minds cause you're psychic?"

"I *am* psychic," Zee said, feigning offense. "And I don't need to read their minds. No one on this island can keep their mouth shut. I know exactly what they think of me."

Chapter 2

Sharp Edges

August 28th 2002

Two weeks before seventh grade Zee dreamt of a tall, tall boy with stinging warm hands glowing with life. She dreamt of the fall of his pale eyelashes on his cheek, the cracking hiccup of his laugh, the knuckles of his fingers all nicked and scraped and scratched red. She dreamt of him standing between her and the rest of the school, the island, bright and shining and safe. She dreamt of covering his skin in marks for protection, for care, for healing.

Nadia called these dreams *pesnya dushi* or soul songs. A melody for her heart to follow in finding the perfect match. At twelve, Zee was obsessed with love magic. She swooned over the women who came to the house, tear streaks on their cheeks and wild-eyed, begging Nadia for answers in the cards or potions. Nadia refused the latter but Zee made them little trinkets of flowers and string and shells she'd picked off the shore. Nadia said the charms were stronger than a little girl had any right to weave a spell, but were safe from working any manipulative magic, so she let the women take them home.

On the first day of school Zee saw the boy standing at the end of the hall. He was tall, tall, tall. Almost twice her height. His hands and elbows were scabbed brown and cracked. His hair was a terrible electric orange, like he'd rubbed a highlighter through the strands, color too loud for the slow changing island, too noticeable. His cheeks were streaked red as people passed him in the narrow hall, as smaller boys shoved against his side and hissed 'someone put the fire out!' and 'move, matchstick!'

Zee watched him from her little locker by the drinking fountain and felt like her whole world had turned into a kind of symphony. The girls' giggles and squeals were the woodwinds, the boys' cracks and cackles the brass section. Her heart was thrumming like a hundred violins, bows vibrating in the air together. And as he walked down the hall, every step was the drop of a mallet on a big bass drum in Zee's head until he continued right by her and into the office.

Zee found him in English. The teacher made him stand and introduce himself.

"'M Johnny Sharpe," the class snickered, "'n I'm from Philadelphia." He mumbled through the words, blue eyes staring down at the bright toes of his new sneakers.

"Go ahead and take a seat behind Zoya Nik-Lane," the teacher said.

Johnny Sharpe's eyes widened, their color turning electric and brilliant, as he walked up the aisle to the desk at Zee's back. She smiled, and her body tingled like the fireflies lighting up the yard in July as she stared back at him. The room was quiet but Zee could feel that music rushing through her blood. *This is a soul song*, she thought. *Here is my match.*

She twisted in her chair as he crumpled down into his desk, knees knocking into the frame of his seat. His face was red, clashing with the awful soda pop orange of his hair, and his gaze was startled as he looked back at her.

"Your hair looks cool," Zee said, smiling, wanting to reach out and slip her hand into his, feel the warmth she knew was radiating there like a sunburn.

He blushed darker, eyes skidding around the room as all the nearest faces watched them, waiting. "Shuddup about my hair," he hissed.

The teacher cleared his throat and Zee jumped and twisted back around, a wave of queasy unhappiness crashing around in her gut, swirling up into her chest.

"Witch," she heard him mutter.

He'd already heard. Aching fissures of pain spread through her chest. Before she could even say hello, he'd heard about her. And from *them*. The fissures filled with ice. She didn't hear another sound, not a word from her classmates or teachers, or a single note of music, until the day was almost over.

That night she thought maybe she had said the wrong thing too. She had only wanted to undo the insults from the others, wanted to show him that it wasn't the whole island who disliked strangeness and newness. But maybe he didn't want to be defended in front of the others. She would try again. Something smaller.

But a week later Johnny Sharpe joined forces with Chris Murphy and Zee's locker was full of slimy toads. She carried them out to a nice shady spot outside and told the toads, and herself, that Johnny Sharpe didn't deserve to share a soul song with her.

The dreams kept coming.

June 9th, 2017

Zee never understood why people thought their house on the cliff was haunted. Because the Nikolaev women were witches? What did that have to do with ghosts? Ghosts hung around for unfinished business, or too much stubborn resentment. Just old energy that couldn't wash out of a place. But witches took care of their shit *before* dying.

When Zee had arrived, six years old and freshly orphaned, she thought the house looked like a place out of a fairy tale, not a horror story. Traveling by boat to a little island off the coast of Maine and moving into a beautiful white house with shutters and porches and towers and a greenhouse in the back that glittered in the sun? Being surrounded by wild gardens and stone paths, flowers blooming right to the edge of the cliff over the sea? It *sounded* like something from a fairy tale. She'd stood at the edge of the white gate lined with big, black hollyhocks, stunned out of the frightened tears she'd been dripping since a social worker had explained that she'd be leaving Virginia (and her home and her school and her friends). Zee wondered if this was the part where they put her in the attic and made her do chores.

But Aunt Nadia was decidedly *not* the wicked witch of stories. She wasn't Glinda either. She was beautiful with hair that shifted in the light, from pink to gold to anger red, like Zee's mother's with added streaks of ash. She was quiet too, voice like a purr, never shouting and doubly frightening for it when she was on the hunt for misbehavior. She let Zee pick her own room and then lock herself in it to cry for a day. The next day she and Sam lured a rumpled little Zee out of the room with the promise of an actual tea party, with tiny sandwiches and mismatched dishes in the garden. Tea time was a regular affair at the house on the cliff and on the first day Sam taught Zee where to find the wild strawberries growing and how to stain her cheeks with flowers.

Now, of course, the house *was* technically haunted. But Zee didn't think Nadia would appreciate being called a ghoul or a poltergeist or anything like that. And while she did still reside in the house out of stubbornness, Zee suspected it was a stubborn love. For the house, and for Sam and herself.

Sam left after dinner to fill orders at their shop, The Lab, an organic health and beauty shop. (The storefront did good business in the busy months of the island, but the online orders came in year round and kept the pair of them comfortable and the property taxes paid.) Zee cleared away the dishes, boxed up Mrs. Humphrey's spelled muffins and then went up to Nadia's room. She knocked three times and opened the door. The spinning wheel in the corner was turning, the treadles pumping, wool tangling on the twirling flyer.

"You're making a mess," Zee said to the room.

She'll need knot magic, something simple, but it won't be an easy pregnancy, Nadia said.

Zee could see a red streak of her hair out of the corner of her eye, and smelled the same perfume Nadia had worn as long as Zee knew her, black tea and roses. She closed her eyes and Nadia grew clearer in the dark space behind her eyelids, hovering just over her shoulder, warm and curious gaze on her cheek.

"I'll spin something pink," Zee said aloud. "She's overrun with boys."

Just make it strong, Nadia said. Her voice was half

there, more rushes of air and creaks of floorboard than words but Zee had memorized every note of Nadia while growing up and her voice had clean edges and the same purring sliding speech in Zee's thoughts.

Zee just wanted a minute like this, with Nadia near, talking together about how to approach a bit of magic. If Sam had been in the room everything would have been perfect.

How do you feel? Nadia asked.

Zee's eyes blinked open.

He's coming back.

"Oh! Not you too!" She was half tempted to stomp her way out of the room.

I'm checking in.

Zee's chest twinged with old pain. This was the family pass-phrase, the secret code for Nadia to worm her way into any one of their conflicts, used most often in Sam's teen years and when Zee left for college. 'Checking in' was a promise not to interfere, but a demand for the sharing of information and feelings.

"It was a long time ago," Zee said. "He wasn't what I thought. What we thought. And it's not his return that bothers me. Just that the whole island seems excited to see him come back and...and what, torment me again? For us to politely ignore each other because we're adults now?"

Fall in love, Nadia said.

"Don't do that," Zee whispered. "Don't do that again. He's not the one, Noddy. He can't be."

She left the room with a stroke of her hand over the door frame.

The phone was ringing downstairs and she ran to answer it. Cell service was spotty by the cliff so either Sam was trying to reach her or...

"Lane?"

"Hey, Adam," Zee said into the phone.

"Lane, I got a bachelorette party of eight staying at the big house and they're drinking me out of stock. Sending em down to you." Adam Banks was sharp, efficient, but he was that way with everyone and not just the Nikolaev women, and he ran several of the most successful local businesses on the island so efficiency was probably a useful tool.

"Oh, gee. Thanks so much. I love cleaning upchucked vodka tonics out of the carpet," Zee said, rolling her eyes.

"I quoted them eighty bucks a pop."

Well, thought Zee, *that changes things*. "Tell them they can have a group rate of six-hundred."

"Aren't we generous?" Adam said and she could hear the smirk. Seventy-five was still high over her usual tourist rate of fifty and it would make sure any of the skeptics got bullied into taking a reading too.

"And tell Howie I'll have some brownies ready for him," Zee added, because if Adam sent his driver Howard with the women, they would actually make it to the house and back again in good shape.

"He better share," Adam muttered and then hung up.

Zee hurried to set up, swinging open the sunroom windows over the rose bushes so that the smell of herbs drying from the ceiling beams mixed with the wet earth and the garden in full bloom. She lit candles and set them on top of glass cupboards full of old family books, bells and ceremonial knives, energy and scrying stones, and the Nikolaev collection of tarot cards. She brought extra chairs to fill the space and centered her own wicker throne-like seat at the low table. She hesitated at the cupboard of *her* tools; tea sets used only for reading leaves, her own personal decks, scrying quartz, and a beautiful, old, hand-carved talking board with its glossy pointer, the ghosts of past fingertips worn into the polished wood.

Zee liked her decks best, but tarot cards didn't like to lie and a bachelorette party didn't want to hear about their tough decisions regarding work, or how they were emotionally stifling themselves at home. And for eighty bucks a person Zee wanted to give the women a bit of a show, if not a few dick jokes. So she laid out a table cloth embroidered with the constellations of Maine at winter, pulled out the tea set for leaves, a perfumed oil for massaging and reading palms, and her least severe deck that was based off the kama sutra. She went back to the kitchen to grab a strong black tea and some munchies - *the better to sober you up, my dear* - and the door knocker clacked in the hall.

Either Howie had sped his little shuttle bus all the way up here or business was going to be hopping tonight.

Grace Harper was standing on her front steps, little red sedan parked under the border oak at the gate. Her blond hair was tangled into a perky top knot, mascara just slightly smeared under her eyes.

"Grace. Hi. I have a party coming up to the house-" Zee said, skipping politeness and aiming straight for dismissal. She knew exactly why Grace was here at ten at night smelling like a bottle of white wine.

"That's fine, it won't take long," Grace said breezily, stuffing a small handful of bills into Zee's raised palm and pushing past her into the house, heading straight for the sunroom.

"You heard already?" Grace asked, a dark smile appearing on her face before it slipped and fell to one side.

"Sharpe is back, yeah," Zee said, hands on her hips and stalling in the doorway, hoping she could still get Grace to leave. "You must be thrilled." Would outright rudeness do the trick?

"Never shoulda married Mark in the first place," Grace said, flopping down into Zee's seat for reading fortunes. "Fucking waste of my twenties."

Wow, Zee thought. *That was a pretty big jump. High school boyfriend—of three months—is back. Good thing I got a divorce this year.*

"I guess you knew he was coming." Grace's eyes were narrowed, as if she were suspicious of Zee.

"Dreaded," Zee said and Grace just blinked.

She's still pretty, Zee thought. *Bitter, and trapped on this island in her mom's old real estate company, wondering about all the other lives she might have lead by now. But pretty.*

"I like these," Grace said flipping through the elicit illustrations of the cards Zee had set out. "Ooh did that with Johnny!"

She flashed a picture of a man getting a blow job. Was Zee meant to be impressed?

"Johnny had the best dick," Grace said, sighing.

"He shared it liberally," Zee said, grabbing a traditional deck from the cupboard. Lying to tourists to give them news they wanted to hear was part of the job, a bonus for the extra charge. Zee never lied to locals. Let them hear the good and the awful, what did she care? They kept coming back. And Grace Harper, who from the age of eleven to twenty three insulted Zee to her face and then said 'jay-kay' with that mincing little smirk? Yeah. She deserved the truth. Zee couldn't hear the letters JK without wanting to punch someone.

"Jealous you never got a taste?" Grace asked.

Zee wrinkled her nose and shuffled the deck in her

hands, a nicked and faded old set from when she'd first learned to read the cards.

"I want these," Grace said holding up the kama sutra deck.

"Those are for the tourists," Zee said still shuffling. "These are real."

This seemed to appease Grace who left the other deck —which was fine and anyway it was Zee doing the heavy lifting—on the table and settled back into the chair.

Zee cut the deck into three piles, and Grace, who'd done this a fair number of times for someone who clearly didn't even like Zee, tipped forward in the chair, her finger landing on the far right pile. Zee restacked the cards and snapped five cards onto the wood in a small arch in front of her. She turned them over one by one.

Five of Cups

The Lovers, reversed

Three of Cups, reversed

Ten of Swords

The Devil

It wasn't good news for Grace. Zee rattled off the textbook definitions of the cards like a novice, trying to keep the mood clinical. Normally she would have interpreted the contents into a clearer picture, given history and context and insight. She would have told Grace that Johnny Sharpe had never been the whirlwind romance she'd fashioned in her memory, just a young man burning energy and having his way with the world. That he hadn't thought of her much when they were together and less after they parted. That the fantasy she'd arranged around him, now more than ever, was preventing progress in her life. That Johnny Sharpe would take less notice of her in the future than he ever had in the past.

Zee felt guilty for the reading, as she always did when delivering bad news, and sorry for Grace. She knew exactly how it felt, dreaming that Johnny Sharpe was a better version of himself than the truth. She did it on a semi-regular basis, even if it was involuntary and unconsciously done. And this was something Johnny had ruined too, Zee's ability to enjoy Grace Harper's disappointment. Schaden-freude was seventy-five percent of Zee's entertainment on the island and Grace Harper had been a thorn in her side since grade school.

But now she was wilting in a wicker chair, eyes focused through the sunroom walls, scanning out over a history of romantic failures, her lips creased in a stubborn purse.

"Do you want coffee?" Zee asked, because expressing sympathy seemed impossible and also like she'd be twisting the knife.

Grace's face twisted into a snarl. "Not with you, Niko-laev," she said standing, then leaning too far to the left before recovering, her feet slapping hard against the floor boards as she stumbled away to the hall, out to the front door. Zee could hear a crunch of gravel and a low bass thumping.

"I saw the way you looked at him when we were kids," Grace snarled, leaning into the the front door of the house. "If you think you've got a fucking chance...out here. This house? Do you honestly think you're a fucking witch?"

Zee took a moment to digest the flurry of accusations in the muddled sentences.

"Do you?" she asked. It was a puzzle she'd struggled with for decades. Did the town think she was crazy? Or were they scared of her? Grace Harper didn't just come up to the house for chintzy fortunes. If she didn't think Zee was a witch, why was she here three years ago on a cloudy morning, begging for a spell to save her marriage.

Grace looked puzzled too, and maybe near to sick, so Zee nudged her aside and opened the front door. Howie had arrived and was helping escort eight tottering women in wedge heels across the stone steps in her yard.

"I was glad to see the back of Johnny Sharpe," Zee said. "That's the truth."

Grace's face was blank as she stood in the doorway, looking at the women in sundresses, the small redhead with her plastic crown and pink rhinestone *Bride* sash across her chest.

"Night, Zee," she said, like she hadn't just been stumbling through cuss words and vague insults.

You're fucking crazy...JK.

"Goodnight, Grace," Zee said. She was happy to see the back of her too.

The bachelorette party was a fun group. They cracked jokes with Zee over the cards and the tea leaves, ate three bowls of snacks, and paid extra for fresh love charms that Zee made from roses in the garden, wild grapevine, and red candlewax. Sam came home, took a shot with the bride and gave her a large phallic candle but warned her that it was meant for fertility. Howie only saved one brownie for his boss.

Zee fell into bed and dreamt of warm hands with hard callouses pressing into the soles of her feet and working away the ache of the day.

Chapter 3

Johnny, Be Good

August 16th, 2008

*T*ink. *Tink.*
     Tink.
     TAP.

Zee blinked up at the ceiling of the sunroom, flooded with moonlight and listened.

Tink. Tink.

It was coming from outside and above, little knocks against the side of the house where her room was.

She left her cards at the table and swung the large bay window of the sunroom out to see Johnny Sharpe standing in a patch of thyme in front of her, arm pulled back and a stone that was certainly much larger than the ones tapping at her window had been in his hand.

"What the fuck are you doing?"

"Jesus! Lane. Scared the crap outta me." His cheeks were dark and there were wet strands of dark blonde hair falling into his eyes. His t-shirt was wet too, like he'd just climbed out of the ocean and up the cliff to her house.

"Why the hell are you in my yard, Sharpe? Get out of here."

"Why the hell weren't you at the docks tonight Lane?" he snarled back, stomping into the rose bush below the window, a sour stench on his breath.

"Why would I be at the docks?"

"Cause we all were! Jesus. Why do you think?'

"We? We as in our class? Classmates who hate me? Who I hate?"

"We don't fucking hate you," Johnny scoffed. "I mean, you don't show up to the party, which is pretty shitty, Lane, I gotta say, but nobody hates you."

"Go home, Johnny. You're drunk," Zee said, trying to shut the window but only bumping it into his shoulder.

"No, wait, I gotta tell you something."

Zee huffed and waited, trying not to notice the warmth billowing off of him and the way his blue eyes glowed in the moonlight, studying her.

Johnny blinked and his head dropped to one side. "Didju say you hated me? You hate me? Never wanted you to hate me, Lane. Just didn't wanna love you."

Zee felt as if, very suddenly, she'd just broken in half. As if there had been a seam holding her together and now it had unraveled and she was falling apart in two separate directions. Her throat was sealed shut and her chest was burning and she could not take a breath.

"You succeeded," she said but Johnny's head was somewhere else, he was staring at her in her cotton night dress, staring at the hem at her knees, and he didn't hear the words.

"Get the fuck out of my yard, Sharpe," Zee said, louder. "Don't ever come back. Get out and go home before I scream for Nadia."

Johnny's face knotted in frustration. "Jesus, Lane, come on-"

"Get the hell away from me. I will fucking curse you!"

She would curse him to forever wonder about love and never feel it. A perfect and fair revenge.

He looked startled and stumbled back, heels sliding in the pebble path behind him. It was the first - the only - time Zee ever used witchcraft as a threat and she couldn't decide if she felt any satisfaction in his fear. She couldn't decide if she felt anything at all.

June 10th, 2017

Zee thought she'd have more time. A small, hopeful part of her wondered if it would be possible to live her life on the island without ever running into him. If they had to, they could work out a schedule. Zee would stay out of town in her free time if he'd stay away while she was working at The Lab.

But instead he showed up the next morning, with the jangle of a string of bells over the door and a flash of sun bouncing off a passing car that hit Zee directly in the eye while she was stocking the shelves with the fruit of Sam's nocturnal labors.

"Can I help you?" Zee asked, wincing at the glare.

"Zee Lane," he said, the exact pitch and resonance of his voice so familiar from so many years of dreams.

He sounded surprised and Zee nearly dropped the jar she was holding to the floor.

"Oh. It's you." She turned back the shelf, adding as an afterthought, "Welcome back."

"Thanks! It's good to be back," the words were rushed and automatic and he sounded winded. Outside, on the street, the traffic was turning into an orchestra. The fan overhead was humming in shifting tones.

Zee put the last new jar in its place and went looking for the burn salve. She took care not to turn to the door. She'd seen a glimpse of wiry muscles under a threadbare T-shirt, and tan knees peeking out of ripped jeans. It was enough. Johnny Sharpe was here and Sam hadn't got out of bed yet and she couldn't just walk out of the shop. A cluster of gulls settled on a roof across the street and started singing.

"I didn't know you worked here," he said, still hovering at the door. "Everyone said you were up at the house...you know."

"Being a witch?" Zee supplied. She grabbed a jar of burn salve. "Sam is a genius but she can't organize for shit." She heard him laugh but refused to look. In her dreams the corners of his eyes crinkled when he smiled now.

"Here." She passed him at the door, dropping the salve into his hands where they'd been shifting over his narrow hips, folding together, twitching through his sun-bleached hair. He caught the jar, just barely.

"Oh. Oh! Hey, thanks. The stuff I have barely works."

"This will," Zee said, sliding onto her stool behind the counter. She pulled out the accounts like now was a good time to worry about numbers. She wished the music in her head would stop.

"I don't doubt Sam. Or you!" he added in a rush. "I don't doubt either of you."

Zee swallowed and looked up. Her heart thumped in time and his eyes stretched wide, gaze skittering around the room. He had a sunburn over his nose and cheeks and it made his eyes look almost chlorine blue. His hair was lighter than before and his face was wider and stronger, and the lines of his shoulders inside the wide v-neck of his shirt were sharp and tanned. She looked back to the book on the counter and the numbers looked like a foreign language.

"Sam's not here," Zee said after a pause. An e-brake on a delivery truck trilled from the road. "If that's why you came."

"Uh, um no. Well kinda," he said. He reached to scratch his head again, and bumped the jar against his forehead. "Shit. Um. I came to, to ask Sam about you."

"About me?"

"Yeah. To see if you'd maybe like coffee. To get coffee. With me?"

"You wanted to ask Sam if I would like to get coffee with you?" Zee said. Her voice was flat, even, and she was afraid to make any sound at all. That it might be a scream or laughter or tears.

"Look." He set the jar on the counter and wrapped his hands around the edge of the counter, bracing himself and making Zee look up again. "I know... I know I was an asshole to you in high school."

"And middle school." The words fell out of her mouth.

"Yeah," he said grimacing. "Definitely then too. And I just... I came to ask Sam if she thought you might... Let me apologize?"

"Apologize?"

"Lane-Zee. I'm sorry, really sorry, for... for all of it. That's not the end of the apology, I swear," he said as she opened her mouth to speak. "It's more than that. And you deserve an explanation, I guess, no, I mean you do. I was crap, and I know it. I knew it."

"And you want to apologize?"

"I *want* to erase what I said and what I did. I know that I can't but I wish that it...that it wasn't a part of...of how we, you know, talk and...interact and stuff. From now on. So.

So...can I- could I buy you a coffee and we could maybe talk?"

Zee felt like she was under water. Everything but Johnny Sharpe was blurry, out of focus. All the sounds and music hushed except for his voice, deep and strangely fragile. Was it his nerves or was he usually this soft spoken? She learned as a teenager not to compare the Johnny from the dreams to the Johnny in real life. But this felt...dangerously close.

"I just would like to start over," he said, every word slow, eyes some wild blue and caught so strongly to hers she felt snared in a trap.

"No." She whispered it, and for a moment nothing changed, not the earnest, hopeful look in Johnny's eyes, or the way he leaned towards her across the counter.

Then the little word sunk in.

He swallowed and she watched his adam's apple bob in his throat. Then he blinked a few times and pushed away from the counter, turning his side to her and staring down at the floor. He nodded his head once, then again after a pause. His mouth twisted and Zee's stomach turned.

"Right," he said, soft and catching. "Right. Yeah."

Zee had the urge to apologize, explain, protest. This wasn't fair. Johnny Sharpe couldn't just pop in after more than ten years with an apology on his tongue and a look in his eyes that she'd yearned for as a teenage girl and just erase the names he'd called her and the bruises he'd left on her heart.

One short, coughing laugh escaped his throat and he ran a hand over his face. "Sorry," he said, half-smiling and barely glancing at her. "Yeah. That's fair. I'll...I'll go-"

"Not coffee." Zee bit the inside of her lip and Johnny froze in place. His eyes crept to her face and she stared out the window over his shoulder. There was a mother and daughter, a summer family who loved Sam and her organic face wash, walking up the steps.

"The whole island would be listening in," Zee said and Johnny grinned, so bright and white. "Just come up to the house sometime."

"Yeah? Really? When's good?" He asked, still grinning, beaming, blinding and warm and obnoxiously handsome.

"Whenever," Zee rushed, pushing the burn salve back across the counter to him. "Just take it. That's about to get infected." She nodded at the jagged blister on his right wrist and slipped out from behind the counter before he could try to pay. She didn't know why she just knew she didn't want his money. And the burn was nasty.

"Hannah, Laura, it's good to see you," Zee said, smiling at the women as the bells rang over the door.

"Thanks," Johnny said. Zee almost jumped when he tapped the base of her back with his hand as he passed her to the door, hand scorching through her linen blouse and callouses snagging at the fabric. "See you soon?"

Zee nodded without looking back at him, pretending to focus on her customers.

June 11ᵗʰ, 2017

Once again, Johnny arrived earlier than Zee (*hoped*) expected. He was walking up the garden path while she was trimming the lavender the next morning. He was looking up at the house when she realized he was there. It was Sunday and it wasn't even lunch yet and he just...came. Twenty-four hours later. She'd come out to the garden to process their conversation and then... here he was.

"Hey," he paused on the path when he caught sight of

her. He was staring, really looking at her, and in old jean cut-offs and an oversized button-down shirt she felt thoroughly exposed by his stare.

"I don't know if I'm ready to forgive you," she said.

He walked to her and settled down to the ground next to her and Zee hated every shift and stretch of it It wasn't right that he was so beautiful, how could one person be so perfectly arranged?

"I'm not asking that," he said. "I'm sorry for yesterday, I just- I'd sort of planned the order out in my head. Of feeling things out through Sam and then, I don't know, bumping into you. But you were just...there. And a lot came out at once."

Who is this person? She wondered. So familiar, but not Johnny Sharpe. Not the teenage boy who'd made a point of stepping on her like an ant so often.

"Okay, so, forgiveness aside," Zee said. "What's the apology for?"

Was he in a program, making amends?

He was plucking at the grass, nervy, and she watched the cords of muscle in his arms working, his scarred fingertips running through the green blades, combing lines. Then she nudged his hands with her toes and when he looked up, caught and guilty like a little boy, she shook her head.

"Leave our yard in peace, Sharpe."

He smiled and scrunched his shoulders up. "Sorry. I, um, the apology. The apology is for..." His fingers twitched and she narrowed her eyes at him. "You gave me a lot of openings," he said finally. "While we were in school. You were nice, even after I was a jerk to you. And I shut you out. I knew I was being a shithead, but..."

"But you were thirteen and new to the island and I was

the weird kid," Zee said for him, shrugging. "If you'd let me in, everyone else would have shut you out."

She went back to work on the lavender while he watched her. His gaze felt like a hand resting on her shoulder.

"That's... A lot of it," he said. She nodded and shifted to put a bundle of flowers into her basket just as he leaned forward to pick a stem out. Their hands brushed and Zee shrunk away like he'd burned her. He had. He was so warm, the feeling more vivid and striking than it had been in dreams.

"Do you want to know the rest?" he asked.

She glanced at him out of the corner of her eye. "Do you want to tell me?" she hedged, snipping at stems with a focus better suited to casting spells than gathering herbs.

"Maybe not yet," he said after a long silence. "I'd still like to get coffee," he added.

Zee cringed without thinking but Johnny just laughed.

"Seriously? Is it me or is it coffee?" he asked.

She rolled her eyes and looked back at him. "Not that much has changed. I'm still the weird kid."

His smile eased and he stretched forward, elbows on knees. She could see the map of scratches and shiny burns on his arms, a singed eyebrow. God, he was a mess. Wasn't he supposed to be *skilled* at glass blowing? Shouldn't that have included a modicum of safety?

"I'm not worried about what the island thinks," he said with just an edge of cockiness. He didn't have to worry now. He was golden. He'd been golden for a long time.

How did she explain to him what it was to be accepted, but not loved. Useful without being appreciated.

"How about I make the coffee?" he said after Zee had spent too long being quiet in response. "You could come to the studio—it's practically finished. I'll make you something since I never paid for that salve. Which, look, tell Sam it's amazing." He showed her the burn on his wrist, the blister had smoothed away and the skin was shiny and white, healing quickly. Still, she wanted to take him into the house and coat him head to toe in the spelled salves they kept in stock, and then an oil for protection for good measure.

"Coffee is fine," Zee said. "I'd like to see the studio."

"You'll come?"

It seemed too easy to make him happy. Yes, she would talk to him. Yes, she would drink coffee with him. She nodded and he looked lighter. He leaned back on his hands and Zee wanted to wrap her hand around his forearm, run her thumb up the sinew of muscle that popped with the stretch.

"I keep expecting Nadia to come out and give me the evil eye," he said looking up at the house, then back to her. "I'm sorry. I heard you moved back when she got sick."

Zee nodded. "She wasn't sick. She just...faded Did you know how old she was?" she asked, feeling a grin creep up her cheeks. Nadia was surely listening, watching from the house, and she would hate for Zee to share the secret.

Johnny pursed his lips, a dimple appearing in his cheek and then guessed. "Sixty-five?"

"Eighty-eight," Zee said and a bell rang angrily in the house.

She laughed at the blank expression on Johnny's face. "No way," he said. "No...she looked- she looked like late fifties, max, while we were in high school! Or a sixty year old who looked forty."

"She was actually my great aunt," Zee explained. "The oldest of the three sisters."

"I don't believe you," he said grinning and shaking his head.

"I have the birth certificate," she said. "I mean, its in Russian, but-"

He laughed and she lost her voice watching him.

"Zee." the greenhouse doors swung open and Sam appeared. "There's a storm coming...Oh. Hello," she said to Johnny, blinking. "Um...it can wait. Well, no, it's a storm. On its way. But we could-"

"It's alright, I'll be right in" Zee said nodding, pretending that sitting in the garden with Johnny wasn't a remarkable thing, hoping Sam wouldn't comment.

Sam hesitated, glancing between the pair of them before nodding and slipping back inside. Johnny sat up and wiped his hands on his jeans, drawing his knees up to his chest.

"I guess that's me leaving," he said.

Zee tried to smile and nod, but she felt a little shaky all over so she just wobbled her way into standing and he followed her up.

"You're coming to the studio though? For coffee."

"Yes," she said. She studied his smile, the way he bounced on his toes, seemed to waver toward her and then back on his heels again.

She smiled back and turned to leave.

"Zee," he said. She paused and wished she could put a screen or a wall up between them, something to break the weight of his stare. "Thanks. For not shutting me out."

She bit her lip, trying to find something honest to say without throwing everything out between them. But her thoughts were tangled and her heart was pounding and Sam was waiting to walk the island wards with her, so she settled on a small smile and another nod.

When Zee came in Sam waited long enough for them to both watch Johnny leaving.

"He's ready," Sam said.

"Please don't," said Zee.

Sam had a sharp edge in her face, the same one that appeared when she was fixing an old recipe to be stronger, or more specific. But it slid into something sympathetic after a moment.

"Alright," she said. "Get your tools."

They walked around the edge of the island, on a hike Nadia and her parents had laid out and she had shared with her great nieces, resetting sigils for safety and peace, checking their warding charms. The storms rolled in and they wove their way under tree cover until they got closer to town. The wind was hard and the rain was heavy, but it was warm out and everyone was tucked away in their houses watching television, so Zee actually enjoyed the soggy walk through town. There were a couple broken charms near the docks, but that was common. There was a lot of traffic here in the summer and not all of it could be innocent tourists. Zee swept up the remains into her bag. She'd replace them later in the week.

It was dinner time when they crossed their gates again, and the storm had moved out over the ocean. Sam stopped in the yard, walking to the cliff to watch the purple clouds swell and flash. A clap of thunder rolled its way to shore.

"Cam's alright," Zee called.

Sam nodded, her back to Zee, a dark sliver of a silhouette against the storm.

It wasn't words of comfort, or not just that. It was a promise, a certainty, Zee had given to Sam after she'd fallen in love with Cameron and he'd left for a year long study of marine weather patterns and tropical storms. For Sam she'd dove into a five day meditation, wiping herself out of visions and dreams and tarot readings for almost a month after. But she was sure. Cameron would always make it home to Sam. They had a long life together.

This was a shorter trip to the arctic, but equally dangerous and while Zee knew Sam believed her, she still watched storms—ones Cameron couldn't possibly be in the midst of—with a wariness like they were a wild animal that might strike out any moment.

A car pulled up to the oak. Zee sighed as Abby Becker, in a bright yellow rain slicker, hopped out of an old Jeep. She was one of the summer flock and another of Johnny's old flings.

This isn't going to end soon, she thought. She knew of at least five more of his exes on the island currently and there would probably be more before the fall. And cards out or not she knew not one of them was going to be happy with her answers.

"He's going to be bad for business," Sam said appearing behind her.

Abby, who had actually always been decent to Zee, smiled and waved.

"I'm mostly worried about me," Zee admitted. If Sam was right about Johnny, she was going to become pretty unpopular. Grace Harper...Zee didn't even want to imagine what she'd say.

"I'll make cocktails," Sam said.

"I'll swing the axe," Zee said, walking up to meet Abby on the steps.

Chapter 4

Fragile Things

August 5th, 2006

Zee watched from the docks as Gabe Andrews, her first summer fling, first kiss, first decent groping in the woods at sunset, turned into a narrow little line of black on the back of the ferry to the mainland. She didn't expect him to wave—his parents were with him and anyway he was a bit of a mall goth. And it wasn't heartbreak to see him go, exactly. His hands were cold and dry and he'd once made her watch him practice dancing with glow sticks for more than a half hour. But he was the first person who'd wanted to spend time with her *for* being a witch. And even if his hands were a little scratchy, his lips *were not* and if she let him play with her breasts over her clothes she totally forgot about the chapped drawbacks in favor of slow, lazy, stirring kisses that went on until she thought her mouth might be bruised.

And he'd liked her. Thought she was cool. Let her talk about spells with a dopey fascination on his face. There was something a little glossy and over done about it all. And she suspected that she would be more of a story to tell his friends than a girl he missed. But being a good story was better than being the girl others crossed the street to avoid, like a black cat on halloween.

"Lane!"

Speak of the devil. Zee tensed as Johnny Sharpe joined her at the dock railing, a plastic grocery bag in one hand. He turned his back to the water and set his elbows on the top bar, leaning into her space and tilting his head to try and force her gaze.

"Your boyfriend was a loser," he said, loud and matter of fact. "You should probably just be glad he's on his way home."

Zee sighed and came back from her mental vacation to the real world.

"He wasn't my boyfriend."

"Well there's the good news!" Johnny said, patting her once, hard, on the shoulder. "Even you shouldn't have to sink so low."

"How's your neck healing up?" Zee asked, taking a step farther from him.

She and Gabe had accidentally run into Johnny and a summer girl rolling around in the grass out by the old one-room school house and they'd surprised the girl so much she'd bit down while she'd been sucking a hickey on Johnny's throat.

"I think it looks pretty cool, actually," Johnny said, tilting his head to the side to show Zee the old bruise, sharp little teeth marks curving into an irritated oval.

Zee laughed despite herself and Johnny grinned and for a moment she wondered, *Is this real? Is this how it might feel?*

Johnny's smile froze and then his face tightened and the expression was forced away.

"Guess it's good the summer brings *someone* willing to talk to you," he said.

Even Zee knew the insult was half-hearted, his attempt at repairing their status quo. So she replied, "And how lucky for you that it brings a fresh selection of low standards for you to sample from."

He snorted, and that ease flickered between them again. Was it so difficult to hate each other? It felt like work to Zee. But she didn't want to be Johnny Sharpe's door mat to walk over so she fought back. Blow for blow. Insult for insult. Until some days she felt like a target that'd been shot to crumbs.

Johnny started fishing in his grocery bag and Zee moved to leave and walk back up to the house on the cliff.

"Hang on," he said, and then he pulled out two Fudgesicles, water condensing on the plastic wrappers. "Here."

She stared at his hand, the treat pointed at her face. "Why?" she asked.

"Because they're melting," he snapped, waving it and nearly hitting her on the nose. "And your little weirdo boy toy is gone and I'm being nice. So just take it."

Zee pinched the wrapper between her thumb and index finger. "Is that the textbook definition of nice?"

"It's as nice as you're likely to get until next summer," Johnny grumbled and then pushed off the railing and marched away from her.

Zee stared at the treat in her hand until she saw a small dribble of chocolate start to melt down the edge. She threw the plastic wrapper in the dock bin and started home, taking long licks and trying not to feel grateful.

June 15th, 2017

Johnny's exes drifted to the house like stray cats after fresh food, trickling in one by one until Zee came home Wednesday evening to find three of them on her porch, looking extremely unhappy to see each other. Sam left the Lab early to help run interference with a pan of brownies and two bottles of red wine. But one after the other his old flames left the house looking more irritated than Zee'd found them.

On Thursday she took a day of rest, leaving Sam to handle the shop while she putzed around the house, tinkering with charms, spinning some wool for Mrs. Humphrey's knot magic, and painting her toenails a light periwinkle blue. The phone rang and Zee's stomach sank even as her heart beat a quick, tell-tale beat. It was Johnny.

"Come to the studio," he said after she answered.

"I will," she said, the 'eventually' clear in the silence.

"No, I mean today. Sam said you're home and I'm just up the road now."

She knew that. He'd bought a parcel of land that'd gone up for sale the year before. She and Sam had been hoping to save enough before it sold. Now it had the unusual looking building Johnny had designed and a small gravel parking lot.

"You haven't been up here yet," he said.

"I didn't realize you meant this week," she said. *Liar.*

"I think I meant, you know, like Monday," he said and then he laughed, abbreviated and a little nervous.

"I was kind of planning a lazy day," she said slowly.

Ten years of no Johnny and now a week entirely full of him, or at least the mention of him. She was drowning.

"I'm not going to make you paint my walls, Zee," he

said. He huffed a little and she wrinkled her nose. Pushy. Too impatient. "My guys are off today," he said, softer now. "So, if you can make it here later, we won't have an audience or anything."

She hummed a little. "Okay, I'll ... I'll see."

He was quiet and then, "Yeah. Okay. I've got to use up some of this first batch so I'll be here. 'Til late probably."

"Okay." She nodded and then thumped her head lightly on the cupboard by the phone.

"Okay."

Zee hung up and moaned into the counter top.

He's waiting for you this time.

"Please don't make this sound easy," Zee whispered against the wood. A soft feeling against her hair, against her back, warmth on her cheek.

Not easy, Nadia said, *but safe. You were always going to land in the same place.*

"Then why did before feel like a crash?" Zee asked.

There was no answer.

Her toenails weren't dry yet so she went to work, pedicure sponges in place, on pounding some sourdough waiting on the counter into submission. Johnny Sharpe could be useful for this—well-kneaded bread. He had been in high school and he would be again. The dough had to rest and Zee decided that the kitchen needed cleaned. And the halls needed swept. And then she invented a few more chores to fill the time, as if she had a checklist that needed completing before allowing herself to leave the house. She chopped dark chocolate and pitted sweet cherries and folded them into the dough before putting it in the oven. She busied herself with cleaning windows and watering the plants in the greenhouse that Sam had given her permission to touch. Maybe, if she dawdled long enough, the day would vanish and she would have missed Johnny entirely.

But at four the house was shockingly spotless and the bread was cool enough to travel, so she packed a basket and walked to Johnny's studio. The building was large and tall, shaped like an old barn but with enormous glass windows on every side and skylights that raised into vents on the steepled roof. It was a clean, bright gray and the garage style rolling door was raised up. Johnny had music playing, some up-beat rock with a guy singing, asking someone not to walk all over him.

He was seated at a bench, his back to her with two fans pointed at him, fluttering the sweat stained blue t-shirt he had on. He had a red bandana twisted up and tied around his head, enormous black sunglasses, and a pair of what looked like old knee socks covering his forearms with burn holes speckling the ribbing. He rolled a long dark pipe on the arms of the bench with a large, red-hot globe of molten glass twirling at the end. He was keeping it centered, adjusting the speed of rotation to balance the soft weight of flexible glass. He stretched, leaning over the side of the bench and lifted a wooden paddle out of a bucket of water, pressing it gently to the glass, water spitting and steam billowing up. The pressure stretched the glass, turning the globe into a longer, smoother vessel.

Zee hung back at the open doors. Johnny had a smooth, almost stern, expression on his face as he worked. It was the first time in a decade that she was getting a chance to just *look* at him, without him focusing on her in return. He was beautiful in a way that made her skin itch to press against his. She'd had *too many* dreams full of textures, sounds, smells of him, but in person the foggy edges of a dream firmed into something unbearably tangible. His hair was sticking up around the edges of the bandana and she wanted to twirl her fingers in the cowlick at the crown of his head, dig her thumbs into the knot of muscle at the base of his neck. She wanted to slide behind him on the bench, straddle her thighs outside of his, and press her chest to his back, put her nose to his spine and take deep breaths of him. He stood and she nearly stumbled back from the door.

This was an unfamiliar creature, she reminded herself. Not the dream and not the bully. Someone new.

He was walking up to a pair of rectangular doors with a basketball-sized opening of heat and fire between them, spinning the hot glass toward the floor in one hand and reaching for a plastic heat shield on wheels with the other, when he caught sight of her in the reflective shine. The pipe slipped to the floor with a crack and a clatter.

"Oh, shit- shit!"

"Ohmigod, I am *so* sorry," Zee hissed, running forward, dropping her basket to the floor.

The glass was turning from orange to red and darker on the floor and Zee wasn't sure exactly what to do, only that this was her fault.

"No, no, wait!" He darted forward, stopping her with a hand on her side, fingers squeezing at her hip for a moment, their chests bumping into one another with breathy 'oofs'. There was another, higher, ominous crack from the floor and Johnny let her go, grabbing the near end of the pipe and running it over to a bucket by the hot mouths of the furnaces. He dropped the glass into the bucket. There was a hiss of steam and then a terrible, slow shattering, little spits of glass popping out of the metal lip and hitting the floor.

"I'm so sorry, I'm so sorry," Zee said, hands over her face.

Johnny wiped his forehead with the sock covered arm,

and flipped up his sunglasses onto his head as he turned back to her. A quarter sized chunk of glass skidded in Zee's direction.

"I'm so sorry," she said again, at a whisper.

His smile was crooked. "It's fine, it wasn't important."

"It looked so nice. I should have said hello when I came in," she rambled.

His eyebrows ticked up. "When did you come in?"

Oops. "Umm...before the wood thing?"

His cheek dimpled and he tucked his hands into his back pockets.

"I would have just ended up smashing it up then," he said. He went to the bench and grabbed a remote, turning down the music overhead. "You surprised me. I gave up on you."

He was looking at her knees where the hem of her skirt hit and she wished she'd worn pants. Or just a tent. Something more like a disguise. She went to back to the door where the basket was laying on its side, the bread still safely wrapped in a towel. She tried not to feel an ache at what he'd just said.

"So what did I destroy?" she asked.

"'S nothing. I was just dicking around. This company sent me a new kind of batch to test so I'm working through it. But I usually just make my own so I kinda want to get back to that. You brought a basket."

"I made bread," she said. "What's a 'batch'?"

"It's the base glass that goes in the glory hole," he pointed to the middle opening against the wall. He walked up until they were barely a foot apart, curling his back to arch over her, and flicked at the towel in the basket. "What kind of bread?"

He was wearing a little smile and Zee had a terrible

urge to press her fingertips to the corners of it and draw him down for a kiss. Her body felt heavy and hyper-aware under his stare. So she blinked and walked around his side, moving over to a small table by a kitchenette on the far end of the room. She was used to being the smallest person in a conversation and having to crane her neck to make eye-contact. She *wasn't* used to feeling dainty. But Johnny's shoulders were broad and his hands were large and she had the strangest sensation of being breakable or delicate standing next to him.

"Sourdough with chocolate and cherries," Zee said. She put the basket on the table and looked over her shoulder. He was watching from the door and he looked *hungry* but she wasn't clueless enough to think it was for bread. "Did you really just call something a glory hole?"

The predator's stare faded away with a boyish giggle. "Uh, yeah. It still makes me laugh, too. But it's where I gather clear glass to blow or add color to. I said I'd make you something."

"You don't have to."

"You brought me bread. Really strange and delicious sounding bread. And I never stopped for lunch so I'm gonna eat a lot of it and you should probably let me make you something in return."

Zee bit her lip trying to think of something he could make that wouldn't take long, or much effort. Something meaningless, something small and quick that she could set aside and forget about. Like a paperweight or...

"A flower," she said and then winced. She'd gone on a date at a fancy restaurant in Providence during college and the table next to hers had received a small glass flower with a long stem for the woman's birthday. She'd wanted one but it'd only been a first date and she hadn't wanted to ask.

Still, they were small, with simple lines. It couldn't take much.

"A flower," he repeated. He wrinkled his nose.

Johnny Sharpe, glass blowing ingenue, probably hadn't needed to make a chintzy little flower since college.

"Or a paperweight," she suggested, trying to see what other face she could draw out.

He narrowed his eyes at her and she tried not to smile.

"You'll stay and talk to me while I work?" he asked. "Till it's finished."

"Sure."

"Alright," he said. "I'll make you a flower. There's fresh coffee in that pot, as promised. And I've got bread knives in the drawer to the left."

"You want a slice?"

"Definitely. I'm gonna set up what I need."

Zee found mugs - one with a little figurine raising a blow pipe that said 'I do all my own stunts' and another that said in large block letters 'Glassblowing Diva' - and the bread knife. She checked over her shoulder to see Johnny setting pieces of brightly colored glass down with tongs, onto a machine topped with a slab of metal.

"What's that?"

"I'm putting your flower petals on the warmer."

"Johnny...you know I meant a little flower, right?"

He blinked at her, all innocent and open, and then slid his sunglasses back down to his nose.

"Yeah, I know," he said.

* * *

You're stupid, Zee thought to herself over an hour later. Johnny had her captive, so to speak, for the rest of the day.

40

And whatever he was making, it wasn't a little flower. It was a massive globe, about the size of a basketball, that Johnny had transferred from one pipe to another where he'd prepped a little blob of molten glass into a foot for the piece while Zee had sat, panicking at the bench and rolling the pipe he'd started with. He'd admitted about halfway through that whatever this was, it was usually a two person job. But he'd coached her through it, and then fixed what she'd messed up.

He'd been opening the small mouth at the end of the globe for about fifteen minutes, alternating heating it in the glory hole with taking it back to the bench to roll and pry the lip open with a pair of special tongs. And the whole time he'd kept a steady conversation moving between them. He asked about college, talked about leaving Swans Island with no intention of coming back and slowly realizing everything he missed about the place. He asked her about her ex-boyfriend, the last one she'd had right before leaving for college, and then about recent boyfriends. When she turned the tables to ask him about all the broken hearts he'd left in Pittsburgh, he blushed and blew her mind a little.

"I slowed down a lot after high school," he said and then he turned to face the kiln as he added. "Had a great boyfriend for a couple years."

Well, Johnny Sharpe wouldn't have been her first guess from their graduating class for who would end up experimenting during college, but alright.

He asked about tarot cards, about Nadia and Sam, about how she ran the little side business out of the house.

"I usually know when someone's coming out," she explained. "Either because of town gossip or intuition, but there's a decent chunk of people who will call ahead."

"How much of the island do you see?" Johnny asked.

He was twisting the pipe in his hand, outlined by the wavy heat from glory hole. There was a heat shield covering half of him, but he kept nudging it to the side so he could get a better grip.

As he hefted the pipe and came back to the bench Zee was hovering behind, she felt she was getting a very clear picture of why Johnny's arms looked so deliciously muscled. He'd been carrying around the weight of the pipe and the glass for over an hour and if he'd broken a sweat it probably had more to do with the three fires in front of them. And she knew from handling the piece that what he made look light and easy to manage, was actually heavy enough to tip out of her hands if she wasn't careful.

"Umm, I have a handful of regulars that I see once a month or so," she said. "And then another couple dozen that I might see once or twice a year. But in the last five years I've probably seen...ninety percent of the island."

Johnny stood and turned back to stare at her. "Seriously?"

She nodded. "Major life events, people like to check in. Get advice or help."

Johnny walked back to the fire. "Your aunt, she helped my mom, back in high school. When she got the diagnosis."

Zee remembered. She'd been working at the old stove when Mary Sharpe had come to the door. Nadia called Sam down to consult, and the three of them worked every spare minute for a month, meditating, mixing, and working hard magics. Zee skipped a day of school to visit Mrs. Sharpe at her home and trace health sigils over every wall. Mary was a single mother, who'd moved to the island with her two children to get away from a nasty ex. It was something that was never mentioned but everyone knew anyways, and even if she'd only come to the house on the cliff the one time, she always treated the Nikolaev family with respect.

"I always meant to say thank you to Nadia," he added.

"You didn't need to. It was the only kind of work she really loved doing," she said.

Johnny was focused on the glass now and Zee watched as it turned softer, growing wide and open, loosening at the end of the pipe.

"So this part goes pretty fast," he said over his shoulder. "Go wait for me by the annealer. When I say, I'll just have you swing the door open, but stay behind it because it's crazy hot in there."

Zee moved over to the big metal cabinet that looked like an old metal fridge. It had six compartments on it, four latched shut with red magnetic squares and two waiting to be filled with green magnets on the front. Johnny checked on her with a glance and then pulled the glass out of the heat, lifting it straight into the air, spinning the pipe in his hands. She stared as the rounded bowl spun and fluttered, perfectly balanced, until it was flat like a pancake. Johnny took two quick steps, looking up at the glass, and then jumped up onto his bench. The pipe twirled down to the floor and the flat plate of glass wrinkled and rippled along the edge. He shifted it back and forth, up into the air, down the floor, until the fluted edge of the bowl cooled and firmed.

She waited by the annealer oven, watching in thrilled surprise as Johnny broke the foot of the piece off the pipe and into his waiting, mittened hand.

"Okay, open!"

She hid behind the door and even then the blast of heat slid over her skirt and down her legs, around the edges of the metal to lick at her arms. It was almost scalding, like jumping into a steamy bath after playing in the snow. His mittened hand appeared and pulled the door shut for her, latching it and then flipping the magnet. Johnny was there, the edges of his face sparkling with sweat, cheeks dimpled.

"Done."

"That was not a flower," Zee said.

"It's a *glass* flower," he said. "So it's subjective."

"I didn't really get to see it."

"It'll look better after its cooled and the colors aren't distorted by heat." He shuffled in step for a moment, before pulling off the mittens and moving them over to the fans. "I could bring it over tomorrow," he said, slipping his sunglasses into the 'v' of his tee and rubbing at the bandana on his forehead to wipe away some of the sweat.

"Oh," she said, a little disappointed to have to wait.

"We could go get dinner together," he added, and then his gaze fixed to her face and she felt herself freeze, like a rabbit readying to bolt.

"Dinner?"

"Yeah." He wiped his hands on his jeans and Zee caught a glimpse of the skin looking too red. The pipe must have gotten hot by the end of the work. "Flowers are sort of customary before dates anyway, so..."

"A date?"

Sentences, Zee. Sentences, not questions, she thought.

"Dinner." He nodded. "Dinner date."

"Is this...part of the apology thing?" she asked.

He scratched at his head and his hair stuck up in place after. "The apology was more of a necessary precursor. I mean- no, shit. The apology was important. And it stands. Very sincerely. But um...a date was also...also something I hoped you'd accept." His shoulders were up around his ears and he was shifting his hands again- pockets, neck, folded arms, pockets again. She wanted to take them in her own and start working salve into his palms, but hers were trembling against the skirt of her dress so she tucked them deeper into the folds.

"I have appointments tomorrow night," she said, because she couldn't seem to focus on the general request, only the specific part. Tomorrow was too soon when she was still standing here with him today.

"Saturday?" he said quickly, looking wary.

He expected to be refused, it was clear. He was leaning back, like he was shying away from a coming blow, eyes wincing as he watched her. She knew that feeling, had been standing on the other end of this exchange years ago. There was a bitter little part of her that wanted to refuse him, wanted some satisfaction for old slights, and she was exhausted to find that in herself.

"Can it be next Friday?" she asked.

He blinked. "Yeah. Next Friday?" He stood straighter, face smoothing back into that golden boy smile she wanted shield herself from, or wanted to bask in, she wasn't sure. "I'm free in the week, if that's better."

"Friday," Zee said, firmly. "I'm...I'm a little overwhelmed, Johnny."

He took a hard breath and she felt his surprise like a punch to her own gut. "Right," he said softly, sobering. "Okay. So, Friday, low-key dinner."

She smiled at that and his face wrestled with a grin.

"It's...it's a date," she said, and she had turn away from the bright beaming of his smile.

* * *

Zee finished up with a summer visitor who was deciding between a promotion at work and starting her own business, and then joined Sam on her balcony. She curled up in the love seat and let Sam twist and elbow her way into her hold, until her cousin was laying half on top of Zee staring up at the sky.

"What are we looking at tonight?" Zee asked, combing her fingers through Sam's soft hair.

"Saturn is in perfect opposition," Sam said, raising an arm and pointing up into the sky.

Zee tried to follow but she'd always been terrible at this part. Sam was practically a telescope and Zee could recall her following the patterns of stars and planets in the sky when they were still both in grade school. Sam had memorized the shifts of universe and the effects on their own world the way Zee had taken to the tarot cards.

"What's that mean?" Zee whispered and she could see straight down the line of Sam's nose to watch her smile grow.

"Upheaval in our love lives," Sam said, smirking. "Commitments. Rejections."

Zee stiffened. She hadn't told Sam about agreeing to Johnny's date or the new face that popped up in her dreams. It was hardly as if either of those were commitments, though.

"You're teasing me," Zee said.

"Yeah, but it's true," Sam answered.

Zee sighed and settled her cheek on the top of Sam's head.

"Johnny's different now," Sam said and she sounded as surprised as Zee felt.

"I know that," Zee said.

"You'll give him time?"

"If he gives me some in return."

Sam wrapped her hands over Zee's on her stomach and squeezed.

"Good, I think you'll need him."

Zee blinked. "Will you tell me what's wrong? You know something."

"No, not really. But there's a puzzle putting itself together and I just...haven't identified all the pieces yet."

"Okay. So not what. When?"

"August, the solar eclipse, I think. Something in August."

August. It was a lot of time to set up guards, lay down protections. Plenty of time for the pair of them. So why was Sam worried?

"We can be ready," Sam said, answering Zee's thoughts.

Chapter 5

Love Spells

December 10th, 2006

Zee found her aunt in the greenhouse. She settled on the top step into the kitchen and leaned into the door frame to watch Nadia trim and coax and praise the plants around her.

"What do you need, ved'mitchka?" Nadia asked, only after Zee was sure that her aunt was unaware of her presence.

"What is this?" Zee held out the journal in her hands, raising it to the open page and turning it, as if Nadia could read the scribbles from across the room.

"Read it to me."

"It's a super grody spell about pouring booze through dirty panties and then serving it with a smile," Zee paraphrased, grimacing at the words.

"Ah," said Nadia.

"It's a love spell?"

"Yes."

"A manipulative one."

"Very."

"My mom *used* it," Zee bit out, trying to force Nadia to meet her gaze. Which was never going to happen. Nadia could drill holes with her stare but Zee mostly gave herself a headache.

"I know, darling," Nadia said.

"You said she didn't use magic."

"Not doing your laundry doesn't take much magic," Nadia mused.

Zee huffed and Nadia set the watering can down on the table, appearing from behind a curtain of spanish moss.

"She came to me...too long after. I helped her undo the spell," Nadia said. "It wasn't very strong and I don't know where she found it."

"She probably googled it," Zee scoffed but Nadia only shrugged.

Zee shrank back against the doorway as Nadia watched her. She flicked the journal shut and set it on the step.

"Ask, Zoya," Nadia said gently.

"Was it my father?"

"Yes," Nadia said.

Zee blinked and took a deep breath. "That's why he didn't stay."

"Spelled love is very uncomfortable, it gives no room to the bearer. Your mother claimed she only needed to draw him in. When she became pregnant she realized that he would be jealous of you. Of her love for you. She thought he would stay. That something real had grown under the lie."

"The charms I make...do they-?"

"No," Nadia answered, swift and soft, joining Zee on the step and drawing her into her arms. "Your charms are the loveliest, neatest, most open-hearted little creations I have ever seen another witch work. They are simple and strong, but they are gentle and they do not force shapes from the world, only draw out the best that can be offered."

Zee hid her blush against Nadia's sweater.

"Your mother would have been very talented too," Nadia said, pressing a kiss into Zee's hair. "I'm sorry my sisters were so afraid of their own lives and made their daughters feel that way too. But I am very thankful for you and Sam."

"Sam and I are pretty lucky too," Zee said easily. "Other people may have cool aunts but they probably don't take them spirit walking on halloween."

Nadia sniffed. "It's the only way to celebrate properly."

Zee wasn't sure that communing with the dead really sounded like 'celebrating' to most people, but she kept that to herself and joined Nadia in harvesting the best of the mint leaves.

June 21st 2017

"Stop twitching," Sam said, as Zee bumped into her while she was picking out crates of strawberries at the farmers market.

"Grace Harper is glaring at me," Zee whispered in her cousin's ear.

Sam flashed a glance over her shoulder before turning back to the strawberries. "Grace Harper is glaring at the price of kale. Calm down."

"I feel like I'm wearing a sign that says 'This idiot agreed to dinner with Johnny Sharpe,'" Zee hissed. She flicked at the strawberries and Sam batted her away.

"Don't put your nervous energy on those, I'm making tarts for that wedding shower," Sam said. "The bride doesn't need your weird vibes giving her cold feet."

"Save the leaves for Mrs. Humphrey," Zee said.

Sam 'hm'd and added, "Don't you think if you were wearing a sign everyone would be doing a lot more than staring?"

"So you admit there's staring happening?"

"Well, the local witch is acting super shifty at the farmer's market, so yeah, Zee, there's probably staring happening. Would you please go get some squash for dinner?"

"Remind me how sympathetic you were about this the next time you need a favor, Sam."

June 22ⁿᵈ 2017

"What should I wear tomorrow?" Zee asked as Sam passed her a cup of coffee over the kitchen island.

"Whatever you decide to put on in the morning," Sam said with shrug. "That's my usual policy."

"I meant the date."

"So did I."

They stared at each other over the lips of coffee mugs for a minute.

"He said it was going to be low-key, right?" Sam asked.

"Sure, but there's low-key and then there's date low-key," Zee said.

Sam took a long, loud, slurp of her coffee. "*Is* there?" Zee thunked her head against the countertop and Sam smirked down at her cousin's tangles, one lock of hair dangling on the mouth of her mug, about to be dipped in. "You seem excited about this."

"I'm anxious, it's not the same thing," Zee said into the wood.

"But you want it to go well," Sam said, with a graceful

sweep of her mug. It was a shame Zee was face down because it was a well-executed gesture of smugness.

"Well, yeah. I want *my* part in it to go well. Ideally, I would like Johnny to crash and burn tomorrow evening so I can go home feeling superior."

"Ah, Got it. In that case you should probably wear a low-key dress."

Zee lifted her head, her hair falling back into place, and hummed as she drank. Sam got up from the table and went looking for her cell phone as subtly as possible so she could text Cameron an update. After getting the long version of the Zee and Johnny history he was firmly team 'Zee tells Johnny to take a hike.'

June 23rd 2017

Zee was trying to be objective about the evening. As objective as possible when it came to her thoughts on Johnny Sharpe. In theory it was a good date. Johnny had checked off the necessary first date boxes with a diligence that made her wonder if he hadn't talked it over with his sister Sarah beforehand.

1. He'd shown up to her house on time, dressed neatly. She'd especially appreciated the rolled up shirt-sleeves because apparently her interest in his forearms was a full-on *thing* now.

2. He was holding the glass flower bowl he'd made her and it was full of floating carnation blooms in pinks and oranges. An odd number too, and Zee could almost feel Nadia's satisfaction filling up the house. Even numbers were unlucky.

3. He'd given her a choice between driving down to town and walking—she'd chosen 'spending extra time with

Johnny Sharpe' over 'a small enclosed space full of Johnny Sharpe'—and the conversation had been easy. He talked about two of the guys he hired to work on the studio and how they'd ended up dating and now spent fifty percent of their time flirting. He asked about Cameron.

"I hear he's either wet-your-pants terrifying or super 'dreamy'" He'd made air quotes.

"He's a teddy bear," Zee said, adding, "But he doesn't let anyone give Sam any crap."

"Fair," Johnny said, smiling at her.

So she told him about when Cameron had shown up at the house because he thought his boat was haunted—it wasn't, he just had a stowaway tomcat eating the fish and making weird noises—and he and Sam had stared at each other for a solid couple of minutes before either one bothered speaking. She didn't tell him about the pesnya dushi, or how Sam had been so determined to dislike Cameron because of Zee's own experiences.

When they'd arrived at the diner, a 'low-key' and wonderfully greasy old shack of an airstream trailer that sat parked in the same lot for over thirty years with picnic tables for outdoor seating, Zee actually felt like she was having a good time.

"Sharpe, shit yeah!"

Until Chris Murphy rose up from a picnic table and walked over to slap Johnny on the back.

"Jesus, man, where've you been? Trying to get ahold of you for...Oh, fuck. Hey, Nikolaev. What're you...guys up to?" Then he'd turned to Johnny and raised his eyebrows, high up onto his forehead.

And Johnny'd been trying, he really had. After shaking off Chris with a promise of beers another night he'd led Zee into the trailer to look for a small table inside. But they ordered lobster po'boys and then ran directly into Tom and Helen Zhang with their perfect little munchkin Maddie on Helen's hip.

"Johnny, man!" Tom had stiffened, halfway through that partial hug, back-thumping thing guys seemed to prefer when he'd caught sight of Zee behind Johnny's back.

"Nikolaev," he said, blinking.

"Zee, hi, how are you?" Helen said, eyebrows heading up, up, up.

Zee appreciated Tom and Helen. The Zhang's were basically model citizens. Always polite, both lawyers, and genuinely respectful. Also, neither one had ever come up to the house for any special requests. They were a happy couple and they had their shit together. But even *they* couldn't disguise the confusion on seeing Johnny and Zee together at the diner. Tom kept looking from her to Johnny with this expectant openness like he was waiting for the punchline to the joke. Zee grabbed a table and tried not to listen in on the quick conversation.

"Okay," Johnny said, after making it to the table. Helen smiled, sort of bemused, at Zee from the door and then walked out, Maddie jumping down the steps beside her. "I guess I see what you meant about coffee."

Zee laughed but she didn't really feel *happy* to be proven right.

"We can go," he said.

But then two women from a couple grades below Zee and Johnny in school stopped by the table to say 'hi'. To Johnny. They mostly ignored Zee until the end and then made a joke of their rudeness with some awkward laughter. Johnny's cheeks started to stain red by the time the women left and his hands were shifting, fidgeting. He looked at Zee, opened his mouth, and the sandwiches they ordered landed on the table between them.

This isn't his fault, Zee thought. But they sat quiet across the table from each other while they started eating.

She's been on worse dates. Definitely more awkward ones. She once met a man for dinner only to discover that he'd double booked his evening and the three of them had sat through an entire meal together. (She hadn't bothered seeing the man again but she still exchanged texts, mostly memes, with the other woman.)

"Look, this isn't-" Johnny started just as Zee said, "Tell me about your favorite work of art."

He paused mid-phrase, hunched over in the seat across from hers. The bell on the trailer door rang and Zee looked down so she didn't have to recognize whoever might be coming in.

"Really?" he asked.

She nodded and took a bite of her sandwich.

"I...I don't know if I have *one*. That's like - that's like, 'what's your favorite song?'" He wrinkled his nose.

"I Put A Spell On You," Zee said. Johnny jumped in his chair, eyes growing huge. "By Screamin' Jay Hawkins," she explained and smirked as he shook off the startled expression on his face. "But I like the version from Hocus Pocus best."

"You're fucking with me," Johnny muttered at his sandwich.

"It's a good song," she defended. "But okay, just give me a ballpark of your artistic preferences."

Johnny chewed, swallowed, and then took off on a tangent about light, color and perspective in the artist Olafur Eliasson's body of work.

* * *

Zee took a long breath as they stepped off the last square of sidewalk onto the quiet road. She could breathe easier outside of town. The mood in the diner had improved, and only one other old buddy of Johnny's had swung by the table to say 'hey' and then gawk at the pair of them. But walking with Johnny became an infinitely more pleasant experience when she wasn't checking house windows to see if the locals were peering out at them.

"Sorry that was…kind of a bust," Johnny said eventually.

The edges of town were falling dark behind them and a little shadow skittered across the asphalt ahead of them, over into the thick cover of trees and brush along the edge of the road.

"It went better than I expected," Zee said.

Johnny huffed and twisted to stare at her but she kept her gaze forward and pursed her lips to hide her smirk.

He cleared his throat and laughter fell out. "Thanks for the vote of confidence, Lane."

"You're the only one who ever calls me that," Zee said, folding her arms around her. It was getting colder now that it was dark and she could feel Johnny's bubble of heat just a foot or so away. Close enough to sense the warmth but too far to soak it up.

"Yeah." Johnny kicked a bit of rubble off into the gravel. "The Nikolaev thing. Does it bother you?"

"It used to," Zee said. "When I was little and I wanted to keep my mom close to me in some way. But now I like the idea of my family honoring its matriarchal line. And acknowledging Nadia's work in raising me. *Not* that that's why the locals use it."

"You're a landmark," Johnny said, and it was just next to sympathetic. Enough to let Zee know that he didn't agree with the island's notion.

"Yep," she said, popping the 'p.' "But I guess that's a certain breed of respect."

He was quiet at her side and she realized that they had slowed down after making it out of town. These loose, dragging steps were probably closer to a stroll than a walk. And for a moment she thought she could just stop in place and stand in the quiet, empty road at night with Johnny Sharpe for as long as she wanted. That this was a peaceful, easy place to be in the world.

"I have something to tell you," he said.

"Ohhh...kay?"

"It goes with the apology."

The Apology. It kept growing in Zee's head, taking on a life of its own and she wondered what came next after it was finished. What was the next act after an apology that spanned weeks?

"Alright," Zee said.

"It's...it's kind of a long thing," Johnny said. "And I am kind of a lot embarrassed about it so...So will you listen and then when I'm done, we maybe don't have to talk about it?"

Zee watched his hands moving, cuffing around his forearms, dipping into his pockets and coming back empty. She was glad he had a tell for his nerves, something for her to read off him.

"I reserve the right to ask one question, if I want it," she said.

His head snapped to face hers and she couldn't decipher his expression other than that it seemed pleased.

"Fine," he growled without any real bite.

They walked, or strolled, or ambled, in silence for

endless minutes. Zee tucked her hands into her dress pockets to resist the urge to reach out to him. It was as if she could see the shapes of the words he wanted to speak vibrating in the air around him, waves of nervous energy.

"I thought you put a love spell on me," he said.

Zee took two steps after he spoke and then stopped as the words sank in. He kept walking, his shoulders inching up to his ears.

"It was...almost right away. As soon as I saw you," he continued and Zee was forced to move or not hear his soft speech.

She opened her mouth to speak. Was he talking about this summer? Or...years ago? But Johnny glanced back over his shoulder, out of the corner of his eye, and she remembered that she'd promised to listen. She jogged to keep pace at his shoulder.

"Chris or one of those guys had probably suggested the idea when they mentioned you," Johnny said.

Watch out for Zoya Lane. She's a Nikolaev witch and she'll probably try and put a love spell on you. Yes, she could see them saying that about her.

"You were nice to me, after everyone else had been little assholes," he said drily. "And you looked like...like some kind of pixie. So *of course* I had an immediate crush on you."

Zee's blood chilled at the evenness of the words, the lack of confusion or struggle. Like it had been inevitable for him to feel this way. A way she'd been so *painfully* unaware of until this moment.

"And I was embarrassed and a thirteen year-old shithead so...I blamed you for it. Told myself you *made* me like you. And it just didn't stop," he whispered. "All through high-school. Kept trying to prove to myself that I didn't- that I was in charge of my own feelings."

Zee felt like someone had plugged her in, she felt charged with high voltage, buzzing and ready to snap. She wasn't sure if the emotion was relief or happiness or a deep and electric rage only that she had never felt so much of something at once and all she could do was step, step, step next to Johnny Sharpe on a dark road at night.

"In college, near the end when I was *less* of an ass I had a friend who was a witch—you'd like her. Eventually I asked her about you. And she pointed out that, well, one—a love spell like that is a shady thing to do and Nadia wouldn't have let anyone get away with it, and two—if you had put one on me I wouldn't have spent six years fighting and questioning it."

She tried swallowing, but couldn't. She was pretty sure she was still breathing. She was, at least, still walking.

"I wanted to apologize then, but it seemed like it was a few years late and... getting ahold of you to say 'hey, that boy that was such an ass to you growing up? Yeah, it was cause he *liked* you,' is a pretty shitty excuse."

Zee nodded at that and the bob of her head felt distant, like she was puppeteering herself from afar.

"But when I knew that I was moving back, and that you were still here...it felt like it might be the right time." There was a long silence and then he asked, "Still want that question?"

Zee could see the light of the house farther up ahead. Sam had left the fairy lights on that lined the gate. She felt like she was dragging her feet across the pocked asphalt, like she might need to just stop here in the middle of the road for the rest of the night to process what he had told her.

Johnny had spent years-

He had felt-

All that time she'd spent thinking the pesnya dushi was-

She couldn't stand it. If all her experiences surrounding her connection with Johnny were turned inside out what was left was everything she'd spent over a decade drawing out of her heart like a poison.

"Not yet," she said.

"I'm sorry, Zee," he said. "It's probably more selfishness saying anything now. I just wanted a chance to be honest with you. And myself."

"I'm not the same girl," she said. "That was a long time ago."

He smiled down at the road. "Yeah I was kind of hoping you'd notice I've changed too," he said, flashing her a grin. He added, "Anyway, you still remind me of a pixie. And seeing you still feels like magic."

That hurt. It hurt in her chest and her head and at the tips of her fingers and deep in her gut, a pain that resonated out of her center to run like an earthquake through her bones and a sharp electrocution through her skin.

"Johnny." It was half-apology and half-exasperation.

They'd made it to the gate and Johnny's car was under the border oak. Zee wanted to push him inside of it and beg him to drive away. But she was fairly certain that if she laid a hand on him she'd end up holding on.

"Let me walk you to your door," he said, unlatching the gate for them and walking inside before she could refuse.

Pushy. She was strangely, distantly, grateful for the character flaw in this new version of Johnny. Something to cling to, even when that persistence seemed to be what found its way through the cracks of shock that spread through her.

She followed him in and startled as his fingers hooked

around hers, not quite holding her to him but chaining radiant links of heat through their hands. With every step closer to the house his hand edged closer to hers until she could feel the raised edge of a scar brush against her palm.

"Does 'better than expected' mean that you had a nice time?" he asked.

Just a few more feet to the front steps and the night would be over and she could breathe again. Could make herself a bath and fall apart in it and try to untangle the nest of emotions clotted up in her chest. She walked up the stairs ahead of him, their hands hovering between them. He was on the stones behind her, face so transparently hopeful that she wanted to cover her eyes.

'Nice' was a very short word for the evening she'd just survived.

"Yes," she said. *It was awful.*

He beamed and followed her up one step. "Can we do this again?" He watched her struggle. Her face was shifting and even she couldn't name the expressions. It was like her brain and her body and her heart were all living in separate moments. "I won't even ask for it to be tomorrow. And the what and where are totally up to you."

She released a long breath and nodded. "Alright."

He grinned and released her hand and then he was standing on the step below her, and it left him just a few inches taller than her and his face close and happy and warm. His hands were on her hips and her whole body seemed to turn to stone, unable to move.

"Zee..."

The tip of his nose brushed against hers and her name out of his mouth was some cue for permission and her eyes were stinging and her chest was burning. She sucked in a breath, thought of pulling away, and only ended up leaning into him, marveling at the span of his hands on her sides and the bright smell of him.

"I swear to God, Johnny, if this is some kind of long-game laugh for you. If I'm one of *them*," Zee whispered, as his nose dragged against hers.

His fingers twitched at her waist and his breath exhaled sharply across the skin of her neck, goosebumps breaking out in its wake. They froze under the lamplight, glancing warily at each other out of the corner of their eyes. As she watched his eyes shutter and the softness in his face sharpen, she wished for small moment that she had some kind of time magic, or a way to erase Johnny's memory of her words. When his lips finally landed it was high on her cheek, resting there for a long second, spreading heat across her face. Or maybe that was embarrassment.

She wondered what would happen if she shifted, lifted to her toes, and set her mouth against his. But he was pulling away and the chilly night air was flooding in around her, waking her out of the dreamy haze of his proximity.

"Not laughing," he said lightly, but his smile was brittle and directed down to the ground. "G'night, Zee."

She meant to answer but the words never found their way out.

Chapter 6

Gentlemen Callers

February 8th, 2007

"See you later, Noddy, I'm off," Zee called from the front door. She was on the front step, w_thout an answer, when a bruise green stain spread out across her vision. A great, heavy rock dropped from her stomach down to her knees she wobbled and leaned against the door frame, sucking in a breath.

"Noddy? Nadia!" she called. She dropped her backpack on the porch and stumbled back inside swinging open doors with sharp bangs until she found Nadia in the sitting room, kneeling on the floor with her hands braced on the frame of the fireplace.

Another wave of *awful* washed over Zee, like cobwebs dragging over her skin and dust coating the inside of her mouth and cement running through her brain and-

"Ground yourself, Zoya," Nadia growled from the other end of the room.

Zee dropped to the floor, pressing her face into the smooth, cool finish of the floorboards. The whiff cf vinegar

and lemon cleared away some of the dense black in her thoughts.

"What *is* this?"

"Someone is trying to break in," Nadia whispered.

"To the house?" She hadn't seen anything in the yard. Hadn't felt anything when she'd stepped outside. They had so many wards, so many warnings, what could sneak up on them?

"To *me*."

Zee took another deep, long, breath. A psychic attack. Sam and Zee had made a joke of them as kids, starting staring contests with each other and then claiming they were practicing mental defenses when Nadia tried to interrupt them. And then, one day, Sam hadn't found the idea funny any more. And now neither did Zee.

"Come here, ved'mitchka," Nadia coaxed softly, and Zee rolled her face against the floor to look across the room. Nadia was grimacing, face white, but her hand was held out to Zee. She flicked her fingers and Zee crawled across the floor to her aunt. "I will take the pressure off," Nadia said. "But you will need to gather things for me. Follow my instructions."

Zee nodded, and then peeking up at Nadia's grave, worried gaze, added, "Anything to miss school."

Nadia sighed and scowled, but the corners of her lips twitched. "Black tourmaline and carnelian. Sprigs of rowan —branches, even. Red ribbons."

"I can make a charm," Zee said as Nadia paused to take a breath.

"Yes, darling, nothing works better than your charms. Black salt. Saint John's Wort. Sulfur. You remember?"

Zee rattled off the list.

"Good. Call Sam, warn her. Make sure she gets the message before we finish today."

"Yes, Noddy. Who is it? Who's doing this?"

Nadia blinked slowly and Zee felt a wretched, slithering, coldness run down her spine.

"Someone is always looking for a Nikolaev woman," Nadia said, eyes creased with tension. "Are you ready?"

"Ready," Zee said.

Nadia gritted her teeth, pulling hard on Zee's hand. Zee shouted, high and aching, and reared back as something thorny and sharp snagged inside of her, catching in her chest, down her arms, out her eyes, until she dropped Nadia's hand and lay flattened on the floor gasping. She whimpered once and then Nadia's hand thumped hard against the frame of the fireplace.

"Go," her aunt ordered and Zee scuttled up off the floor and ran out the room to hunt down ingredients.

June 25th 2017

On Sunday Zee woke before dawn after dreaming of the other man.

The one who wasn't Johnny.

This one was still too tall for her, but his touch was cool and his hair was dark and when he whispered in her ear she felt drowsy. Drowsy in a dream. He didn't stand at a distance, but surrounded her, smelling like the deepest part of the woods. His arms banded around her, wiry and as strong as steel.

"Moon bloom," he said against her skin, and she shivered.

Zee sat up with a start, heart pounding and skin running hot and cold from the man's touch in her dream.

Could it have been only a dream? Just a figment man touching her in her sleep. But this wasn't the first time she'd seen him in her sleep. He was significant. Another pesnya dushi?

"Noddy?" She called, holding her breath, wishing for her aunt to appear in the room, to make sense of the turmoil in her chest.

Was it possible to have *two* pesnya dushi? Or did this mean that she and Johnny were well and truly never meant to be together? Nadia never came, always liking to leave the largest puzzles for her nieces to work out on their own.

Zee threw back the covers and tiptoed down the stairs to work her anxieties out on a loaf of bread for breakfast. Sam appeared when the sky had bloomed into wild tangerine and rosy hues. Far too early for the average Sam, she must have felt Zee's unease soaking into the pores of the house. She made a pot of hot water that Zee had to recycle back through the coffee maker, that time with the grounds included, and sat to write half-formed notes while Zee chopped vegetables for a frittata.

"Do the dreams stop?" Zee asked. Maybe the date had been enough for the pesnya dushi. Maybe she and Johnny were moving in the right direction and for once a dream was just a dream.

They never talked much about Sam and Cameron's connection. Sam didn't want to upset Zee and, to be honest, Zee hadn't wanted to know what life *could* be any more than the visions she suffered through at night.

"For the most part," Sam said. "Sometimes I get a little glimpse, a head's up or a warning or...just a little comfort. But it's not like it was...before."

Before Cameron arrived at the house and fell in love with Sam on the spot.

September 17ᵗʰ, 2015

Zee was half waiting for the visitor, rocking in the chair on the front porch, the King of Cups sitting face up in her lap. It had been a persistent card for weeks, popping up uninvited in readings, appearing wedged between cushions as if forgotten there.

She wasn't fooled.

Someone was coming. Someone important.

Sam was sleeping in, or trying to sleep. Zee had heard her haunting the house at night for weeks. When she quizzed her on it Sam only said "problem solving" as if Zee was meant to believe that she were dreaming up new potions. As if she didn't know her cousin's, her *sister's*, habits. A potion problem happened in the kitchen. A problem that left Sam crossing the halls at night, wandering out to cliff to stare at the sea? That was a heart problem. And at night? Zee knew. Sam was having the dreams. Her pesnya dushi was coming.

And with a card like the King of Cups Zee decided she could be happy for them.

When he arrived, in all his huge and beautiful glory, Zee understood.

Cameron Johnson walked up the road and stood at the gate, a broad shouldered giant with a mane of curling reddened black and brown skin shining. He looked like a cross between a lumberjack and an artist and Zee's first thought was that he was probably three times Sam's size altogether.

"Um, I'm looking for the Nikolaev sisters?" he called, standing at the gate, waiting for his invitation in.

"They're dead," Zee answered, pleased to get to use that joke again.

The man's head cocked, reminding her of a puppy. "Does the island know that?" he asked.

She laughed and waved him in, the gate wards releasing. Behind her, in the house, she could hear Sam's light steps creaking on the floorboards.

"Zee? Who is it?" Sam asked, the door creaking open.

Zee sat, wobbling in the rocking chair and watched them catch their first glimpse of one another. The man, stopped in his tracks, halfway to the house. Sam, on the porch, looking like the world was falling out from under her feet.

"I won't love him," Sam whispered, lips barely moving.

Zee's heart broke, a little for Sam and a lot for herself. "Yes. You will."

June 25th 2017

Zee spent the day fretting, flipping over one card after the other. *Strength. Ace of Cups. The Lovers.*

She didn't really like reading her own tarot. She prefered stubborn denial in the face of change.

Sam sent her out of the house so that she could get work done, so Zee fretted at the tea table outside. She picked a daisy and plucked its petals, feeling guilty all while keeping track of the number. Even or odd? Is he or isn't he? She didn't remember which phrase came first, making the daisy is a moot point. Johnny Sharpe might not be her *pesnya dushi* any more. He might not come back. She could live with that. She was less certain about the dark haired man with iron tight arms and the kissing voice.

But she was left grateful when a man arrived at the gate. (Even if she was half hoping the car pulling up to the house was a different make and model.) Until he stepped out, tall and wiry with a dark sweep of hair smoothed back. He looked a little like an insurance salesman, polite and cold. Nothing like the simmering feeling he'd left her with in the dream, but Zee knew it was him.

"You must be Samara," he said, voice smooth and lilting.

Zee looked him over once more. He was dressed for an office instead of for - well Zee had always felt Sunday was for pajamas but maybe that was just her. Was he different? Did she *want* him? Was the world singing? It was—a quieter, tentative tune of whispers in grass and birds far off.

"Zoya," she said. "I'm the fortune teller, she's the herbalist and she doesn't work from home so you'll have to wait till the shop opens tomorrow if you need to see her."

He blinked and looked over to the white house before turning back to give her a smile that didn't reach anywhere but his mouth. "My mistake, I must have confused the names. I came for a reading," he said, eyeing the deck on the tea table.

"Sixty dollars," she said, because pesnya dushi or not— and she really didn't want to decide—he *was* a tourist.

He'd already had his wallet out and she saw him smirk and slip a crisp fifty dollar bill back into its place before pulling out three sharp-edged twenties. She took them from his hand and ran her thumb across them, but there didn't seem to be any deceit woven in. He felt like a witch, like a big giant secret, but without an ounce of magic on his skin.

"Do we sit here?" he asked, gesturing to the tea table. "Or can we step inside? I'm not really dressed for summer."

Zee gathered up her cards - this deck was for *her* only, anyway - and led him to the house.

"It's very beautiful," he said, and his tone was shifting, growing more polite as if he'd picked up on her dislike. "Your family built it?"

"Wow, the locals really talk a lot, huh?" she asked.

"I ask a lot of questions," he said, grimacing in what would have been a charmingly apologetic expression if it weren't for the fact that she could tell the whole thing was one perfectly packaged lie.

Either she was so burnt to the pesnya dushi that she couldn't see him clearly, or that dream the night before had been a different kind of trap.

Nadia was a glimmer of red and black in the hall leading to the kitchen. *Keep Sam preoccupied,* Zee thought.

"What kind of wood is this?" the man asked, stroking the toe of his shoe along one smooth floorboard.

"Cherry," Zee said.

"But the beams are...oak?" he asked, as if it were a guess, pointing up at the ceiling.

"Yeah it's a bit of a mish-mash," Zee said. Cherry for grounding. Oak for protection and power. "Are you a real estate agent?"

He laughed and cleared his throat. "No. No, sorry. Just nosy and a lover of late victorian architecture."

"What was your name?"

"Ah, right. Lucas Wolfe." He shifted to hold out his hand to her but Zee turned to the door before he finished so she could pretend not to have noticed. "Luke."

"Well, Lucas, here we are." She swept her arm into the sunroom for him to walk ahead of her. "Take a seat and I'll get organized."

He prowled around the room and Zee pretended not to watch him cataloguing the items in the cases as she put her personal deck away and grabbed the standard. He was sitting, face a smooth, innocent mask on his face, when she finished.

Definitely a witch. Disguising himself—poorly—as a tourist. She wished she hadn't let him in the house.

"Who taught you how to read the cards?" Lucas asked, leaning across the table to her as she shuffled. "Or is it something that comes from instinct?"

He was smirking as if she should find the thought funny when in fact she *had* picked up Nadia's deck without asking and started reading the cards aloud to herself like a story.

"I taught myself," she said. Because Nadia was special and he hadn't earned the right to know her. She placed the three stacks of cards down on the table between them and stared at him.

He was handsome and he had vivid green eyes that stared back at, giving away more than he probably meant. Laughter, and an edginess that reminded her of drug addicts, and the faintest wince of pain.

"Pick one," she said and watched the corner of his wide mouth twitch. He tapped the deck on his left. Contrariness. Hardly anyone picked the left stack.

The cards hated him. They spewed gibberish, laying out contradictory messages side by side until ending in a chaotic clash of swords and wands, trouble and conflict one after the other. Zee hadn't seen anything like it since Nadia had thrown up psychic blocks as a test. Which meant that Lucas Wolfe, or whoever he was, was here for reasons other than a tarot reading. And that eerily blank facade he wore, coated in normalcy and blandness, was there to keep Zee from noticing any strains of power.

Better to get him out of the house sooner than go digging for answers, she decided.

"You're in over your head," Zee said, ignoring the cards spread between them and meeting his eyes again. "You've been manipulated and abused and the person at fault isn't going to be there when things fall apart. You'll end up drowning in the mess. You should start planning your escape route now."

There was a flinch, and an accusatory stare at the cards, and when he looked up again his face wasn't bland at all but lined with tension and anger.

"That's what those cards say?" he asked.

No, she thought. That's what I say. "Yes," she said."

He leaned over them, his face reflecting up from the glass table, and taped on the seven of swords. Then he rose up from the chair.

"It was a pleasure meeting you, Zoya." His tongue wrapped around her name, recalling the feel of it on her skin from her dream, and Lucas Wolfe left the room.

Chapter 7

Turn Around

June 27th 2017

After another night, dreaming of Luke Wolfe holding her close, fingers skimming her skin and voice crooning in her ear, Johnny returned to her dreams.

It couldn't be simple. Not one man to dream of and not want to crave, but two.

It was their first serious fight. As a couple.

She was angry with him for springing last minute travel plans on her, always expecting her to leave the shop and house to Sam so she could go to the city gallery parties with him. He turned the argument around to her reluctance to make any progress in their relationship, putting off moving in together and make plans farther out than a month or two. The small, mincing accusations grew longer and more specific, calling out words spoken, excuses made And Zee brought up their past. And Johnny brought up her secrets - the pesnya dushi that took too long to come to light.

And then he left the house.

(The scalding ache in her chest at his departure stretched out of the dream and Zee caught herself rubbing at the spot for the rest of the day.)

But the dream didn't release her after one fight. She lived through an entire day, spent the night crying at the kitchen counter and scribbling charms for forgiveness and hexes to forget people into her notebook before scratching them out again.

And she was there when Johnny came back to the house in the morning, glass-eyed and gray-skinned, carrying breakfast in a white sack that he left in the kitchen before bundling a wincing, weeping Zee up in his arms. He carried her upstairs and settled them both atop the covers to get some sleep.

Zee sat up in bed after finally waking. It was a dusty blue outside with a line of pink along the coast. She stretched her fingers across the mattress, half-searching for the weight of him next to her, the cloying heat he radiated in his sleep, the tangy smell of him. But the bed was empty and that was for the future.

Not necessarily, she thought. She had botched the end of their evening. *But he always comes back.*

In the dreams. He always came back.

June 30ᵗʰ 2017

Zee stood in the gravel parking lot, chewing at her lip and listening to some kind of surfy guitar rock pour out of the open garage doors. She could hear a harmony of male voices barking orders and insults and jokes at each other. She just couldn't bring herself to walk in. She'd spent the week waffling on what to do next, waiting for Johnny to call or appear at the house, hoping that her accidental accusation on the porch might be the end of their story.

Not that she wanted the alternative.

She'd thrown herself into digging through old Nikolaev journals, and the internet, and the household collection of book of shadows for protection charms. She'd scryed for whoever Lucas Wolfe claimed to be and come up more than empty, it'd been like bouncing off a mirrored wall. He covered his businesslike ass neatly. Sam had, thankfully, gone on a potions bender, stocking the Lab in her working hours and filling the house with a dense perfume of herbals tinctures at night. She was too distracted to notice that Zee was in her own kind of frenzy.

And Zee just kept thinking about those few recent moments where she had someone other than Sam to talk to, to listen to. The small flow of conversation between her and Johnny had felt, if not always easy, honest with a new and gentle kind of cautiousness. Something close to friendly. She may not be able to tell him about the witch pretending not to be a witch, or about whether or not her feelings for him were being replaced with a new *pesnya dushi*, but it would be nice just to talk.

She walked up to the garage door and found three unfamiliar men working around the room. The first to notice her was a giant of a man, with waxy skin that rippled and pulled over half his face and down both his arms. He was leaving the glory hole, blow pipe in a dense fist, and walking up to the bench when he saw her and seemed to try to shrink into himself.

Burns. She blinked and then gave him a small smile and nod.

"Johnny's not here."

Zee turned to the gruff voice. Two men stood together,

pulling dense bricks of textured glass out of the annealer and loading them onto a cart. One stepped forward, arms folding across his wide chest. He had long, dark hair pulled back into a pony tail, and a long sleeve covering one arm, a prosthesis. He was smirking at her while the blonde man behind him continued working, glancing at her out of the corner of his eyes. The blonde looked familiar, and a little like Johnny. The former soldiers Johnny had told her about. The ones who were dating now.

"He left for the night," the smirking man said. "Sorry, hun."

She had passed Johnny's CRV on her way in, but there was something in the man's amused gaze that told her this was a routine for him now. And one he found humor in.

"Right," she said. "Sorry. Tell him Zoya Lane stopped by."

"Zee Lane?"

She glanced back to the man at the bench who was exchanging wide-eyed looks with the other two.

"Wait here," he said. "I'll go get him."

"Brian, wait-" said the dark haired one, reaching out with his sleeved arm. The sleeve ran all the way down to cover his hand. "Damn," he said, when Brian left the room and then he turned back to her with a narrow gaze. "So, you're Zee."

"Will," the blonde warned.

"We have heard a *lot* about you," Will said, grin spreading. "Johnny's been a pouty little shit-stain this week 'cause of you."

The blonde sighed and shook his head. "To be fair, Johnny's usually some kind of little shit-stain."

Zee barked out a surprised laugh and then cocked her head. She remembered that lovely deep voice.

"You're Johnny's cousin," she said.

"Eric," he said, and then lifted his hand in a small wave.

"You know, I honestly didn't think Johnny had very good taste in women but..." the other man looked her up and down and Zee tried not to preen.

"Jesus, Will," Eric sighed.

Will turned back to him with a sheepish smile. "What? She's a peach."

"Thank you," Zee said. Brian seemed to be taking his time, and she was feeling pretty grateful at this point. "I take it Johnny is here, then?"

"Oh yeah, he's here," Will said easily, as if he hadn't just told her the opposite. "But you should've seen the parade that was comin' round the last few weeks. So we keep pretty boy in the back now. Tell me, doll, they put drugs in the water on this island?"

Ah. It was official. Zee really liked this guy.

"Haven't they told you?" Zee asked, waiting for Will to perk up with interest. "It's the witches up on the cliff. They're out there casting love spells all willy nilly."

Will laughed and Eric grinned and said, "That's funny, I heard they were the good kind of witches."

Zee shook her head. "No, no. The incompetent kind."

"Shut up, shut up, everyone shut up," Johnny panted, running into the room. He halted a few yards back from Zee and stared at her for a long second, taking in her smile, and then narrowed his eyes at Eric and Will. "What'd they say?"

"I hadn't even started to tell her about what you said about her knees being the-"

"I will rip off your other arm, Jackson," Johnny said quickly, pointing a bandaged finger at Will.

"I'd still be better looking," Will said with a shrug, and

Eric nodded sympathetically at Johnny from the background.

"Shit," Johnny said, shoulders drooping and casting short, furtive glances at Zee. She wasn't sure if he was conceding to Will being better looking or was frustrated at her presence.

"Is now an okay time to talk?" she asked. He could say 'no' this way. That he was busy. And she would walk back home and that would be an end.

"He's free. He's been twiddling his thumbs all fucking week," Will said from behind her.

Johnny winced and glared at the other man before looking back at Zee and nodding. "Yeah. Yeah…let's…let's talk somewhere these assholes can't chime in."

"I dunno, I kind of like this peanut gallery," Zee said but she walked up to Johnny and he stumbled back a few steps.

"You come back when you're done with him, doll," Will called.

"Will, just, go make out with Eric or something," Johnny growled.

"You said we had to act professional in the shop, though," Eric said, light and teasing.

"Okay, well now I'm saying have at it," Johnny said.

"Oh, thanks," Brian said softly from the bench. He had scrapped the first pipe when Zee arrived and was starting over again.

Johnny huffed, looked hard at Zee, who was feeling a little more at ease with him off-kilter, and then rubbed at his face with his hand. "Let's go in the cold shop."

Zee followed Johnny back to the swinging doors Brian had vanished behind earlier. They walked into a cool, open room, with a long metal table lined with more finished textured bricks of glass. There were a few tools sitting out that looked like they'd been abandoned unceremoniously in the wake of her arrival.

"I like your guys," she said as the doors swung shut behind them.

"They're assholes, don't listen to them," Johnny said quickly. He took a deep breath and released it slowly, eyes darting around the room like he'd just invited her into his bedroom and was checking to make sure no porn or dirty underwear was left lying out. He added, "But yeah, they're okay, I guess."

She smiled and lowered her chin to try to hide it.

"I wanted to call," he said and she looked up to meet his eyes. "But I know I dropped a bomb last week and then I..."

"Do you want to go out to the park with me on Sunday?" she asked. "I can pack a picnic."

Johnny dropped back onto a stool, never looking away from her face. "You don't have to do this," he said. "If I fucked things up too much in the past. You don't have try."

Zee rolled her eyes and walked over to perch on the stool next to his, trying not to be offended by the way he seemed to shrink away from her. "Look, dude. You've had how many years to think about this? To come up with apologies and plans and dates. And to think about...about," she waved her hands between them. "You know. This. What you want. And I...I thought I closed the door on the Johnny Sharpe saga a long time ago."

"I know. I know, Zee," he started.

"No. You don't." She stiffened in place. "I just...You have this whole map in your head of where you want to go and I am...blind in this. But I know it's not a joke. I'm sorry I said that."

"I don't blame you," he said. He was rubbing his hands over the knees of his jeans and it reminded her to ask.

"What *did* you say about my knees?"

Johnny coughed out a breath and bent at the waist, shaking his head down at the floor and muttering something about 'arms.'

"You owe me," she said, testing the waters.

He peeked at her between the longer strands of hair in his face. "I said they were pretty," he muttered.

"You said my knees were pretty?" She asked, surprised.

He groaned and sat back up, leaning against the table behind him. "I said they were the prettiest," he said, sharp and clear.

"The prettiest...knees."

"You know," he said shrugging. Which, no, she really didn't. "Knees are just...knees. But yours are nice."

"The nicest?" she asked—for clarity, of course—and he laughed and blushed. "Is 'knees' a euphemism or..."

Johnny's laugh grew louder and she watched the smile stretch across his face, squeezing at the corners of his eyes. "Shit. Don't get me started." He turned and looked at her from underneath thick lashes and Zee felt herself go hot.

Right. That was stupid.

"You invited me to a picnic," he said, as if he'd just managed to digest her words.

"A second date," she said.

"On Sunday. This Sunday?"

She shrugged, "Or next."

"No, this Sunday."

Johnny's growing smile was interrupted by the door swinging open and a red faced Eric creeping into the room.

"Just looking for...a thing," Eric said under his breath, edging around the room, scanning the shelves while continuously checking on Johnny and Zee from the corner of his eyes.

Johnny rolled his eyes on the stool and mouthed 'Jackson' at Zee.

"Hummm," Eric said. "Maybe it's *not* here." He scratched his chin and Zee stifled a laugh behind her hand as he shrugged at them, all exaggerated shoulders and open hands, and then backed out of the room.

"I should go," Zee said.

Johnny frowned a little and then nodded. "I'd convince you to stay but Will would just pop in after another couple minutes and I think it's better if I limit his opportunities to talk to you."

"Yeah, I am definitely planning on getting more out of him," Zee said with a laugh. "Fair warning—he's my new best friend."

Johnny stood and she had to arch back to get a good look at the smile on his face, soft and wicked and fond all mixed together making her light up from head to toe.

"I'm gonna kill him," he said in a tone better suited to whispers in bedrooms. "Don't be mad."

Johnny was very close, and Zee realized it all at once. The toes of his sneakers were nudging at hers and he smelled like bitter sweat and lemon and eucalyptus. She wondered what his shoulders would feel like under her hands. Would he have to bend if she rose up on her tiptoes? She'd told herself she *hadn't* come for that kiss. She wasn't here to learn if the taste of him matched the flavor in her sleep—salt and chapstick and mint gum. But being this close felt like laying out in the sun, falling asleep on a blanket all boneless and safe and she just *wondered.* What would it be like?

His fingers caught against hers and Zee looked down to see him curl his large hand over hers. *Dainty.* His thumb pressed into her palm and the scrape of skin sent a thick curl of pleasure down her back and into her belly. He released her hand and stepped back.

"I'll see you Sunday," he said.

"Yeah." She blinked. *Damn*, she thought. She turned to go, trying to ignore the weightlessness in her feet.

"Should I bring anything?" he asked.

She almost turned back, but she didn't trust herself not to take a running leap and give Will something to crow over when he walked in on them any minute.

"Surprise me," she said.

Will was suspiciously close to the door as she walked out, and even then it was Eric who jumped guiltily from across the room where he'd been watching.

"Aw, doll, you leavin' already?" Will asked sweetly.

"You guys can come up to the house, *anytime*," Zee said, patting Will on his shoulder as she passed, waving to Eric and Brian in turn. "I'll make you dinner and read your cards free of charge."

"We'll take you up on that. But do we gotta bring Sharpe?" Will asked.

"Not without warning me first," Zee said under her breath and Will cackled.

"Jackson, whatever you're doing I don't like it," Johnny yelled from inside the cold shop.

Zee buried her grin and hurried out to her bike, flipping on the safety lights now that it was dark out and starting home. The trip home was cool and she found herself continuously fighting off a smile. She decided she liked baffled, nervous Johnny. And she very evidently liked intent and pleased Johnny if her reaction to him in the cold shop was anything to go by.

After the initial shock, and anger, and earth-shifting change in perspective from his confessions during the date, she thought she might have found something to understand in their current interactions. This wasn't a new twist to Johnny's feelings that she had to weigh the risk in trusting. This was a new perspective on a very old problem. One she understood better now. She was still shocked, and still angry, but she thought maybe, *maybe*, she could find the upper hand in the dynamic. Johnny would push them forward, but he backed off when she asked him to and...

And he kept coming back.

It didn't solve the question of Lucas Wolfe, but she wasn't sure she wanted that answer when she could have...

Johnny.

Zee rolled up the gate and stepped down from the bike and the ground wobbled below her feet. She paused in step, glancing down at the dirt - still firm - and then around her. She leaned forward and the air in front of her seesawed, like something left too far to the edge of a table. She reached out to the gate and felt the threads of the property wards loose around her fingers.

Shit.

"Sam!" she called, dropping her bike to unlatch the gate. She ran up the stones to the house. "Sam!! Sam, the house—"

Sam stretched her body out the window of the kitchen. "The wards are loose," she said, mouth tight.

Zee skidded in step and then hurried to meet Sam in the greenhouse.

"You're alright-"

"I went to the Lab and when I came back-"

They both took a deep breath and then Zee jumped forward to wrap her arms around her cousin.

"I'm okay," Sam said. "The house is okay. The wards are still up, but..."

"But those were *Nadia's*," Zee whispered. "Who could even find a thread to pull on those?"

"I don't know. But they didn't get in. And they were long gone when I got back." Sam squeezed Zee once more before pulling back. "Is she here?"

Zee took a breath, trying to shake off the grip of dread that had squeezed at her heart. She closed her eyes and searched for the bright spot of Nadia's presence nearby. The grounding strength of the house surrounded her, settling the trembles in her hands. Sam's fizzy, sharp energy was at her side. And somewhere, but not near, there was a soft brush of affection and care.

"Close," Zee said. "But not here."

"If we needed to worry, she would be here," Sam said with firm surety.

Zee nodded. "Okay. Okay. I have to tell you something."

And she unloaded the tale of Lucas Wolfe. The dreams, his coming for a reading, asking for Sam, scoping out the house and their sunroom, giving the bogus fortune before chasing him back out again. Sam's brow furrowed as she listened.

"That's why you keep putting Patchouli oil in my conditioner?" Sam asked.

"Umm...yes. He said your name and I was afraid maybe he was looking for you," Zee said quickly.

"No one like that's been in the shop so it's probably more likely that it's *us* and the house," Sam said with a wave of her hand.

"Okay... what do we do?"

"Make tea," Sam said, as if it were obvious. "And get to work. Do you think you can reinforce the wards?"

Zee considered this. Her wards weren't *bad* but they weren't Nadia's. But her magic worked well with her aunt's and the magic in place might take hers without much struggle.

"It'll be a patch job," she said.

"It's a start," Sam said. "I'll start pulling books. We might need to lay a few snares."

Chapter 8

One Week

⟶)ᴐꬱ)●((((⟵

July 1ˢᵗ 2017

"We *need* banishing magic," Sam grumbled, flipping through dusty pages.

"The moon is waxing," Zee said.

"I *know* the moon is waxing, Zee," Sam said, lifting up a heavy tome to hide the scowl on her face. "And *I* didn't even have to look at the calendar to tell."

Zee narrowed her eyes at Sam and then went back to her own collection of books. "We could make an egg tree."

"We don't have any dead trees," Sam said. Oh, yeah, Zee just got to that part. "So unless you want to get pregnant..."

Zee huffed and sank back in her chair, pushing at the piles of books in front of her and barely scooting them an inch. "What are we doing? We have charms and sigils and wards up the wazzoo, but if this guy can get in..." She pulled her glasses off her face and rubbed at her eyes.

"He didn't get in," Sam said.

"I *waved* him in," Zee said. "He has been *in* the house, Sam."

"Yeah, when he came to scope it out and get a phony reading," Sam said, setting her book down and reaching across the dining room table - which only ever ended up used for study and never eating - to take Zee's hand. "But he didn't *break* the wards."

"He could have," Zee whispered. She met Sam's eyes and their faces were mirrored and grave.

Sam sank back in her own chair. "Where is Nadia?"

"She's hiding. She wants us to solve this," Zee said.

"I'm thirty years old. I don't need another lesson," Sam said, with just a hint of petulance.

"Come on," Zee said, slipping out of her chair. "It's three in the morning and we have to be in the shop tomorrow. The house will stand for the night." She held out her hand and waited for Sam to take it in hers.

"You wanna sleep in my room?" Sam asked, leaning into Zee's shoulder.

"Yeah, I do."

They slipped into Sam's old four poster, Zee falling back onto the pillows and Sam clamping herself around Zee's middle. In another hour she rose - Sam had tossed and turned until she was spread eagle across her half of the bed and a bit of Zee's body - and gathered every blue stone she could find in the house. She bundled up the Aquamarine that sat on the windowsill in the bathroom, and her own raw sapphire earrings, and the sodalite chunk on the mantle, and the iolite encrusted trinket box from Nadia's room. She snuck them out into the chilly night and settled them at the four corners of the property before tiptoeing back inside.

She slid back under the covers, trying not to jostle Sam

more than necessary - the little woman could cover a standard king bed as if she were the size of Cameron.

"Good thinking," Sam whispered at her, half-asleep. She wrinkled her nose and pulled away. "Your toes are cold and wet."

July 2nd 2017

Johnny was laying across the old plaid blanket she'd laid out for their lunch, his arms stretched back and head laying in the palms of his hands. His eyes were closed, face turned into the sunlight, and Zee was cataloguing the number of things she wanted to do in that moment.

She wanted to tease the the edge of her fingernail up from the cuff of his t-shirt, around the muscle on the inside of his arm where the skin was paler, down to the hollow of his elbow.

She wanted to lean down and stroke her nose along his temple, hear his quiet breathing in her ear, feel the prickle of his stubble on the tips of her fingers while she turned his face to hers.

She wanted to press her palm down onto his chest until she could feel his heart thumping against the cup of her hand.

She wanted to settle astride him and tuck her face into his neck and take deep breaths until her lungs were full of him.

Johnny turned his head and blinked one eye open, smile creeping across his face and dimple winking at her. "Am I being boring?"

Zee blushed, grateful she'd left her hair down to hide behind. "Nope. Came out here for the quiet."

He hummed. "Yeah, don't think I ever really came out here for the nature before."

Zee blinked and her stomach rolled. Right. The park was where Johnny brought his dates so they could mess around. She smirked bitterly and twisted in place, leaving him her back so she could pretend to dig for a snack.

Now she wanted to be one of those girls, spread out on a blanket under the hot weight of Johnny Sharpe. She felt her hair shift, felt a snag worked loose, and then the barest brush against the back of her blouse. She ignored the prompt and scooted to the edge of the blanket to put a line of food between herself and Johnny.

July 3rd 2017

Zee sucked at her bruised thumb, grimacing at the juniper sap flavor she found. She pulled another sprig up from the pile and set back to work, weaving the pieces through the spiral of willow she'd twisted together into a large hoop.

"Here," Sam came out the open front door, carrying a basket of brown and white feathers on one arm, and a bowl of steaming ward water in her hands. "That's huge. Is it going to fit on the door?"

"I took measurements," Zee said. "Bigger can't *hurt*."

Sam stepped carefully down the steps and then reached back to pull a small paintbrush from out of the nest of her hair. She dipped it into the water and then stroked the bristles along the edge of the first step.

"I've been scrying," Zee said.

Sam nodded while she worked. "If you'd found something you'd have told me."

Zee slipped an iron nail through a gap in the branches under the juniper and then covered the glimpse of it with a speckled feather. "It's like…It's like a one-way mirror. But I'm on the wrong side."

Sam stiffened and then pulled back from her work. "Then you should stop."

Zee nodded, focusing on the hoop in her lap, pinning a bit of lavender through the juniper. "That's what I thought."

July 4ᵗʰ 2017

Zee was reaching that lovely, fuzzy place in meditation where she lost track of *her* and just became breath and a beating heart when someone knocked on the front door. She flicked it away from her mind and took another slow, sliding draw of air, settling back into her pattern. There was another knock.

"Zee! Door," Sam hollered from the kitchen.

Zee sighed, resisting the urge to shout back, and unfolded from the sunroom floor. She padded down the hall, reaching little tendrils of curiosity to the door. It felt friendly.

Will was grinning on the other side.

"Hey, doll."

"What are you doing here?"

His smile only grew.

"Sorry," Zee shook off her surprise. "I mean, hi, Will."

"Came to see if you and your cuz wanted to join us at Johnny's. He's got a deck with a good view of the docks, so we're grilling burgers and watching the fireworks."

Zee looked around the edge of the porch to see Eric leaning out of the driver's side of a truck. He waved and she waved back.

"Does Johnny know you're here?" she asked.

"No, but he said I could bring somebody."

"He meant Eric didn't he?"

"He did mean Eric, yeah," Will said, shrugging.

"Well. I guess he should have been more specific then," Zee said. "Go get Eric out of the car cause it's gonna take a bit to tear Sam away from a project and I'm not going to a barbecue in my yoga pants and sports bra."

"But you look so cute," Will said with a wink, before turning and waving Eric over to them.

"Are you here doing Johnny a favor or are you trying to irritate him by showing up with me on your arm?" Zee asked, smiling.

"Don't see why it can't be a bit of both," Will said.

Eric met them on the porch and Zee led the pair inside and through the entry and dining room over to the kitchen. Will followed close, but Eric stopped at every framed photo and side table covered with stones and candles. They both paused at the coat rack where a tidy line of brooms in different lengths and woods hung, ready for use.

"For cleansing," she said, before rolling open the door to the kitchen.

A cloud of honeysuckle and lilac fragrant steam poured out, revealing Sam over the cauldron, a fire burning bright in the old stove. The room was humid and the smell was cloying and Sam's hair was damp and curling around her intent and sharp expression.

"Witches." Zee heard Will whisper the word but it was touched with a bit of awe so she moved farther into the room and let them follow.

Zee watched as Sam wrinkled her nose, standing up on tiptoes to peer inside the black pot, before turning to the island and pinching a few rose stems up between her fingers. She pulled a short, sharp knife out from the back pocket of her jeans - Zee would be having words with her about that - and sliced the thorns off the stem and directly into the pot.

"So...what's cooking?" Will asked. Eric spun slowly in place, lips slightly parted as he took in the room with wide eyes.

"Body armor," Sam said.

Eric stopped and he and Will exchanged a startled look.

"Sam, we have company," Zee said.

"I see that," Sam said, even though she hadn't looked at the men yet. She dumped a small bowl of ash into the pot and went back to whisking. "Who are they?"

"Friends of Johnny's."

That stopped her. She looked over from the pot and gave Will and Eric two long, examining stares, squinting at Will and making him shift in place. "Why are they here?"

"To take us to a party."

"Are we going?"

"Yes."

Sam met Zee's eyes and she tried to press to her cousin, *please don't make me go alone.* Sam couldn't read her mind exactly. But it was a very close thing after all these years.

"Alright," Sam said, tapping the whisk against the cauldron and setting it to the side. She ducked into the pantry and came out again with a small silver tin. She stepped up to Will and pressed it into his hand. "For the nerve damage," she said, glancing at his sleeved arm. Then she went back to the stove and ladled out a helping of the guarding water into a jar and passed it to Zee. "Put that on after you change."

Zee smiled at a stunned Eric and Will with a small shrug. "Feel free to wander, but don't touch anything that looks weird. Sam, make polite conversation."

Sam grunted over the stove and Zee decided to hurry.

But by the time she made it back downstairs, in a soft old dress and smelling faintly of flowers, Will had Sam giggling and blushing and Eric was sitting up on the island, licking chocolate from his fingers.

"Don't know why your house was s'posed to be so scary when we were kids," Eric murmured to her.

"Just rumors," Zee said with another shrug.

"Johnny was always trying to convince me to sneak up here with him," he said. "Think he just wanted to come inside."

Zee hummed, shying away from the topic and Sam damped down the fire. As they left the house, Sam's pan of emergency brownies in hand, Zee hung a rusted key on a red ribbon from the inside of the door wreath. She turned and Will was there, eyes flicking between her and the key.

"You having issues, doll?" he asked.

Zee skipped down the steps ahead of him. "Nothing serious," she lied.

When they walked into Johnny's apartment as a group, the room went quiet. It was only Johnny, Brian, and Sarah with her husband and kids. Zee wondered for a moment if this was really the place for her and Sam to pop-up uninvited. Johnny was standing, taking up a narrow doorway with his broad shoulders and a foil lined tray full of grill tools. His arms dropped for a second and the tools slid noisily to the edge of the tray before he righted them.

"Hey," he said.

"Sharpe," Sam said drily.

Zee half-smiled and glanced to find everyone's eyes ping-ponging between her and Johnny.

Johnny grinned, eyes fixed to her face. "You want a drink?"

Later, after they had eaten and the fireworks had started, Johnny joined Zee against the wall of his deck. A warm palm found the base of her back and she let herself lean into his shoulder.

"I guess I won't kill Will," Johnny whispered into her ear as fireworks spiraled up into the sky with a whistle. The bang of the explosion hid her bubble of laughter. "Can I drive you and Sam home, after?"

Zee thought it over. She and Sam could always walk home. Or they could leave whenever Eric and Will decided to call it a night. If they waited for Johnny they would be the last ones to leave. Sam turned to look at Zee over her shoulder from where she was sitting between Sarah and Eric. She nodded once.

"Alright," Zee said, and then she leaned a little further into Johnny's side until his arm was around her back and his hand was curling around her hip. "Want to go watch the movie in the park with me this Friday?"

They were playing Bell, Book, and Candle—which was one of her favorite oldies. She suspected it was a nasty joke on Grace Harper's part-who had *definitely* been glaring at her in the coffee shop the other morning—given it was about a witch casting a love spell on a man and having the consequences backfire onto herself. But it had a happy ending and Kim Novak played the witch, so Zee didn't really care. It would be their third planned date. And even more public than the first, since there wasn't much else to do on Friday nights on the island. But Zee *wanted* Johnny to sit next to her in the dark, and she wanted him to walk her home, and she wanted to kiss him on her porch and not mess it up this time. She wanted to *try*.

"Yes," Johnny said firmly.

July 5th 2017

The docks were quiet and the moon, only a few days from full, was staring back at Zee from over the water. Sam was working in the Lab and Zee had taken a walk to check her protection jars at the docks. They were all broken.

She nudged the shattered glass with the toe of her sneaker and it clinked gently. She crouched down, carefully flicking the sharp edges to the side. The rusty nails and herbs were missing - had been *removed* from the collection - so she brushed the rest of the debris into the water below to be purified and washed away. Lucas Wolfe was pulling bricks out of the Nikolaev walls that protected the island and Zee was ready to start throwing hexes around.

She rose up and turned back to the town, eyes reflexively seeking out the balcony deck of Johnny's apartment. She could see lights on through the blinds and she had an urge to go knocking on his door. She liked the feel of his arm across her back and wondered what it would be like to curl up against his side doing something as mundane as watching tv together. Would she be able to pay attention to the screen? Or, if they were alone this time, would she stretch against him, press her face into his skin, take a taste of the back corner of his jaw, just below his ear where there was a line of three freckles?

He hadn't tried to kiss her again, even when Sam had rushed out of the back seat the night before, leaving them alone in Johnny's car together. He was waiting for her, just like Nadia had said, and Zee felt paralyzed with the choice in her own hands. But he touched her, her hands, her back. He'd set his hand at the back of her neck at one point while she'd been talking to Sarah in his kitchen, running his thumb back and forth across her shoulder, and she'd very nearly crumpled against him.

A shadow crossed the light of Johnny's blinds, his shadow, a hand flicking them to the side as he reached for the handle. Zee pulled her hoodie up and marched herself back to the Lab to drag Sam home for the night.

July 6th 2017

Zee came up from the Lab basements, hefting a box of jars for Sam to fill, and found a to-go cup of coffee waiting on the counter for her.

"Johnny dropped it off," Sam said, smirking as she took the box out of Zee's arms. "He brought me one too, but he didn't write a note on the sleeve."

Zee waited until Sam went into the back to pick the coffee up off the counter.

See you tomorrow. There was a scribble underneath the words, something firmly covered in black sharpie and then a little :) to the side.

She took a quick sip and pressed her lips together to fight off her smile. Who had given him her coffee order?

Chapter 9

Open Doors

July 7th 2017

Zee tried not to enjoy the look of utter outrage on Grace Harper's face as she watched Johnny spread a blanket out on the ground and then wait for Zee to take her seat first. She failed. But she tried.

"I'm gonna need you to fact check this movie for me while we watch," Johnny said.

"It's all nonsense," Zee said immediately.

"Now, see, that is a disappointment," he said. "Because I was really looking forward to you taking me to an underground beatnik witch club."

"Oh, no, that part is accurate. You're right." She grinned at him and his eyes flicked to her mouth.

And then another couple, unfamiliar summer renters, settled their own blanket nearby and the moment settled and drifted away.

They sat, stretched out, side by side for the first half of the movie, fingers brushing together on the blanket. Johnny seemed a little embarrassed at first by the love spell plot, and he grimaced at Zee and whispered another, shorter apology which she shrugged off with a light bump against his shoulder. He shifted a few minutes after that, inched closer to her so that their arms brushed. The warmth of the day was rolling off the island back out over the water and goosebumps were raising on her arms and neck. Zee tucked her hand - the one that wasn't soaking up Johnny's preternatural heat - inside the sleeve of her sweater.

"I'm cold," she whispered to him halfway through.

He blinked and frowned, sitting up and reaching for the zipper of his sweater shirt. "You want-"

She shook her head and shuffled up onto her knees, trying not to block anyone's view.

"Just, let me..." She pushed his knees to either side and then crawled into the space available, biting her lip as he sucked in a breath.

She settled back slightly, just barely leaning against his chest. "Can I...?"

Johnny folded himself around her, filling in the gaps with warmth and closeness. His arms wrapped around her middle and she rested her hands over his sleeves, body softening against him. She could feel his face against the side of her head, heard him take a long breath.

"You might need to fill me in later on what happens in the second half of this movie," he whispered into her hair.

Zee smiled up at Kim Novak's pout on the large screen. Johnny re-tangled their arms together, taking her hands in his and curling her up tighter in his hold.

* * *

Johnny was a surprisingly smooth driver for only using one hand. His other was linked with Zee's on top of the center console. The car was quiet, but now it was a comfortable silence between them. And every so often...

Johnny squeezed Zee's hand in his and they both looked out their windows to hide their smiles.

He was going to walk her to her door again and this time-

"Is that smoke?" Johnny asked, straightening up.

Zee leaned to look out his driver's side window and saw it immediately, a small trail of blue smoke in the night sky, and a faint dome of orange near the ground.

"That's the house," she said. She dropped Johnny's hand and tried to perch higher in the car to see better. A sharp stab of dread pierced her stomach and she dove to the floor, knocking her head lightly against the dashboard. "Sam." Where was Sam?

"Did she light a bonfire?"

"She was supposed to be at the Lab," Zee said. Maybe Sam was safe but what did that mean for the house?

They were bumping faster along the road now and Zee wanted to spare a thank you to Johnny for the urgency, but she couldn't find her damn phone in the dark and why did her purse have so many fucking receipts in it? Her fingers slipped over the smooth case and she pressed hard against the home button.

No signal.

"Fuck," she muttered.

Johnny reached into his own pocket and pulled out his phone, grimacing at the screen. "Sorry. Almost there."

The tires kicked up stones as they sped around a corner, headlights swerving and flashing over to the house.

"The gate is open," Zee said. She was unbuckling her seatbelt before Johnny had even started to brake.

"Zee! Wait for me!"

But he was still putting the car into park underneath the border oak when she was jumping out of the passenger's seat. The world spun at the gate for a moment and the sound of Johnny's car door slamming was amplified in her head like a gunshot.

The wards were broken. *Shattered.*

Johnny caught up to her inside the property, halfway between the house and the small, innocent looking fire that was burning up her juniper door wreath.

"It looks like brush," he said. "Is Sam-?"

"It's not brush. It's a protection charm I made for the house," Zee said, whirling on Johnny. "Our wards are broken. And Sam's not here. But someone else is, and I think you should go back to the car."

Johnny reeled back at the sharp bite in her voice and she pushed past him. The house was dark, but she could see the front door hanging open and she stormed over to the steps. She was going to tear Lucas Wolfe a new asshole for breaking into her home. Magically and physically. She was going to bind him up so tight he'd have trouble catching a breath to answer her demands.

Johnny's hand clutched around hers as she was inspecting the ash footprints on her doorstep and she whipped so fast around that she saw him flinch away from her swinging hair. She opened her mouth to rip into him. His free hand wrapped around her waist, warm and firm and solidly reassuring. Her mouth shut as a horrible wave of nerves and longing swept through her and she battled the irrational urge to curl into his chest and cower there.

"I believe you," he said in a whisper. Zee blinked, startled. "I believe you that this is out of my depth. But I'm not letting you go inside alone, okay?"

She sagged slightly, and Johnny's thumb stroked against

her ribs. She nodded, squeezed his hand, and turned back to the footprints. She ran one finger through the ash and lifted it up to her nose.

"Magic dust?" Johnny whispered.

Oh dear, thought a farther corner of Zee's brain. *He's got a lot to learn.*

"Chicory," she said and Johnny looked puzzled. There was blood in the ash too and Zee wiped it off on her jeans. "It's like a magical invisibility trick."

There was a rustle from deeper inside the house, on the south end near the sun room.

Zee ran in, Johnny close at her back.

"You're supposed to call the police," Johnny whispered. "For intruders."

"The police are asshats and they won't make it in time. But sure, phone's in the kitchen," Zee hissed.

Johnny didn't answer, just followed her down the dark hall, hands at her waist.

At the door to the sunroom something uncoiled in Zee's a stomach. A thick, spinning, queasiness that had her wavering in step. It reminded her of the psychic attack on Nadia when she was younger, but this time it was sludgy and liquid and rising up her throat. There was a shadow in the room, amorphous and quick, and her eyes were blurring, the taste of gasoline at the back of her mouth.

"Oh," she said and then slid in to the doorjamb and down to the floor.

"Zee!" Johnny's exclamation startled the shadow, and it sent one of the old glass cases crashing to the floor.

Her insides were doing strange, rearranging dances in her chest and stomach and she slapped a hand over her mouth to try and keep everything inside.

There was a bright flash in the room and Johnny

charged in, but Zee had to tuck her face into her shoulder as her eyes watered and stung from the light. Everything was silvery bright and blinding, angry explosions of fireworks behind her eyes and clanging through her head.

"Johnny," she whimpered.

She could hear Johnny grunt and then a hiss and crackle of fire and she winced and tried to stare in the room. There was something burning on the floor, and Johnny was grappling by the window with a dark shape that was more ink and smoke than it was person. Zee crawled into the room and gagged as another rush of syrupy poison rolled in her gut. It was a book of shadows on the floor. It was Nadia's.

"Johnny," she said again, but it was barely a breath.

There was another crash and shatter and Johnny fell back onto the floor as the darkness scrambled out of the window. Zee thought she saw simple black pants and shoes for a moment but then they shifted back into a gauzy shadow and disappeared into the depth of night.

"Fire," she said, catching a gasp of air.

Johnny twisted on the floor and Zee blinked itchy tears out of her eyes just in time to see Johnny slam his bare hands down onto the burning book.

"No!" she cried out. "Oh, you idiot."

She scrabbled forward through the glass shards and gathered up a large brass bowl meant for mixing tonics before slamming it down over the smoldering pages, Johnny pulling his hands free just in time.

"Glass," Johnny said, staring at her.

"You set your fucking hands on fire, Johnny," she said, glaring back at him.

"Not the first time," he said, sitting up and glancing down at his hands. There were bright splotches of damage across the palms. "What the fuck was that? The bogeyman?"

Zee fell to her forearms on the carpet, slivers of glass scratching against her skin. "Witch. Bad witch. He wants something from the house." *Also, he might be my soulmate,* she thought, *and you might not be.*

"Stop," Johnny said, stumbling up from the floor. "Stop laying in glass, Zee."

"Stop setting yourself on fucking fire, Johnny," she yelled. "Why are you a walking, talking burn mark? Don't they teach you anything about fire safety in glassblowing school?"

Johnny snorted softly and then crouched down at her side. "You okay? C'mere. Put your arms around my neck."

Zee sat up and brushed the glass off her arms - she wasn't *that* scratched up - and then held on to Johnny's shoulders as he used his forearms to scoop around her waist and under her knees, lifting her off the floor.

"Kitchen," she instructed him. "I need tea."

"You need to call the police."

"I need to call *Sam.*"

They exchanged unhappy expressions, Johnny's stern and tense and hers scrunched with the effort of keeping a scream inside. But the anger crumpled quickly and Zee pressed her face into Johnny's neck to keep the tears at bay.

"Are you alright?" she whispered.

"Yeah," Johnny said, leaning his cheek against her hair. "I'll heal. Might not pick up a blow pipe this week, but it wouldn't be the first time."

"Not that," Zee said leaning back to fix a glare on his face. "I can fix that. I meant...you know...you fought a shadow. You tried to punch a shadow."

"Hey, I *did* punch that shadow. That shadow had a face

underneath it. Which...is freaking me out a little, yeah. Which way?"

Zee pointed him to the kitchen and she flicked the light on as they passed the wall.

"Set me down," Zee said.

"Kinda don't want to," he said, wincing and squeezing her a little closer.

"Set me down so I can make tea, and fix your hands, and call Sam."

"The police," he said.

"Johnny, the police won't listen to us," Zee said. "You just admitted that you punched a shadow in the face."

"I'm not putting you down until you agree to call the police. It's breaking and entering even if it is a shadow. They have to do something and you need to have this on record," Johnny said. He looked a little wild-eyed, and the logic wasn't quite sound, so maybe calling the police was Johnny's last grasp on finding some reality for the situation.

Zee sighed. This wasn't going to go well. "Fine."

"Call first," he said.

"Johnny, your hands!"

"I'll go put them in cool water. Call first."

She growled but nodded and he bent - oh, wow, he was tall, she was really *high up* - to set her gently back to the floor. Her knees wobbled and her stomach flipped, but she made it to the phone and waited until Johnny had turned the faucets on with his elbows before picking up and dialing.

"Yes, hello. I'd like to report a breaking and entering at 700 Forest Way. 700 Forest Way. No that's...it's the house on cliff. Yes. The Nikolaev house. Yes. This is Zoya Lane. Yes a breaking and entering." Zee was fighting the worlds' biggest eye roll with Macy Steele, the police dispatcher. "I don't know yet, but there are damages. And a small fire was set. No, the intruder is gone. No, I don't know how old they were. I didn't get a good look. I'm not alone. I'm with... Johnny Sharpe. Yes. Johnny Sharpe."

At the sink the lines on Johnny's forehead were deepening with his frown. Zee turned her back to him so he couldn't see her own frustration bleeding out of her eyes.

"Yes. Fine. Thank you." She took a deep breath and released it slowly. "They'll be here soon. I'm calling Sam."

Johnny murmured from the sink, but she couldn't hear it over the water and the ringing in the phone.

"How was the date?" Sam asked. It was loud in the background and Zee thought she heard a familiar male rumble.

"He broke the wards. Where are you? Who are you with?"

"The bar with Eric and Will, hang on-"

"No, no," Zee rushed. "Stay inside. Stay with them. Make them bring you home. But not yet. Johnny had me the call the police."

"The police?! Why would you call those backasswards idiots?"

Will was laughing in the background.

"He ripped the wreath down, burnt it. Oh god—there's a fire on the lawn, I forgot. He broke a case in the sunroom. Nadia's book of shadows." Zee's throat filled up and suddenly Johnny was there at her back, arms looping around her shoulders with his hands held carefully out, some kind of silly, hopeless-idiot's hug. "It's burnt. I don't know how bad."

"I'm coming home," Sam said sharply.

"No, just wait. Stay with the boys. Watch out for greaseball insurance salesman look-a-likes. You come home while the police are here and it'll just get more ridiculous. Johnny's here. He set himself on fire," Zee added the last bit with a soft headbutt back to Johnny's chest. He pressed a kiss to the top of her head as an answer.

"Are you alright?"

"Yeah. There was some kind of whammy but it's wearing off now. Nothing tea and a couple band aids can't fix."

Sam was quiet for a long minute, the bar noisy in the background. Zee heard Eric ask her to explain what was going on.

"The wards," she said finally.

"Yeah," Zee said. "They're gone."

"Shit," Sam breathed across the line.

"Full moon tomorrow at midnight," Zee said.

"You just read that on the calendar didn't you?" Sam huffed. "Yeah. We'll put them back up then. I love you."

"Love you," Zee answered and hung up.

Johnny stepped back and set her free to fill up the kettle and flick the stove burner on.

"Wait here," she told him, pointing to where he stood by the kitchen island. She went to the pantry to grab muslin strips and a jar of ointment and then out to the greenhouse to trim off three spines of aloe. Johnny was waiting at the counter, palms raised, kettle rattling softly as it heated.

"That was stupid," she said, as she sliced open the aloe spikes and cut away the spiky edges.

"What'd the plant do?" Johnny joked.

With his hands rinsed clean of soot, it didn't look so bad really. He must have put the flame out straight away. But still. He was an idiot. Zee slid the aloe strips gently across the red welts of burn, the gel leaving shiny streaks.

"If you stick around I'm fire-proofing you," she said.

"That would be extremely handy," he said immediately. "Can you do that?" Zee delivered one (what she hoped was) stinging glare and then went back to work. "Hey." He nudged the toe of her shoe with his own. "I'm sticking around."

He sounded so sure. So certain of his decision even after an experience that was definitely in her own ranking of Top Worst. She twisted open the jar ointment and smeared it liberally across his palms.

She needed to tell him about the pesnya dushi. She wasn't even sure if she believed in them now, after dreaming of Lucas.

"Let it soak in a minute."

"This definitely smells better than usual," he said, bringing a hand up to sniff at a safe distance.

"Don't eat it," she said. She put together two cups of tea, Johnny could take it or leave it, she was too wired to care either way.

"So...wards are...?" Johnny's head was tilted, eyes still a little too wide and dilated, but she was impressed with his ability to make easy conversation. Every time she opened her mouth she was fighting back a scream or tears or just outright insults for no reason.

Zee joined him back at the counter, setting his mug down to one side and hers to the other and started wrapping his hands up carefully with the muslin.

"They're like...well, not a security system. Not ours at least. But they're meant to be a barrier for bad intentions." And for no good reason that she could think of, Zee found herself explaining to Johnny about Lucas Wolfe, and the wards being tampered with earlier, and she and Sam scrambling to put every immediate safeguard available in place.

"Why didn't you tell- tell anyone?" he asked. He was

growing in front of her, shoulders broadening and bristling with anger.

"You mean like, 'Excuse me, Swans Island, our invisible barrier at the house got hacked. Can ya'll be on the look out for a boring to posh dude who may or may not be involved?'" Zee faked a cheesy little shrug of her shoulders and then scowled back at him.

There was a knock at the door and Zee and Johnny both jumped in place. Her heart hammered in her chest and Johnny let out a rough breath, arms halfway around her back as if he'd been impersonating a shield.

"Hey there," a voice called from the hall. "Miss Niko-laev? It's Officer Doyle."

Zee sighed and Johnny put his arm around her shoulder to lead them both out in the hall.

"Coming," she called.

They'd walked to the kitchen in the dark, Zee too shaky and Johnny's hands too injured. Zee flicked the lights on as they moved to the front door. There were rusty, caked ash prints on the floorboards. Everywhere. Johnny's arm tightened over her shoulder, muslin mittened hand hanging loose.

Jasper Doyle stood in her entry hall, face amused as he watched their approach. When Zee had first moved to Swans Island, Jasper had just moved back home after college and joined the local police force. And for whatever reason, he was *always* on duty when someone called down from the house on the cliff for break-ins or teenagers running around outside the house in the middle of the night, or unruly customers who'd had too much to drink before arriving to see Nadia. As Sam and Zee got old enough to clean up broken glass, and chase off teenagers, and subdue drunks, they'd agreed as a family to stop calling Officer Doyle up to the house.

"Heard you had yourself some trouble with the local kids, again, eh Nikolaev?" Jasper asked, giving Zee that indulgent little smirk she wished she could tear off his face with her fingernails.

"It wasn't a kid," Johnny said at her side. "It was a man. He set a fire outside on the lawn, and down the hall here, in the sunroom."

"Sure hope you put that one out." Jasper laughed at his own joke and Zee walked ahead of them both, taking more care not to step in the footprints on the floor boards this time. Everything was going to need a very deep cleansing.

Zee stopped in the doorway, staring at the wreckage in the room, the contents of the old case spilling out across the floor. Jasper walked in and absently kicked a black onyx seeing orb off to the far corner of the room. Zee chewed at the inside of her lower lip as he looked around.

"He came in through the front door, and jumped out the window here. But I haven't looked to see where else he was in the house before we pulled up," Zee said. At Johnny's gaze drilling holes into her face she added, "I think it was an island visitor, a man whose cards I read a couple weeks back."

Jasper turned, eyes wide and making the lines in his forehead deepen. He had his uniform hat still on, covering his bald head. "What makes you say that?" he asked.

"A feeling," she said. It was simple, but true. Truer than Doyle was going to think, anyway.

Jasper rolled his eyes a little and glanced out the window to the fire still burning on the lawn. "I wouldn't start spreading that kind of accusation around, Miss Nikolaev. You rely on the tourists' business as much as the rest of us," he warned.

"Doyle, look," Johnny pressed. "This was not a kid. This was not a prank."

"You know, I never thought I'd see you two together," Jasper said after turning, eyes narrowed and smile intolerable. "Still working your way through the island, Sharpe?"

Zee was pretty non-plussed, all things considered. She'd learned a long time ago that anything that came out of Jasper Doyle's mouth was a pile of trash. But Johnny's face turned a deep shade of red and a muscle in his jaw ticked angrily.

"Nikolaev knows the drill," Jasper said, apparently unaware of the fact that Johnny was clenching his *burnt*, wrapped up fists like he was about to start throwing punches. "Kids make hitting this house a competition. Somebody just got a little overzealous this time. Or who knows, maybe you pissed someone off with a nasty reading, huh?"

Zee settled a palm against Johnny's spine, could feel him almost vibrating with tension.

"I'm sure Zee appreciates your due diligence, Johnny. But these women, they just get this stuff coming at them all the time, right?"

"We sure do," Zee said, nodding along.

Johnny was gritting his teeth almost audibly and glaring at Doyle like he was ready to do permanent damage. And there was a tiny part of Zee that was enjoying the whole thing. But she really didn't want to mend broken knuckles *and* heal the burns tonight so it seemed like it was a good idea to get Jasper Doyle off the property and Johnny Sharpe drinking his cup of tea.

"Well, I better go put that fire out," Zee said in the

pause that followed. She turned and looked hard at Johnny until he met her gaze and added, "Before something blows up."

He nodded once, face still hard with the dark blush across his nose and cheeks. "I'll come help. Just give us a minute."

Zee hesitated and he nodded again, expression softening by a small fraction.

"Okay," she said. "Thanks for coming by, Officer Doyle."

"Anytime, Nikolaev."

Zee ignored the note of invitation in the older man's voice and walked down the hall.

"Look at those hands, Sharpe," she heard Jasper say. "Won't be much of use tonight with her. Maybe she'll do all the work for you, huh?"

She heard Johnny's voice answer, hard and sharp but too quiet to make out the exact words so she left the house and turned on the garden hose to put out what was left of the small wreath fire. She walked to the four corners of the yard gate and found the blue stones still in place on the posts, letting out a small ring of safety.

They worked. Your charms.

"Nadia," Zee sighed out, shoulders drooping with relief. Nadia had been scarce since her wards were tampered with and having her back in this moment turned things half-way to rights again. "They didn't," she said.

They did. He didn't find what he was looking for. And my book isn't too worse for wear, just a few old, useless pages lost.

"There was nothing that you ever were or ever made that is useless to Sam and I," Zee whispered.

She felt a bloom of Nadia's love and pleasure and then

the front door was opening and Johnny was standing, arms folded across his chest, as Jasper Doyle walked down the stone pathway and out the gate. He was silent, and he didn't look back at Zee once, but he wasn't bleeding so it couldn't have gone that badly. Zee met Johnny on the stairs.

"I'm sorry for not listening to you," he said, still glaring at Doyle's police car as it drove off, and a growl in his tone.

"Thank you. Now, please, let me fix your hands," she said. She grabbed at his elbow and dragged him down the hall.

"You did fix them," Johnny said. He looked down at his hands and realized that the muslin was crumpled and coming loose from all of his frustrations. "They feel pretty good, actually. Kinda tingly."

Zee ducked into the pantry, grabbed the best jar of the burn salve—the one that had erased the nasty welt on the back of her hand after she'd whacked it against the hot iron —and came back to jump up and sit on the island. She took a quick slug of tea and and then held her hand out, waving for Johnny to come closer.

"What is it?" he asked, scooting the jar in a circle on the counter, looking for a label.

"Your salvation," Zee said, and then grabbed his wrist and tugged him forward until he was standing between her knees. She started unwrapping the bandages, happy to find the skin had blistered and was toughening. "Drink some tea."

"That's," Johnny leaned close so their heads were side to side. "That's healing really fast."

"Magic," Zee said. She opened the jar and scooped out a chunk, turning Johnny's palm up and rubbing the salve over every new burn and then over all the old scars she saw as well. He was holding himself still in front of her and she could see him watching her hands, then looking up to her face. She linked her fingers through his so she could massage the salve into the rough skin, listening carefully for any hiss of discomfort.

"Doyle's an ass," Johnny said.

"He is. But I just try to remember that Nadia hexed the hair off his head and it makes the experience of dealing with him a little easier," Zee said.

"Wait, really?" Johnny took a tiny step closer to the counter. The sharp lemony edge of his scent was bright and tickling in her nose.

"It went with very little effort," Zee said. "So it was probably going to happen sooner rather than later." She finished up with his right hand and set it down, open, on her thigh before starting over with his left.

"Can I say that this feels...really good?" Johnny asked. Zee made the mistake of looking up and the smile on his face was was soft and grateful with a hint of expectant hunger in the slant his eyes. "Do I need to keep burning myself for more hand massages? Does it help my case if I say that they cramp up a lot from carrying the pipe?"

"Well, it's going to take me awhile to fireproof you, so... you should be good. Please don't inflict any more damage until then."

"Can you really do that?"

Zee smiled down at his hand in her lap, her thumbs spiraling around the pink edges of a burn blister. "I think so. Sam's a genius and if I ask her to do it, and say it's okay if you're just fire resistant she'll probably invent something entirely new to prove just how good she is at her work. I helped her come up with something to make Cameron more buoyant so he wouldn't drown."

"Life jacket?"

"Bubble baths," Zee said and Johnny snickered. "Lots of bubble baths from what I heard."

"What kind of baths do I get?" he asked, grinning and wiggling his eyebrows in away that made Zee want to flick him on the forehead or tackle him to the floor, she wasn't sure.

"We'll leave treatment up to Sam. She's the professional." But if Zee could make a request it would be something that required Johnny stripped bare on her bed while she spent an excessive amount of time working the magic into his skin. "What did you say to Doyle while I was outside?"

Johnny sighed and grimaced, the dimple in his cheek flickering away. She played with his fingers while she waited for him to answer until she found a scratch down the length of his ring finger to attend to.

"Is everyone really like that here?" he asked. "Just dismisses you?"

"Not entirely," Zee said. "But yeah, when the house gets broken into, people assume it's just kids. And as far as they're concerned, it's not a problem that kids want to prank the house because we're witches. That's just part of our role here."

"I never did," he said quickly. "Just so you know."

"Yeah, I know," Zee said. It had actually been a pretty peaceful few years for the house while she was in high school. And maybe Johnny had headed off some of the trouble with the others.

"I told Doyle he needed to do his fucking job," Johnny said, voice low and harsh. "And that if anything happened to you, or Sam, or the house, I was holding him responsible. And that Cameron probably would too, which I dunno, I'm guessing is true. Not that I have anyway of clearing it with the guy."

Zee stopped her work and held Johnny's hand in both of hers. Her heart was swelling and a sharp edge in her chest was turning soft, mending itself. Johnny glanced at her out of the corner of his eyes, and twitched his lips in an embarrassed little smile.

She dropped his hand and lifted hers up to his jaw, fingers slipping across the prickly shadow of stubble. She was at just the right height to lean in and set her mouth against his, pulling his bottom lip into her kiss. So that's what she did.

She got one firm press and then Johnny's surprise vanished into reaction. His hands slid, barely brushing, up her thighs to the backs of her hips before he pulled her tight against him with one sharp movement, her legs bracketing his hips. The kiss was long and tight, the pair of them holding firmly together. She could feel his exhale, a shaky puff of air against her face. She leaned away and he chased her so she slid her lips apart to flick her tongue out and taste him. The chapstick was missing, and the mint too, but the salty, tart flavor of him was there and when his mouth parted with a soft groan she hunted for more.

He was keeping her now. The resolution was in the press of his fingertips on her spine, the hand at the back of her neck that she leaned into as he arched over her. He was letting her lead the kiss, following her searching tongue, her soft nips along his lips, and somehow even that was over-powering her. She was sinking into his hands, pulling him over her, dragging soft sounds from his throat as she tried to take and take and take. Find every flavor of him, every texture of a kiss, all the little catches of breath she had dreamt about.

She would stay with him. It was in the way she was turning softer in his hold, reclining back as he half-bent over her. One hand, slippery with salve, slipping into his hair to clutch him against her, the other hanging tight to his shoulder as if to keep from falling. She needed to catch her breath but she needed the fantasy—*reality*—of the kiss more so she stroked her tongue along the back of his top teeth and whimpered as he pressed their hips harder together.

He dragged his mouth away, over to her cheek, and her breath came out in short pants.

"Zee," he said, all rasp and grit that just made her want to pull him back, kiss him more, forget for longer that the wards were down and the house was a mess and everything was tits up, even the part where she was kissing Johnny Sharpe like he was an antidote to all her griefs.

He was mouthing along her jaw, swirling wet patterns with his tongue and raising goosebumps with scrapes of his teeth, making his way to a spot on her neck that would have her toes curling in no seconds flat. Zee thought she might have been glowing with the way her whole body was tingling and her pulse was drumming. But something snagged at the back of her mind and she winced.

"Sam just pulled in," she said. "Oh!"

He had found it, his lips circling around the thrumming beat of her pulse and she was drooping, melting, trying to suck in air and turning her head to offer Johnny more of her throat, more of *her*.

"Hmm?" he hummed into her skin and she shivered.

Huh? She wondered. Oh. Right. "Sam. She's home."

"Kay," Johnny said, lifting his head up. She blinked sluggishly at him and wondered if she should be concerned by how smug and pleased with himself he looked.

He pulled her to sit up straight again, and her hands settled on his shoulders. She was pouting, she realized. Were they done? She didn't want to be done.

And then his mouth slanted across hers and this time he was leading, and taking, and she was clutching at the shoulders of his sweatshirt and trying to pretend that all the little moans and gasps weren't coming from her this time. The front door opened and slammed shut and Johnny's thumbs brushed just below her breasts and she wanted to tackle him to the floor, and not care what Sam walked in on.

"Zee?" Sam called from the hall.

Johnny pulled away once, and then again after another briefer kiss, before stepping out of the ring of her legs and over to her side. He was taking a long drink of cooled tea and Zee was staring wide-eyed at the floor when Sam walked into the kitchen.

"Shit," she said. "I should have taken Will up on that last drink."

"Hi Sam," Zee said and Johnny grinned at the cracked note in her voice.

"Hi Zee," Sam said, all amused. "Johnny."

"Hey," Johnny said. He had one arm crossed across Zee, his hand cupped around her hip, and she wanted to smack the pleased smile off his face or drag him upstairs to her bed to kiss him stupid again. "So which of those fancy brooms in the hall should I use to clean up the glass in the sunroom? You should check the rest of the house together."

"No magic brooms for trainees," Sam said.

"I'll get it," Zee said, batting Johnny's hands away as she hopped down to the floor. She was only a little wobbly.

Sam snorted from the doorway and wouldn't meet her eyes until Johnny was walking down the hall, plain broom and tray in hand.

"The pair of you have salve handprints *all* over you," Sam said, raising an eyebrow.

Zee looked down and, yep, there were too-large greasy

hand smears all up and down the side of her clothes. "Shut up," she said.

"Maybe I should go clear up the glass and you and Johnny should go check on your bedroom," Sam whispered.

"That was not where it was going," Zee said. Was it? It was a kiss that didn't seem to have a destination. Would they have ended up in bed together all at once?

"You're forgetting I have been on the other end of a pesnya dushi kiss, Zeezee," Sam said as they headed up the stairs. Sam sniffed at the brown footprints and wrinkled her nose. "If I'd been out tonight you and Johnny would have christened the kitchen. And then the stairs. And your doorway. You might have made it to the bed eventually."

"Stop," Zee groaned and then paused at the top of the stairs. A small bell rang in Nadia's old room and they both hurried down the hall.

It looked like a hurricane had been set off. The mattress was torn open, springs and foam and feathers everywhere, and the closet looked like someone had set off a cotton and linen bomb. Every scrap piece of paper—and this was Nadia's room and she shed notes like strands of hair and they had saved everything she touched, really—was littered across the floor, and her desk was toppled over.

"He thought it would be here," Zee said with sudden clarity.

Sam, frozen in shock, turned sharply to her. "What? What do you mean?"

"Noddy said he didn't find what he was looking for. But he checked here first. He thought it would be in *her* room," Zee said.

"What did you tell him about her?" Sam wondered.

"Nothing!" Zee cried. "I never even mentioned her."

Sam sagged against her side. "This is going to take forever to clear up."

"I'll go to the shop early tomorrow morning and put an emergency closed sign up. Stay in my room tonight?" Zee asked.

"But Johnny-"

"Johnny's not staying. I'm not ready for that. And we have too much to do."

Their hands squeezed tightly together. The tension that had seemed to melt away five minutes ago on the kitchen counter doubled back in Zee's neck and shoulders. This man wanted something from them, about Nadia. Their Nadia. He was going to be in a world of trouble if he ever got close to hurting her aunt. She might be a ghost, but her soul was still here, holding their family together. She just wished that her aunt was still alive, she would have had a better idea of *how* to keep them safe, and Zee wasn't so sure she could keep that promise on her own.

Chapter 10

Waxing, Waning

July 9th 2017

Moonlight pooled over Zee's skin where she lay in the grass. Her shift was getting damp from the ground and her skin was tingling with the chilly air, but the clear soft glow of the moon on her body was soft and gentle, seeping in and filling her stiff bones with light and warmth.

It was after one in the morning and she and Sam had expended a lot of magic in the past twenty-four hours. But the wards felt tangible and strong from here in the grass and Zee was satisfied, if not excessively tired. She needed to get up and go inside, join Sam in the kitchen to eat cake and drink tea. She could roll into her bed to lay in the moonlight once she got upstairs. If she got upstairs. She was feeling very, very lazy at the moment.

Gravel crunched and an engine hummed and Zee craned her neck back to watch as a car pulled up to the house. She squinted against the headlights and then smiled as they flicked off. What was Johnny doing here in the middle of the night? The wards fluttered as he reached the gate, the gentle flames licking in the back of her head, but they released and let him through. She raised one arm out of the grass and waved until he spotted her. He was dressed in sweatpants and a threadbare t-shirt, padding over in a pair of flip-flops with his hair at odd angles as if he'd just jumped out of bed.

"Hey pixie," he said. He was looking down at her like he'd been looking at her in the kitchen the night before, awed and wanting, glancing over to where her shift ended at her knees. She lifted them up a little to tease him. "What's the night time version of a pixie?"

"I really have no idea, I'm not sure they're especially fussed about what time it is," Zee said. She reached her hand out to him. "Come down here."

Johnny settled down on the ground next to her, frowning a little at the grass until she snuggled up to his side and settled her chin on his shoulder. Then he looked very happy to be where he was.

"Why are you here?" she asked.

"Sam called," he said. Zee narrowed her eyes at the house before he added, "She said you needed a...'recharge?'"

Zee smirked. "Did she explain that to you?"

"No." He shrugged. "But then again, I didn't really ask questions past 'you should come see Zee.'"

"Moonlight is kind of restorative for me," Zee said. "It's like a magical boost for a lot of witches, really. And so is this..." She sat up a little and leaned forward, pressing her lips softly to his.

Johnny smiled as she pulled away. "Lane, did you just admit that kissing me is magic?"

Zee raised an eyebrow. "If you have a differing opinion,

please share."

"No, no," he said quickly. "Feels like magic. Here, let me help some more."

His hand slipped through her hair to the back of her head and he pulled her down for another, sliding his lips back and forth against hers for a moment before pressing softly. Zee hummed, a pleasant buzz of energy bursting in her heart and running out to the tips of her toes and fingers. Johnny smiled, drawing a way for a second to catch her eye. He grinned, dimple popping out, then his arms snaked around her body and he rolled them over.

She got half a laugh out before Johnny was swallowing the sound with another kiss, his mouth wrapping around her bottom lip to suck and soothe with a flick of his tongue. One hand slid up her back through the grass until he was cupping her neck. With every pound of her heart there was another spark of magic zipping through her, up her throat, down into her belly. Her hands clutched at his lower back, rucking up his t-shirt until she found his skin, heat spreading up through her chilly fingers. Johnny gasped into her mouth and Zee pushed up into his chest, chasing the taste of him. Their legs were starting to tangle together and his hand was clutching at her hip, arm holding her tight against him as they passed the lead of the kiss between them.

He retreated again, loosening his grip on her waist and Zee sucked in a breath. Her whole body was singing in his arms and one of her legs was wrapping around his hip. She felt *charged.* She felt electric. She felt like she could show Johnny what it really meant to be a witch, the brightness that filled you up while working magic. The dizzy, heady strength that burned through you.

Johnny ducked his head and took a taste of her neck, his

lips pressing wet, open kisses over her pulse and down to her clavicle. She shuddered and her fingers dug into his shoulder blades.

"What about this?" Johnny said against her throat. "Does this recharge you, too?"

His teeth scraped against her skin and choked giggle escaped Zee.

"It's not ineffective," Zee said, voice breathy.

Johnny nuzzled against her neck, breath hot and damp, chilling fast along her skin as a breeze skimmed them in the grass. She could feel his shoulders shake with quiet laughter. His knee was pressed between her thighs, propping him up slightly from the ground, and it was taking every ounce of her restraint not to arch up and press herself to his thigh for a sharper edge of energy, something more than restorative. Something creative.

"Just trying to help out," he said. He made a pattern across the base of her throat; suck, nibble, and a wet swirl with the tip of his tongue until she felt like she was wearing a necklace of kisses.

Another stroke of wind washed up over the cliff, and Zee shivered in the grass, caught between the cool air and Johnny's warmth.

"We should go inside," she said as he started to make his way back up to her jaw.

"'M not done with my job yet," he said, and dropped three firm, popping kisses on her cheek next to her ear.

"You can continue upstairs in bed with me," she said, laughing, and then trailing off as she realized what she'd implied. Johnny stiffened above her and lifted his head up with a frozen, stunned expression. She rushed to add, "If you don't want to drive home and want to sleep here. Next to me."

He blinked twice and then smiled, his eyes softening and wrinkling at the corners. He kissed her, soft and careful, just once. "Nice save, Lane."

"I just meant-"

"No, I know," he assured her. "And yeah, I want to sleep next to you. Does your offer include me being the big spoon?"

Zee laughed and tried to hide her face but there was nowhere to go with Johnny hovering over her.

"If you can give me an outline of appropriate touching zones I promise not to disappoint," Johnny said and Zee couldn't tell if the eager earnestness in his face was a joke or...well, earnest.

"You're teasing me, I take it back-" She tried to squirm out from under him but he caught her close with the arm at her back.

"Nope, nope. I promise to be a gentleman," he said.

He pushed himself up on his knees and gazed down at her. Zee was suddenly very aware of the fact that she was wearing her plain white shift for working serious magic and...nothing else. Johnny appeared to be taking this in as well if the way his gaze darkened was anything to judge by.

"Hey," he said, voice throaty. "You're really beautiful."

Zee blushed and sat up, trying to push the skirt of her shift back down to her knees. Johnny stood and held his hands out to help her stand.

"You're not too shabby either, Sharpe," she said while turning away to the house to hide her growing smile.

"I dunno," He said, keeping her hand in his as he followed her to the greenhouse. "Someone once called me a walking, talking burn mark, which is probably more accurate."

"I don't appreciate my panicked declarations being

quoted back to me," she said.

"Hang on," he said. He tugged on her hand to stop her just before the steps up to the greenhouse. "Moonlight."

And then his head was dipping down and Zee was on her toes to reach him sooner, mouths fitting together in perfect pieces. With her arms over his shoulders Zee could only just touch her toes to the ground and Johnny wrapped an arm around her waist to drag her up against his chest. There was a rumble of pleased humming rising up out of his throat to vibrate against her lips. She landed back on her feet and Johnny left another quick peck on her lips.

"You're shivering," he said.

Trembling, she thought. There was a difference.

She took his hand and pulled him in through the greenhouse, tugging him along before he could get distracted by any of Sam's experiments. Sam was mysteriously missing from her usual haunt, the kitchen.

"Are there *always* brownies in your kitchen?" Johnny asked, snatching one up off a plate at the center of the island.

"Chocolate is very important to witches," Zee said.

"Hm," Johnny said, and then he held the brownie out for her to take a quick bite.

All things considered, Johnny was a pretty quick learner.

Sam was back in her own room for the night. She and Zee had finished cleaning up Nadia's space and fixing the furniture, and the door was closed now. There was a small tea candle burning on a dish in Zee's room and the slightly romantic touch had Nadia's signature all over it. Zee twitched as she crossed the threshold.

She was bringing Johnny Sharpe into her bedroom.

She was asking Johnny Sharpe to sleep next to her, in

her bed.

She had clothes piled in the armchair by her dresser, a bra hanging from the knob of a drawer, and a spread of spellbooks sitting across the covers of her bed.

He set his hands on her hips and Zee jumped.

"Hey, if we need to take a step back…I can head out whenever you ask me to," he said. His hands soothed stripes up and down her sides.

"No, no, I want you to stay," she said, but to her own ears her voice sounded uneven and when she turned back to him, she could see the edge of a frown from the light of hall. "I'm not ready to have sex with you," she said all at once.

Johnny's hands slid from her waist and he stepped inside of the room, shutting the door behind him. The candle was flickering dimly but the room was flooded with blue moonlight and she could make out the soft, tired smile on his face.

"I know," he said. He shrugged his shoulders and Zee watched the muscles shift under the soft fabric of his t-shirt, and almost *almost* regretted her words. "And if you aren't ready then I'm not ready, okay?"

She stared up into his eyes, their color almost shining in the dark. Something taut and brittle in her chest softened, and she felt her shoulders relaxing as he stared back at her.

"Okay," she said. "I'm going to change. Bed's there." She gestured to the center of the room where her bed was sitting at an odd angle.

"Are those wheels?" Johnny asked eyeing the feet of her bed.

"Yeah, I move it around a lot," Zee said, grabbing the first sleep shirt and shorts she found. They weren't a match but they weren't a total disaster and they were definitely less provocative then the gauzy dress she was wearing now.

She heard a squeak of rusty old wheels as she shuffled to her connecting bathroom and looked back to see Johnny pushing the bed into a pool of light falling to the floor from her giant windows. The sight made her heart clench in her chest and she hurried out of the room. When she'd finished she came out to find Johnny on the left side of her bed, covers pushed back and his toes tucked under her sheets. The sweatpants were gone and he was laying back in his tshirt and boxers against a cluster of pillows, his knees bent up as he stared hard at the cover of an old book about using ley lines to charge home wards.

Zee considered going back into the bathroom until she could name the exact emotion she suffered from after seeing Johnny Sharpe in her bed, looking comfy, and reading the back cover of a spellbook in the moonlight.

"I didn't know which side to pick," he said.

"The blue pillow behind you is my favorite but other than that you're fine," she said.

He sat up and retrieved her pillow and she watched as he pressed it to his nose for a long breath in. Then he fluffed it and put it on top of her share.

"What's it take to be a witch?" he asked, as she picked up the books off her bed, plucking the one out of Johnny's hand.

"Practice," she said, and set the books down on the sill as she opened the window to let the cool air in. It was what Nadia had always said.

"Okay, but it's a little different for you, isn't it?" he asked. "Corey, my friend in college, she was a witch but she never said anything about shadow men that could make you sick or set things on fire."

Zee slid into the bed and Johnny immediately pulled the sheet up over both of them. Like this wasn't its own kind of magical phenomenon, the two of them in a bed together... talking about witchcraft. He scooted down until she could see the white blurs of his feet under the blanket, sticking out of the bars of her bed frame.

"To be fair, I've never really seen anything like that before either," Zee said. And then she settled down against her pillows onto her side.

"C'mere," Johnny said, lifting his arm up along her head board. She shuffled closer to him, blue pillow tucked into his shoulder. She was glad she'd opened the window because he was toasty under the covers.

"You're really warm," she said, shifting a little closer until she'd found a way to fit herself along his side.

"I run hot," he said, as he wrapped a heavy arm across her back. "A little under 100."

Zee blinked and tilted her head back to stare at him. "Oh."

"Oh?" he asked. His eyes popped wide and a grin spread across his face. "Did you think it was cause I'm hot?" He waggled his eyebrows.

Zee snorted and kicked her legs against him. Which was a mistake. The friction of their bare skin together sent tingling shocks of electricity up her body to settle between her thighs. Johnny took the challenge with a quick laugh and rolled her beneath him, one arm cradling her neck and the other framing her to the bed. He was heavy against her and the weight made her pulse pound under her skin.

"Or did you just think that was what it felt like when we touched?" he asked, leaning down until the tip of his nose stroked along her cheek, breath puffing against her neck. "'Cause it does feel different than anyone else..."

"You're supposed to be kissing me," she said, not entirely sure if she was trying to distract him from the dangerous train of thought they'd landed themselves on, or if she just badly needed him to kiss her.

He started to smile, she could feel it twitching against her jaw, so she clasped his face in her hands and brought it up to snag his bottom lip between her teeth. His breath hitched and he sank a little harder against her hips on the mattress as he kissed back, swallowing a happy whimper from her mouth and answering her with quiet groan. She could feel the moon on the backs of her hands as they threaded through the strands of his hair, tugging gently and making him shudder over her.

Full moon magic was meant for lovers.

* * *

Zee woke once in the night from dreaming that she was floating in the water to find that the bed was scooting across the floor. She rolled over to see the fuzzy shape of Johnny pushing carefully at one of the bed posts. He smiled at her and Zee's stomach flipped at the picture of his hair sticking out in soft tufts.

"What're you doin'?" she asked, voice scratched with sleep.

"Puttin' you under the moon, pixie," he whispered back just as the bed shifted enough for the light to stretch across her skin.

"You're hired," she said.

Johnny huffed a laugh and crawled back into the bed, immediately pressing close to her back. He nuzzled the hair of her shoulder out of his way so that he could stroke kisses over the curve of her neck.

"Go back to sleep," he said, and she was halfway there already.

April 18ᵗʰ 2005

Nadia's head peeked in through the cracked door and Zee curled up tighter on the bed, springs squeaking and sobs catching and bursting from her throat.

"Oh, ved'mitchka," Nadia said, sighing and slipping into her bedroom. She shut the door behind her with a silent click and hurried to the bed to cover Zee's body with her own like a shield. "I know, my love. I know."

"Why?" Zee asked with a gasp of breath. "Why won't they stop? Why won't they stop?"

Nadia brushed at long dark strands, unsticking them from wet cheeks and working deft fingers through the tangles.

"He hates me," Zee sobbed.

"Shhh," Nadia murmured. "That isn't true. I have seen that boy, Zoya, and he does not hate you."

"He got the whole class to ignore me today," Zee shouted and Nadia's lips pursed. "No matter what I said, no matter who I spoke to, they all pretended as if I wasn't there."

"Your classmates are especially prone to suggestion," Nadia growled.

"I hate the dreams," Zee whispered. "I could hate Johnny too if it weren't for the dreams. God, Noddy, why can't I stop dreaming?"

The sniffles started again and Nadia hurried to stroke long patterns along her back, encouraging slow, even breaths.

"They will not stop," Nadia said. Zee looked up at her face and found pain etched into the lines there, carved around her aunt's eyes and lips. "Those dreams will not stop, my love. They will never stop, not while you are apart from him. And you must bear that. You can, I know you can."

Zee found herself gaping for a moment before she swallowed another sniffle. "You...have you-"

"You are beautifully strong, my ved'mitchka," Nadia said firmly. "You can bear that."

July 9th 2017

Zee spread herself across the sheets in the morning. Johnny was missing from the bed, but his citrusy sharp smell was in the pillows behind her and she pressed her face against them to inhale. Falling asleep had been hard with him in reach, equally uninterested in not touching, not tasting, not holding each other tight enough to fuse together. But his hands never more than *teased* at the places he might touch her with her permission.

She sat up in bed and folded her knees close to her chest. Johnny must have moved the bed again before the morning because a glass of water on the windowsill was now in reach. She drank half the water and stood on wobbly legs out of bed. It'd been a long time since she'd spent a night rolling around a bed with anyone, semi-innocently or otherwise, and feelings of the night before were imprinted on her skin. The scratch of his stubble on her neck, the outline of his hips over hers even as he tried to hold himself away the longer they touched, the evidence of his arousal growing. Even the grip of his hand around hers, the way his knuckles had tightened against her fingers as she'd sucked his earlobe into her mouth the night before.

She wanted to see him. Needed him to smile at her and remind her that he'd been glad to be here. Happy with where they'd started and stopped the night before.

But when she made it to the kitchen to find Johnny hunched over the counter staring into a coffee cup and Sam shifting restlessly with arms folded over her chest by the toaster, Zee's nerves flared. Sam glanced once at her and then actively avoided her gaze. Johnny didn't look up at all.

"Did you just give him a shovel talk?" Zee blurted.

Johnny's eyes flicked to her but his head didn't lift and he went back to staring down the mug in front of him.

"I..." Sam trailed off, biting her lip and looking up at the ceiling. "I might have made some assumptions about what you two have discussed."

"Umm..." Why did she feel like there was ice running through her veins?

"The dreams," Sam whispered and Zee felt her heart stutter.

"Pesnya dushi," Johnny said, brow tight as his mouth fumbled over the words, sounding out the syllables too carefully.

Zee turned back to Sam who winced and mouthed 'I'm so sorry.' Zee let her eyes fall shut and nodded, listening to her cousin's feet pad quickly out of the room and down the hall. When she opened her eyes again Johnny was staring at her and there was something painfully absent from his expression, some kind of hopeful softness that he'd been wearing ever since that first day he'd walked into the Lab.

"It doesn't have to mean anything," she said, adding, "If you don't want it to."

His expression grew tight, eyes sharpening as he looked at her and she felt pinpricks on her fingertips.

"I'll come back to that, what you just said. But first I want you to tell me what it might mean," he said. "Tell me the *whole* thing."

"What did Sam-?"

"Zee." He sat up on the stool, his arms falling into his lap and Zee almost flinched at the pale exasperation on his face.

"I have dreamt of you. Since we were twelve." She lined the words up between them, like little tiles, and waited for Johnny to knock them down.

"What kind of-?"

"All kinds," she said. "At first...at first it was just...you. What you looked like. How you..." How he smiled. How his hand would feel in hers. "How you were. And then it was things you might say to me. Conversations we might have."

"Like the day we met?" he asked.

The day he had rejected her friendship and snarled 'witch' at her. "No," she said. "They were...dreams about us as if we were...happy. Usually. None of them came true."

His face was slack and he looked down at his untouched mug of coffee as if it had bitten him. "I don't think I had...I mean. Zee, I dreamt of you but..." He turned a little pink as he glanced at her.

"No it's...it's something a witch experiences," Zee said.

"Why? Why dream of me?" He asked.

Zee swallowed and tried to think of anything to say, anything at all that might be true but wouldn't leave her feeling like she had torn herself open in front of him. "Johnny, I - I can't-"

"Come here," he said. When she hesitated, her eyes felt hot and wet and everything was fuzzy in front of her, he stood and joined her at the other side of the island. His arms went around her and she finally released the breath she'd been holding. He was curving over her, setting his mouth to the top of her head. "Please tell me," he said.

"You were meant for me." She whispered the words. She wasn't even sure if she said them loudly enough for him to hear. But then his hands twitched on her spine - was he going to pull away? - and she rushed to fill the space. "Nadia said it was what happened when a witch's life was entwined with another person. That the threads of memories and growth and change and experiences all get tied together and it falls into our dreams."

The fingers on her back slid up and down, light and almost ticklish, but not another bit of Johnny moved around her.

"But, that doesn't mean that...that anyone has to..." She didn't know how to say the words without putting Johnny and herself in the implications. Pesnya dushi's did not always stay together. Fate giving another person impact on a witch's life didn't always mean the impact was good. "Nothing is written in stone," she said instead.

But *so much* was possible.

"Since you were twelve," he said. "That's how long you've known?"

"It doesn't have to mean anything." She meant it as reassurance but when she stepped back from him she caught the end of a frustrated twist in his face.

"Please stop reminding me of my possible insignificance to you," he said.

"No. No, it's... obviously yo- a pesnya dushi is significant," Zee said. "But it's not...there's always a choice."

His eyes narrowed at her for a moment and his mouth shifted, words near to bursting out, before he shook his head. He stepped away from her, fingers combing through his hair, pulling at the strands.

"Why didn't you ever say anything?" he asked, folding his arms and looking down at the floor.

"Johnny, really? When? When we were twelve?" She almost had. She almost had so many times. "When we were sixteen? While we were in college? I was trying to forget about you," she said. The words went off like a gunshot and Johnny's head shot up. He looked stunned. She fought for any explanation, wrestling the words out of the choking tightness in her throat. "You always...It seemed so clear that you wanted nothing to do with me."

His mouth firmed into a thin line and she watched him swallow hard, twice. He turned his back to her scrubbed his hands over his face and Zee felt wet streaks running down her cheeks.

"You keep saying it doesn't have to mean anything. But it could, right?"

Zee nodded, but he wasn't looking at her so she cracked out, "Yes." And then slammed her eyes shut as he turned back toward her, afraid of what she might see.

"If we want it to?" he asked.

She nodded again and there was no way to voice a word.

There was a little glow of warmth in front of her and then Johnny was gently lifting her face. When she tried to turn away, his thumbs were on her cheeks, smoothing tears on her skin.

"I know that I ruined a lot of years of potential," he said. "I didn't realize how badly. But I would really like to enjoy some of that potential now. If you think it's still there."

She hadn't even realized that her fingers were knotting into the fabric of his t-shirt until she was pulling him down to her, darting up on her tiptoes to kiss hard against his mouth. He grasped at her, exchanging three fierce, firm kisses before pulling away again.

"Zee, I'm not freaked out by you dreaming of me," he said, trying to lift her chin up while she tried to burrow her face against his throat. When she was too stubborn he settled for soothing his hand down the back of her neck. His free hand sought out hers, fingers stroking over her clenched knuckles until she loosened her fist and held onto him. "As much as I wish I'd known...that you'd been able to tell me sooner, I get why you didn't. What I'm upset about is that you don't seem to realize how much I *want* it to be true. I'm going to keep trying to prove that, okay?"

She tried to answer but all of her emotions were swollen bruises in her chest and throat so instead she turned her face up, new tears slipping out.

And, oh shit. This wasn't even the end of it. Lucas. She had to tell him about those dreams too, didn't she?

"Need to kiss you," he said, even as he was bending down and fitting their lips together. Zee could barely breathe in the kiss but she could taste him and touch him and the urgency of that eclipsed the one for air. His mouth dragged and sipped hers, trailing over her cheek as she gasped a breath, settling at the top of her neck by her ear.

"I promise," he said, voice ragged. "Zee, I promise. I'll-"

She cut him off, pulling him back and swallowing the words she hadn't learned to trust yet.

Their rhythm grew hard, bodies pushing against each other until he had her lifted up in his arms and pressed against the back counter. This she could believe. That Johnny wanted to feel her, kiss her. That she could make him groan by rolling her hips and scratching her fingers down his back. That they could find a way to fit together with him curling over her, with her surging up to meet him, stroking her tongue along his, letting him chase her. That his hands could be everywhere at once and still holding her safely against him.

"Hey," he said as the broke apart, by barely an inch, to take sharp gasps of air. She tried to catch him again, pull him close before he could think straight. "Wait," he said, leaning away. His hands were sweeping down her arms, her still sleep tousled hair, her back, as if it could erase the sexual energy or turn it softer. "Tryin' to distract me?" he asked with a smile.

He must have seen the trouble on her face, the guilt in her eyes. He sighed and she slipped down his body to rest on her own feet again.

"There's something else," she said.

He stiffened, waiting.

"I haven't told Sam, even," she whispered, widening her eyes. Johnny flinched and nodded and she swallowed twice before she could force herself to say the words. "The dreams started again, after you came back. With Lucas Wolfe."

Johnny stared at her for a long time. Then he blinked. "Wait... do you mean..."

"Nadia never told me there could be more than one. And at first I thought it meant you and I weren't... but I dream of you too and I don't- Johnny, honestly I don't know what it means."

"He broke into your house!"

"It could be- we could be twined together for- for, I dunno, awful reasons!" She said throwing her hands up in the air. "I don't know, I don't know. I'm sorry!"

Johnny left her standing there, pacing down the length of the kitchen, and she thought he'd just walk out the greenhouse and leave. But he turned around again, came back and stopped inches away from her, eyes pale and gray instead of their usual blue. He leaned forward, setting his forehead onto her shoulder, arms braced against the countertop. She cupped her hands over his shoulders. "I should go, Zee," he said.

She stiffened below him and one hand lifted from the counter to wrap around her waist.

"Why?" she asked.

"I'm not trying to put distance between us," he said. "Well, not emotional distance." He turned his head and kissed along the line of her sleep shirt where her skin appeared. "I'm just not sure where my head is at. And I don't want to make a mistake with you. Not another one."

He stepped back and Zee had to drop her grip on his shirt. His eyes were still tight as he looked over her, and the line of his jaw was hard, a little pulse of tension popping by his temple.

"Do you need me to stay?" he asked with a worried twist to his frown.

She didn't want to think about what she looked like. She had to be a mess. She wasn't a pretty crier. (Was anyone?)

She shook her head. "No I'm...I'll be alright."

His hands twitched at his side. And she understood. She wanted to wrap herself around him. She wanted him to leave. It was all tangled up.

"I'll call you tomorrow," he said. She nodded and her mouth wobbled and then Johnny was against her again, soft kisses against her mouth. "I'm not walking away, okay?"

"Okay," she said. They kissed again, holding together, lips wet and breath passing between them for a long minute until she pushed softly at his chest. "Okay," she repeated.

He wavered in place until she looked away, her eyes felt heavy sore from bad sleep and crying, and then he was leaving the kitchen and walking away down the hall. She stayed leaning against the counter until the rattle of his car started. She crossed the kitchen to take his barely touched cup of coffee upstairs to bed with her.

Chapter 11

Setting Traps

July 11th, 2017

"You know you saved me, right?" Luke asked her, his head on her chest, arms pinning her into the grass.

She ran her fingers through his hair, scratched at his roots and felt him purr against her chest. *This is a dream,* she thought.

"I didn't even know you needed saving," she said. She felt lazy and wonderful, staring up at the maple with its leaves turning wild red above her. It was getting cooler out but down here in the earth, with Luke, fall felt perfect.

"Yes you did. From the very beginning."

He rose up, twisting and sliding over her, tall and lanky and trapping her underneath him. His smile was gentle, green eyes reflecting her in the iris, the grass making the color deeper.

"Where's Johnny?" he asked.

She woke at that, the bed a little damp beneath her, summer turning muggy. She could smell Lucas Wolfe in the room, the woodsmoke and deep forest heaviness of him. And then a breeze came through and Nadia's hair flashed like a prism in the corner of the room.

"Why won't you tell me what you know?" Zee asked her.

Why won't you admit you already understand? Nadia answered.

* * *

"And I am telling you, Mr. Hunt, that you have never tried my potions," Sam said smugly, arms folded across her chest as she stared down at Brian, Johnny's quiet glass crew member. He was sitting in one of their little iron tea chairs, filling up the edges like it was meant for a child rather than a full grown adult. And he was trying to shrink under Sam's glare, slinking down against the back of the chair, his legs bumping up against the table.

"Don't bully the man," Zee said to Sam.

"Bullying is malicious," Sam snapped back. "I'm being helpful."

"Let her wear him down," Eric said under his breath to Zee. "Brian could use a little magic on his side."

"Hey Zee," Will called from the greenhouse. "Can't find the corkscrew. Can you give me a hand?"

She narrowed her eyes at him, half hanging out the door. She'd left the corkscrew sitting directly next to the bottle of wine in the kitchen. She glanced over at Eric who was unsubtly focusing all his attention on Sam lecturing Brian on the benefits of white light healing and meditation.

"Okaaay," she said, rising up from the chair and heading over to the greenhouse. "What's up, Will?"

"Just need your help," he said, but his voice was pitched too high, playing innocent.

She glanced back at the others, outlined by a pink and tangerine sunset, Eric smothering his laugh as Sam's hands wrapped around Brian's head in some kind of exercise. "Finding the corkscrew?" she asked, turning back and following Will into the kitchen. "Because unless you hid it..."

"Test the pasta sauce," he said. "Think it needs something."

His hair was up in a little knot at the top of his head and he had one of Zee's flour caked aprons over his clothes. The corkscrew was sitting next to the open bottle of wine on the counter.

"Pour me a glass to go with that side of bullshit you're serving me," Zee said to him with a lift of her eyebrows.

Will grinned and went to the cupboard to pull down two glasses while Zee took a quick taste of the sauce simmering on the stove.

"This is really good," she said, and then went to her spice cupboard to add more fennel and the dried lemon basil from the garden. Will snorted behind her and a glass of wine appeared on her left.

"So," he said, the word drawing out too long and making Zee's hackles raise. "How are things with Johnny?"

Her teeth clenched and she stirred at the sauce for a long minute. Will was patient behind her. There was a rustle of movement and the sound of bread being sliced.

"How about you just skip the small talk and ask the question you're working up to," Zee said.

The bread knife thunked on the counter and Will joined her at the stove, leaning in to meet her eyes.

"He's beating himself up about something, and I just

want to know if I need to help him with that," Will said. "What'd he do?"

Zee sighed and turned the burner off, passing the spoon to him for a taste test. His eyes lit up at the flavor.

"I think, this time, the blame is mine," Zee admitted. "But...we'll be okay. I think we'll be okay. We've been talking. I'm coming to the grand opening on Saturday."

Johnny had kept his promise and called her, asked her to be his date at his studio opening that weekend. The conversation had been fragile, both choosing their words like they were being tested on them. And making plans together had hardly been a step back, even if Zee did want to erase the awkwardness and go back to the night of fooling around and cuddling in her bed.

"He doesn't act like it's your fault," Will said and Zee thought the way his brow furrowed was adorable.

"Not fault," she said with a shrug. "We just have a lot of history and I've been carrying more of it than he realized. And now he knows more...just more. It's a lot. We'll be okay."

"He's not giving up on you," Will said. Zee glanced at him and tried to keep the hope off her face. "I've known Johnny a long time. And even before he ever mentioned you, I knew you existed. I knew there was *someone*."

Zee wiped at her cheeks. It was the *steam*, nothing else. "Where's the manicotti?"

Will smiled, pecked a kiss on her cheek, and went to the sink to pull the soft pasta shells out of the strainer.

July 12th, 2017

She fingered the bloody scrap of black cloth in her hands, running her thumb back and forth over the grain of the fabric. The furniture in the sunroom was pushed to the side, the glass swept away and the un-homed artifacts lined up along the windowsill. Zee had been taking customers outside on the wrap around porch, cloaked with citronella candles and handwoven afghans for the chilly nights. The sunroom still had an icky, sticky residue in the air. Something sage bundles and salt washes hadn't been able to erase yet.

But that was alright. A little bit of that black magic was just another thread to grab onto for what she needed to do next.

She lit the burner of herbs sitting on the floor in front of her; anise and lemon peel for strengthening psychic vibrations, bay for protection. She tucked her hair back with Nadia's old chrysocholla hair pins and paused at the soft hand on her shoulder.

This is dangerous little witch.

"I know," Zee whispered.

I cannot follow you on the mental plane.

"I can do this, Noddy," Zee said. "I can do this."

A kiss pressed into her hair at the crown of her head and then Nadia was gone again.

Zee leaned into the smoke from the herbs, closing her eyes and breathing deeply. She buried her cough at the thick licorice stench and took another deep breath, thoughts spinning. But the sour flavor of magic that clung to the walls of the sunroom was sharper and the fabric in her hands tingled at her fingertips. It felt like little needles, the quick stabs of cold at the touch of ice.

That was what she was looking for.

She leaned away from the smoke as the shiver of power ran under her skin into her bones, up her arms and throat, making her teeth throb and her cheeks cramp and her eyes tear up until the chill was in her thoughts, a cloak of cold. She could chase Lucas Wolfe down like this, slip into his head to dig and tear until she found answers. Or until she left him weak.

Her head fell back with the weight of the ice and when she opened her eyes again, the world around her was gray and blue with violent, worming threads of red, the stains of magic. They slithered in the corners of the room, streaks running over a few of her family's tools, and a dark heavy stripe dragging across the floor and around the edges of the bay window. She took a deep breath and as she released it - so slow that it didn't even disturb the smoke drifting in the air in front of her - her frost-lined consciousness drifted away from her body.

She had practiced this when she was younger, with Nadia. It was not quite like floating. Nadia said that was because the brain supplied the memory of what a step felt like. She imagined it was similar to walking on the moon, weightless and aimless, every motion accompanied by the urge to catch flight and lose direction.

This time was easier. Her toes clung to the greasy red streak of magic across the floor and the path to the window dragged on her like a magnet. She followed it, skipping along the trail in static bursts of time and space. She was on the windowsill, her fingers brushing through a clean crystal globe with a glimmer of old memory - Nadia so, so young, eyes sharp and forehead knotted as she stared into the sphere of light and dug for answers - and then she was outside on the lawn, and at the gate.

The red spots thinned outside of her home boundaries, little glances on the road, a shimmering stain outside of the Lab, and then a glossy wash of red at the docks. There was a border of crimson ringing out over the beach, washing up with the ocean scurf, battering at the shining blue Nikolaev wards around the island.

Two more skips passed - the mainland docks, a graveyard - and then she found him in a one room cabin in the woods, a rickety looking thing painted green with moss and new trees sprouting out of the gutters. The walls were streaked with oily red magic. It pooled over the bed and slithered across the floor. Power patterned like frost crystals shaded the windows and mirrors barring view and reflection. Lucas Wolfe sat cross-legged on the floor of the cabin, wearing plain dark pants that tied around his narrow waist. His wiry chest was bare and his pale skin was patterned with a red tinged ash. There were bones, and knives, and rusted iron rail stakes spiraling out on the floor around him.

His eyes narrowed as she appeared. He looked different, the clean cut insurance salesman transformed back into the witch, a feral look around his eyes. She hovered in the corner, studying the room for any signs and clues to who this man really was. But this was a space designed to hold magic. There was no cell phone, no computer, no little suitcase. Not even a car outside. This was a workspace and now, to Zee, it felt like a trap.

"I know you're here," he whispered into the space. "My little moon bloom."

The red streaks of magic pulsed as he spoke and the ice crackled. The magic she had used to hitch a ride here felt tighter around her, more like a cage and she immediately began to draw on her own, the clean light, to push against his and give herself breathing room.

He grinned, eyes unfocused, scanning the room aimlessly, drifting over her.

"You made a mistake in coming here, darling," he said, a crisp hint of British accent appearing.

Yeah...she was beginning to realize that.

"Did you think you could catch me unawares?" he asked. "Sneak up on me? You, with your charming wreaths and gentle wards. I've heard stories about the Nikolaev women. I never imagined they'd have grown so *soft*. Your aunt must have coddled you."

Zee smiled and began to circle him on the floor. The tools around him were a trap. She wasn't stupid. Maybe Nadia had been gentle on them, taught them the sweeter parts of magic, focused on what could help people rather than what might make them stronger witches. But she hadn't left them completely in the dark no matter what this man thought.

"Come closer, moon bloom," Lucas cooed. "I can almost taste you. That honey flavor from my dreams."

Zee tried to shift away and found a frozen wall at the back of her thoughts and a sharp jab of power striking her dizzy. She grimaced and gasped and Lucas Wolfe startled in his spot, his eyes fixed to where she was, but seeing right through her. Icy lightning zipped through her and pain rung out. Zee tugged and pushed and tried to chip at the power around her, but the walls grew denser, colder, closer as she fought. Her head felt muddled as Lucas stood up from the floor and turned to face her, and the soft touch of the fabric in her hands on the island grew fainter. The feel of the floor under her legs softened and flickered. He was cutting her consciousness away from her body and she grappled for a foothold out of the projection and back into her home.

"You feel like silk, my darling," Lucas murmured. "Such a delicate heart. So fragile for a grown woman."

Now that's just rude, she thought. And now she could feel him tracing through her, the ragged edges of his chilly aggression, the scraping sensation as he dug through her memories.

She built guards up in her mind, walls to surround her love for Sam, her ache for Nadia and her mother, her fear of Johnny breaking her heart again.

"Musn't have secrets amongst lovers, Zoya," he said and the strange red ropes of power circled her like sharks in the water.

She was sluggish and fuzzy-headed, and when a memory of Sam soothing her horrible respiratory infection floated in she clung to it for a moment, basking in the teasing sarcasm of her cousin, the bright flavor of her tonic. Then Lucas chuckled and Zee moaned and shoved the memory away. She had let him in.

She tried to shore up the blocks but they crumbled under his grip just as quickly.

He found Johnny next, just a dream, a startle of his surprise in her thoughts. He hadn't realized she had another one. He watched the perfect little vision of her and Johnny facing each other in bed, naked and sleepy and talking over their day, an echo of heartache running through them both. An old dream, one that she had clung to even in college when she was determined to forget him. Lucas hummed as it ended and then the dream started over again, from Johnny pressing a kiss to her lips, stroking back a lock of hair, and asking her about the customer she'd been reading for when he'd arrived home.

"Pesnya dushi," Lucas said, but his voice rattled strangely, as if there were an echo inside of it. When he continued, the echo had faded. "The Witch's Joke. Did you know that's what it's called?"

Nadia had called it that once, when Zee was young,

spoken it in a bitter tone and then distracted her with a magical treasure hunt around the house.

"A witch is not a lover. We are conduits, moon bloom, we are forces of change," he said, and it sounded recited.

Nadia had always said a witch was a force of growth.

"He was never going to stay," Lucas whispered into the air, just inches from where she was caught, tangled in red and anchored in ice. "He was never meant to love you, only to tighten the grip on your heart so you could learn to break it."

She had never learned to break Johnny's grip on her heart.

Zee. The voice was soft, no competition for Lucas Wolfe's hisses and whispers. Cold burned at her cheek like a caress.

"Now, tell me all about *her*," Lucas said. "The powerful one. Your aunt."

"Fuck you." The words were surprisingly firm, even said over a channel of distance. Lucas's brow furrowed and she wondered if he could hear that.

But Nadia. Nadia he could not have.

Zee? Zee, what's happened?

The burn was over her throat, at her wrist, and she cried out, pulling away.

Zee!

"*He's found her*," said a voice, all rattle and grit. And as it spoke the red threads pulsed and squirmed in around her and Lucas's eyes sparked with crimson. "I'll have her shredded before he can do anything," Lucas said. "I promise you."

"Johnny," she said. The name was miles away from the cabin and clumsy on her cold numbed lips.

Zee, what- what's happening?

The burn stroked at her cheeks, soft and gentle. It wasn't the stinging tear of cold but the brilliant flash of sun and fire. Johnny was at the house.

"Help," she murmured. She tried squirming away from the red strands curling around her wrists and ankles, snaking around her waist, but only bumped against the hard shell of ice.

Shit. Zee? Zee, you gotta tell me what to do.

He was so warm. Even in her thoughts he glowed like the belly of the ovens he worked around. She was soaking in the heat, sapping it into herself to try and combat against the shattering cold of Lucas's power turned against her. She was horrible and selfish and maybe giving Lucas Wolfe access to Johnny's strength, his shocking brightness, but she needed it wrapped around her.

Zee! Zee, babe, c'mon. C'mon. Tell me what to do.

"We have her," Lucas said.

"Rowan crown," she said, or tried to say, the words all stuck together on her tongue. "By the window."

She could feel Lucas's fingerhold on her thoughts now and his amusement was spinning in the background, laughing and twisting her head. Johnny's warmth vanished from her side and Lucas and the inky, oily shadow lurking inside of him were all that was left. Zee shied from every brush in her mind, every greasy fingerprint on a memory, every attempt to cut away at something precious of hers, to chisel at the stronghold keeping Sam safe in her mind.

When Johnny reappeared at her side, she had no sense of her own body left but his glow was there and it battered back at the intruders. He spoke her name, but instead of the word, his strength surged through her. She clutched at Lucas as he tried to retreat another step and her grip answering his seemed to spin the control between them.

"Not yet," she managed to Johnny as something vivid and clear scratched against her hair and for a moment, the room at home was in focus again.

When the tables turned Zee was ready. Weak, but desperate, she pierced and kicked and swam upstream against Lucas' invasion. She dug all the sharp edges of her power, all the fierce teeth that Nadia had trained her with but never demanded she use, into Lucas Wolfe.

And found that he was not alone.

They were little glimpses. He was better at guarding than she was.

A younger version of Lucas, sweeter and closer to her dreams of him, with a backpack over his shoulder and the famous silhouette of the onion dome churches in St. Petersburg. A coven of unfamiliar faces, tired dark eyes watching him, drawing him into a rich library of magical texts. A staircase underground. The creeping shadow that swarmed his dreams, the color of dried blood.

And then the shadow was rushing at her, Lucas—no, his resident parasite chasing after her, a tangle of white flesh and black eyes!

"Now!" she cried out and then cabin split apart in little fractions of light until she was back in the sun room, thin branches tangling in her hair and Johnny kneeling before her, white-faced and wide-eyed.

Zee tossed the scrap of fabric to the side and threw herself against Johnny's chest. He caught her with a soft burst of breath and fell back on his heels, holding her tight against him.

"Johnny," she said followed immediately by a sob.

His hands were clutching at her back, gathering up her legs and drawing her up into his lap. His head nudged against the crown of branches in her hair and she snapped up a shaking hand to hold it steady.

"What was that?" He asked. "Are you okay? Jesus. Zee, are you okay?"

"I think so," she said. "No. No, I'm going to be sick."

To Johnny's credit, he didn't throw her off him, only snatched the poor misused bowl that had put out the journal fire the other night, and held it expectantly in front of her face. She might have smiled, but her face was still numb with cold.

"Need the floor," she said instead, gingerly crawling off his lap, all while Johnny continued to pet at her, appraising her condition. He guided her wobbling arms down to the floorboards, sweeping her hair back over her shoulder as she pressed her cheek to the warm grain of the wood.

"Zee," he sighed, leaning forward to set his forehead gently onto her shoulder. And oh, that helped too. Could she ask him to lay over her, cover her in that safe fire glow of his? "What happened?" he asked.

Zee opened her mouth to explain and after a choked pause, another sob fell out. One hand soothed at her spine and Zee clutched at the front of his button down and pulled him down to the floor and next to her side. That was better. She still wanted him closer.

"Shh... hey. Hey, it's okay. It's okay."

"I was so stupid," Zee said, gasping the words out in shuddering breaths as her chest pounded and her lungs burned. "Oh my god, Johnny. I was so fucking stupid."

Johnny bundled her up in his arms again so she was draped half over him. But it was alright she supposed, he seemed to be another grounding force for her to soak up, just like the house. She just wished she could get ahold of herself. She was rattling in her own skin like one of those little wobbling wind up dolls that skittered across the floor and she could feel Johnny chasing the trembles with his hands as if he could iron them away with firm comfort.

"I went looking for him," Zee whispered in hiccups. "I tried to spy on him."

"Him?"

"Luke- Lucas..." Zee shuddered again and turned her face to the side to as a dry heave kicked up her throat.

"You what?" Johnny said with a furrowed brow. "Why?

There was a little nervous vulnerability in the whispered question.

Zee tucked her face against his neck as the nausea passed. "We don't know what he wants. Why he's after us, what he's looking for. It has something to do with Nadia. I projected myself, followed his magic, tried to track him down." When Johnny stiffened, she added, "It was a trap."

He exhaled hard. "Why wasn't Sam here?"

"I didn't tell her," Zee whispered.

Johnny flinched under her. "You're probably gonna tell me it's none of my business, but Jesus fucking Christ Zee, even I know you shouldn't do shit like that alone."

I agree with him.

"Not now," Zee said with a huff.

Johnny reared up. "Um...yeah now. Now is the time, Lane."

"No, I didn't mean you, I meant Nadia."

"...Nadia?"

In for a penny, Zee thought. "Yeah. Nadia. She's a ghost. She lives here too." She twisted in his arms to watch as Johnny blinked, eyes glancing out of the corners as if he might see her. But Nadia was curled up like a cat in one of the pushed back arm chairs at the far corner of the room.

Tell him I said 'hi'.

"Don't tease, Noddy."

Johnny's head thunked softly on the floor again. "Okay," he said. "Okay, you need tea right? I could use some tea." Zee made to move off him but his arms clamped tight around her. "No, wait. Not yet. You're really okay? I have more questions but...you're okay?"

Zee reached up with the arm that wasn't trapped by Johnny's cuddle and shifted the crown on her head. "I think so."

They released you, Nadia said. *We are alone here.*

"They wanted to prove they were stronger," Zee said.

"They?" Johnny asked.

"Umm...yeah. That's the bad news." And then she explained what she had seen, the two auras of magic and the cabin in the woods and the second voice from Lucas' mouth. The way he had dug through her memories and feelings. The fragmented scraps of memory that she'd stolen in return. She skipped what Luke had said about the pesnya dushi, partly because she wasn't sure if it was still a sore topic between her and Johnny, and partly because she didn't want to give those words any credence.

She *didn't* want to believe that Johnny wasn't meant for her.

She trailed off as she realized this fact. How long had it been since she felt that way? Since she was a kid at least.

"You okay?" he asked, and he sat up from the floor with her held close, shuffling them both back to lean against the wall.

"I'm sorry," she whispered. He leaned back to catch her eye so she continued. "I'm sorry for never telling you about the dreams. I don't know how I could have, but still. I'm sorry."

Johnny's face relaxed and he leaned again, pressing his face close to hers until their breaths mingled.

"I'm sorry for thinking you put a love spell on me, instead of realizing-"

She shifted, swallowing his terrifying confession with a press of her lips. He followed her quickly, hands spanning around her waist to draw her into his lap and Zee knocked the Rowan crown off her head before digging her fingers into his hair. It was just this side of too long and she loved the way it felt sliding through her hands. His grip on her hips rocked her against him and Zee gasped, leaving Johnny's mouth sliding down her neck and over to the spot he'd discovered just nights ago that left her pliable and melting backwards in the nest of his arms and legs around her.

"Please don't change your mind," she whispered.

He paused at the corner of her jaw and then pressed one firm, closed mouth kiss there that left her shivering.

"I won't," he rasped against her neck, opening himself up to give her room to hide under his chin against his chest. "I won't, Zee. Don't shut me out, okay?"

Zee opened her mouth to make the promise and then swallowed. She sat up to meet his gaze.

"I'm trying not to," she said, and it was as honest as she could be.

He nodded and they kissed, softer and lazy, his hands sliding up and down her spine. Then, all at once his hands froze and he stiffened under her.

She pulled back immediately, searching his face for discomfort. He was looking out the corner of his eyes again.

"Shit," he muttered. "Is Nadia still in here?"

Zee barked out a laugh and some knot of fear and tension burst with it until the giggles spilled out one after the other and she could barely catch her breath. Johnny just rolled his eyes and carried on soothing at her back with his hands.

"Look, you *just* told me that your Aunt is a ghost living in the house and...you can see her, yeah?" Johnny asked as Zee tried to bury her giggles under her hands. "I just, I don't want Nadia watching me debauch you or-"

"We haven't even gotten to the debauching yet," Zee said.

"Yeah," he said, grin growing. "But when we do, it can be private, right?"

She bit her lip to stifle another flurry of laughter. "She left a while ago. And as much as she loves chiming in with her opinion, she's still very discreet."

Johnny shook his head. "This is wild. This is fucking..."

"Crazy," she said for him, slightly touched that he had stopped himself. "Yeah. It is. Hey. What're you doing here?"

"Oh. I brought you a new case," he said, nodding towards the old wood and glass cases that held the family tools. "I took some measurements and pictures Friday night and sent them to friends of mine. It should be a pretty close match."

Zee blinked and stared as Johnny's cheeks started to turn pink.

"It was gonna be a surprise," he said.

"It is a surprise," she said. And then after another pause she asked quietly, "Even after Sunday morning?"

"Zee," he sighed, one hand sliding up to stroke his thumb at the back of her neck right over a knot of tension. How did he always know how to find those? "Yeah. Especially after Sunday."

He drew her close, mouth coaxing hers with careful patience until all her nerves and worry had faded and been replaced with a mellow hunger. How could Lucas be this to her? His soul must have been a darker thread tangled with hers, but Nadia had sworn those threads couldn't be untangled and that thought terrified her.

Johnny drew back when her thoughts drifted and she stretched up for another kiss. He turned it into a short press and smiled at the way her bottom lip popped out.

"We need to call Sam," he said.

She tried not to frown. "I don't want to scare her."

Johnny tilted his head slightly and raised an eyebrow. "You're gonna keep her in the dark?"

"No! No. I just...She's still at work and there's nothing she can do so..."

"So you just want to put off her being angry with you for putting yourself into a dangerous situation?" Johnny said, an old, familiar smirk sneaking onto his face.

Zee's eyes narrowed. "Maybe."

He grinned. "Well, I'm kinda looking forward to it," he said. "So how about we go to the kitchen and I'll make you tea and call Sam."

"I'll make the tea," she said quickly.

"I won't mess it up," he said.

"I'll make it," she repeated. "But wouldn't you rather just make out until Sam gets home?"

He snorted and then stood up, Zee burying a squeak as he lifted her along without so much as a grunt. "We can do that too," he said brightly.

But as Zee was waiting at the stove for the kettle to start steaming, and Johnny was grinning at her while he cradled the phone against his ear with his shoulder, she wondered if she shouldn't have let him make the tea while *she* called Sam. Because Sam was barking inflamed orders over the phone loud enough for Zee to hear the consonants. And those orders included 'Not leaving her alone for more than the two minutes it takes her to come up with another crap, kamikaze plan.'

Johnny arranged for Eric and Will to pick Sam up from the Lab as it closed and bring her back to the house. He then roped them into helping him haul in the display case from the back of his car to the sun room while Sam and Zee faced off across the kitchen island.

"I can't believe you did that," Sam said, voice ragged after firing off snarky, bitter questions all through Zee's explanation of events.

Zee ducked her head for a moment, like a child, and then straightened again. "I know. Neither can I."

"They are stronger than us," Sam said. It was a statement with the tilt of a question.

Zee nodded. "I didn't give them anything about Nadia, I promise."

"It's not that," Sam said firmly. "You gave Lucas and... the other one, access to *you*, Zoya."

Zee only bit her lip.

"We need more help," Sam said, just a breath of sound. Zee stared at her, eyes wide.

"Nadia's not-"

"No. Zee, we need...people." Sam said, her own eyes growing big. "We need a team."

"A coven?" Zee asked. They'd worked with Nadia and been a coven of three. And then together as a pair but... more witches? They'd met more, of course. Nadia had introduced them over the years but to *work* with them...

"Actually," Sam said, blushing, "I was thinking...friends."

"Oh."

"Yeah."

From the other end of the house Will cackled at something Johnny did - he *always* laughed at Johnny - and Zee and Sam both leaned to look down the hall.

"I like them," Sam said.

"Yeah," Zee said, a little startled. "Me too."

"And Cameron is home next week," Sam said.

"Oh!" Zee let the beaming smile spread across her face. "Good! Good. So...we have...people?"

"Yeah," Sam said, nodding. "I guess we do."

Huh.

Chapter 12

At the Opening

July 15th 2017

Had they needed to convince Eric and Will to become staples at the house? It seemed to happen naturally, practically overnight after they had helped arrange the case with Johnny. The way Will helped himself to the kitchen utensils to cook dinner without Sam raising a fuss. The way Zee found Eric in odd corners of the house, nose buried in obscure magic texts, before she even knew he had come by.

Like how she'd found him nosing through her books in her bedroom when she'd gotten home after work and started to get ready for the studio opening.

"Do you and Sam make your own incense?"

Zee leaned past her bathroom mirror to peek into her room where Eric was sitting cross-legged on her bed with a family recipe book. He was dressed in a pair of crisp black pants and a blue button down with a black vest over the top. Will had picked it out and brought it over in a garment bag to keep Eric from getting it wrinkled. Which it now absolutely was. And covered in the fuzzy lint from her blanket.

"We do," she said. She went back to her mirror to brush mascara over her eyelashes.

"You don't sell it at the Lab," he said.

"We don't sell magic at the Lab," Zee said. "Just at home."

"Why not?"

"Magic should be specific to the person receiving it and you can't do that in a shop where everyone wants to come in for an aromatherapy lotion. But good ingredients used correctly can do a lot even before magic," Zee explained.

Eric appeared in the doorway, looking rumpled but dapper.

"Am I taking too long?" she asked. "You and Will should have gone ahead."

"Nah, you're fine," Eric said, eyeing her up and down. "You look beautiful."

Zee caught her cheeks pinking in the mirror. He hadn't meant it as a come on, not the way Johnny or even Will (teasing) would have. But it was nice to be admired and Eric was easy on the eyes just like his cousin, even if he didn't set her heart pounding.

"Thanks," she said. She reached for her lipstain but one look in the mirror reminded her that she'd already applied it. Twice.

"Nervous?" Eric asked.

"Umm..." She was going to say no. Except she couldn't stop checking her reflection for lipstick on her teeth or a weird bump in her curls - they were curls, for chrissakes, there were loads of bumps. "Yes. Yes, I am."

"Johnny is too," Eric said and Zee's eyebrows shot up in the mirror before she turned to face him.

"He is?"

"Yeah," Eric said, sly grin spreading. "He's worried 'bout his fancy art contacts not being impressed with the studio. About the island not getting his work and not being ready to support him. And he's worried about you bolting," he said.

Zee wobbled in place at that, and took a step away from the sink. "Bolting?"

"With the locals around tonight," Eric said and Zee found herself suddenly facing a new man, one of hard lines and firm resolve, the former soldier giving her his whole attention. It wasn't a mean look, but it also wasn't very forgiving. He continued, "With Johnny having to do his peacock act for the patrons."

"I wouldn't..." she started.

"That's what he said," Eric said, with a little smile. "But he's worried. Just a head's up."

Zee clenched her jaw shut and looked down to smooth away wrinkles in her dress. It was a clingy knit fabric and it'd been hanging up in her closet for over a year. There weren't any wrinkles.

"Come on beauty queens, what's taking so- jesus, look at you, punk," Will said from her bedroom.

Eric turned, the severity melting into sheepishness as he looked down at his blank pants covered in purple fuzz. It was worse in the back but Zee decided she didn't feel like saying anything. She followed him out of the bathroom, resisting the urge at the threshold to go back and double check herself one more time. Will whistled as she appeared and Sam popped up on her tiptoes to see over his shoulder.

"I got you that dress," she said, proudly.

"Fits just right," Will said with grin.

It was a little tight, specifically around the bust.

"Letch," Zee said, grabbing her nice purse and wiggling her way out of her bedroom, leaving the others to trail behind her.

"Aww, Eric, look at your ass. You're a mess." Will huffed from the end of the line.

Outside Sam and Zee slid behind the bucket seats of Eric's truck onto the bench and watched as Will retrieved a lint roller from the glove box. He barked instructions to Eric and gave them a private wink from outside, until Eric was more or less de-purpled and it was really time to get to the studio.

Zee and Sam had maintained to the last minute that they could have made it to the studio on their own. But once Eric and Will were filled in on the situation with Luke and the house wards being torn down and put back together, Zee and Sam had been outnumbered. And the weird thing was, Zee didn't even really mind. It felt good to have the house filled up with voices, to have others to talk to. She and Sam could converse in glances and the shift of shoulders most of time and it was nice to remember how to make full conversation with someone.

Also, she'd so far been managing to get herself out of dish-washing duty after dinner. It was too easy to convince Johnny and Eric to do the cleaning up. Their mothers had raised those boys with manners as it turned out.

The truck pulled into the gravel lot and curved around the tidy lines of cars that had already started forming, circling to the back of the building. Zee tried to ignore the butterflies in her stomach. The ones that felt more like eels twisting through her guts. Will helped her out of the back and gave her hand a squeeze as she stepped down. And then Johnny was in front of her.

Will moved away with a half-laugh of exasperation as Johnny leaned down and grabbed a quick kiss from her lips.

"Hey," he said, eyes lighting up as he pulled away. His breath was short, like he'd sprinted through the studio to meet them at the backdoor. "Wow. Wow. You're - you're here and you look amazing."

"Thank you," she said. "You have guests."

"I do, yeah," he said, nodding. His hand was at the base of her back and he was leaning down again.

She slipped out from between him and the car. In the past couple days, unless they were confined to a bed, Johnny seemed to have a hard time keeping his hands off of her. But then night came and he stayed over and held her without so much as a teasing touch in sight. But she needed to keep her head on tonight and not let Johnny catch her in a corner somewhere where they might get caught and embarrass themselves.

"Come on," Zee said, pulling him to the back door as it shut behind a smirking Sam. "Do you really want to leave Will to represent your work?"

"Well, no," Johnny admitted, but he tugged gently on her arm. "Gimme a sec though."

This time as his arms circled her waist she didn't fight it, just met him on the tips of her toes. The nervous eels in her stomach vanished with the swooping feeling that followed his kiss. He always seemed to manage so much as he kissed her, his hands fanning up her back to press her closer as his toes nudged between her feet until she was pressed up the length of him, grasping his shoulders to keep from turning into a puddle on the ground. One hand appeared at her cheek, thumb rubbing along her jaw and he pulled away once, twice, and then successfully on the third try.

"I might have done a thing," Johnny said and Zee's kiss-sedated eyes popped open.

"A thing," she repeated.

"Yeah...I asked Sarah to hang out with you when I couldn't," Johnny said his expression doing a strange dance between an encouraging smile and an expectant grimace.

"Oh. Okay, I like Sarah."

"Sarah likes you," Johnny rushed to say.

Zee fought off a smile. "Is Sarah my babysitter? To make sure I don't knock anything over? Or that I don't offend any of the money bags?"

"Look," Johnny said, and Zee tried not to sway into him at the wicked grin blooming. "I just don't want you taking all my donors back to the house and giving them upcharged readings."

"Aww, but come on...they're just leaking money. I can smell it on them," she said. She started to pull back to the door but Johnny stopped her again, his smile eeking away.

"She's...more like your bodyguard," Johnny said.

"Johnny if Luke shows up..." Her arms flapped at her side. If Luke showed up, Sarah was going to need *her* help first.

"Not from him," Johnny said. "More just...you know. The usuals. Just to keep people out of your hair."

"Sarah's my social buffer?" she asked.

"Yes! Yes. That's a better term for it," he said, nodding. "She knows not to let anyone corner you and tell you potentially discouraging shit about me."

He was starting to blush and he nudged her toward the door as she stood, startled, at this confession. She hadn't really been worried about what people might say about *Johnny* so much as what they would say about her.

"Who's going to guard you from all your old girl-friends?" Zee asked.

"Brian. And he's got permission to bring Sarah's husband Roger into it if it gets serious. Or if it looks like Roger is pissing off the donors."

Zee laughed and Johnny kissed her neck before leading them both down the hall into the bustling hotshop.

Her first thought was that maybe this was an event that would have been better held outside in the gravel parking lot. From where they entered, the ovens were blasting heat and Zee could spot at least three people - Chris Murphy included - who didn't seem to have much sense of self-preservation in regards to their proximity to the glory hole.

"You're gonna set yourself on fire at some point tonight," Zee said with a sigh.

Johnny grinned and pressed a kiss to her cheek as Sarah appeared.

"I said the same thing," Sarah said. "I'm glad you're here. I know Johnny wanted me to protect you, but I think I might need you to save me from the small talk."

"I despise small talk," Zee said, beaming back at Sarah.

"Good. Because I have a lot to talk to you about as soon as he walks away," Sarah said with a nod in Johnny's direction.

"Uhhh..." Johnny frowned at his sister. "I thought...we said..."

"Someone is waiting to talk to you," Sarah said sweetly point over to an attractive older woman with a haircut of steel and heels that must have been a bitch to walk in over all the rough stone.

"Yeah, yes. Okay," Johnny said, giving them a worried look over his shoulder as he moved away.

"So, I was thinking I'd start with the time that Johnny

accidentally burned down our old garden shed with a single match," Sarah said, linking her arm with Zee's.

"I'm having such a good time," Zee said over her shoulder to a horrified Johnny.

* * *

Surprisingly, that remained true.

Sarah was good company and a master at deflecting bad company. Like when Grace Harper slipped into their huddle—smile dripping acid and backless dress clinging perfectly to her narrow frame—and started chatting about bumping into Johnny at the deli the other day and catching up on old times. Zee wasn't too impressed. Sarah just glanced at her, rolled her eyes, and then smiled at Grace like butter wouldn't melt.

"Yeah, Johnny's changed a lot over the years. I think high school is a great tool for embarrassing him now," Sarah said. "Which reminds me! Zee, did I tell you yet that my mom and I used to have a drinking game for every time we could get Johnny to start talking about you? I got to drink a lot of wine coolers on Saturday nights thanks to his obsession with you."

Grace moved off to a new corner of the room pretty quickly after that.

"She was always jealous of you," Sarah said, satisfied.

When someone from town made a point of ignoring Zee while talking to Sarah, Sarah made a point of including Zee in the conversation. When Jasper Doyle started toward them, Sarah found them a good hiding spot by the appetizers in the kitchen area.

Sarah Sharpe-Day was kind of Zee's hero of the night. Being stared at, being whispered about, it was all fairly tolerable with Sarah heckling the room around them under her breath.

"Oh, look," Sarah nodded to where Will and Sam were being cornered by Roger and a patron. "Hang on. Someone needs rescued. Not sure who yet. Bring the cheese platter." Sarah rushed ahead while Zee tried to figure out how to balance a glass of wine in one hand and a cheese platter in the other.

She had just managed to get her palm under the platter when a sliver of ice pierced her thoughts. She dropped her hands and the cheese skidded to the edges of the table before settling, the lip of her wine cup catching at her fingers. She left it on the table and hurried around the table, scanning the room in a panic.

Sam was still with Will and Sarah and the others, and there was no sign of Luke around them. She scrabbled to find the spike of cold in her head, to push it away from herself while finding the source. She shifted to the doorway, trying to stand at the tip of her toes to see above the button downs and cocktail dresses. She braced herself against the frame of the garage door, slipping the toes of her left foot out of her shoe and into the gravel, searching for grounding. She searched the dark of the parking lot and then turned back to the studio.

He was there. A completely different version than the one she had first met, than the witch in the cabin of the woods. Luke fit in with the art scene, leather jacket and a black button up, dark hair rumpled and the knees of his jeans threatening to tear at any second. He was standing next to Johnny who was smiling, shoulders back, gesturing to the furnaces and pointing up at some of the works that lined shelves high up on the walls. Luke's eyes were drinking Johnny in, oblivious to her watching, and Zee was frozen in place, trying to decide between grabbing Sam and running home, or storming over to Johnny to push Luke through the glory hole. He wouldn't fit.

She didn't grab Sam either.

They were flirting, Johnny's hands doing their nervous shift through his hair, over his arms, at his pockets. Luke's eyes caressing over him. A little flare of heat burned under her skin. Shit, she wasn't even jealous.

Luke looked directly at her and smiled, and she might have believed it was sincere if it weren't for the sharp focus of his gaze. He turned back to Johnny, said a few short words and then they both smiled, wide and friendly and Johnny shook his hand with faintly flushed cheeks before Luke walked away. He circled the room, looking up at the glass for sale in cases and on shelves, and Zee's heart pounded as he passed close to Sam.

The gravel scratched against her feet but she dug deeper into the dirt, trying to summon up strength and a wall of safety to hide behind as he prowled closer to her.

"You look lovely tonight, Zoya," he said, voice purring, face shadowing out of the light of the garage.

He looked friendly, at ease, and she was as aware of the hunger in his gaze while he looked at her as she had been when he was with Johnny. But Zee could feel the snarl of power around him now that he wasn't hiding behind a cloak of mundanity.

"I'm going to burn every trace of you off this island," Zee whispered.

Luke laughed, a throaty rattling sound, and the party sounds dimmed beyond them. Johnny was schmoozing and Sam was laughing and Sarah was whispering in Roger's ear and Will and Eric were kissing softly. And she was alone with Luke, shrouded in his magic. Even the cicadas and cries of the bats from the woods around them were dimmed, like she was shrouded in a heavy curtain.

"I find you infinitely more interesting than your cousin," Luke said, head tilting off to one side. "Your instincts are stronger at the very least. You never liked me did you? Sam seemed to find me charming."

Zee's hands formed fists behind her back. "Sam is good at faking," she said.

Luke raised an eyebrow, like he could tell she was lying. "I know your dreams, moon bloom. I've lived them too. I don't know how he resisted you so long. He certainly wasn't resisting me."

Zee glanced over at Johnny again at those words. Had Luke done something to him? How would she find the poison to suck it out again?

"You haven't solved the puzzle yet, darling," Luke said and Zee jumped when she realized he was less than a foot away from her. "Soon enough. I am curious though. What's so worth protecting in him? Why waste all that power on a man that's broken your heart so many times? He's sure to do it again."

"I figure he's got a few good tries left in him,' Zee said, shrugging her shoulders. "But I'd like to see his face when you suggest to him that he's not sticking around this time. I guarantee he won't like it."

Meanwhile she tucked his words away for perusal later. He'd been circling Johnny for a reason, not just to torment her, and found something of interest there.

"Have you spoken to your aunt recently?" Luke asked, inching closer.

"My aunts are both dead," Zee said, pressing her lips together.

"She hides in your house, nursing her cuckoo children

even now that they are grown," Luke said. His voice was strangely resonant, an echo hiding in the smooth sliding notes, something dark and rough. "But she cannot hide there forever, Zoya. She has debts to pay."

Zee felt the metal guide of the garage door digging into her back as she tried to keep her distance from his looming figure.

"I don't know who you've been speaking to," she said, quiet and low, "But Nadia can do whatever she damn pleases. And if you didn't already know that, you're working with some very suspect information."

Luke's eyes twitched, he looked irritated, frustrated.

"What are you doing here?" Zee asked.

"Enjoying the party," Luke said, smile smoothing away his ruffled feathers. "I wanted to see my pesnya dushi. Both of you."

"Whatever you're looking for isn't here," she said.

"What I'm looking for is exactly here," he said, glancing down the length of her, and then over to Johnny.

"You are scum," she whispered, watched his face harden. "You are a knot in my threads, not a part of me. Not to mention that you're acting as someone's puppet. Find another mark. But let me tell you this, if you go after Nadia I will shred you. And I won't be alone. I may not be as strong as you, but I will never stop pricking holes in your defenses if you hurt someone I care about."

She was leaning forward now without even realizing it. But Luke took a step back, the smug and charming washing off his face to leave a blank coldness.

"You should speak to your aunt," Luke said, sharp and clipped. "You're playing this game and you don't even have a full hand of cards."

He turned away from the light of the party and slipped

away into the falling dark with that parting shot. A hand appeared at the base of Zee's back and she jumped and spun directly into Johnny.

"Hey, hey," he soothed, grinning down at her. "You know, I thought that guy was kinda cool till I saw that look on your face. You okay? You're cold, c'mere-"

"Johnny that was him," she snapped, nerves feeling fried. "That was Luke."

Johnny stiffened and then darted forward, but Zee caught him by the waist, stepping up against his chest to hold him still.

"Not here," she said. "Not here. Not tonight. Just let him go, please."

"Are you kidding me?"

"No, I am not. I am not ready to go up against him again," she said staring up into his eyes. He was shadowed by the dark but she could make out the wide gaze, the edge panic in his shoulders. "I'm okay, but we are better off with him walking away right now. Trust me."

Johnny's arms circled her and she pressed her face into his chest as he scanned the dark parking lot, waiting for the chill of Luke's company to burn away.

December 12th, 2003

Nadia shut and locked the door behind Olivia Grant, resting her forehead against the wood for a moment, palm pressed open.

"Love is not always beautiful, my darlings," Nadia said in the quiet.

Sam and Zee snuck out from their hiding spot under the dining room table.

"Will she be alright, Noddy?" Sam asked.

"Let's hex him," Zee said, nose wrinkling as she tried to push the words she heard spoken out of her head.

"She will," Nadia said to Sam. "And I don't like to hear that kind of talk from you, Zoya."

Zee had already thought of at least three things she could twist into a charm as a perfect punishment for the man.

"Come in to the kitchen my ved'mitchka," Nadia said, her eyes sharp on Zee's face as if she were reading her mind. "It's time for a story."

"I'm too old for fairy tales now, Noddy," Sam said.

"Are you now, Samara?" Nadia asked, voice raising in feigned surprise. "I see. Well, then you may take your chocolate and toast away with you and leave Zoya and I to our chatter."

Sam frowned at that, and then darted out into the hall, following Nadia to the kitchen with Zee catching up at their heels. Sam pulled down the mugs from the cupboard as Nadia lifted the pan of hot chocolate off the stove—Zee hadn't even realized she'd been making any, and thought it might have been magic.

"Where I came from," Nadia started, and the words were as familiar to Zee as the phrase 'once upon a time' was to other little girls. "Very, very long ago, there was a lovely girl. The village called her Alina, because she was bright like a star."

Zee dragged a tall chair over to the counter, and used it to climb up to the top to sit. Nadia said her growth spurt would come sooner or later, but so far it only arrived in centimeters, one year at a time. She took the first mugful of rich chocolate, splashing in a little cream, and bringing the cup up to her nose to breathe in the smell. She had yet to crack the recipe.

"She was sweet and good and all of her neighbors knew that she would marry young and have a dozen little babies for her husband, whoever that might be," Nadia continued. "And soon, the towns to the north and south knew of her reputation too. And not long after that the towns to the east and west had heard. And so many people were very interested to see who little Alina would fall in love with."

"This is a lousy story to follow up hearing about Olivia Grant's-"

"Hush, Samara," Nadia said, passing the older girl a mug of chocolate. "By the time Alina was sixteen, she was more beautiful than ever, sweeter than ever, and smarter than all the boys in the villages for a hundred miles. When a boy came to the house for her hand in marriage she would ask them a question and if they gave the wrong answer she would ask them to leave. This went on until there were no men left at all to ask."

"Who did she fall in love with?" Zee asked. Had Alina had a pesnya dushi too? No, Nadia hadn't mentioned it.

"One day," Nadia said, ignoring the pair of them and taking a sip of her own chocolate, dark as night without a hint of cream. "One day, a man came to the village. He was handsome, and had cunning eyes, and beautiful clothing made from the richest fabrics. He had a dark carriage and glossy black horses. He came to Alina's door and she answered."

"It's Koschei the Deathless, isn't it?" Sam said, chin in her hands and eyes narrowed. "He's always picking on the lovely girls."

"The man told her that he was rich, and she could be rich too. That he would live forever," Nadia hushed Samara before she could speak, "And Alina could live forever too. That he ruled a kingdom, and she could rule at his side.

And so Alina said to the man 'I will only ask one question and you may only give one answer. It must be a true answer. I am good and honest, but I can see a lie when it faces me. So, tell me, why do you want a wife?'"

"Oh shiiiiit," Sam whispered with a giggle and then Zee giggled too and Nadia swatted them both on the head.

"Alina had heard many answers to her question. A wife to clean, to bear children, to cook meals, to soften a bed. None of them pleased her," Nadia said, with a raised eyebrow. "And so she watched the stranger's face as he struggled with his answer until his pale white skin was red with effort. But he did not lie when he spoke. 'Only one reason,' the man said. 'I want a wife to hurt.'"

The kitchen was quiet and Zee felt tears rise up in her cheeks.

"Alina asked the man to leave, and he did," Nadia said.

"Who did she marry?" Sam asked, frowning into her chocolate.

"She never married," Nadia said. "A woman does not have to marry fools who don't appreciate her, or men who only want to make her suffer. She can be happy on her own, if she finds nothing better."

Nadia drank her chocolate then, at the counter with her nieces, her eyes staring out into the dark greenhouse.

Chapter 13

By Night

July 16th 2017

It was after one in the morning when the wine ran out and the last of the locals slinked away in their cars, or in the back of Harry's limo-taxi service. Sam spread out in the backseat of Johnny's car, folding herself up into a sleepy little knot with her face tucked against the leather. Johnny folded Zee's hand in his and drove the quick trip up to the house.

The three of them stood together in the entry hall for a long minute.

"The house is safe," Sam said.

"Nadia is hiding," Zee added.

"Good. I'm too tired for that," Sam said. "Goodnight, you two."

"I'll get us water," Johnny said, kissing at the top of Zee's head. "Meet you upstairs."

Zee hesitated in her room. Johnny was giving her time to change and get into bed. He'd created a careful routine for them. One that was gentle and considerate and painfully stilted. She moved into the bathroom and turned the warm water on in her tub. She dumped in a heavy handful of herbs and salts and oats and stirred with her arm.

She heard the door of the bedroom click shut and then Johnny's head appeared around the edge of the bathroom doorframe.

"Hey," she said, standing and letting the water drip from her arm. "Come unzip me."

She turned her back to him and kicked her shoes off, waiting for Johnny to close the space between them. She was about to turn around to see if he'd run away when she felt his hands slide her hair over one shoulder. She held it in place as the zipper snick-snicked its way down her spine, the tip of his finger drawing a warm line in its wake. She shrugged out of the shoulders of the dress and shimmied it over her hips, her panties catching and dragging down a few inches.

"Umm..." Johnny hummed, even as his hand spread across the bare skin of her lower back.

"If you're tired you can go to bed," Zee said, reaching her arms back to the clasp of her bra. Johnny's hands beat her there, fingers slipping beneath the elastic and undoing the hooks.

"I'm...I was tired," he said. "I'm not now." His fingers slid up under the loose shoulder straps and drew them down her arms and she pulled herself free. He was pressing up against her back, his clothes brushing against her skin and raising goosebumps. She let her bra drop onto the tiles and Johnny's hands slid against her ribcage.

"Like this," she said, covering his hands with hers and lifting them up to work away the ache and strain of tissue from her underwire. She sighed as he took over and let her head drop back to his shoulder. "That's always a relief," she admitted. "Kind of hurts, but feels great too."

Johnny hummed, his hands cupping over the front of her breasts to slide her nipples between his fingers. He peppered kisses down her neck and over her shoulder and she shivered in his hold.

"Kind of can't believe you're letting me do this," Johnny whispered into her shoulder, the words barely audible over the water filling the tub.

Zee just turned her head and found a spot near his temple to kiss before hooking her thumbs into the hips of her panties and pushing them down, kicking them off her legs. She felt Johnny gulp as he gazed down the length of her, his hair falling forward and hiding his eyes from her. She nudged his hands away from her breasts and walked forward to step up into the bathtub.

It had been a treat to herself from the inheritance, a copper tub big enough to stretch out in, to share. She settled at the back and then rested her chin on her arm at the edge of the tub, staring up Johnny.

"You in or out?" she asked. She popped her knees up out of the cover of the water in the hopes that might help sell her case.

His eyes were dark as he looked back at her and she watched his throat bob with another swallow. Then his shoulders shifted and she watched him unbutton the top three buttons of his dress shirt before shrugging his way out, pulling the back collar over his head and leaving it in her pile on the floor. She stared at the lines of him, the tangles of muscle over his shoulder, the firm planes of his stomach, soft hair running a line down and circling his belly button before disappearing lower. She smiled up at him after finishing her study, licked her lips slowly, and then glanced down to where his hands were hesitating at his waistband.

"Feel like there should be some heavy bass playing for this," he mumbled.

Zee grinned. "Want me to get out and go put some on?"

He blinked and his eyes went unfocused, jaw dropping slightly at the thought of her rising out of the water. She laughed as he shook himself. He snapped the button on his pants loose, jerked the zipper down with a firm tug, and then pulled the dark slacks and what looked like boxer briefs down unceremoniously. Zee perked up from the water, taking a long look at the strong thighs that appeared and the gently bobbing erection between them. Johnny took two quick steps to the tub, leaning into Zee's space so that she settled against the back edge, and drew her into a hard kiss. He pushed against her, teeth tugging at her bottom lip before slipping his tongue into her mouth to stroke against the back of her teeth.

"Mm!" She cupped his face in her hands and tried to find her place in the kiss. Water shifted around, lapping at her collarbone, and then Johnny's hands were behind her hips, pulling her up to press along the length of him as he settled in front of her. Her thighs bracketed his hips and water sloshed over the rim of the tub, still pouring out of the faucet, as they wrestled closer together.

"Jesus Christ," Johnny growled as the lips of her pussy slid across the soft skin of his cock. He drew away for a moment and Zee caught a glimpse of his forehead knotted, eyes dilated and dark before the momentum of the water rocked them together again, both of them groaning.

"I- I need to turn the water off," Zee managed as Johnny gasped against her throat and tried to hold himself still.

He made a soft wounded sound at the back of his throat,

tongue flicking out to catch the water beading on her neck. She meant to push him back, give herself room to think straight, but instead her wet hands were snagging in strands of his hair as she tipped her head back. He nipped at her pulse, sat up on his knees and twisted in place to turn the water off.

Zee floundered at the sight him in front her, water droplets sliding over contours of muscle, cock skimming across the top of the bath water like an invitation for her to lean forward and lick at the tip. The color flushed a deeper red and she glanced up to find Johnny staring down at her. His expression was dark and more serious than any she'd seen him wear yet, it left her feeling hot and pliant in the water. And it took a long moment for her to realize that despite everything he could see in the clean water, his eyes were fixed to her face.

"Hey," she said, rubbing her knee against the side of his thigh.

He smiled but it only made the strength of his stare burn deeper into her skin. "Hey. Where do you want me?"

She bit her lip to restrain her first thought and Johnny's nostrils flared slightly.

"Lay next to me?"

Johnny sighed and sank into the water, turning and sliding back as she shifted to her side and faced him. She lifted one arm over his shoulders and snuggled up, the other hand settling on his chest and down to his stomach. He caught the wanderer, muscles jumping under her fingers, and tangled their hands together.

"I'm ticklish," he said, tapping his forehead to hers, brushing his mouth to catch and kiss at her lips. "If I have to keep my hands to myself-"

"I never said you had to keep your hands to yourself," she said.

He swallowed hard and stared at her for a moment. Then the arm that was under his side shifted between them, stroking his fingers gently where her thighs were laying pressed together. She let one leg float up and then propped her knee over his hip. His eyes slid away from her face for the first time and she watched him mapping out the terrain under the water, his hand spanning across the inside of her thigh, fingers spreading until his pinkie was barely grazing her outer lips, making her whimper behind her closed mouth. He squeezed at the back of her leg near her ass and dropped his head back onto her shoulder.

"Fucking Christ, Zee. I want to touch you."

"So touch me," she said, tilting her chin to nuzzle at his jaw and then leave kisses behind. "I want you to touch me. I want to touch you."

He huffed and his body froze and for a moment Zee had a terrible uncertainty. *Did* he want her? Was it more than respect and patience that made him hesitate recently? But then his hands were in action, wrapping around her back to pull her closer at the waist, hitching her thigh higher on his hip to spread her open. He released her hand on his stomach and then his hand was dipping down, drawing spiraling patterns against the soft skin of her pussy.

Her laugh of surprise broke into low moan, mouth hanging open against his jawline by his ear. Her breasts were pressed to his chest and when she tried to lift herself up, his hand on her waist held her tighter, his face turning to swallow another note of pleasure with his lips, curving her back into one long arch as he rolled her clit gently under his thumb. She tried to shift, to rock closer or pull back or wrestle against him enough to reach down, wrap her hand around the hard length of him that lay bumping against her thigh.

She tried to make an argument, some sensible collection of words to make her case, but all that came out were two meek and throaty words. "...Touch you." It was half mumbled against his lips and it fell apart as he pressed a finger inside of her, barely up to the knuckle.

"Not yet," he said and it was all rasp and it echoed in his chest and the water was shifting against her back and as his finger slid deeper she couldn't remember what she had just asked.

"Not yet," he repeated and he leaned back to watch her expression knot, lips shaking, as he pumped a digit slowly inside of her. "I'm too close. Just wanna watch you, see what you like. God, Zee, I wanna be in you the first time. Is that okay?"

How was he talking? She could barely make a sound. Everything was knotted up in her chest, ready to shatter out. Her arms and legs shook, cheek brushing over the top of the bobbing water and a creaking moan crawled up out of her throat as a second finger joined the first, shifting against each other and stroking up into her. His thumb was pressed into her clit, just enough pressure to keep her wired but without any friction.

"Is that alright?" he asked again.

"Fuck yes, yes," she said. She finally managed to find purchase for her hands against the planes of his chest, and her toes gripped to the end of the tub. She pushed down onto his fingers and groaned, her forehead falling to his shoulder.

"I want you inside of me, Johnny, please," she said, and the water was so close it brushed and caught on her lips.

He pulled her up by the waist again, twisting his wrist

and stroking his thumb against her as she shuddered with heat. "Not yet. Gonna watch you fall apart, here, like this, in my arms. I've been dreaming of this."

"I have too." The words fell out with a whimper and Johnny caught them against his mouth, lips prying and pulling at hers, drinking all the short gasping sounds she made as he worked his fingers inside of her, his thumb dragging and swirling between her bucking hips.

"Tell me," he said. "Tell me what I do to you in the dreams. Tell me what I do to make you come."

She was so close, her breasts dragging and sticking against his chest, his mouth sucking at her pulse, teeth nipping in time with the rhythm of his fingers. There was heavy burn of pleasure swirling just below her gut, flaring a little hotter with every roll of his thumb. She could barely think of a gesture from a dreamed Johnny when the real one was under her hands, his bright smell filling up her lungs, strong legs bracing hers apart, hand unravelling her in quick desperate strokes.

She shook her head, nose dragging against his cheekbone, unable to find the words for instruction.

Which was fine. Johnny found his way, as he was always going to. His fingers curled in, pushing at the tangled nerves inside her and her head fell forward again with a shout. The hand at her waist slipped up into her hair and pulled gently back until she was caught under his eyes.

"Let me watch," he said, pressing in again, harder this time and Zee's toes curled as the heat flashed out of her, licking down her legs and up her spine. Her expression crumpled in the onslaught, waves of pleasure sparking through her as Johnny watched, expression fixed and yet tender. His eyes scanned her, memorizing the way she bit hard into her lip, the color spreading over her cheeks, the battle of her eyelids wanting to fall shut.

His hand in her hair loosened and pulled her close, tongue sweeping across her bruised lip and into her mouth. She kissed back lazily, arms sliding back over his shoulders, hips still twitching against his hand as little aftershocks flickered through her body.

"So beautiful," he murmured, pulling away. "You have no idea how long I've wanted to see you that way, touch you that way."

She did though. She'd wanted as much for as long. She *still* wanted.

"Take me to bed," she said, dragging him back for a kiss, while trying to shift away from his persistent fingers.

She hadn't meant it as a command, but Johnny was rising up out of the water, with Zee attached around his neck, barely before she'd finished the words. She whined and hid her face in his neck as he dragged his fingers out of her to lift her out of the bath with his hand under her thighs. He was halfway to the door, with her laughing in his arms, before she realized he was kind of single-minded.

"Towels! Towels, you dork," she said, trying to bury her giggles. She could feel him pressed between her legs, twitching with the way she shifted against him as he walked them. "We can dry off a bit before we get in bed right?"

Johnny blinked at her, hair sticking up in damp tufts, pupils blown wide and dark. He turned in the middle of the room, Zee dangling down the length of him, still shaking with barely contained laughter.

"Your two o'clock," she said.

Johnny finally spotted the towels, and even put her down onto her own—unsteady—feet but the process of drying each other quickly became less about towels and more about hands stroking new skin.

"Shiiiiit," he breathed out as she *finally* wrapped her fingers around his cock, felt the pulse of it under her fingers. She stumbled back to the door, forgetting the cold drips of water at the backs of her calves, the wet ends of her hair, in favor of focusing on the way Johnny followed, mouth hungry against her, voice strained in wordless groans.

The bed was near the window and Johnny took both her hands away from all the spots she'd discovered, trapping them between their chests as the backs of her thighs bumped into the mattress. She pushed herself up onto the bed and crawled back, falling onto her sheets without really caring what direction she was pointed in relation to her pillows. She just wanted Johnny laying over her, pushing into her, clinging to him as she rode her way back up to the heights she'd just fallen from. She knew he could do that to her. She'd been thinking of it for weeks now.

Johnny followed her onto the bed, arms bracing himself up above her. She slid her legs apart and grinned as he watched, lips parted and breath panting out.

"Come closer," she said.

He looked up, into her face and she paused in her teasing, one leg half hooked over his hip. There was something caught in his expression, startled and frozen.

"Are you real?" he asked, whispered it. Zee stared up at him and his eyes widened. "Are we for real now?"

She pushed up with her elbows, pressed her cheek against his, absorbed the warmth of him against the contrast of the cold window behind her, and then sealed her lips against his for a long minute.

"Yes," she said, retreating back down into her sheets. "We're real now."

He surged down with that promise, mouth locking to hers, tongue sliding into her mouth, hand reaching down to pull her leg around his back. He bucked on top of her, cock nestling against her, slipping in the wetness. He drifted down from the kiss, tongue licking a trail down her neck to her chest. Zee gasped as his lips wrapped around her nipple, sucking lightly, and she knotted her legs behind his back, lifting her hips up to press and hitch against him, the tip of him tapping at her entrance.

"Johnny, please," she said, fingers digging into his shoulders, heels pressing into his ass to try and drag him closer, deeper.

He nudged softly, carefully, and Zee reached down to help guide him inside of her where she was still swollen and wet from his care in the bath. She watched his face turning slack, breaths huffing against her collar bone.

"More," she said, and her own face fell open as he pushed deeper with a roll of his hips.

Johnny's strength seemed to falter and he sank forward onto his forearms, their bodies pressing together.

"Fuck," he whispered, forehead knotting and hips kicking gently forward like he was trying to resist the motion.

"Johnny," she started, distracted by another perfect moment of pressure that ended with her pulling at his bottom lip with her teeth. She tried again. "Johnny, I won't break. I want you. I want to feel you."

"Don't want it to end," he whispered against her cheek, wet lips tracking on her skin. "Feels so good. You fit me..." he lost the words with a groan as her heels pushed him deep inside her, deeper until he bottomed out and they both released aching cries.

She was inclined to agree though. Nothing had ever felt

so right, like the shape of him around her, filling her up inside, was what her body was designed for.

His hesitation vanished then in a furrowed brow concentration, his hand unknotting from the sheets to burrow between them. He surged inside of her, fingers working quickly at her clit, tongue laving at her pulse as he groaned and choked out pleasured notes against her throat. Zee's breath had left her. Her hands clutched at his shoulder blades and her legs clamped around his waist, absorbing every shock of their hips with a gasp bursting from her lips and an aching burn that rattled through her.

She was sore from sudden use and felt as if she were burning bright and fast in the bed, the pleasure almost stinging in her blood. But she kept her eyes open, watching the glow of Johnny's back rocking in the dark, muscles shifting like the blue white waves under the cliff lit by moonlight. He turned his face to her and she met his eyes, took in the shock and the relief in his gaze, the mix of urgency and the desire to drag out every pull of skin, every catch of breath.

His free arm slid under her back, shifting her until he was thrusting perfectly inside of her, every shift inside of her coaxing a cry from her mouth, her walls clutching and fluttering at him. His lips fused to her, their voices echoing between their mouths as she arched up into his hold and ecstasy snapped out of her center.

The darkness was bright with colors behind her eyelids as she quivered in his hold, feeling the snap of his hips into hers, the hot rush of him inside of her as his sob of relief melted into her kiss. They sagged together, Zee holding tight to his back as he tried to shift.

"Not yet," she said.

He relaxed over her and the careful crush of his weight

was soothing on her frayed senses. He trailed his mouth across her forehead in something that was half a suggestion of kiss but really more of a lazy sigh.

"Gonna do better next time," he mumbled sleepily.

She laughed and let him shift down to her side, trying to bury the hiccup of sound as he pulled slowly out of her. He turned her in his arms to curl against him and she decided she'd worry about the mess in a minute...or two.

"You did pretty good for a burn mark," she said, kissing his shoulder and settling her legs in a tangle around his.

"My pixie," he said, pulling her tighter against him. He murmured out a last word before nuzzling his sex addled smile into her hair and falling asleep.

"Perfect."

Chapter 14

Lovers and Madmen

July 16th, 2017

They were trying to get out of bed. Really, they were.

"You taste like breakfast," Johnny mumbled, hands covering the tops of her breasts as he smeared wet kisses across their soft undersides where she said they ached at the end of the day.

"Kind of a weird compliment," Zee said, a little breathless. "But I'll take it cause I like what you're doing."

"Think I just meant..." he said, muffled by her skin. "You know, that we could skip going downstairs...for today. I'm good here."

He nipped at her and she jumped. And then three quick knocks sounded outside of the door and they both jumped.

"Umm, I think Nadia is waiting for us?" Sam said in a tight voice through the door.

"Is she-" Johnny whispered.

"No, she's not in here," Zee answered, sitting up and

pushing at Johnny's shoulder to roll him away. "We're on our way, Sam!"

She was scrabbling for a bit of blanket, not realizing that Johnny was just as quickly pulling it through her fingers.

"Stop, what are you doing?" she asked, yanking on a sheet.

"Trying to make you smile," Johnny said, eyebrows raising.

Damn. She *was* smiling. She dropped the sheet and leaned forward, landing a kiss halfway between his mouth and his nose. He tried to follow as she drew away, crawling out of the bed, but landed on his chest alone in the blankets.

"I appreciate that," she said, dodging one of his hands as it reached over the mattress for her. "But I feel like you have an ulterior motive that will get in the way of me talking to Nadia. She has answers for us and it's about time she coughed them up."

"Will I see her?" Johnny asked.

Zee made the mistake of looking back behind her and seeing Johnny stretched down the length of her bed, outlined by sunlight, all lean lines and bedhead.

"Umm..." she said, and Johnny grinned at her and stretched himself a little more. "No. Probably not. But you might be able to tell she's there. Maybe you should stay up here."

"Saving your place?" he asked, smirking.

A little bit that, yeah. "It's just gonna be weird," Zee said. "You watching me talk to her. I'll look a little crazy."

That got Johnny out of bed. Zee wasn't sure what was more distracting. Johnny naked in her bed. Or Johnny naked out of her bed, all tall and strong and within reaching distance. Or pouncing distance.

He pressed a kiss into the top of her hair. If her hands settled on his ass...well, sue her.

"I'm coming down," he said. "Weird or not, I want to be involved now, okay?"

She wrapped her arms around his waist, smushing her face against the warm skin of his chest and he stepped closer against her. Zee didn't think she'd ever just had a hug this way with a man, skin to skin without any intention of it leading to sex. Johnny's fingers spread across the skin of her back, little nicks and scars tickling her in their travels. He patterned a message of kisses into her hair before another series of knocks at the door had them both sighing and pulling back.

"Got it, Sam," Zee said as Johnny scuffled into the bathroom to hunt for pants.

She grabbed a handful of clothing off a chair and dressed on her way to the door. Sam was waiting for her by the staircase.

"Told you," Sam said brightly. "Once it starts-"

"Shut up," Zee said, trying not to let the grin on her face break her jaw. She pushed past Sam and hurried down the stairs, pausing on the landing when she heard the rustling in the library.

"I said she'd been waiting," Sam said.

Johnny looked suitably stunned when he walked into the library to find books laying out in a starburst pattern on the floor, pages flipping back and forth in an agitated little dance. What was missing from the picture for him was Nadia zipping around the room flashing in and out of sight, pulling spines from shelves before pressing them back again with bursts of frustration. Sam was curled up in the window seat, a throw pillow clutched to her stomach and she patted the space next to her for Johnny to join her.

He edged sideways around the room after checking on Zee.

"What's going on, Noddy?" Zee asked. She knelt down onto the floor and reached for one of the books, but it scooted away from her fingers, pages flicking faster.

I thought, when I left, you'd be safe. Nadia turned to face her and Zee winced at the foggy shapelessness in her expression, the way the faint red of her hair faded almost to a baby pink.

"Safe from who?"

Nadia sank against the bookshelves, just the dark stain of her eyes and lips peering out. And then all at once she was crouched down in front of Zee, pale eyes sharp and vivid. The books nearest them shuddered on the floor and Zee jumped, Johnny flinching forward at the window until Sam pulled him back.

I never loved him. I was only a little girl when he found me.

"Nadia," Zee breathed. She eyed the books on the floor. They were heirlooms, gilded Russian texts. Things brought over from the old country.

Let me show you ved'mitchka, Nadia murmured in her ear a cool, gentle sweep of air surrounding Zee on the floor.

"I'll be right back," Zee managed to warn the others before falling under.

* * *

They were only nightmares at first. Bad dreams of a giant man with a face like a mountain side, all robed in soot gray with red snakes swirling at his wrists and ankles. He had a woman in his shadow, a woman who was a shadow, with cold blue eyes and hair like blood. Her hand rested in the folds of fabric and the red snakes twisted around her like shackles.

She dreamt every night of the giant and his shadow woman. She dreamt of the two of them creating terrible, foreign shapes together, all skin and bared teeth. She dreamt of the man sitting in a dark throne, circled by robed figures, red shadow woman at the heart of the room pulling screams and sobs from broken figures on the floor with a lift of her eyebrow and a pinch of her lips.

She woke in her bed each morning, stiff from terror, teeth sore from clenching, palms bruised from her nails digging.

It was her mama who pulled the truth from her lips first. It was her papa who gave it a name.

Pesnya dushi.

It sounded like a curse to her, not a song.

They moved out of the city. Her younger sisters loved the house, it was bigger and it came with ponies and private lessons to shirk and their mother taught them about the plants in the woods and the shape of the stars in the sky.

She had her own room.

But the dreams didn't stop.

Visitors came and went from the house. Witches and friends and family that extended across the continent.

She learned spells to stay awake.

She learned how to take rest in short bursts.

She grew a little and looked in the mirror and realized that the red shadow woman was going to be her someday. She softened the color of her hair with lemon and vinegar glamours and learned how to heal broken bones and bad fevers and torn flesh. She took care of the ponies.

One day a man and his coven came to the house. He was as tall and as wide as the doorway with a face like the side of a mountain. Her father's skin was white as the snow outside as he let the man enter the house. Nadia kept her face pointed to the floor for three days but the man and his travelers would not leave the house.

He found her in the pony barn.

"It is time for you to stop hiding, my princess," he said.

Nadia's hand was behind her back, fisted around the long black pritchel, sharp edge pressed into the folds of her skirt.

He stepped into the barn and his body filling the door stole the light from the bright winter outside.

"You're nearly grown now," he said, words soft and coaxing as if he were speaking to a skittish filly. "Your courses will arrive in a few short months and it will be time for you to take your place as priestess in the coven."

"I am still learning, sir," Nadia said, using the careful deference her father used with the man. Her mother had not spoken in days.

"You are learning a woman's craft," he said, the words like stone. "I will train you to be as strong as the Titan gods. You need not worship the moon when it will do your bidding."

He spun words around her, painted a canvas of skill and deference, of foreign places on earth and in worlds her mother had only allowed her glimpses of. He offered her a library of knowledge, a dragon's hoard of delightful tricks to entertain herself, and a freedom to choose her magic. Before he left the barn his hands were on her shoulders and she felt as strong and as tall as the giant before her. Her fingers were loose around the iron.

That night she dreamt of an ecstasy outside of the boundaries of skin, one that could only be met in a pool of magic so vast and infinite it might have been the universe itself.

The giant and his coven had gone in the night and her family members were like ghosts at breakfast, all sagged in their chairs, not with relief but exhaustion.

"He has given you three months to join him" Nadia's father told her as she sat down.

And for one month she thought she would leave her family in a few weeks. Her dreams were heady and she looked forward to being the red shadow woman.

And in the second month she caught swirls of red at the corner of her eyes, in the reflections of glass as she passed windows and mirrors. When she dreamt, her dreams were beautiful visions of the men and women who would worship her, of the structures of spell work she would invent and weave around the world. And in the dreams she wore a necklace and bracelets of curling red magic.

And in the third month she woke, bleeding into her sheets, bed smothered by red snakes of magic, thoughts cloudy and stomach queasy.

And in the third month her family found a boat to take them to America.

* * *

"Nadia."

Zee woke on the floor, body half lifted onto Johnny's lap. He squeezed around her shoulders and helped her shift against him to sit up, hot palm against the back of her neck, thumb working against a knot of muscle. Sam was crouched on the floor next to her, fingers digging into the word work.

Nadia was sitting at the heart of the explosion of books, thin but clear to Zee. She looked half the grandmotherly figure she had when she'd passed, and half the delicate child in the horse barn.

"Oh, Noddy," Zee sighed.

I could have changed the world. It was wistful and apologetic.

"Not for the better," Zee said and watched one slight shoulder lift and fall in acknowledgment. "How can he possibly be alive still?"

He will never surrender.

It felt like a warning.

* * *

Zee's thoughts were still in a Russian winter as the three of them spread out on blankets under the sun. Nadia had faded into hiding - or, as Zee was beginning to fear, somewhere farther away and potentially more permanent - not long after releasing her from the memories.

Sam was chewing on sage leaves as she digested everything Zee had returned with. Johnny was quiet, but he had his head pillowed on her stomach, one hand tangled with hers and the other arm curled around her hips, as if to pin her safely home.

"What can this- this-" Sam stumbled on the name.

"Kasimir Chernov," Zee whispered.

"That guy. What does want from *us?*" Sam asked. "Nadia? She's...well even if she isn't gone it isn't up to us to deliver her to him."

"Maybe not, but she's shaken," Zee said. "She's never seemed so...like...like a ghost. Like she was haunting the house instead of living in it?"

Johnny's hand squeezed hers. He did that every time

her voice started leaning higher with nerves. She squeezed back and he nestled closer against her.

"What does Chernov have to do with Luke?" Johnny wondered.

Zee let her fingers comb through Johnny's hair as Sam hummed in agreement.

"He's manipulating Luke," Zee said. "He's got him on strings like a puppet. Like he wanted to do to Nadia."

"I am...lacking sympathy over here," Sam mumbled through her sage leaf.

Johnny grunted in agreement against Zee's stomach.

"But he teamed up with him for a reason. And Nadia was his pesnya dushi. If he wanted her..." Zee chewed at her lip as the thought abandoned her. It had been there, a little wisp of Luke's memory that skittered away when she reached for it. She shook her head when Johnny and Sam both popped their heads up to look at her. "Lost it."

Johnny shifted up to stretch out alongside her and she rolled in to rest her head on his shoulder.

"We'll figure it out," he said, face in her hair again.

She didn't even mind that he didn't sound very optimistic.

July 19th, 2017

Cam's boat came in on Wednesday morning. Sam left the lab after frittering around in the back for two hours, promising to return with Cameron and lunch.

Zee waited until two in the afternoon to call Johnny.

"Hey pixie, everything good?"

He did this now. Every greeting accompanied by a quick and ever so slightly nervous edged urgency.

"I am starving," she admitted. "Sam and Cameron are

definitely not bringing me lunch and also, can I stay at yours tonight?"

"Yeah? Yeah!" he answered. "Of course. You need to grab your stuff or-"

"Nope," she said with a pop. "Not stepping in that house until I get some kind of all clear from Sam."

"Huh?"

"They are really loud," she said, "It's a thing."

Johnny laughed on the other end of the line. "You need lunch?"

"Yeah... you think you can get one of your lackeys to swing by?" she asked, fighting a smile.

Johnny snorted. "Sure. I'll find a guy."

Which is how she ended perched on a table in the back room making out with Johnny like of pair of teenagers listening for the door to open so they wouldn't get caught.

And *that* is how she ended up testing Sam's new bruise cream formula on a pair of mid-afternoon hickeys. Johnny swore he hadn't meant to. Which was probably bullshit, but she hadn't meant to rub up against him like a cat in heat so that when the bells over the door did finally ring, Johnny hung out in the back room waiting for his erection to subside.

Whoops.

Still. She was taking her revenge.

Johnny's bed in his apartment was not picturesque and mobile, but it *was* a lot less squeaky and he looked very handsome spread out underneath her with his hands pinned to the mattress.

"Zee- Zoya, jeeezzz..." The rest of whatever words he had chosen fell apart with a gasp.

She framed her teeth around the freckle right over his pulse point and sucked hard into the skin. Johnny's hips bucked beneath her, dick slipping futilely against her wet lips as he squirmed below her.

"You're...you're fucking evil," he managed through short, hard breaths of laughter.

She was not about to be distracted from her goal, so rather than pull away to argue, she only worked her hips back and down to drag over the length of him. She felt his arms tense under her hands and an extended, low groan rumbled up out of his chest. She pulled harder, rolling her tongue against his flesh and Johnny managed to nudge the tip of his cock inside of her, his whole body shaking with tension below her.

She released him with a sharp draw of breath and sank down several inches all at once.

"Fucking- damn it. You feel so good," his eyes were squeezed shut, bottom lip already swollen from biting.

He felt good too. She was trying to remember her goal of the evening, to drive him as insane as possible before letting them both get some satisfaction. But the stretch and pressure of him inside of her, and the picture of him at her mercy... She looked down between them and found herself whining slightly at the sight of where they were joined, the look of her wrapped around his cock, bodies red with blood rushing.

"Oh god," she whispered.

Johnny's wrist twisted under her hand and she released him as she lifted up slightly and then sank down farther again.

Johnny grunted, and it might have been a word, but Zee couldn't make it out for the rushing in her ears. His arm wrapped around her waist and he pulled her flush against him.

"One day," he ground out. "One day we're gonna go so slow."

She abandoned his other wrist in favor of giving herself leverage against his chest. "Not tonight," she said.

His hands wrapped over her hips and his knees bent to brace against the bed. "No. Not tonight."

Their rhythm was rough, rushed at first, both fighting to set a pace. Johnny pushed himself up to kiss her, teeth pulling at her lips, dragging against her chin, down her neck as he let her take control. She wanted to be patient, to drag every rise and fall out. But with every broken note from Johnny's lips burning into her throat, she tried to fit them tighter together. With every dig of his fingers into her curves, greedy and anxious, she needed the sharp buzz of friction burning between them.

"Johnny." His name fell out of her mouth before she knew she was speaking and then again, into a chant until she realized she was begging.

His kisses circled up her jaw to her ear. "I've got you."

Zee whimpered as she worked herself down onto him, chasing at a hot throb that bloomed and then faded again. Johnny wrapped an arm around her waist as her legs started to shake, his hips bucking up to meet hers. His other hand pressed between them, fingers swirling over her clit.

Her head fell back with a shout and Johnny was twisting them on the sheets. She landed with her head trailing off the edge, arms reaching back to grasp onto the corner of the mattress as he thrust into her in short, hard presses that dragged at her walls and pulled high notes of pleasure from her throat. His arm behind her back shifted down to pull her leg up, pressing it to her side. Every time he bottomed out inside of her she felt it ring out from her toes to the top of her head and then back down into her center. She could hear her voice cracking in the room, Johnny's breaths spilling over her neck and down her chest.

But her focus was between them where his thumb was pressing and rolling at her clit, bright sparks of electric pleasure bursting out until they were shattering through her, leaving her limp and barely aware of Johnny following after.

Zee was still hiding her blush, face down in Johnny's pillow, when he came back from the bathroom after cleaning them both up. The bed dipped as he joined her and she grabbed the hand that he set gently on her waist, pulling him tighter against her back.

He kissed her shoulder and pulled her hair back from her face. "You okay?" he asked. His hand was caught in hers, pressed against her stomach and she could hear the note of concern. She rolled on the bed until her hair was wrapped around her head again and her face was pressed against his chest.

"I'm not usually loud like that," she said into his skin.

His chest shook with repressed laughter and a bark of it escaped as she pinched his hip. "Sorry!" he said, half-giggling. "I believe you, I just...can't say I minded. Hey, you made this hickey kind of visible. Can I have some of that bruise cream?"

"No," Zee said, pushing her hair out of her face to smirk up at him. "I want Will to see it tomorrow."

Johnny grimaced. "He won't shut up about it all day."

"Yeah, tell him to send me pictures. Hang on, I'll just text him." She rolled to reach her phone and Johnny pounced over her, body weighing pleasantly over hers as they wrestled to reach the side table. She had to cheat and search out his ticklish spots. His arms were too damn long.

They both ended up abandoning the phone, hands shifting restlessly, mouths drinking from each other.

"Am I... is this too much?" he mumbled against her skin as their legs untwined and twisted to fit him between hers again.

She shook her head against his kiss. "Don't want to stop," she said.

Sam *had* warned her.

July 20th 2017

Johnny parked the car in the drive the next morning and moved to get out.

"You don't have to," she said.

He paused, half-leaning out of the door of the car. His face was still and she realized he was trying to decide what she meant.

"If you need to be at the studio," she tried again. "You can come by later. Cameron will be around. You don't have to do the... you know, *meeting* thing now."

His shoulders relaxed and he got out of his car. "This guy thinks I'm an asshole. I'm not gonna delay meeting him. Besides, I can make a good impression."

She followed and met him at the gate where he held it open for her.

"You're right," she said, perking up on her tiptoes to steal a kiss.

"Zee!"

She fell back to her heels with a grin and looked up at the house to see Cameron—a shirtless, freshly showered, barefoot Cameron, waving from the deck.

"Holy shit," Johnny muttered. "That dude is...a cartoon right? He's like...crazy buff."

"Makes you question your sexuality, doesn't he?" Zee asked.

Johnny shrugged. "My sexuality is flexible, to be honest."

That brought up the memory of him speaking to Luke at the studio opening and she brushed the memory away. She refused to fantasize about Luke. He was enough of a problem in her dreams never mind the reality of him.

Zee took Johnny's hand without thinking about it, like that was where it belonged, and walked them up to the house. Where Cameron promptly met them on the grass and lifted her up and out of Johnny's grasp.

"It's good to be home again," Cameron said, in his serious and sincere way that he seemed to use with absolutely no irony at all.

"It's good to have you back, buddy," Zee said, chin propped on his warm shoulder as her legs dangled. She patted his back. "So, this is Johnny."

Cameron turned and set her down two steps up to the house before facing Johnny. He had his arms on his hips and Zee was pretty sure he was flexing. Johnny gave her one, startled glance over Cam's shoulder before Cameron stepped forward. He was a little taller than Johnny, but mostly he was *bigger*. And Johnny made her feel kind of dainty generally, although that might have had more to do with the way he touched her. But Cameron was barrel chested with limbs that young trees could be jealous of where Johnny was tapered and tightly muscled.

It was both terrifying and thrilling to watch them face off.

"It's really good to meet you," Johnny said, his voice lowered and strangely casual. Dude talk. "I've heard a lot about you." He reached his hand out to shake.

"I've heard a great deal about you as well," Cameron said, words rumbling like thunder at a distance.

Oh shit, Zee thought, when Cameron went in for the handshake. She winced in sympathy as Johnny's attempt at a friendly smile turned into a comical grimace.

"Cameron," Zee said.

Cameron pumped Johnny's hand three times in a somewhat over enthusiastic gesture before stepping back to smile up at her.

"I hope you are happier now, Zee," Cameron said, all bright and friendly. Johnny stuck the probably injured hand in his back pocket and paled.

"I am very happy now, Cameron," she said, wondering if she might be allowed to burst into flames now, on the porch?

"What's taking so long?" Sam asked from behind them. "Cameron, were you male posturing?"

"I'm not familiar with that term," Cameron lied.

"Why aren't you wearing a shirt for this?" Sam asked. "Were you showing off?"

"I wanted Zee to know that I supported her," Cameron said, blinking big blue eyes up at a baffled Sam. "And I wanted him to know I could break his bones if he hurt her."

"Cameron, no," Zee said, covering her face with her hands.

"Dude, I believe you," Johnny said.

"You wanted to support Zee, without your shirt on? Go get dressed." Sam shook her head as Cameron shuffled up the stairs and into the house. "Sorry," she told Johnny. "He's a total teddy bear, really."

Johnny joined Zee on the steps and she heard him mutter 'grizzly bear' under his breath.

"Ohhhh did you bring coffee for everyone?" Sam asked, eyeing the drink carrier in Johnny's uninjured hand. "See, Johnny, you'll be fine. It's *my* vote that matters."

This time Johnny took Zee's hand. "You're happy?" he whispered.

Had she said that? She had said that. There were megalomaniac witches after their house, or Nadia, or maybe even her. But she had said that. It was true.

"Yeah," she said, squeezing his hand. He hissed. "Oh shit, sorry, he got that one didn't he?"

Chapter 15

A Cliffhanger

July 21st 2017

"**S**o your aunt gave up like...world domination, huh?" Will said, twirling a blow pipe in his hand like he was one of those baton girls at fairs.

Johnny scoffed and Zee wobbled her hand in the air. "I mean... maybe regional witch domination. But yeah."

Eric was wiping down the metal marver counter, scooping away bits of glass frit to save for later. He set the rag down and then jumped up to sit, Johnny's lips twitching irritably at the misuse of the space.

"What does this tell you about Luke?" Eric asked.

Zee and Johnny were sharing a bench, Zee smoothing salve over an old red streak down his forearm she'd been going to battle with for the past month. Johnny was leaning back into her, free hand fiddling with the frayed strands of her jeans over her knee.

"Nothing, unfortunately," Zee said. Johnny's head turned on her shoulder to prompt her with a raised eyebrow. "Not enough. We know he's been under Chernov's thumb for years." She opened her mouth to say that she didn't know why Luke was sent to them. But she was beginning to have an inkling.

If Chernov knew that Luke was having pesnya dushi visions of her, of Nadia's niece, wouldn't that be a perfect excuse to send him to the house?

"Chernov has his brain all twisted up," Johnny said.

"How do you keep a ghost safe?" Will asked, joining Eric on the marver. "Or, other end of the question, how do you capture a ghost?"

Brian was sitting on the free bench, rubbing Sam's miracle salve over the backs of his hands, stretching and flexing the stiff muscles as he listened.

"We're still researching that," Zee said. "It would help if Nadia weren't hiding, but I suppose it's a way of keeping her safe."

Johnny's fingers slipped down the hole of her jeans, resting against her skin. Zee wasn't sure if it was the pesnya dushi bond stretching its wings now that she and Johnny were together, or if it was the stress of everything going on at the house and with Luke. But all she ever wanted to be doing was keeping skin to skin contact with Johnny. She'd never been a very demonstrative person in a relationship. (She'd never felt very strongly for someone in a relationship.) But she'd grown up tactile around a tender Nadia and a cuddly Sam and now she found herself constantly resisting the urge to curl up against Johnny, searching for somewhere warm to touch. Or not resisting the urge, if she was being honest. She gave up working at the old scar and let her chin fall to his shoulder and her arms circle around his chest. He immediately covered her arms with his own.

Will was smirking from the table, but Zee just ignored him. She wasn't going to be embarrassed. Not in the hot shop, at least, where all the guys were plenty aware of just how mutual Johnny's affection was for her.

"So, what do we do?" Brian asked.

Zee wondered absently if anyone had ever mentioned to Brian that he had a pretty spectacular aura around him. All oranges and glimmering silvers with dark, bitter reds in splashes. She wondered what he would do if she told him and decided to save it for later.

"*We* are going to make ornaments," Johnny said.

The others' noses all wrinkled simultaneously.

"Told you," Johnny said, bumping his head against hers.

"Sam and I are going to charge some ash and iron flakes and Johnny's got a special glass chem compound coming in for them," Zee explained. "We're hanging them up around the island before Luke and Chernov find anymore cracks in the wards. Johnny already got the island to agree to it— they're happy to boast about the local talent."

Johnny scoffed and Zee bumped her head back in retaliation.

"Wait, we get to do magic?" Eric asked, perking up.

"Yeah," Zee said and she and Will exchanged a smile at Eric's spreading grin. No one who looked at Eric would've guessed he'd become such a massive nerd about witchcraft in so little time.

"I've been practicing meditation," Eric said.

"It cuts into our morning sex, but he's been very dedicated," Will added.

"This is the A-team?" Johnny whispered.

"That's perfect," Zee said to Eric. "I'll be generating a lot of the power, but everything you can add will help."

Johnny's fingers threaded through hers. He had also been very patient the past couple evenings as Zee had meditated and made teapot after teapot and taken charging baths with herbs and stones and candles surrounding her. And he hadn't even complained one bit when she told him that sex was a powerful magical boost. He'd been *very* supportive of that method, in fact. And even after a day of dealing with a fussy mother of the bride who wanted a very specific selection of products in every single one of her gift baskets for a wedding party, she was still feeling head to toe electric with magic. Largely due to the handful of orgasms Johnny had insisted on giving her with his mouth at dawn.

"And if Luke shows back up?" Will asked.

"We've...decided to try and reason with him," Zee said, glancing at Johnny. "I mean, Luke might be a lost cause. But there was... something worth saving in him at one point."

There was still something worth saving in her dreams too, although she tried not to let them change how she saw him.

"And if he's too far gone?" Brian asked.

Zee thought of the cabin in the woods, smeared in red, the voice that had crawled up out of Luke's throat.

"I don't know," Zee said. It hurt to admit. She and Sam had been trying to keep their words positive and Johnny and Cameron had backed them up in that effort.

They were Nikolaev witches. They were strong. They would block Luke and Kasimir Chernov out, build an impenetrable defense against them.

But that hadn't happened.

"I don't know," she repeated and Johnny's fingers were firm around hers. "I don't know how we approach Chernov directly. I think...I think I could try to break the link between him and Luke."

Johnny stiffened against her. They'd only broached the idea briefly the day before and given that involved her developing another link to Luke's thoughts, or manipulating what was left of the original, he had been firmly opposed to the idea. Cameron and Sam had too. And then she'd dreamt of Luke sleeping between her and Johnny, brow tangled and skin damp with sweat until they'd woken him with gentle calls.

"Is that safe?" Brian asked, and Zee suspected he'd seen something on Johnny's face.

"No," she said. "It wouldn't be. It's only an option."

"Not one we're taking," Johnny said, thoroughly stubborn.

She opened her mouth to argue and then thought better of it, and tucked a kiss behind his ear.

As it turned out, Johnny was right. It wasn't an option they would use.

July 22nd 2017

Johnny walked into the shop fifteen minutes after closing while Zee was wrapping up a customized gift basket for the customer she'd been gently pressing into making decisions for the past hour.

"They're closed," the woman at the counter said helpfully to Johnny. She was from the mainland and had held an extensive email discussion with Sam over the past few months until Sam ended it with an abbreviated 'I think you'll find our storefront very informative on scents and packaging.' Figures Sam would take the weekend off to spend with Cameron when Ms. Details finally did come around.

"He's just waiting for me," Zee said, finishing off the ribbon bow on the basket.

The woman gave Johnny, who was leaning against the cupboards and rubbing in a little tester of body butter onto the back of his hand, a longer look. When she turned back to Zee she raised her eyebrows and said, "Sorry for keeping you."

And Zee was pretty sure she was being sincere. She buried her laughter and locked the door after the woman, flipping the open sign to closed in a reflex. (Some days she turned back after making it halfway down the block because she couldn't actually remember whether or not she locked up.)

"You know I know the way back to my own house, right?" Zee asked Johnny as he followed her to the back room while she flipped the lights off. "You don't have to come all the way down here to give me a ride back."

"By all the way down here I take it you mean...the three minutes of driving it takes?" Johnny asked her. "And that we're just gonna ignore that Luke could be...anywhere at this point?"

"Not *ignore* it," Zee said, scrambling for an argument against him. She swiveled in step after locking the door and popped up on her toes to kiss him softly, lingering against his lips to settle on, "I missed you."

Johnny's lips twitched as his eyes narrowed. "Damn," he said. "That works every time."

She tried not to look too smug. She *was* letting him taking her home after all, despite all her protestations. She was going to have to start taking walks for *exercise* if Johnny was going to make her healthy habit of biking and walking to and from town moot.

She filled him in on the indecisive day on the drive up, he told her about Eric's small disaster in the kiln turning into a new project for him to experiment with and they pulled up to the house before Zee even had time to regret the fossil fuels.

She'd barely made it out of the car, swinging the door shut, when she heard the shouting.

"Let her go, Luke!" It was Cameron, in the backyard by the cliff, voice cracking out like a gunshot into the quiet afternoon.

Zee was running through the gate with Johnny at her heels. There was a sliver thin tear in the wards at the gate, the violation so subtle that it only scratched at her thoughts as she ran. Luke had charmed his way in, probably fooling Cameron with some bit of glamour. Sam was still feeling the violation of the break in keenly, constantly checking locks and having Zee add charms in the border gardens or to hang from the windows. She would have caught the deception.

"Zee, wait," Johnny said.

She hushed him with a wave of her hand, trying to make out the words in the smooth glide of Luke's voice behind the house.

"Call for Zoya," Luke growled. "Before I do permanent damage."

Zee stopped in place as she reached the corner of the house and saw Sam on the ground, clawing at the grass, mouth gaping in a silent scream, eyes clamped shut. Cameron was at her side, glaring up at Luke who looked as tidy as ever. But Zee could see the snarls of red that wrapped around his head and wrists and chest.

"Sam!" she screamed. She wove through the gardens, pebbles kicking up behind her.

Luke turned and smiled at her approach, as if he were actually *happy* to see her.

"Let her go," Zee spat. "We all know why you're here and it isn't Sam!"

"If your aunt would come out of hiding-" Luke started.

"Nobody is hiding anything here, *you idiot*," Zee said. She felt like there was a drum pounding inside of her. The evening was hot, the air heavy with a storm boiling closer to shore, and her blood was thumping hard through her veins, magic gathering in her palms.

"My master-" Luke turned back to Sam as Zee passed him and sank into the grass next to Sam.

She pressed her hand onto the center of Sam's back and winced as her cousin whimpered at the touch. She tried to spread love and healing, to clean out whatever poison Luke was using on her, but found herself too spiky, all the sharp edges and bright anger she had needed to use against him when she was on her own.

"Your fucking master wants what he can't have," Zee said, turning to see that Johnny was frozen a few feet away, clearly struggling to push against whatever block Luke had set against him. "And he's using you like a puppet. Aren't you stronger than this?"

"Where is Nadia?" Luke hissed.

Zee rose up from the ground, pressing a current of magic down into the earth by the soles of her feet, sending the power to Johnny until he stumbled in her direction, stepping up to her side.

"Nadia is dead," Zee said, the words tearing at her heart. "She made her choice about Chernov decades ago. I don't know what crap he's been feeding you but the dreams aren't a promise. You only stay with the pesnya dushi you *want*."

She didn't feel sorry for the flinch on his expression, not really. Not with Johnny nearby. But it still tasted like a lie on her tongue.

"Zoya," Cameron said, rising up to his feet, still standing

guard over a Sam who seemed to be gaining ground against Luke's attack.

Zee made herself blink to clear away the clotted red that swam around Luke, and see the way his brow furrowed and his eyes twitched around the yard, down to Sam and over to Johnny.

"You touch him, I will break the bones in your hand," Zee hissed.

Johnny was warm at her back, hand looping around hers. Luke snarled and paced away from them, closer to the cliffside, eyes narrowed and restless. His fingers trembled and the elbows of his jacket looked worn thin, as if Zee was suddenly seeing through a glamour he'd concocted.

"Your aunt," he said, rounding at Zee.

"Is dead," Zee said. She stepped closer. She was building something up in her chest, something that rushed through her, sweeping in circles around her heart. "She's gone. She's barely even in the house these days. What does your puppet master really think he's going to do with a wisp of a ghost?"

"There are ways around death," Luke said, all smooth and purring.

"Disgusting," Sam spat from the ground.

"You *play* at witchcraft," Luke snapped, furious in a moment as if he were the wild-eyed Jack bursting out of the box, after too much winding on Zee's part. "You squander generations of power, of history, and for what? *Body wash?*"

"Do you really think you're here for yourself?" Zee shouted into Luke's face. "You're just a pair of legs for Chernov to exploit. And do you know why? Because he knows that's all you're good for, and he's too decrepit to come take care of it himself!"

"Chernov is nearer to a god than the imaginings of the devout," Luke snarled.

"He's weak," she said. Johnny fingers were wrapped around her wrist, gently warning and she wanted to throw him off her.

Before she could, long cold fingers were wrapped around her throat.

"Don't you fucking touch her," Johnny snarled, arm around her waist. It was too late. Luke had a good grip.

"Luke, let her go," Sam growled, diving forward and yanking at his legs. But it only served to have Luke stumble closer to the edge, dragging Zee along with him.

"Jesus, everyone, stop!" Johnny barked, and his touch was hot on her skin.

"What have you been storing up for, little moon bloom?" Luke hissed, fingers hard around her neck, making the air in her lungs thin. He bent his face down to hers until their noses were barely inches apart, eyes narrowing to thin slits of ice surrounded by threads. "Were you looking for a fight?"

"Zee," Sam whispered on the ground and Cameron rushed to her side.

"I was preparing for one," Zee gasped out before swinging her free hand up to wrap around Luke's neck in a mirror image of his hold on her.

There was a charge of power, a circuit of magic that clashed painfully in Zee's chest as it spiraled between them. Her only reassurance was that she could feel him falter, the brittle crack of his control as she swept through like a tide. She was digging in, searching for some loose thread in the web Chernov had woven through Luke's mind, even through his skin. The armor magic, the secrecy, and something like a veil over his perceptions that colored everything in bitter anger and an urgent need for destruction. Luke faltered a step and Zee advanced.

There were hands digging their fingers into her stomach- Johnny trying to hold her back.

"Let him go, Zee," Johnny whispered in her ear.

But he didn't know that Zee had just found Luke's grip on Sam and she flooded it with bright magic until she heard Sam gasp sharply behind her, breaths heaving from her spot on the ground.

"You're a puppet," she managed to say to Luke, words barely catching enough air to make a sound. His grip tightened as he snarled and she choked, gray creeping in at the edges of her vision.

"Stop it!" Johnny yelled, voice close and sharp, and Zee shut her eyes, trying to focus just as he reached out and wrapped a hand around Luke's on her throat.

She felt nails scratch the skin of her neck as Johnny grappled to free her. Sam was shouting her name behind them, Cameron trying to soothe her and command Luke to release Zee all in the same breath. Zee tried to swallow, tried to sweep through the corruption in Luke's mind just as Johnny managed to pry the other man's fingers away from her. She sucked in a breath that was too deep just as she released the magic.

And suddenly, from nowhere, a tiny bundle of cotton and soft blonde hair was charging into Luke's stomach, knocking him out of Zee's grasp until his toes were at the edge of the cliff and he was sliding off.

"Sam!" It was barely a sound but Zee was diving forward, catching hold of her cousin's hand just as her own feet were skidding on crumbling grass.

Johnny was clambering to the edge, a black sleeve in his grasp, boots digging into the earth as he tried to drag Luke back from the fall. His head was turning between the drop of the cliff to where Zee was pulling a weak-kneed Sam back to the grass, Cameron's arms clamping tight around their waists as they collapsed, all knees and elbows into a pile.

"Reach up" Johnny growled, forehead knotting, fabric slipping through a nervous grip. "Come on, man! Reach up!"

"He has me." The words were soft and strangely light. Almost surprised.

"Luke. Reach your hand up, I will - I can pull you up," Johnny begged even as his knees slid forward.

Zee tried to wrestle her way free of Sam and Cameron, wondered if she wanted to help Johnny pull him up, or convince him to let Luke fall. It was an ugly thought and as Sam wrapped her arm around Zee's shoulder, scooting them back farther from the edge, she hid her face against Sam's neck.

But she could still hear it.

"He has me."

"Luke!!" Johnny bellowed and Sam screamed behind her hands and Cameron broke out in a sudden startled cry as earth broke apart on the cliffside. Zee folded herself in the grass and covered her ears with her hands, biting into her knee to keep from screaming, a wounded sound crawling up from her throat.

Cameron scrabbled to Johnny's side and both men released pained yells as the steady waves that beat against the cliff were broken with a sharp splash.

"Oh god," Sam whispered.

Zee squeezed her eyes shut and when a small hand wrapped around her foot she reached down to squeeze back, to anchor herself. There was a siren in her ears that was drowning out the sound of the waves, the sound of her own breathing—if she even was breathing. Everything was numb and tingling and raw and she realized that she'd pushed away every last thread of magic she'd been saving up. Sent it into Luke and the air and the ground until she felt boneless and sore and jangling.

"...My boat. Need to go down to the water," Cameron was saying as the ringing sound softened in her head.

"The rocks," Sam whispered. "Be careful."

"I'll manage them," Cameron said. Everyone sounded gentle, or careful like they were tiptoeing around glass. "It's high tide."

Zee lifted her head up and her neck ached with the effort. Sam lifted her hand off her foot and stood up, hanging back from Cameron, face fragile and open. Johnny hit the grass heavily at her side and Zee let him pull her up by the elbows. She could hear Cameron murmuring to Sam and she pressed her own face into Johnny's chest. His thumbs pressed into her shoulders, finding knots, and he buried his face down into her loose hair.

"I'm going with Cameron," he whispered. "Stay in the house, okay?"

"Sam and I can call..." Zee started but then stopped. Her eyes popped open as she remembered Sam barreling past her into Luke's chest.

"Wait," Johnny said. "Wait for us to get back okay? We'll decide what to do then."

There were protocols on the island for drownings, ones they had grown up with in school, lessons in health class. Because of course there was always going to be a few idiot teenagers who thought of daring each other off the edge of a cliff, with half a pack of beer or a bottle of cheap vodka. None of the protocols included waiting to call the authorities. But Zee didn't want to call the authorities. She didn't want *Jasper Doyle* showing up here to investigate a fall...a...

"Go in the house," Johnny said, lifting her face up to meet his gaze. "Stay in the house, okay?"

"Okay," she said, tongue heavy in her mouth. Johnny pulled back and she could see Cameron and Sam too close to the edge of the cliff, Cam's hand at the back of her head, lips moving at her ear, free arm wrapped tight around her waist. When Sam nodded briefly Cameron moved them farther into the yard. Safer, Zee thought, a bubbly light-headedness taking over.

Sam's hand was in hers, their fingers loose, and Zee watched Johnny and Cameron walking across the yard, down the stone garden path, heads bowed. Sam kept stopping on their way to the greenhouse doors, pausing in place, eyes scanning around them, landing back at the cliff.

"Inside," Zee prompted, tugging softly on Sam's hand.

"Car," Sam murmured.

"That's Cameron and Johnny leaving," Zee said.

"Zee- Zee, I-"

Zee stopped on the greenhouse steps and looked down into Sam's stunned face, pale and slack.

"Come inside, Samsam," Zee coaxed, gently pulling her cousin up the stairs, lifting at her elbows when her feet missed and stumbled. "I'm making tea."

Valerian root, lemon balm, passionflower. What would Sam mix? Add lavender.

Zee pushed Sam onto a stool at the kitchen island, sliding a small plate of leftover brownies in front of her before pulling them away again with a glance at Sam's greening face. She lifted her back up off the stool and guided her to the sink, twisting her hair into a quick braid as Sam bent and retched into porcelain.

Ginger for nausea.

No, that was too many flavors.

Zee bit her lip and stared up at the ceiling, rubbing Sam's back and willing the tears trying to slide free back into their ducts.

What would Nadia do?

Vodka. They needed vodka.

Sam gagged softly and Zee winced. Ginger tea first. Then vodka.

* * *

Cameron and Johnny made it back to the house after dark. Cameron was wet, head to toe, like he'd dove into the water and gone swimming in the search, and Johnny had rope burn around his palms. But they came back alone.

"No sign of him," Johnny whispered to her, and he leaned heavily against Zee at the kitchen counter, face burying itself back into her hair, nose nuzzling behind her ear. She worked around him, spreading Sam's best potions into his hands. "You smell like alcohol."

"Been drinking," Zee said.

"It help?"

"Nope."

When they made it back to the library, Cameron was sitting in front of the fire, steaming in the heat with his hands firmly around Sam's.

"We aren't calling anyone," Cameron said firmly, and Sam's head drooped a little further as if she'd just lost the argument.

Neither Johnny or Zee spoke. She didn't feel as if it was really up to her. They'd all stood there together. Fought against Luke. And Sam...Sam had pushed him. She looked up at Johnny and found him studying her, brow furrowed, something frightened in his gaze.

She felt a little sick now too.

"Where's the alcohol?" Johnny whispered.

"Here," Cameron answered before taking a swift chug and holding it out to Johnny.

Johnny crossed the room to take the bottle and Cameron lifted Sam up from the carpet to hold her against his soaked chest in front of the fire. Zee stood in the doorway watching Johnny take a long drink, grimacing and gasping as he pulled away, and felt her heart sinking.

Chapter 16

Cracks in the Amor

July 23rd 2017

"Y**ou've been avoiding me.**" Johnny sat down in the grass at her side, wrapping his arms around his knees and propping his chin in a mimic of her own position.

"I don't know what to say," Zee said.

There were crickets trilling around them in the dark. It was a new moon and Zee wasn't sure if that was why her body felt like someone had stitched her up with rocks under her skin, or if it had to do with the day before.

"I don't need you to say anything," Johnny said.

"Then why are you out here?" Zee asked. "Go home, Johnny."

The words hit her first, the choking sound from Johnny's throat second, the sudden shift of him jumping up from the ground and leaving her in the grass third. Her eyes were burning as she lifted her hands up to cover her face, screaming silently into her palms. Her heart was punishing her with a sharp tearing feeling when warm fingers wrapped around her wrists pulling her hands back from her face, gentle and firm.

Johnny was there, eyes tight and lips hard, but he was in front of her.

"Stop doing this," he said, and the words were harsh. "Zee, you have to stop doing this. I don't know if you're testing me or-"

"I'm not, I swear," she said, twisting her hands in his hold to grab at him in return, clutch at him to keep him from running.

"I'm not going anywhere," Johnny said, eyes growing open again. "But you fucking shut me out like this and- I'm not going to force myself on you, okay? I need to know if you want me to be here."

"I want you here." There were tears falling out of her eyes and she was trying to pull them closer together even as he was resisting. "Johnny somebody *died*. You were here and Luke died, and it's *our* fault-"

"It's not."

"It's my fault that you're here. That you're part of this. That you had to *witness* that."

Johnny's face broke, crumpling, and then he had her wrapped up in his hold, face pressed into the spot just below his throat she always found. Her fingers clutched at his t-shirt as dry sobs broke free from her chest against his.

"It's not, it's not," he chanted into her hair. "It's not your fault. I'm always going to be here."

"We could go to jail," Zee whispered.

Johnny's fingers slid into her hair, lips pressing to the top of her head. There was nothing to say to that. None of them really knew what would happen if Luke's body turned up. Although Zee had run countless scenarios through her head.

He would never be found.

His body would wash up and be unidentifiable.

It would be identified but no one would ever know why he came to the island, what business he had at the house on the cliff.

He had a plan for this to incriminate them, insurance against any violence. Jasper Doyle would gladly turn on the Nikolaev women. Sam would be put in, maybe the both of them, left to wither without magic in a cell. Johnny would move on without her.

She wrapped her arms around his waist as if to keep him there with her, to guard against all the worst possibilities.

"Stop it," Johnny said into her ear. "Stop torturing yourself. Come inside with me."

"I can't lose Sam," Zee whispered. "I can't lose you."

He sat back on his heels, untangling her arms from around him and smoothing her hair away from her face. She leaned into his palm.

"It's not gonna happen, okay," he said. "I'm on your team. Zee I-" he broke off and Zee looked up. She knew what he wanted to say and she was both ready to hear it, and sure that today was not the day for the words.

She wrapped her hands around his arms. "Let's go inside."

Johnny stood up and pulled her along with him, drawing her against his side to lean there. "You want Sam? She's been in the kitchen for a few hours and Cameron says it's better if he leaves her there."

Zee appreciated that Johnny sounded a little skeptical of the idea. "He's right," Zee assured him. "Sam's processing or avoiding or maybe she's just...working, but it's better to let her do her thing right now. Cameron knows how long to let her stew before making her take a break."

Johnny hummed and his thumb stroked along the back of her hand and they passed the greenhouse to leave Sam in peace in the kitchen.

"So, what do you need?" he asked. He caught her looking at him and gave her a half-smile. "I don't know these things yet. And I don't want to bother the others so...what should I do?"

Zee bit her lip as they walked up the front steps and into the house. He'd already broken her out of the spiraling panic outside. She didn't know what else to ask for, or how to go about the asking. She'd tried to think of what Nadia would have done when she was young and her heart was breaking almost every day at school. Or how she and Sam coped after Nadia died.

"I need to focus on something other than myself," Johnny said.

He'd been in bed with her when she woke up in the morning, although he'd been downstairs drinking when she slunk away from the others. And he'd woken up hungover and quiet. There were still dark circles under his eyes, and his shoulders were tense and high.

"I'm going to steal some tea from the kitchen," Zee said and stepped into his chest to settle him down from the flinch in his eyes. "Find a book to read and meet me upstairs."

"Ohhkay," he said, frowning a little. But he didn't press when she left him to walk down to the kitchen.

Sam didn't look up as she entered, but she passed Zee the chamomile without looking. Zee stepped up to her cousin's back and wrapped her arms around her shoulders, holding loosely until Sam's nerves settled and she relaxed for a moment. Zee squeezed, once, and then let her go back to work, waiting for the kettle to steam.

"Take some to Cameron for me?" Sam said into the old pot above the wood stove.

"Of course," Zee said.

Cameron was in the living room by the fireplace, staring at the few flames left licking at the remains of old logs. She set the tea down next to him and started to retreat.

"It wasn't her fault," Cameron said.

"I didn't say it was," Zee said. She had seen it on his face after Luke had fallen, when he'd returned with Johnny after searching the water. There was no resentment there. It didn't make things simpler for Sam. "Just don't let her stay in the kitchen all night. Make brownies."

"She hates my brownies," Cameron said, looking up at her finally, face puzzled, eyes red and tired.

"Yeah it'll help distract her," Zee said.

Cameron scoffed and the corner of his mouth lifted for a moment. "I don't mind him so much, now," Cameron said, glancing up at the ceiling.

"Yeah. Me neither," Zee said, smiling.

"I am glad you are in good hands," Cameron said, somehow making her feel small in front of him despite staying relaxed in his armchair by the fire.

"I'm glad Sam is," Zee said, patting Cameron lightly on the shoulder. "But if you need her right now you should tell her. She's just ...afraid."

Cameron's eyes flickered over to the door and back to Zee. "Do I give her time or not?"

Zee checked the clock. "Give her an hour if you can stand it."

Cameron shifted slightly in his chair, sniffing at the tea. Zee figured he'd wait another thirty minutes now. And given the curl of Sam's hair in the kitchen that should be just about the right timing for pulling her out of her project.

Johnny was waiting upstairs in her bed, pushed against the window, two books in his lap. One was a magical text on drawing down the moon, the other was a well loved book of short stories. Zee crawled into the bed and settled down against Johnny's side, putting the magical book down on the window sill with the mugs of tea. She picked the other one up and thumbed through until she found the one about the ice maiden who fell in love with the scorching desert prince. She passed the book over to Johnny.

"Read to me?" she asked.

Johnny startled beneath her, hands fidgeting along the book.

"I'm not a very good reader," he said.

She remembered him from school, steady and simple and slow. She'd always liked it, but maybe she had just enjoyed hearing his voice without the sneer or the sarcasm.

"It doesn't matter," Zee said, burrowing down against his side. "I just want to listen."

"Kay." He propped the book in one hand and the other drifted down to tangle his fingers in her hair as he started the story.

* * *

There was copper on her tongue and something like warm, wet, velvet running over her skin. She opened her eyes and everything was a dense, shifting red, like theatre curtains pulling away to reveal the scene. But when she tried to call out the color flooded in, cloying and thick like syrup, bitter like blood. She thrashed and her movements were milky and loose, floating in space with the pulsing glow sliding over her skin like a tongue. She screamed and air gurgled in her throat, liquid filling her lungs.

"Zee! OW!"

She sat up and she was in bed, her hand fisted in Johnny's hair, yanking his face back on his neck. Her fingers were tight on the strands for a long moment, his startled blue eyes vivid in the dark. Her chest burnt and she let go of him with a gasp, sucking air back into her lungs and realizing she'd been holding her breath.

"Hey, pixie," Johnny whispered slowly, as she curled away from him. "Hey, hey, it's okay. Bad dream, just a bad dream."

It *was*, she realized. She'd woken up from a nightmare. Johnny's hands were soothing down her side, gently tugging her back to face him. He brushed at her cheeks and there were wet tracks there, she'd been crying.

"It's okay. Zee, you okay?"

"I-" she took another deep breath. "I don't remember it? The dream," she added at his blank look.

"Yeah?"

She nodded, brain scrabbling for some foothold in her own terror, some concrete image to remember and make sense of her racing heart and shaking hands. Johnny gathered them up in his own, laying back against the pillows and drawing her down against them, gently pinning her trembling arms between them. His hands slid over her ribs to tangle in the ends of her hair.

"Bound to have bad dreams hanging around," Johnny murmured.

Zee had her ear pressed to his chest and the notes of his voice hummed in her head, ushering away something slick and sinister that'd been slithering around in the background since she'd woken up. She shifted and settled into a more comfortable spot, leaving Johnny surrounding her as she fell back asleep.

"We're okay," he said as her eyes fell shut.

The words were soft, vibrating beneath her cheek.

July 24ᵗʰ 2017

Johnny said it first, over warm cups of coffee in her bed the next morning.

"We won't tell the others."

Zee swallowed, hands wrapped around the black soup bowl sized mug she'd found at the grocery store around halloween that read 'Witch, Please' in curly white letters.

"They're our friends. They'll want to know what happened," she said. She agreed with Johnny. It would be better to leave the others out of the...event with Luke. The moment on a cliff she couldn't wrap her thoughts around and couldn't close her eyes without remembering, vividly.

"They'll want to know why Luke isn't a problem anymore," Johnny said, as if the two weren't connected. "And we can say...we reasoned with him. It's..."

"Almost like the truth," she said, looking up from her mug into Johnny's weary eyes.

He stretched past her to set his coffee down on the window ledge and then settled back to wrap his hands around her shoulders, ducking his head until she met his gaze.

"I don't like it either. And I trust those guys, I do," Johnny said, scooting forward across the sheets and drawing her closer. "But right now I'm going to focus on you. And if I know you, you're gonna focus on Sam."

Zee nodded and bit her lip.

"Are you still waiting for me to decide I've had enough

and walk out?" Johnny asked, voice dropping gently, thumbs brushing softly over her shoulders.

"A little," she answered in a whisper. Johnny took a deep breath, looking down at their laps and she rushed on, "I know...I know you won't." He blinked and looked up at her and she tried to smile for him. "I'm just...This is so much more than high school feuds and the island pariah dating the golden boy."

Johnny made an uncomfortable face at the last bit and shook it off. "It is. It's...I'm not done processing either, okay? I don't know if we've done the right thing, I can barely think straight about what happened but...we're in this together. I chose that when I walked into the shop last month, and when I fought a shadow and...It's definitely a different dating experience than I predicted," he said, somewhat dazed.

Zee found herself laughing against her better judgement and buried it as quickly as she could, stuffing giggles behind pursed lips.

"I feel a little insane," she said when she settled.

"I don't know what I feel," Johnny said. "Someone died and I couldn't do anything about it and I don't know if I'm responsible or if I'm relieved or what I should be doing to keep it a secret. I thought about googling it but I figured we wouldn't want that in my search history if something turned up later."

"What if he isn't..." Zee whispered. They hadn't found Luke in the water and while it seemed *impossible...*

"I..I've thought about that and I...don't know what to feel about it either," Johnny said. "It would be...would it be good?"

Zee wasn't really sure either.

* * *

The shop was thankfully quiet that Monday. Zee hadn't expected Sam to come with her, although she couldn't verbalize why without cringing. It felt strange to be facing the shelves, cleaning the tester displays, smiling as the door opened with the ringing bells. She and Sam passed each other with soft touches, rousing one another from empty stares, and for the last half hour they stood together at the counter like eerie statues waiting for the minutes to tick away.

"Cameron went out in the boat today," Sam said as Zee locked the front door.

"Oh."

"He didn't find anything, he just texted."

"Should we...should we look?" Zee asked as Sam turned the lights off. Sam paused with her hand on the light switch. "Should we scry for him?"

Sam turned, face flat and eyes anxious. "Should we?"

They stood in silence for a long moment before Zee walked forward and took Sam's hand in hers, leading them out the back door. Johnny was waiting for them at the back of the shop. Sam slid in behind Johnny and Zee hopped into the passenger seat, Johnny's hand finding hers before going to the gear shift.

"What did you tell them?" Sam asked.

Johnny frowned and pulled out onto the street. "That they had to wait a few more days to come up to the house. You and Cameron are still..." He glanced at Zee as his lips hung open. He'd probably managed to pull it off as a joke with Will and Eric and Brian, but in the car with the three of them it was never going to land.

"I miss them," Sam whispered. "But I'm not ready to see them."

"Well, they were being shits in the studio today so I'm glad for the break," he said with strained levity. Zee squeezed at his knee and his hand came down from the steering wheel to tangle their fingers together.

When they arrived home Nadia was in the garden, tearing up plants.

"Zee?" Johnny asked, urgent, nervous.

Not that she could blame him, nothing good ever followed her rushing out of the car.

"It's just Nadia," she said over her shoulder and she heard Sam and Johnny murmuring together in her wake.

Streaks of white and soft red were zipping up and down the garden paths, daffodil roots lying on the ground, branches of rosemary and juniper scattered across the pebbles.

"Nadia what's going on?"

Cold and heat stroked up her arms. *I've caused so much trouble, ved'mitchka. Causing so much trouble.*

"It isn't your fault, we know that," Zee whispered, scooping herbs and flowers up off the ground and finding a horrible ache in her chest as she catalogued every plant.

Won't be much more now. Won't be much longer.

"Oh, Nadia, please," Zee said, her voice cracking as Sam's palm landed gently on her back. "Please, calm down. Please don't do this."

Need to take care of my girls, ved'mitchka. There was a bright kiss at her cheek and a snap of a sage branch. Sam plucked the bundle from Zee's hands as fat tears rolled down her cheeks. Johnny picked up the sage from the ground and hurried to Zee, startled by the broken cry sobbing out from her throat.

"What? What is it?" Johnny asked, sage leaves brushing at her cheeks as he lifted his hands to her face.

She pressed herself against his chest, wanting to tear the sage out of his hands and stomp it into the ground, but needing the solid feel of him more.

"It's Nadia," Sam said, soft and sorry. "I think...I think she wants us to exorcise her."

Johnny squeezed Zee's hand in a vice grip as she tossed the collection of plants over the side of the cliff. Sam sagged in the greenhouse doorway, face in hands. Cameron made it back to the house shortly after, finished with his fruitless search. Johnny made grilled cheese sandwiches as Zee tried to talk him into going back to his apartment for a break from her, from the house, from all of the magic and horror. Cameron vetoed her suggestion and ate three of the sandwiches himself.

July 26th 2017

Fingertips brushed at her shoulders as she walked down the street. There were flowers everywhere and their fragrance was as heavy as silk over her cheeks. Sam was...there! Just down the alley, out on the sea and the waves with Cameron. They waved. She waved back, and Caleb Carver stopped and knelt at her feet. There was a kiss at her ankle, wide brown eyes gazing up at her, and then he rose and left.

All the words of the people in town were sweet, welcoming, grateful. All their faces were smiles, all their touches were gentle.

She felt warm and soft. Like she was floating.

There was someone missing.

No. No, this is perfect. This is what you deserve.

There was nothing missing.

* * *

Zee opened the front door at the crack of dawn, near to growling, to find Will and Eric on the porch, coffees and pastry bags in hand.

"We're calling bullshit," Will said. "Let us in."

"Don't wake anyone," Zee said, stepping back to let them shoulder in. Will passed her with the food and drinks, heading for the kitchen, but Eric stopped for a long hug until Zee had to push him away or burst into tears.

There was a coffee and a little egg scramble pastry waiting for her on the counter when she managed to coax Eric into following her without checking on her every other second.

"You look tired," Will said, nudging at the coffee cup.

"You woke me up," she said, and she let her voice be as whiny as it wanted.

"Johnny's distracted in the studio," Eric said, breaking up his triple chocolate muffin into crumbling pieces as he ate.

"I know," Zee said. She had dealt with the fresh burn the night before, wrestling an irritable Johnny into a chair, ignoring his eye rolls as she lectured on safety.

"Zee?" Johnny mumbled from the hall before tripping his way into the kitchen. He stopped in the doorway, grimaced at the sight of his friends and then padded over to her side.

"Cover it up, Sharpe," Will said, cheerfully snipping at his favorite opponent who was shirtless, eyes heavy lidded with sleep.

Johnny ignored him in favor of taking the coffee Eric passed him. "Told you guys to stay out of our hair."

"They can't fuck like rabbits *every* hour of the day,"

Will said. "And even if they could you and Zee wouldn't look so completely miserable about it cause you're just as bad yourselves."

Johnny couldn't seem to decide on whether he felt offended or proud of the accusation and the result was a sleepy compromise of a disgruntled shrug and a possessive arm over Zee's shoulders. She let it slide because it was chilly in the kitchen and Johnny was perpetually cozy and warm.

"There was a blow out with Luke," Zee said.

Johnny stiffened at her side and lifted the coffee cup up to his lips to hide his expression.

"What happened?" Eric asked just as Will sat up straighter and asked, "Why didn't you tell us?"

"It was...everyone's still a little sore about it," Zee said. "We're all fine. No one...nothing happened. But it was ugly."

Eric's brow furrowed. "Where is Luke now?"

"Gone," Johnny said.

"We think," Zee added. "We think it's...resolved, I guess."

Johnny's fingers made spirals over her shoulder and she wasn't sure if it was meant to soothe her or if he was fidgeting under the lies.

"Seriously?" Will said, face twisted and eyebrows raised. "You think he's just going to give up."

"No," Zee said, not meaning to, but thinking of Chernov and finding the word already spoken.

"So we're going to go ahead with the globes?" Eric asked.

"Yes," Zee said.

Johnny was looking at her, face blank. They hadn't discussed the globes. But it had been their Luke Plan and she supposed that they had all mentally dropped the idea. Now she couldn't shake the idea that they should stay.

"Best case scenario," Zee said, turning to stare back into Johnny's eyes. "They'll help protect the island. Just like we've always done."

Johnny nodded softly just as Sam and Cameron entered from the hallway.

"Oh my god," Will whispered.

Cameron was also shirtless and bleary eyed but he smiled gently at the two strangers as Sam practically sleep-walked her way to the coffee Eric held out to her.

"You must be Eric and Will," Cameron said, more morning person than anyone else living in the kitchen. "I take it I have you to thank for making Johnny less of an ass than the stories I've heard from Zee and Sam."

"No," Johnny said. "No they are not-"

"You absolutely do," Will said, beaming at Cameron as Eric nodded, his head bouncing rhythmically as he eyed Cam's bare chest.

July 27th 2016

Johnny grunted softly, face down on her mattress, bare from head to toe, as Zee worked Sam's newly designed burn protection potion into the planes of his back.

"Feels good," he mumbled, face smashed against her sheets as she dug her fingers into the tops of his shoulders, smoothing circles of oil over his skin.

"The magic or the massage?" Zee asked, smiling.

He had protested her wearing anything, but she wasn't sure she'd be able to focus for long if she was stretched over him, the pair of them naked. She was fairly certain Johnny wouldn't have let her finish her work in that state. A little nightgown wasn't really proving much protection from the temptation as it was. She'd started at his toes and worked her way up the backs of his legs and Johnny had shifted restlessly beneath her hands the whole way.

Now at least he seemed to be relaxing. He had yet to answer her question. She tiptoed her fingers up the back of his neck with firm presses until they were sliding through the soft strands of his hair.

"Mnnnoo, mnot ma hair." Johnny's voice slurred but he barely even twitched until her nails were scratching behind his ears.

"Every inch," she said working along his jaw until his mouth was hanging loose, just a little smile at the corners. "I know you well enough to know that there's no spot safe from you finding a way to burn it."

He huffed a little and then hummed as she rubbed circles into his temples. His eyes were shut and his breaths were slow and deep, back rising and falling beneath her thighs. She stroked her fingers through his hair as she watched him doze, ran a finger over the worry line on his forehead, at the edges of his hair that were starting to gleam gray instead of blonde. He snuffled softly and shook himself awake as she ran one fingertip down the shell of his ear.

"Roll over for me," she said.

He blinked for a moment and then squirmed and rolled between her legs, arms thrown back over his head to flop on her pillows as he stared up at her. She poured a small dollop of the oil into the palm of her hand and warmed it up before leaning forward to start at his hands.

"I'm going to get hard," he said. He already was a little.

"I know," Zee said. She focused on his thumbs first, then his index finger, and so on, giving every joint equal attention as her thumbs dug and spiraled around his palms.

His breath was brushing over her throat, warm and heavy as her fingers circled his wrists.

"Zee," he breathed, something needy in the back of her name.

"I'm taking care of you," she said, leaning down to leave a dry kiss at his jaw pulling away as his mouth sought out her throat. She sat back on her heels and lifted up her nightdress to pull it over her head. Johnny's hands spread over her ribs, sliding up to push her breasts up, fingers framing her nipples to pinch them lightly. She shuffled over his hips, pushing her underwear down and trying to find a way out of them that didn't involve getting out of the bed.

Johnny shifted his hold to her back and pulled her down against him, their chests pressing together as he kissed her, tongues stroking together as he helped her wiggle out of her panties. She pushed him back to the mattress as he tried to roll them over.

"You're so wet," he said into the skin of her neck. "Lemme touch you, please."

She swung her leg back over his hip and took his arms from around her back to lay them back above his head. "You can touch when I'm done," she said.

Johnny's forehead knotted and he started to muffle a groan of disappointment, until she lined them up, the head of his cock sliding against her wet slit, before sinking down onto him in a slow glide. Then he groaned openly, baring his throat to her as he arched back, hips bucking gently.

Zee bit her lip, swirling her hips lightly until they both sighed as he bottomed out inside of her. She took three long breaths, watching Johnny's chest heave below as he looked down his chest to where they were joined and then up into her face, brow furrowed in confusion. She reached for the oil, trying to ignore the way he shifted inside of her, the drag and stretch of him. She rubbed the potion in her palms until they were smooth and slippery and then settled them down onto his chest.

"Every inch," she said again with a smile.

Johnny laughed a little, grinning back at her, before his face tightened in pleasure as she leaned forward, rising up off him to spread her hands up over his shoulders and along his arms until she reached his wrists. As she worked her way back down his forearms, making sure to work oil into every scar and over every bit of miraculously unblemished skin, she sank back down onto him one fraction at a time.

"Diabolical pixie," he said through gritted teeth.

She pulled off again until just the tip of him was inside of her and then rocked there for a long moment, her breaths panting as she coated his elbows.

"I don't know what you mean," Zee said. "I never said you couldn't *move*."

Johnny's eyes opened at that and Zee grabbed more oil as she felt his legs shifting behind her. She braced slippery palms on his biceps and let a cry bounce free from her throat as Johnny began to buck beneath her.

Chapter 17

Dark Waters

July 31st 2017

Her feet dragged through the wildflowers, long grasses and soft leaves and heavy scented petals twining around her ankles and making every step a warm, lazy effort. There was a crowd in the distance behind her and she could hear their bells and cheers and praises, cheering for her. And ahead...at the other side of the field was...

Something was missing.

Yes, that's what was at the other side of the field. That missing thing. The pang at the back of her chest. The music in her ears. She just needed to keep walking and then she would get to it and everything would be...back together again.

Her feet hurt. They were tired. She'd been walking...a long time? But it didn't seem like the field was that big.

No, she'd been walking before the field too.

It was very cold and the air was wet.

No, it was sunny out. The grass in the field was wet and it wrapped around her legs and tried to hold her close, and the ground was hard and uneven and that's why her feet hurt.

Why was she barefoot?

The sky was nearly yellow with sunlight, but the full moon was out and the stars glinted blue and Zee felt dizzy when she looked up.

Her family—no her family was Sam—the audience…no the island, her friends, were farther back now. Had she traveled this far already? Her feet cramped with every step and her skin was covered with goosebumps and the skirt of her nightgown stuck wetly to her legs.

Why was she in her nightgown?

I should wake up, she thought.

You're almost there. Everything will be settled once we're together. A little further.

A little further, just to see, she thought. To remember what it was, that gap of memory, the disorientation of missing something as if she kept driving straight past her house in the dark at night.

Her chest burned with cold and her feet felt stiff, plodding in the muck below.

And then all at once her feet slipped out from underneath her and brackish water slipped between her lips. The sky was dark and the moon was overhead and then it was dancing and twisting behind churning water as Zee sank. Salt water burned at her eyes and she sealed them shut against it and held still, surrounded by cold sea with seaweed fingers tethered around her ankles. She blinked up and the moon had grown smaller, slithering like a white snake on the surface of the water several feet above.

You're drowning, stupid, said Sam's voice in her head.

Her heart kicked her in chest and Zee thrashed in the water, legs spiraling and seaweed looping and tangling until her ankles felt knotted together. She couldn't tell if she was rising or falling, but her lungs stung and her head pounded and she could no longer see the moon. There was something dark passing in front of her eyes and she squirmed in the cold grip of the sea.

Something tangled through her hair and she bucked, swinging her arms in sluggish sweeps over her head. Warm bands wrapped around her wrists and for a moment she tugged and wrestled against them, but that would leave her sinking. She winced up into the water and saw white arms reaching down for her.

Johnny or Cameron or Sam or all of them! Hell, it could have been Doyle at this point and she would have been grateful. She choked on air as she broke water and coughed up salty water. Her hair was over her eyes in streaks and it wasn't until she was clinging to the side of a meek little boat that she saw her rescuer.

Luke.

"Lemme go!" She rasped and began to thrash again, trying to push herself off the boat, scratching at his arms and hands where he held her. Water sloshed and sprayed them both in the face, Luke wincing away and nearly dropping her back into the water like an uncooperative fish.

"You're going to tip us over!" He growled, and she wasn't sure if he was shaking her or just couldn't hold her still.

"Let me go! Help! Hel-"

"I'm trying to save you, Zoya!" Luke snapped.

It was more surprise than cooperation that had Zee

drooping still, water up to her chin again, but Luke took it all the same, dragging her out of the water by her armpits and draping her ungracefully half into the boat and practically upside down.

She hesitated for a moment, knees still in the sea, and then scrambled the rest of the way in as Luke sat back and steadied them on the water. He threw a scratchy blanket at her face before she could get her bearings. She glanced down, realized she was in her nightgown—had she sleepwalked?—and wrapped it around herself quickly, pushing her hair away from her face.

Luke was at the other end of the boat, yanking on a chain for the motor with an irritated snarl on his lips.

"Where are you taking me?" she whispered. She wasn't sure if he could hear her over the rattling of the resistant motor, the salt water had scratched at her throat.

"Back to the island, where do you think?" Luke snapped with a quick glance at her. The motor flared to life with a roar.

"Not to Chernov?"

Luke's lips pursed as he stared at her, and then over her shoulder at the dark. She glanced over her shoulder and saw the small collection of lights from the island.

"Your... magic, not to mention the attempted murder, shook a few things loose from my mind," Luke said quietly, his voice blending with the hum and growl of the boat. "Chernov being one of them. He thinks I'm dead for now. I'm hoping to keep it that way."

There was a warning in his tone.

"He can't...find you?" The way he had found her. Waking, asleep, it didn't seem to matter.

"Not if I'm careful," Luke said with a huff, and it was a weary sound.

Zee wrapped the blanket tighter around herself and folded down to rest her head on her knees. "I don't understand. I don't understand why you were out here. Why you'd bother to..."

Luke had saved her life. She wrinkled her nose against her cold lap.

"Maybe I just felt like playing a different role tonight," he said.

She rolled her head to look at him. What role? The hero or her... pesnya dushi? Swallowed in a sweater, hair wet with sea, that intent gaze on the horizon that she knew from her dreams. It was the way he looked at her while she was sleeping.

"Chernov has...trouble with water. His hold wouldn't have lasted much longer on you, not that it'd have mattered. But out here, even the island, it's a safer place for me to be at the moment than on the mainland. Until he finds a new body to dig his claws into."

"So he can't see us now?" she asked.

"I fucking hope not," Luke muttered.

"Can I tell them?" The others. Luke wasn't dead. *Luke was alive.* Sam had pushed him off a cliff and that was...well it was a serious offense, but Luke had broken into their home and threatened them so they were probably going to call it even, right? Because he wasn't *dead.*

"Sit up, look at me," he said.

Zee almost stuck her tongue out at him. But she rolled her shivering shoulders back and sat up, tugging at the edges of the blanket to keep the wind off her frozen skin and wet dress. Luke leaned forward and his eyes glanced off the moonlight, glowing faintly green. There was a soft riffling feeling against her forehead and Zee brushed her hand against the spot.

"Stay out of there," she snapped but she was cold and tired and felt all used up and paper thin.

Luke was in and out of her thoughts in a few gentle sweeps.

"He lost his hold on you when you nearly drowned," Luke said, drawing back. Zee blinked and he raised one eyebrow. "Not unlike he did with me. With a bit of help from you *reaming* my brain out on that cliff."

"You're welcome," Zee said and his lips twitched. The island was creeping up to them and Zee glanced over her shoulder. He was taking her back to the docks.

"I need somewhere to stay," he said as she watched the island grow brighter, larger in their approach. She wasn't sure she'd ever been so relieved to see the island's silhouette before. He added, "Somewhere warded. I'd rather not be back on his radar again."

"Our wards haven't had a great track record against Chernov."

"Your wards haven't had a good track record against *me*," Luke said, voice a little smug. "That's my specialty."

"Is that supposed to make me feel better?" Zee asked.

There was a pause. "Your little protection charms have more power than they ought to. It wasn't easy."

She grinned at the island and heard his irritated huff behind her. "Well thank you, I guess."

The pause was longer this time. "You're welcome."

She wasn't sure how sincere he sounded. But she was hardly about to accuse Luke of being a prickly but effective guardian. She doubted he'd see the need of coming to their rescue more than once. This was about debts paid.

"Chernov is old," Luke said. "And yes, physically he is weak. But don't underestimate him."

She twisted back to face him. "How could I, after everything that's happened?" She couldn't *see* his face clearly but she could feel his stare and it made her want to squirm.

"Your family has a legacy," he said.

"Oh, not this again!" Zee wiped wet hair away from her face with a huff and rolled her eyes.

"He'll find someone else to do his legwork for him," Luke continued. "Just to distract you from dealing with the problem of him directly."

"He's powerful," Zee started.

"So are you! So is the other one," Luke said.

"*Sam*. Her name is *Sam*. Why is that hard for you to remember?"

"I have an issue with being pushed off cliffs,' Luke snipped.

"Psh, you're fine. Get over it," she said.

There was a sharp silence and then a soft snort from the other end of the boat. But Luke was someone who clearly liked to have the last word.

"Quit pretending to be so harmless," he said, softer, something almost sweetly intimate in the words.

Zee chewed at her lip, resisting the urge to fall to the bait. "What the hell does that mean?"

"This island, the role you're playing. Little witches who grow herbs and read tarot cards and run a cute bath shop on main street," Luke said. "Trying to *blend* in. They fear you and they have good reason to. He should fear you too. Quit hiding."

Zee turned back to the island, swallowing the accusation he'd thrown at her and studying the way it sank heavy in her gut. The boat rumbled up to the docks, prow bumping softly against the ladder.

"Thanks for the assist," Zee said.

"Keep the blanket, you have a long walk home," Luke said and his head was framed by the crescent moon hanging behind him. "Well..."

She blinked at him and remembered what he'd said earlier. "You could stay at the house."

Luke stared back at her, expression frozen.

"I don't know if that's... safe enough for you," she said. "Obviously we've had some security issues."

"Aren't you concerned that I've been lying to you?" Luke asked, brow furrowing. "What if I'm still helping Chernov?"

"I can't be more useful to him alive than I would be at the bottom of the sea," Zee said and she wondered what the pained twist on Luke's face meant.

"I would help reinforce your wards," he said in a rush, like he thought he had to advertise his usefulness.

"Alright," she said.

"The others..."

"Will be very glad to see you aren't dead."

He looked surprised by that announcement. "I'm concerned about your self-preservation," he said finally. "But thank you."

Luke docked the boat in a spot that Zee knew for certain belonged to a local. She supposed boat theft wasn't his worst offense. The air was harder up above the water, running in off the sea to beat at the walls of the island. It became clear, quickly, that her feet were badly beat up from her nighttime travels and the blanket wrapped around her shoulders wasn't in much better shape. Luke was looking a little soggy on his own after wrestling her out of the water.

"Do you want me to..." he nodded down at her feet and then grimaced. "I dunno, carry you?"

Zoya choked on a laugh and tried to turn it into a cough, lungs still aching from the salt water. "I'll be alright," she said. "Come on. We've got a walk."

There was a tall clock at the end of the docks and she winced her way across rough wooden boards to read it.

2:22

For a moment, she closed her eyes and wished like she had when she was younger and the numbers lined up on the digital clocks at school.

I wish someone would take me home.

But it was after two in the morning and the island was asleep.

Someone up at the house might be looking for her. If Johnny had realized she wasn't in bed he might have looked through the house. Or he and Sam and the others could just have easily been sleeping under some sway of Chernov's. She had no phone and her only allies in town were Sarah and Roger. It didn't seem like a good time to go knocking on their door, soaked to the bone with a strange man.

A light came on across the street at the front of the Inn and Adam Marks walked out of the bar door, locking it behind him. He turned, and Luke stepped in front of Zee, the pair of them standing frozen by the clock as if it might make them invisible.

"Nikolaev?" Adam hissed, leaning forward slightly and squinting.

"Hi," she said, stepping out from behind Luke.

Their voices were quiet but carrying in the silence of the sleeping town.

"Who is that? What the hell happened to you?" Adam asked.

"Umm..." she bit her lip, checked the road out of some strange force of habit, and started mincing her way across the bruising gravel to them, Luke following close at her back. Adam leaned away as if they might have been some kind of contagious.

"Do you have a cell phone I could borrow to call up at the house?" Zee asked, ignoring his other question.

Adam's eyes flicked between her and Luke. "Sure, but how about I drive you home?"

She wondered if she should object, but she *couldn't* and then Adam was running to get the car and Luke was pulling off his sweater and tugging it over Zee's head. The sleeves were wet but it was warm from him and when she looked at him in question he ignored her.

The seats of the car were heated and Adam waited as Zee brushed seaweed and stones and muck off her feet and onto the street curb before she would fold her legs in.

"He's coming too," Zee said, sliding across the back seat, Luke following and shutting the door, hunching down and staring out the window.

Adam passed her his cellphone, his eyes narrowed on Luke until he started the car forward.

Will answered the house phone after a long series of rings, voice snarling with sleep.

"It's me," she said.

"Jesus, where are you? What happened? What the *hell*, Zee-"

"Zee!?" Johnny had stolen the phone. "Where are you?"

"Adam Marks is driving me and Luke back to the house," she said. Luke's head whipped around to stare at her.

She could hear the gasp, felt him struggling in the quiet, could hear the others layering questions behind him.

"I was sleep walking," she said, quieter, turning her head to avoid seeing Adam's. "I'm okay. Luke found me."

"I...okay," Johnny said, voice strangled. And then fast and and sharp, "Stay on the phone!"

"Alright," she said. "Will you ask Sam to start a bath for me?" He echoed the request over the phone and the sounds of shuffling in the kitchen followed. "Is everyone up?" she asked.

"Hmm? Oh yeah. Sorta shouted the house down when I woke up and couldn't find you anywhere. How close are you?" Will's voice was rattling in the background and there was a rustling and then a brief growling sound from Johnny.

"Just turned onto Forest Way."

"Where did you sleep walk to?" Johnny's tone was gentle but she could hear the stress and struggle underneath the words, the tightness in his throat he was trying to swallow away, Will hassling at his back for answers. "Are you safe with him?

Adam twitched in front of her and Zee said, "I am. I promise. And...the docks," and left it at that.

"Was it Chernov?" Will said in the background.

"Yes," she whispered and Johnny's breath hitched over the phone. "I'm okay. Almost to the house."

There was an abbreviated note and Johnny 'hmm'd for a moment. "Okay. I'll be at the gate." They both paused and she could hear him sigh over the receiver. "Okay. Hang up."

She pulled the phone off her ear and passed it back to Adam, her chest suddenly hammering as the lights from the house peeked through the brush and trees on the road. She had an urge to jump out of the backseat and run the rest of the way up to the house, as if that might get her to Sam and Johnny and the boys faster.

"Is there..." Adam hesitated. "Is there anything I can help with?"

"Everything is alright," Zee said. She bit her lip. "Thank you. I'm...sorry about this."

Adam grunted and Luke twisted to stare at Zee with something that crossed confusion with frustration, but they were pulling up to the gate where there was a line of tall, broad-shouldered men waiting.

"Well. Guess you're in good hands now," Adam said, with a dark glance at Luke.

"Thanks again, Adam."

Zee was halfway to the gate, Luke shutting the car door behind her, and Johnny was halfway out of the gate, his eyes flying over every wet and mussed and dirtied inch of her, when he stopped dead at the sight of Luke.

There was relief on his face, and Zee knew that he'd been playing that moment before Luke's fall over and over again in his head. And then Johnny's arms were around her and she was lifted up. Her face immediately sought out the heat of his shoulder, cold nose tucked into his neck.

"Christ, you're soaked."

She opened her mouth to say that she'd almost drowned, that she'd been sinking in the sea and Luke had lifted her out, that it wasn't *just* Johnny who had been what was always missing from those sickly sweet and lulling dreams Chernov had sent her. But they were both shivering together now and it was probably better to make it inside, rinse the muck off her, and say it all at once for everyone.

Bright headlights pulled away from the house and Johnny carried Zee through the gate, warm hands from the others brushing over her shoulders. Over his shoulder Zee watched Will and Eric flank Luke, marching him up to the house. Johnny took her straight upstairs to her room, rinsing the worst of the sea off in the sink before taking her into the bath with him, never letting her toes touch the floor.

* * *

Zee and Johnny made it back downstairs to find Luke surrounded by the others, no one speaking. Sam had surrounded the chair Luke sat in with candles and black stones and rowan branches.

"Time to catch us up," Will said, sitting up on the counter, his prosthetic arm tucked against his chest as he watched Luke like a sniper waiting for permission to shoot.

"Luke says I cleaned Chernov out of his head," Zee said, joining them in the circle. "I'm inclined to believe him."

"I thought you told us you 'reasoned' with him," Eric said. The expression on his face was a good reminder of how far bullshit did *not* go with him.

Luke snorted in his seat, and when Zee caught his eyes there was a hint of a smile, but it wasn't cruel and sharp like it'd been when Chernov's magic was running through his veins.

"Okay, yeah," Zee said, and then she caught their friends up on the real story. Silence followed for a long time.

"Do you believe him?" Sam asked her.

Did she? Or did she *want* to? Johnny's hand was on her back and she turned to look up at him. The same struggle was on his face, anger and suspicion and hope, and she wasn't sure how to break it down into a feeling that made sense. Zee turned back to the others.

"I do," she said.

I can watch him. Nadia was soft, by the cauldron on the old wood stove. Zee tipped her face in her aunt's direction, trying not to be too obvious about the visitation. *He won't know I'm there.*

If Nadia was right, she'd be the perfect one to keep an

eye on Luke. If she was wrong, if Zee was wrong about him, Nadia would be too vulnerable against Chernov.

"He can stay in Nadia's room," Zee said. Will and Eric had the only guest room anyway. It was the last place left in the house.

"What?" Sam breathed and Zee met her eyes. It only took a glance and Sam's shock settled. "Alright."

Cameron, Johnny, Will and Eric seemed satisfied to leave the decision between the cousins. It was Luke that looked gobsmacked, surrounded by guarding magic, still a mess from the sea, his mouth open but no words falling loose.

Cameron rounded on him, all six feet eight inches of muscle and none of the usual cheer to be found. "If you put my family at risk," he growled.

Zee felt her heart stutter. Family. It was true too, that big guy was her brother in all but name. Sam was her sister by everything that mattered. Will and Eric had a place in this house and she'd only known them for weeks. And Johnny...

Johnny was home, every bit as much as the house they stood in.

Luke didn't look entirely unaffected by the threat, he nodded to prove he understood and then looked at Zee.

"I don't mean any offense," he said. "But I'm more afraid of the scramble she could leave in my brain if she wanted. I'll be on my good behavior."

Johnny's hands squeezed around her waist. "You should be," he said to Luke and Zee's eyes popped wider.

She'd known she had worked some whammy on Luke at the cliff, but the understanding between the two men that she could somehow do the same under anything less than desperation was a surprise to her.

"Come on," she said. "Let him out of that and let's all go to bed."

"We should start defending the house- the island, now," Luke said as Sam nudged the stones and branches away from the front of the chair and blew out the candles.

"We should sleep," Zee said. She didn't know any more defenses. She didn't know any more spells. She just knew that if she didn't rest she was going to fall over.

"Zoya," Luke said and everyone but the two of them raised their eyebrows.

"Sleep," she said, turning away under the cover of Johnny's arm over her shoulder.

"I know you don't like when I ask," Zee whispered when they were back in her bed, and Johnny stiffened against her back, his arms wrapped around her. "But are we still...are you still..."

His shoulders loosened and his chin fell to her shoulder, lips brushing along the curve of her neck. The touch sent a surprise trail of goosebumps down her spine. She'd thought her body was too tired from the night to feel any kind of thrill, but then he kissed under her jaw and the goosebumps curled over her collar bone.

"We are still a team," he whispered. "I'm still here."

Something loosened and burned gently behind her ribs and she leaned back into the circle of his hold, turning until their noses were almost touching.

"I love you," she said, as if she hadn't fretted over the words for a month or fifteen years.

Johnny sighed, a long release of breath as he melted into her mattress. He brushed her hair over her shoulder to kiss her neck as she digested the moment. There was no moon, and no strength in her bones, and a thousand worries hung in the air. One of them was laying in a bed just down the hall. But she was warm and safe in spite of all that, and time was running faster in all the trouble. She was glad to have said it, finally.

"I love you, pixie," Johnny whispered, lips resting against hers, a barely kiss. "Not going anywhere."

Chapter 18

Luke Wolfe

July 31ˢᵗ 2017

The dreams had a strange sense of timing.

Johnny was turning Luke into a moaning, panting mess on her sheets while she watched from the bathroom doorway. Tan skin pinning Luke's pale body to the bed, the pair of them straining, Johnny's hands holding him down as his tongue ran long stripes up and down Luke's cock. The picture of them was hazy and sun streaked.

"Zoya," Luke groaned, his head tossing on the mattress until he caught sight of her. "Come closer."

One hand fisted into the bed as Johnny hummed his agreement, and the other reached out for her, arm shaking with the effort of holding himself back.

Johnny rose up and turned to her, face flushed and sunburnt. "Hey, pixie. Wanna taste?"

* * *

Luke was waiting for them when they all woke up, pacing the kitchen, dark stubble growing in over his face and eyes tracking the room without ever meeting anyone's gaze. Not that she liked to look anyone in the eye at seven in the morning after two scant hours of sleep.

"We have to get started, the pair of you need to learn to defend yourselves," he said, almost barking the orders out across the counter. "The full moon will be here in a week. We need to make the most of it."

"We need coffee," Zee rasped, glaring somewhere around his chest, afraid she might see something like the dream reflected back in his stare.

"I bet he didn't have to look at the calendar either," Sam whispered.

"Shut up."

Luke braced himself against the counter, a baffled kind of anger on his face as the rest of the house trudged into the room with lagging steps. No, he didn't look like he'd been dreaming of her and Johnny last night. He didn't look like he'd been sleeping at all.

"Don't," Zee said, pointing her finger in his face as he opened his mouth to speak.

"You have to act, and act fast. Before Chernov catches up," Luke said as if he hadn't heard her. "There are chargings to do, your mental defenses need work, I can break through the wardings in the root cellar like they're tissue paper."

"Who's coming in through a root cellar?" Sam grumbled.

"It's Monday, we have to open the shop. We have to pretend to be normal. We have to get ready for the music festival starting tomorrow," Zee said. "Who knows what

Adam Banks has already told everyone. So yes, we have to prepare. But first we have to work a day job."

"Your *day job* is insignificant," Luke hissed, green gaze flashing against hers.

"Our day job pays the fucking bills!" The words came out louder than she meant, some thin thread of panic from the night before finally snapping. The room bristled and she held up her hands before anyone moved, slowing her breathing. "Look. I get it. You've been living in his world for years now. You've been eating and breathing and dreaming magic and you know, better than any of us, what he's capable of. And don't get me wrong, I plan on taking advantage of that. But this house is our home, and we have to take care of it. This island knows us, and when we have solved the problem of Chernov we will have to continue existing here as if nothing ever changed. We can't erase the facts of our lives just because they're too mundane for you. So you're going to have to work around them, just like we do. Every day."

Behind them, near the stove, the coffee maker gurgled to life. Zee thought a private blessing to whoever had taken the time to start the machine while she was ranting.

"I see," Luke said and she was still trying to figure out how he managed to be haughty and sheepish at the same time. "Should I just come with you and... make bath bombs then?"

"You know your way around the house," Zee snapped back. He'd broken into it after all. "Why don't you stay here and get started without us?"

"I can take him to the studio," Johnny offered, words soft against the back of her neck. She could feel Luke studying them as Johnny kissed the spot his voice landed against and there was heat in the gaze. "Put him to work with us on the globes."

Zee shrugged but reached back to squeeze Johnny's hand in gratitude.

"Globes?" Luke asked, and some of the frazzled energy in him seemed to wane.

Eric was the one to explain the project to him, covering every significance of the materials they were using. And surprisingly, Luke didn't growl at the other man and point out that he already *knew* the significance of iron, although when Zee glanced over from the cupboard she could see Luke's jaw working with restraint.

"I don't see him as a team player if I'm being honest," Sam whispered after the first few sips of coffee.

"I didn't see myself as a team player before two weeks ago," Zee said. She hadn't told Sam about the dreams yet. She hadn't even really covered the full scope of it with Johnny. And somewhere in the last month telling Johnny the truth became as essential to her as the honesty she shared with Sam.

"Alright," Sam said, scanning Zee's face. "But can I pay him back for the bath bomb comment?"

* * *

Johnny and the others got back before dinner and Luke walked straight through the kitchen and out into the back-yard, without a glance at her or Sam.

"How did it go today?" Sam asked with feigned innocence.

Johnny arrived at the oven just as Zee was pulling a tray of garlic and rosemary stuffed chicken thighs. He shrugged when Zee looked at him.

"Guy has got an ego on him," Will grumbled. "But. Technically. He didn't fuck anything up."

"He was fine," Johnny whispered to her. "After he got over burning the shit out of his arm when he wouldn't listen to us about the whole sock thing."

Ah. The arm socks. To keep from burning all the hair right off your skin when you got to close to the kilns.

"Do you wanna take the salve out to him or should I?" Zee asked, raising an eyebrow.

Behind them, Will and Cam were tossing their worst attempts at a British accent back and forth to each other and Eric had taken over chopping ingredients for a salad.

"Maybe we should both go," Johnny said, keeping his voice lowered, away from the others' ears. "There's a connection there, isn't there?"

Zee looked down to the floor, but Johnny caught her chin with his fingers tipping her face back up to his. He bent, kissing her lips and then whispered there.

"I mean. Not just between you and him. Right?"

Oh.

"He said he dreamt of you too," Zee said, sliding her lips to his ear. Johnny nodded against her cheek and she added, "I choose you. I love you."

Johnny grinned and kissed just before her ear. "I love you." He straightened and there was a little blush on his cheeks. "And I know we're a long way off from what I'm about to suggest but... you don't have to choose, if you don't want to." And then his eyebrows waggled, and he wasn't even trying to be funny. "Just saying."

She tried not to think of the dream from the morning. Tried and failed.

"I'll grab the salve. You put together some food for us before they eat everything," she said. Johnny kissed her cheek again and then got to work as she left for the pantry.

She cut through the greenhouse out to where Luke was collapsed in one of the wicker chairs. His eyes traced her approach and she held out the jar to him.

"It's only hedge witch magic, but it will help," she said.

Luke didn't hesitate to take the salve, opening the jar and sniffing it, eyes growing large. "The pair of you put such power into such small works," he said. "And I don't have anything against hedge witches. My grandmother was one. She taught me my first magic."

He slid his jacket off his shoulders, wearing the same old t-shirt from the night before. Johnny's things would fit him, maybe a little looser but close enough. Zee sat herself on the chaise across from him, saving room for Johnny, and watched as he smoothed the salve over the welt on his arm. His eyes fluttered shut with a sigh as it began to work its magic.

"We don't sell that at the shop," she said.

Luke smiled a little and looked at her. "What was the charm you put on him...Johnny? He saved me from myself today and never so much as flinched."

Zee grinned at that. So Sam's mixture was working. Good. She'd reapply with Johnny later tonight just in case. "More of Sam's touch. She's a genius with herbs and tinctures. She'd teach you... if you asked nicely."

Luke nodded, looking back down at his arm. "Chernov makes his followers focus on manipulating raw power. Without aides. Pure magic."

Zee scoffed and then Johnny was coming out of the greenhouse, two trays of food in his arms.

"I'm sorry for the way I spoke to you this morning," Luke said, his eyes on Johnny.

"Just this morning?" Zee said and got a glimpse of that smile again.

"Fair enough," Luke murmured.

"The others are staying inside," Johnny said, passing Luke his dinner before crossing to Zee to share a plate with her.

Luke tossed a look and a frown back at the house. She couldn't explain it but she understood the expression on his face. The sense that you were the person others were avoiding, a familiar old bruise twinging in her chest.

"Sam and I aren't usually used to this much…togetherness," Zee said to Johnny, but the words were for Luke. "After last night we probably all need a break."

They sat in quiet for a stretch, Johnny groaning around the chicken thigh in a way that Zee found distracting.

"What magic did you use to get that man to give us a ride last night?" Luke asked after a beat.

Johnny looked at her, sucking juice off his thumb, and Zee blinked.

"There was magic," Luke said. "Just a bit of it."

"Oh. No, it was 2:22," Zee said. "You know. Like on the clock. You just make a wish when the numbers line up."

Luke's eyes narrowed and he leaned in. "You made a wish? Wish magic is notoriously unreliable."

"It wasn't wish *magic*. It was just a wish. A normal one."

"You're a witch," Luke said, eyebrows raising. "Of course it was magic. What did you do to charge up before… you threw me off the cliff?"

"Hey! I tried to pull you up. You didn't reach," Johnny said, very quickly and Luke smirked in answer.

"Um… meditation. Charged baths. Sex," Zee said.

Luke's smirk went a little sideways at that. "I think Chernov is wasting his time with the wrong witch. None of your techniques should add up to as much power as you gather."

"Maybe you're just learning from the wrong teacher," Zee said and Luke blinked. Johnny grinned, bumping his shoulder against hers. "You never met Nadia. She put meaning into everything, even the smallest workings."

"I suppose Chernov was partial to the prestige of the more cryptic areas of magic," Luke mused, more to himself. "Zoya-"

"Zee—" she corrected.

He paused and then that smile of his spread into something sweet and terrible. "I like Zoya," he said, drawing her name out. He cleared his throat and continued, "You should start your routine again. Before the full moon next week."

And then he leaned back into his chair, eating his dinner and watching her and Johnny with a level of observance that made her skin feel electric.

August 1st 2017

Maria James' heels clicked against the floor of the shop, the strains of a fiddle following her in from the street. Sam was on the floor, managing to make conversation with the tourists while Zee managed a steady line of people checking out at the register.

The Sweet Chariot Music Festival was in full swing, the island was packed to the rafters, and every so often Zee caught herself feeling like everything was normal. Even with the addition of Luke in the house. Meditating shirtless in the sunroom. Flirting with a sleepy Johnny over coffee. Perhaps it was the addition of Johnny, as if he had settled some unevenness left from his years of absence. Maybe it was both of them. Two pesnya dushi come to roost, threads starting to twine together.

And then she would catch a glimpse of Nadia in the corner of a room, shadowy and faint, and the world would wobble and Zee's heart would stutter again.

"You got away from the committee," Zee said, managing a smile as Maria made it to the desk, three gift baskets balanced in her arms.

"Barely," Maria said with her own tight smile. "And only by coming up with an errand that needed running. Does Sam have any..."

Zee had already turned behind the counter and grabbed a bottle of Maria's preferred scent off the wall.

"At last," Maria said, with a sigh. "Someone who can read my mind. I'm leaving these baskets with Adam for a few of the artists. Pop 'em into their hotel rooms. Drum up some interest for you."

"We appreciate it," Zee said sincerely. "Anyone I shouldn't miss?"

Maria shrugged and it managed to feel diplomatic. "To be honest," she said under her breath. "I don't really care that much for folk music. But don't tell the island. The tourism alone saves us from going obsolete."

Zee hid her snort and finished tallying Maria up. The perfume she left off the bill. Maria was always sending people into The Lab or up to the house. And lately she'd even managed to be *gracious* about it.

She packed the gift baskets into a large canvas tote for Maria and caught the woman biting at her lip and studying Zee's face. She smiled when caught and blushed slightly.

"I don't mean to listen to gossip," Maria said, voice lowered, and Zee's stomach flipped nervously. "But I caught on to the stir about you and Johnny Sharpe. All I'll say is...

I'm glad you're happy. And I don't mind if some of the local mom squad isn't."

Zee coughed, or laughed, or some combination of the two and found her mouth shifting between a grin and a slack jaw.

"I've got some of his earlier works around the hotel. And his crew seems nice. Good to see a few men around who I didn't go to highschool with. We should all get dinner sometime," Maria said. "Cameron and Sam too."

"That sounds great," Zee said, because there wasn't anything else to say and it was an invitation she'd never imagined getting. What would Maria say if Luke came too? God, she wasn't ready to think that far ahead.

"See you around the festival I'm sure," Maria trilled on her way out.

Zee rang the next customer up three times before getting it right.

Chapter 19

Odd Fellows' Hall

July 8th 2013

It was sticky out. Hotter than usual for the island with the sun burning up the sea into a damp haze in the air. Nadia was stretched out on the wicker chaise lounge, cheeks turned pink again with the heat.

"There you are," Zee said, dragging a chair to sit by her aunt.

"Still breathing," Nadia teased weakly.

Zee wrestled with the wild animal in her chest begging to kick and tear and bite at those defeated words. "Amazing," she said instead, "Considering it's hard to catch a breath in this heat."

"I like it," Nadia mused.

She was always cold lately. Even now she had a little knitted blanket thrown over her legs. Zee, meanwhile, was sweating in her sundress. But Nadia seemed to have shrunk in the past year, vanishing away into the delicate old woman she ought to have looked like at least a decade ago.

"Will you help me with a spell for the Anders family?" Zee asked. "The restaurant burned down and-"

"Ved'mitchka," Nadia stopped her with a small, steely smile. "You and I both know you can manage a fortune charm well enough on your own."

Zee turned away, folding her sticky arms over her chest and glaring out at the sea.

"It's time for me, Zee."

A thin, cold, hand landed on Zee's lap and no amount of stubborn denial could stop Zee from taking it up in her warmer grip and holding on tight.

"Sam will be back next week," Zee said.

"That's good," Nadia said, voice turning dreamy and slow. She'd be napping again soon. "You'll need her when..."

"It's just a visit," Zee reminded Nadia who just blinked lazily, pale red lashes fluttering over the blue circles under her eyes. Sam was just getting ready to set up a shop in Connecticut selling her concoctions.

"She'll stay," Nadia said, glancing at Zee out of the corner of her eyes. "You'll need her...when he comes. He's coming. Zee...he's coming...after I'm gone."

Zee felt the warning like a punch to the gut. The old wound of Johnny Sharpe she thought her aunt had let close years ago.

"Don't say that," Zee said, voice breathless with surprise. "Don't say that Noddy. Johnny's gone. He's not coming back."

Nadia's brow furrowed. "He is. But...you'll need Sam. The other one too." Her eyes blinked shut and then stayed closed.

Zee released a slow breath, heart pounding and then Nadia whispered it again.

"He'll come for you after I'm gone."

August 3rd 2017

Cameron was handy in a crowd, towering over the sea of heads around them in Odd Fellows' Hall while a band with too many musicians to count trilled a sea shanty on the stage. The old town hall was packed to, and probably past, its limits with locals and tourists out in force.

"His head is quite large, yes?" Cameron called down to her.

Zee's face scrunched, puzzled, and turned to catch Sam's eyes.

"Yeah that's him," Sam answered for her.

"This way, he's by the bar," Cameron said.

He wove a path through the room and Zee and Sam—who could practically fit side by side in the space he cleared in his wake—followed close behind until they reached Johnny at the bar with Eric, Luke, and Will.

"There you are," Will said. He grinned and pulled Zee out of Johnny's reach to press a kiss to her cheek.

"There you go again, stirring up the locals," Zee said. "They've only just got their heads wrapped around me dating Johnny."

"And me dating a man," Eric added in a softer tone.

Zee backed up to Johnny's chest, leaning against him for support and taking a long swig from his beer bottle that was sweating in the warm hall. Luke was standing at their side, beer sweating in his hand, arm close enough to brush against and she told herself that when they did, it was an accident.

"Good end of festival?" Johnny asked into her ear.

She nodded. "Lots of orders to fill. And lots of people

coming up to the house before the week is up." She hadn't been doing many readings for the past couple weeks and she could feel a wave of business coming on between the tourists in for the festival and the locals who had been biding their time. It was good, nest money for the winter when The Lab slowed down to online orders. The timing, however, was off.

A little trumpet blared on stage and Zee flinched as the sound pierced her ears. Johnny's fingers appeared under her hair against the back of her neck and she sighed.

"Headache?" Luke asked, lips close to her ear so she could hear over the music that was reaching a wild raucous party level on the stage. Zee could see Sarah on the floor with her kids, spinning one with each hand, Roger standing to the side grinning at his family.

"Storm coming," she said nodding. "The pressure's got me all out of whack."

"We don't have to stay long," Johnny said. "And it'll be your turn for a massage when we get back to the house." She smiled at that and her shoulders eased as Johnny carried on in digging the tension out her neck. Luke's stare was heavy on their faces, eyes darting between them.

Some moments, it felt like all he needed was the invitation. Other days he held himself so distant, remained so cold, that Zee felt certain he'd weighed his options and decided against them.

"We'll be taking a break up here for the moment," said the shaggy haired guitar player on the stage. "But our Molly should be able to keep you entertained and keep those feet flying on the dance floor."

A waifish blonde young woman—who had come to The Lab and bought Sam's line of Earl Grey bath products—stepped up to the front of the stage, red violin perched on her shoulder and bow poised to play. She struck high and quick, bright notes filling the hall over the low sound of conversation, and Roger took to the floor in what he probably thought was a good approximation of a jig. (Eric and Will turned away from the sight with embarrassed expressions on their faces and Luke hid his grimace behind the beer bottle.)

Zee's head panged, a sharp and sudden squeezing in what felt like her brain, and the windows of the hall darkened suddenly. She looked at the nearest one and the sky outside looked nearly black, setting sun blotted out by the storm clouds rolling in. A note of music soured from on the stage.

"I hope the people on boats have somewhere to go," Johnny said.

Zee twisted in his arms, looking out the windows. "Luke."

"Hmm?" He tore his eyes from the girl on stage and they widened, catching the weight in the air around them.

"Zee," Sam whispered but her voice was clear. "Zee, something is..."

Something was wrong. The air in the hall was heavy, not with salt water and locals, but the smell of sweet smoke like a cake burning. The sound of the violin wobbled and swooned in Zee's ear and she pressed her cheek against Johnny's chest trying to sort out the noise.

"Feels sleepy in here?" Johnny murmured.

"Dark magic," Luke said and Zee reached over to pinch at the inside of Johnny's elbow sharply.

Sam swatted at a listing Cameron.

"Where are Will and Eric?" Zee asked.

"They went up to...they're up closer by the stage," Johnny said pointing. The light in the hall yellowed and then turned crisp and orangey, the color outside of the windows was bloody. "What's going on?"

The woman on stage fiddled with urgent, swooping gestures, but her eyes were blank and the music she created was a dark moaning sound, like a wild animal.

"Is he here?" Sam's fingers clutched at Zee's hand and she spun in place, pushing around Cameron's body. "Zee, is he here?"

Zee stared at the back of a tall man with hair the shade of dust. Her breath was caught in her chest, trapped there for a long minute until the man turned to her, expression flat. He was familiar, a local.

"He is not here, Sam," Luke said softly, and a string on the violin broke with a wicked scream but the woman kept playing.

Zee stepped up to a familiar woman—Gretchen who worked at the coffee shop—and waved her hand in front of her face, but there was no response.

"Get the boys," Zee said to Luke. "Johnny, grab your family. We need to get outside."

"The town-" Johnny started.

"I don't think this is about the town," Zee said and her voice cracked.

Johnny's eyes flashed and his hand reached out to squeeze softly at her arm as he pushed through the crowd.

"I'll help him," Luke said to Zee. "Get Sam and Cameron outside."

Zee pushed Sam ahead of herself, Cameron weaving them back through immobile neighbors and tourists, stiff bodies pushing back as they squeeze past. Zee tried to convince herself that she was imagining the glares the hypnotized audience gave her until they had almost reached the door and a man leaned down to snarl with bared teeth directly into her face.

"Cameron!" Sam shouted, hands pounding on his back. "He can't hear me."

There was an accordion playing now, something familiar like a tune Nadia had hummed to her at bedtime, and entirely unconnected to the song of the fiddler and the wilting trumpeter that had joined in the fray.

"He can get out," Zee said, less worried about Cameron and Johnny with all of their bulk than she was for herself and Sam against the increasingly ferocious looking crowd around them.

She put her hands next to Sam's on Cameron's back and together they pushed him forward against the tide of the crowd. She took a glancing elbow to her side (one she answered happily and less lightly) before Sam seemed to realized the situation and was shoving her boyfriend forward through the last ring of people around them and breaking out of the front doors, dragging Zee along by the wrist.

The sky above them was twisting and black, screaming and rushing with hundreds of wings crashing together.

"Crows," Sam breathed.

"Shit, what- what happened?" Cameron asked, spinning in place.

Zee's back bumped into the opening hall doors as Luke and Johnny came running out, Johnny's nieces in each of their arms, with Sarah, Roger, Will, and Eric standing in the open doors behind them. All their faces but Johnny's pointed up at the sky.

"This is him?" Johnny asked.

"This is him," Luke said, voice low.

"Chernov," Zee said, turning back and watching the

cloud of crows spiral in the sky over head, downy black feathers raining to the street.

"What the hell?" Roger muttered from behind them.

Johnny shifted Cara in his arms and pointed ahead of them. "Zee, the docks."

Sam was walking down the steps with jerky, clunking motions. The water was red from the streaks of sunset bleeding through the black storm clouds on the horizon. Tourists stood and pointed up at the spiraling birds as they swooped down nearly to skimming the ground. Sam flinched back onto the steps and Luke passed a sniffling Olivia over to Sarah so he could stand as a shield on the ground, hands raised. Zee could see the ice and green of power spreading out from his fingertips.

"I feel like you guys have been keeping something from us," Roger said under his breath.

"We need to get back to the house," Sam said and then crouched as another wave of birds, cawed in a sharp chorus and dove for their heads.

"I never really liked Hitchcock," Will said.

"We'll never get the girls through this," Sarah said, softer and to Johnny.

"Don't take them back inside," Zee told her. She trusted the birds more than the hypnotized strangers waiting behind the doors. Even now she felt like she could feel the air shifting from inside the hall, bodies moving restlessly. She didn't want to wait for the crowd to follow them. She looked up with the others and then back down to the ground, searching for some kind of shelter they could use to escape the scene.

"The torches," Zee said, pointing down the steps to the citronella staffs lighting the walkway up to the hall. "If we carry them-"

Luke nodded from steps below and rushed ahead as the crows swooped over the docks before circling in the air to turn back to the hall. Sam yelped as the swarm dove closer, Cameron dodging in front of them, the birds rearing back like a black wall, screeching and rising in the air away from the flash of the torch.

"Go," Johnny said, hand at the base of Zee's back as the group of them ran down the stairs, grabbing up the torches in pairs. "My car is around the block."

"We're just up ahead," Eric said.

"Take them back to their house," Johnny said to him, passing his niece over into her dad's arms.

"Johnny I don't under-" Roger started.

"We'll explain," Zee said. "We'll explain later, but please, get home and stay inside."

Sarah and Roger grabbed their girls as Eric and Will braced themselves in front of them, torches held aloft. Johnny grabbed at Zee's hand and they met Luke with Cameron and Sam at the corner. Zee turned at the sound of a wild shout, a nearly animal roar from behind them.

The doors of the hall were swinging open and the audience was rushing out, another wave of irritated motion like a mirror to the squirming black above them.

"Zee!" Johnny shouted over the screams from the scene in front of them. His hand swiped at hers but she pulled away.

"What are they doing?" she asked, voice drowned out.

Sam and Luke appeared at her sides, shoulders brushing against hers as a long dark mass of bodies pushed and shoved their way down the hall stairwell and across the empty road over to the docks. The birds paid none of them any mind, only followed the shape and direction of the crowd to the edge of the water. Johnny's heat was at her back, Cameron's bulk a shield behind them all, and together they held their breath as the crowd from inside the hall and the swarm of birds hovered at the water's edge.

As one, the crowd screamed and rushed towards the water, crashing off the dock like a wave in the wrong direction.

* * *

Johnny parked at the gate's edge. Zee blinked and saw again the strange vision of person after person, crow after crow, diving into the water just at the edge of the dock. The crowd had dispersed along the frame of the wooden walkway. It was too crowded, too many bodies clustered together, wrestling and treading water. She wasn't sure what happened to the birds.

"What do we say?" Sam whispered from the back seat, squeezed between Luke and Cam. "Do we...do we tell the island?"

The house was still, quiet, safe. Zee could feel the wards glowing from here.

"How?" Zee asked. "How would we explain what just happened to them?"

"I can help," Luke said. "Put a film over the memories. It won't erase them, but it will make them less concrete. More confused."

"Let me talk to Sarah and Roger," Johnny said. "I have more to cover with them and... I don't want to lie completely. They'll have questions."

Questions about her and Sam, Zee guessed. She stared into her lap until Johnny's hand joined hers.

"We're alright, pixie," Johnny whispered.

A smile wavered on her face without her permission. "Let's get inside. Fill in Nadia."

"Is she...?" Luke trailed off.

"She's around. Feeling better as far as I can tell." Zee decided not to mention that Nadia was in charge of keeping an eye on him. So far she'd had nothing to report other than that Luke 'seemed nice.' Luke did not seem nice, not as far as Zee could tell. But he was... learning to be pleasant. And there was more too, a sort of vividness that surrounded him. Johnny had become her grounding force, but when Luke was near she, and Johnny too, felt on tenterhooks, waiting for something electric to happen.

Johnny was on the phone with Sarah and Roger as Sam made tea and they waited for Eric and Will to make it back. Zee listened to Johnny pacing the hall, fragments of his conversation floating to her ears.

"No, no, I know Sarah, but don't go back... Zee and Sam they... we're not sure. No, it wasn't... it's not...*you* be careful."

Luke appeared from the sunroom, arms piled with books. "You worry about whether or not he'll stay?" he asked, leaning against the wall near her.

"Not really. Not now," she said, watching the head of Johnny's shadow reach as far as the foyer before retreating again. "But you saw how we started."

When he'd gone hunting through her memories, looking for hints of Nadia.

"I know where you'll end up too," Luke said, something soft and calling in the words.

Zee rolled her head to look up into his face, craning her neck back. Why couldn't one of them have been just an average height?

"Yeah, you do," she said, and it was easier than it should

have been, in all the mess and the crows' screams still ringing in her ears, to smile up at him, to soak up that shocking green gaze fixed to her face.

And then a car door slammed. Eric and Will were safe, the wards giving way for their familiar touch.

"I'll take these to the kitchen," Luke said, looking kind of dazed and confused on his own as he pushed off the wall.

Zee opened the door, catching Will's expression from halfway across the yard. Narrowed eyes and lines around his mouth, a pulse ticking in his jaw from clenching his teeth. All the ease and calm and peace he wrestled for in life, smothered under the attack from Chernov. The soldier back in place. Eric was wearing the same expression too, but more tired.

"Sarah called the police and the hospital," Johnny said. "Should we go back? Help people out of the water?"

"An emergency vehicle was at the docks when we passed on our way back here," Eric said.

Will grabbed Zee's arm on his way in through the door, the grip a little too tight.

"Will." Eric was up against his back, voice soothing.

"There's tea in the kitchen," Zee said setting her hands on Will's chest. His eyes had turned a thundercloud gray and the lines were fine and white in his pursed lips. "Get a fire going in the library and meet us in the kitchen," Zee said to Johnny who was looking at Will's hand on her arm like he was about to try and tear it off. "Go."

"He was in my head," Will hissed in her ear as she led him down the hall to the kitchen. "How did he get in my head?"

"It's a specialty of his," Luke said, clear enough for Eric to hear as he followed behind them. He stood in the doorway of the kitchen, eyes fixed to Will's grip. "Chernov can slip into anyone. Let her go."

"It's alright," Zee said, because she could feel the tremble in Will's touch and see the sheen of tears on his eyes.

"He's here?" Eric asked.

Sam was at the cupboards, pulling boxes of tea blends down from the shelves as Eric filled the kettle. Zee went with Will to stand stubbornly at the center of the room, fingers loosened but still grasping, holding onto her like an anchor. She held his gaze and lifted her hands slowly, resting them on his chest. He didn't flinch as she pulled some of the white light power in her chest and let it trickle into him, hunting for any of Chernov's smoke and shadow.

"He doesn't have to be here," Luke said. "He just needs to know enough about what is here to catch a hook in the fabric, then he can drag his consciousness over."

"He's gone now," Zee whispered to Will. "No sign of him left."

"What was the point?" Will asked her, hand dropping. "What was the point of...of-what the hell did he even do?"

"He put the hall in a trance," Sam said. "He projected it through the fiddler, the music, but the influence was all over the hall."

"But why?"

"Because he can," Luke snapped. "He did it to show that he can."

"Can you do that?" Eric asked.

Zee, Luke, and Sam glanced at each other and she knew that Sam felt that same sharp pang at the nervous tone in Eric's voice.

"I don't know," Zee said.

"We would never try," Sam said, more firmly.

"Probably," Luke said with a shrug. "But I don't want to."

Zee caught his eye, a tilt of her head. *You couldn't have thought of something more comforting to say?* She wondered. His brow lifted for a moment and she almost heard his voice in her head. *You wouldn't want me to lie.*

"Is this all for her?" Will asked. "Chernov... is this whole thing about...?"

"Nadia," Sam said, scooping herbs into a ceramic pot.

Eric and Will both looked up and Zee resisted the urge to snort. Why was it everyone always looked up when they mentioned their ghost aunt? It wasn't like Nadia was likely to hover over everyone's heads all the time.

"It's all I know," Luke said although he looked at Zee.

Shit, she felt it again. Like he was whispering in her ear. *If he were smart, he'd be after you.* She turned her back to him, not prepared for anymore of his thoughts.

"Is that even an option?" Eric asked.

"Of course," Luke said.

"Not for us," Zee said.

"Chernov's decided it is and I suspect that's enough for him," Sam said, more diplomatic. "I don't know if he's trying to draw her out by terrorizing us? Or if there's something he thinks we can do."

"Which we won't do," Zee said, staring at Sam.

Sam glanced up and there was a flicker of something, some hypothetical Sam's scientific brain would consider that Zee couldn't bear to.

"No, we won't," Sam said, meeting her eyes.

August 4th, 2017

Luke was in the garden, reading one of Nadia's journals, and talking to the deadly nightshade.

"He's a bit like she was, isn't he?" Sam asked her, leaning against Zee's legs as they shucked peas on the porch in late summer.

"He keeps his secrets," Zee agreed. "And the locals certainly seem about as terrified of him as they were of Nadia."

"I think that has something to do with the way he stares anyone down who looks twice at you or Johnny," Sam teased.

Just then, Luke set the notebook down to the ground and looked at them, eyes red. "*It was only a warning, my pet. You will surrender,*" he said, in a borrowed, hollow voice.

Zee sat up in bed with a gasp. Johnny, who must have been twisted around her side, rolled over with an irritated grunt and smashed his face against the pillow he had claimed from her pile. The sky outside was just starting to turn pink with dawn and her heart was hammering in her chest. There was something oily at the back of her mouth that she couldn't swallow away, and a deep ache in her head that had hung around for days now.

She crawled over Johnny out of the bed, smiling as his hand came up to cup the back of her thigh, handsy and affectionate even in sleep. She grabbed a pair of sleep shorts to put on under her t-shirt and one of Johnny's hoodies thrown over the back of a chair and padded down the stairs to make coffee. They would need a bigger pot with all the extra bodies in the house. The light was on in the sunroom —Luke, up researching. She debated going to him but she was craving comfort and the right sources for that at this moment were all up stairs.

Instead she started running the list of ingredients for pancakes through her head—a treat for the house to make up for the terror of the previous night—when she found Nadia in the kitchen.

Someone's coming.

Zee's toes skidded on the floor boards at the sight of her aunt, crisp and clear, alone in the kitchen. Ice ran through her veins at the warning. She opened her mouth to ask for advice. What could she do *now* against *Chernov* at dawn? Before coffee and breakfast?

She could get Luke.

No, not Chernov, Nadia soothed, and Zee's heart pounded at the safety that wrapped around her like a blanket with this return of *her* Nadia. *It's the idiot. Go answer the door, I'll get Sam.*

Maybe her brain was just too slow before coffee because it wasn't until she was reaching the door, swinging it open to reveal the blue uniform that she realized which idiot Nadia was referring to.

"Doyle," Zee said dully. Couldn't she just...go *back* to bed?

"Miss Nikolaev," Jasper Doyle said, looking down at her bare legs peeking out from under Johnny's hoodie.

"It's very early," Zee said, trying to clip her words with that same irritated tone Nadia had always used when dealing with the man.

"I've just left the hospital," Doyle said, and this time he didn't bother with any attempt at charm. He just stared at her legs and then up at her face, looking disgusted. "I was gathering statements from-"

"From everyone at Odd Fellow's Hall," Zee finished, adding, "Are they alright?"

"You're aware of the incident?" Doyle asked, sounding not at all surprised to hear it.

"I was leaving with the others when everyone rushed out of the building," Zee said. "Do you know what happened?"

Doyle rolled his eyes. "Oh I have a few guesses," he said and Zee's palms itched, seeing the next blow against her and Sam coming from a mile away. But not the direction they'd expected. "Why was it you were leaving early? Can't have been there long."

"Zoya?" Luke called from the hall.

"No," Zee said to Doyle slowly. "But everyone was acting so strangely. We got uncomfortable."

Doyle scoffed and opened his mouth to speak but was, blessedly, interrupted.

"Zee?" A sleep addled Eric stumbled into the doorway, shrinking in his t-shirt and boxers from the cold breeze flooding in from the open door. "Wassgoin' on?"

Luke appeared from the other end of the hall at the same time. "Is everything alright, Zoya?"

Doyle blinked once at the two men before sneering. "So much for Sharpe, eh?"

"What about me?" Johnny asked from the stairs, feet landing heavily as he made his way down to Zee's side, a parade following behind him made up of all the others.

Doyle took a step back from the door at the sight of the crowd. And Zee couldn't really blame him. She couldn't think of a single time the house had ever been so full of people. Of guests or friends or...family. Whatever it was she seemed to be surrounded by at this moment. She wondered if even Nadia could have named a time.

"It's the ass crack of dawn, Doyle. What the hell do you want?" Cam snapped, dark circles under his eyes and Sam drooping against his chest.

Zee and Johnny barely glanced at each other but it was enough. Who knew Cameron Johnson could possibly wake up on the wrong side of the bed?

Doyle looked cowed for half a moment, probably thrown off course from terrorizing the local crazies (her and Sam) by the sight of actual upstanding citizens. But he squared his shoulders and took an uninvited step inside the house.

"I'm going to need your statements regarding the events last night."

Chapter 20

Full Moon

August 5th 2017

Luke was behind the counter at the bookshop, feet propped up on the edge of his cash register, eyes lost on the page.

Zee cleared her throat.

He didn't look up.

She rang the little bell on his counter.

"Just a minute," he said, from behind the book. It was an old dusty text on magic in the South Americas that she'd found online for him.

"I'm looking for a book on how to make my boyfriend pay attention to me," Zee said.

There was a pause and then, "I hear food is good for that sort of thing," Luke said, without setting the book down. "If that fails...try lingerie."

She snorted. "You're such a shit."

He snapped the text shut—he had a spell for finding his spot again—and appeared, grinning. "Hello, moon bloom."

"Did you know the shop closed ten minutes ago?" she

asked him, and enjoyed the baffled double take he did at the clock on the wall. The one she and Johnny had got him after too many nights coming home late.

"Can I finish my chapter?" he asked.

Zee woke from the dream, biting her smile.

* * *

She was a prism of white light, reflecting the world back on itself, shielding herself in cool, hard, glass. The magic was thrumming inside of her, twisting and shimmering in her veins, almost hot to the touch. Something shivery and soft trickled down her back, ice melting, and Zee sighed inside the shell of power.

You let me in again.

Her eyes popped open as she grimaced, Luke sitting across from her in the grass, the world pink with sunrise. His eyes were on her face, the others around them in a circle, legs folded and eyes closed.

Samara does a better job of shielding than you, Luke said in her head. *They* all *do a better job aside from Johnny.*

Zee rose up from the grass as quietly as she could and Luke followed, the pair of them walking over to the greenhouse. Johnny's eyes popped open, tracking them.

"You don't feel like Chernov in my head," Zee said.

"Thank you," Luke said with a shrug.

"Has it occurred to you that Johnny and I *can't* shield you...because...you know," she said, a limp hand gesturing between them.

"You can't even say it," Luke said, grinning. But Zee was learning the flavor of his moods on the air and that grin was bitter, frustrated.

"Are you ready to talk about it?" she asked. The only

284

time Luke had ever openly acknowledged the connection between them was while he was under Chernov's control. Did he want them, her and Johnny? Were they having the same dreams? Most nights now she woke up demanding Johnny satisfy a need that wanted two mouths, two pairs of hands, another body at her back.

Luke's eyes drifted from Johnny back to her. His gaze was unlike any other's she'd ever met, she thought he must have learned her by heart down to every eyelash.

"Not yet," he said, words cracking. "After."

After Chernov was gone. If they were all still standing.

"You're right," he added, taking a deep breath. "You won't be able to block me out. I should start teaching the attack. You and Samara can practice on each other."

Zee blew a dismissive sound out from between her lips. "So you think Sam and I will be any better at blocking each other?"

Luke frowned at her. "Must you be so open-hearted, Zoya?"

"I must," she said, reaching out and catching his hand. It was an unconscious thing, just a touch of acknowledgement between... whatever they were at the moment. But Luke's fingers twined and tightened around hers, his grip desperate. Just as quickly he released her, passing her on the lawn to return to the others, still meditating.

Zee slid into the greenhouse. It was time for coffee and toast and probably four skillets of bacon with the appetites now filling the house.

Johnny padded into the kitchen just as she got the stove going.

"Sorry," she whispered.

"You know you don't have to be, right?" Johnny asked.

She held her palm over the skillet, waiting for the heat

to glow. Johnny surrounded her back and the warmth from him, even after the morning chill, was stronger. They leaned into another.

"We haven't really talked about it," Zee said.

"Okay. So let's talk about it. You should kiss him," Johnny said, and then he kissed the top of her head. "But would you be mad if I did first?"

Zee bit her lip to fight her smile and shook her head, hair ruffling against Johnny's chest. "He said something about waiting until...after this whole thing is taken care of."

Johnny hummed and together they dropped slices of bacon into the pan, fat sizzling.

"Would you be mad?" Johnny asked.

"No. Disappointed, if I wasn't there to watch it happen."

"Now, there's a solid idea, pixie."

She thought about it too often. "He's yours too," she said.

* * *

Zee ducked her head as a man spat at her as she passed him at the corner. The wet glob narrowly missed her ankle and she picked up her pace, trying to make herself relax, hold her chin up, stare them all down. She could feel their eyes pressing into her back, all the people who had jumped from the docks that night. It was Saturday and it felt like the whole island was downtown. Staring out of windows, glaring at her from behind the coffee counter, crossing the street to avoid walking too closely to her.

Doyle hadn't made a secret of the fact that the first people he spoke to regarding the 'incident' were Zee and Sam. He had probably been less forthright with the fact that there was nothing to accuse them of outright, other than escaping the same strange hypnotism as everyone else in the hall.

The door to the shop opened too fast, banging against the wall before swinging noisily shut behind her. Will stood with Sam behind the counter, eyebrows raised sympathetically.

"I woulda got you coffee," he said.

"She only went to prove a point," Sam muttered, crossing her arms and turning her back to Zee.

"I didn't know you were coming," Zee said. She passed Sam's coffee to Will instead and listened to the affronted squeak with only a little bit of pleasure. Will snorted and passed the coffee over to Sam.

"I arm-wrestled Johnny so I could be the one to come by," Will said, smiling at her.

"Liar," Zee said, smiling back as some of the tension from outside the shop faded from her shoulders. "Johnny's not stupid enough to arm wrestle you."

Will's laugh was a bark as Sam sidled up to Zee and settled an apologetic chin on her shoulder. Zee leaned into the touch.

"He's dealing with a fussy account over the phone because *thankfully* he's the only one who has to do that kind of stuff still. But we wanted you both to know that we're almost ready to blow the globes. Could be tonight if you want."

"Full moon's on Monday," Sam murmured at Zee's ear.

She nodded, "We'll come tonight."

* * *

The garage door was up at the studio, letting the nearly waxing moon's glow fall in. The lights outside and overhead were turned off but there were small lamps on around the work areas so no one was left fumbling in the dark with burning hot glass at hand.

The first half dozen globes had been messes, too small or crooked or melting right off the pipes and cracking across the floor. The guys had warned them it would be like this, that it would take a few practice rounds before they had their movements down as a unit so the three witches had left magic aside for a moment to focus on learning the pattern and rhythm of heat and breath and the smooth, intuitive rolling of the pipe to keep the glass balanced at the end of it. After the process was less of a fumbling comedy routine and more of a steady ritual, and they'd each helped make three full and rounded globes in what Johnny promised was going to be a nice clear crystal blue after it cooled down, it was time for the real work to start.

Zee leaned back, shoulders brushing against Will's chest, as Brian took the pipe to the glory hole to flash heat over the little bulb of glass she'd just breathed a spark of magic, and air, into. She glanced over to the bench at her right, where Johnny was framed around Luke, his arms keeping the the shape of the glass even while Luke filled the orb with magic. A feeling that wasn't quite a thrill—softer and gentler and warmer—rolled down her spine at the sight of them, Johnny's strong thighs bracketing Luke's. As if he had felt it too, Luke glanced over, face showing a rare peace. Johnny was studying the back of Luke's neck the same way he looked at Zee's knees, baffled and hypnotized.

On her left, Cameron had Sam surrounded, having practiced controlling the pipe while Eric took care of flashing it in the heat.

Brian returned to Zee with the pipe and Will's hands took it from him, rolling along the bar of the bench as she set her lips to the mouth and released a breath full of that feeling. Safety, warmth, a bright...love. She inhaled through her nose, body shifting from one end of the bench to the other as Will spun the pipe, and exhaled until the globe was thin and round, glowing softly.

Brian took the pipe away again to finish off the end and Zee leaned back, closing her eyes and charging herself up for the next round.

August 7th 2017

"It's past moonrise," Luke said after dinner, standing at the sink and washing. Zee was pretty sure she was going to live the rest of her life without ever having to wash more than a teacup, but she didn't mind this compromise of putting things away in the cupboards. The domesticity of the routine was more thrilling than it had any right to be.

She and Sam both glanced out the kitchen window to where Cameron and Johnny and Will and Eric were all dicking around at the fire pit, trying to one-up the others with log placement.

"We could tell them to shoo for a few hours," Sam suggested.

Johnny yelped from outside, snatching his hand back out of the flames after throwing in another log. A shower of sparks spiraled up into the dusty sky.

"We could let them stay," Zee said glancing between Luke and Sam.

"We've never had others involved," Sam said. But the words were speculative rather than a refusal.

"We're still vulnerable," Luke said shrugging and

rinsing off the last of the plate, setting it in the drying rack for the night. "It'd be better to have someone watching the house while we work. And they have... a kind of energy, to say the least."

Sam was leaning against the counter when Zee turned. Her arms were crossed over her chest, a loose hair bun tilting off one side of her head matching the leaning smirk of her lips.

"Johnny grounds me," Zee said, shrugging her shoulders. "I feel stronger with him around."

Sam grinned triumphantly and then let it fade. "I understand the feeling," she said. It was better than 'I told you so.' "Alright, let's get ready."

By the time she and Sam made it out of their quick baths and into their white shifts—Luke had inherited a pair of old cotton pajama pants from Eric—the campfire had become a roaring bonfire, almost as tall as Will. Johnny blinked, fast and stunned, as she and Luke approached and Cameron's gaze went soft on Sam.

"Hey, pixie," he said. "Luke."

Zee bit her lip to fight her smile, thinking of the night the month before when he'd joined her in the grass after this same ceremony.

"Hey, burn mark," she said, the smile blooming. "It's a full moon. We're going to work magic."

Eric made an abbreviated, excited sound from the back of his throat and Will nudged him with a teasing grin.

"You want us to head out?" Johnny asked. His voice was even but she could see the brief tightening around his eyes.

"Actually we'd like it if you all wanted to join us," she said.

"Yes," Eric said immediately.

Johnny's hand found hers and he squeezed as Cameron answered, "We would be honored."

They moved as a group into a square of moonlight peeking through the trees. A ring of the glass orbs surrounding them in the grass, glittering reflections of the sky on their surfaces.

Sam had rewritten their small ceremony in the bath. She gave Johnny the candle, Cameron the the cup of water, Eric the incense, Luke the bright quartz globe, and Will the small potted succulent Zee usually held herself. She met Zee in the center, surrounded by their odd new collected family, and joined hands. Zee lifted their arms up into the air, wide and open, cool light and shadow sliding down their bare skin. She closed her eyes, tilting her head back to soak up more light, and took long, even breaths until she and Sam matched, bodies nearly touching with every inhalation.

There was a little, soft well of warmth in her chest, the prism of light glowing stronger. The firm tower of Sam was at her front and a pool of heat at her back, Johnny focused on her every movement. Around them was Cameron's wave breaking and scrambling against the shore, and Eric shifting from storm cloud to easy breeze, and Will's roots tangling deep into the earth below them. And Luke, a sharp shard of cold power, something between a lightning strike and a blizzard, running like a current through the men making the circle.

Sam's fingers squeezed gently at hers and Zee opened her eyes to the moon overhead and began to chant.

August 8th 2017

Luke found her in the garden, huddled up under a blanket on the wicker chaise, and he sat down in front of her so slowly she thought he was afraid of spooking her.

"You didn't go with the others?" he asked.

Johnny and the boys and Sam had left a couple hours ago to hang the globes out around the island, a small collection of island locals and tourists expected to join them. Luke had given the event a hard pass, retreating to the sunroom at the first mention. It hadn't been two weeks yet but she was learning him in pieces. That his guardedness had more to do with being an introvert than any sign of hiding anything. He was the opposite of Johnny in this way and the rare sharing of a moment together was as meaningful as Johnny's open-hearted confessions.

"A little girl burst into tears when she saw me on the sidewalk this morning," Zee said, lifting the blankets up to her chin. She wasn't cold exactly. Maybe tired. She'd put all her energy from the week into the those globes and no matter how many times Johnny moved the bed into moonlight last night, she still felt the strain.

"Samara went," Luke pointed out.

"Sam... she was always a little better with the island than I was. And she's not the one who tells them the hard truths of their lives over cups of tea," she said.

He rested his elbows on his knees, looking down into the grass. Her toes rested against his hip and she wondered if he'd give her a dirty look if she tucked them under his thigh to keep warm. When she tried he only moved his hand to cover the tops of her feet like a blanket.

"It's been a long time since I tried to live outside of magic," he said to the ground. "When my parents were alive... we lived away from towns. I went to public school until I didn't have to anymore."

"Did you like it? Living only magic?" she asked.

He shrugged, head tipping to one side to meet her eyes. "It was my life. Did you like growing up known as a witch?"

"No," she said and his eyes opened wide. "I hated it. I wanted to be normal. But I wasn't and I knew that I couldn't be. So I learned how to live that life."

Luke blinked, stare drifting back to the horizon over the cliff. "I was very lonely," he said. "There weren't many other children amongst my parents' friends. There was nothing like what you have here in this house. My parents practiced privately—I made magic on my own, in the woods."

"What about amongst Chernov's followers?"

He shook his head. "We were all out for ourselves, for his favor, to be something other than his battery," he spoke the last word with a spitting anger.

"You have us now," she whispered. When he didn't respond, didn't even so much as glance at her in acknowl-edgment she added, "And if you need to leave, for yourself, you can."

"I'm not going anywhere, Zoya," he said, an uncon-scious echo of the promise Johnny left her with regularly.

"What about...when we've defeated him?"

"Would you let me stay?" Luke asked, turning slowly to face her. "Let me share this with you?"

Eric's truck pulled into the drive first, then Johnny's car, doors shutting and voices calling, heading into the house.

"Yes," she said.

Neither Zee nor Luke moved and Johnny found them there, collapsing between them, his body draping over Zee and his legs landing in a motionless Luke's lap.

"How did it go?" Zee asked, watching out of the corner of her eye to see if Luke bolted.

"Fine," Johnny said, too heavily for that to be the end of it. "You should have come."

"You didn't need me for that part," she said. "It's better if the island doesn't know I'm a part of the project."

He 'hmphed' and nestled back tighter against her while Luke seemed to relax, hands behind his back bracing against the foot of the chaise.

"I just don't think you should have to hide out from the town. They need to get over this whole..." Johnny trailed off.

"They should," Zee agreed, combing her fingers through his hair, scratching at the back of his neck to make his eyes fall shut. "But they probably won't. It will come and go but Sam and I will always be available as scapegoats. At least this time they're partly right. We are responsible-"

"Zee," Johnny groaned and tried to twist to face her.

"Bullshit," Luke grunted.

She wrapped her arms around Johnny's chest and pulled him back down, glaring over a tuft of blonde hair at Luke. "It's Chernov's fault, I know that. But it's my family that drew his gaze. But the island will never understand how that works, it's too..."

"Magical," Luke said.

Zee hummed. It wasn't the word she was thinking of, but it worked. The Nikolaev women stretched the imaginations of the island at the best of times. In a case like this...

"Do you think he'll come here?" Johnny asked him.

"I don't think he can," Luke said, nearly whispering, like he was half afraid to say it aloud, that it might catch to the wind and carry back to wherever Chernov was lurking against shadows like an old stain. "But I don't want to count on it."

Johnny's hands found her knees under the blanket and squeezed. "Let's go inside. Pixie, you want a bath?"

Zee grinned up at Johnny and the tired tightness in his eyes vanished, replaced with intent. Luke was shifting and she could see his knuckles whiten on the wicker.

"Definitely," she said, winking at Johnny. Couldn't they make it hard for Luke to resist them? "I have plans for you."

They left him, jaw clenched, and pulse jumping, on the chaise. A prickle of ice teased down from the top of her head to the backs of her thighs, but he never moved an inch.

Chapter 21

Hex and Burn

August 11th 2017

Luke came into The Lab with a rattle of bells on the door and an icy snap of air. He stopped stone still in the doorway, finding Zee helping a handful of teenage summer girls spend their babysitting money and Sam busy with a phone order.

"We'll be right with you," Zee said, in her best retail voice, bright and smooth, eying the ratty looking bag in his hand where a muddy feather was poking through the fabric.

"Er...right. Thank you," Luke said, drifting over to a corner and finding himself staring at a wall of massage oils.

The girls giggled and preened at the sight of him and Zee fought her smile, directing them back to the sweetest of Sam's clay mask mixtures. Zee tried not to track him in his wander around the small shop but her eyes drifted there, called by the whisper of his shuffle across the floor, the light click of him returning a jar back to the shelf. That damn song again.

Her dreams were turning sweeter at night, small

glimpses of the three of them traveling together for Johnny's gallery shows. Her and Luke tooling around in cities to burn time, him and Johnny bickering about directions as she dozed in the backseat. The three of them grabbing dinner together at the docks to the bafflement of the island. Luke opening a rare bookshop with a secret door leading to his stash of occult texts that he hoarded like a greedy dragon.

It was a life she was trying very hard not to crave.

The summer girls left the shop, small bags in hand, with parting glances at Luke as Sam finally finished on the phone. Luke came up to the counter, dropping the bag in front of them.

"Why and who is leaving kitschy hex *trinkets* around for us to trip over?" He asked, nose wrinkling. To be fair the bag had an odd smell, mucky and herbal at the same time.

"I find them sort of...endearing," Sam said, opening the bag. She pinched the odd tangle of feathers and mud and nettles in her fingers and frowned sympathetically at the cluster.

"I know what you mean," Zee said, shrugging. She looked up at Luke who was frowning and staring at them like they were both insane. "Where did you find these?"

"Outside your gates, in front of the shop, behind the shop, behind Johnny's tire," Luke rattled off.

"Johnny's car?!" Zee asked, eyes widening. She hadn't expected the island to go after Johnny even if they were dating and it brought up a little of that early anxiety about their relationship.

It might have been more concerning if the hex...*globs* weren't so apparently flat and devoid of any actual power. Scooping them up off the floor and tossing them into the waste bin was along the same lines as brushing a stray ant off your arm at a picnic. Annoying, but harmless.

"Are they effective?" Sam asked.

"They're offensive," Luke said, but his eyes were on Zee's face, watching her lips press tight together. "No, they're useless."

"Well... I'll say this much for you, Lucas," Sam said, nudging the bag and it's stink back in his direction. "At least you would have made it scary."

In the wake of Luke's relieving reappearance to the land of the living, Sam had absolved herself of the guilt of pushing him off the cliff and enjoyed the opportunity of gentle antagonization as often as she could. Luke didn't seem to mind, only smirked in response.

"I guess it's kind of creative of the locals to try and fight us with magic," Zee said. She took the bag from the counter and walked through the back room to take it out to the garbage bin.

"I don't see what's so creative about Googling," Luke mumbled from inside.

"Give it a week and they'll have lost interest in us or we'll have I dunno...dog shit on our windows or something," Zee said, coming back inside and flipping on all the shop lights.

"Wow," Sam said, one eyebrow raised as she frowned at her cousin. "Now I'm really looking forward to it."

In all honesty, the scene at the docks and the island's suspicion as to Sam and Zee's part in it was taking a small toll on their business. Tourist season was almost over and with everything that had happened over the summer Zee had barely taken half her usual number of clients at the house. Sam's online sales were strong, but the shop was deadly quiet aside from the few summer visitors who'd arrived *after* the festival and a surprise contingent of islanders. Zee was going to bake Maria

James the most exquisitely sweet gift baskets for Christmas this year.

"I think you should both take this more seriously," Luke said, eyes narrowed. "I'm going out and making sure there aren't any around Johnny's apartment or Cameron's boat."

Sam's face twisted uncomfortably as Luke pushed off the counter and headed to the door.

"Thanks, Wolfe," she called, before he left.

He raised a hand in goodbye and glanced at Zee as the door swung shut behind him.

Aug 15th 2017

"You're not paying attention again," Sam snapped, pushing a jar of sleepy time body lotion into Zee's chest.

"I am," Zee said, blinking and trying to remember what Sam had been saying. And then when that wouldn't come she tried to remember where her mind had been. But that wouldn't come either.

"You are literally drifting off again, right in front of me," Sam said and then added more quietly, "That's *my* schtick."

"Doesn't today feel...off to you?" Zee asked.

Sam blinked and frowned. She glanced around the Lab, at the sun streaming in through the windows, everything bright and tidy across the shelves, a heavy bouquet of flowers sagging on the counter.

"No," Sam said slowly, forehead wrinkling. "Is it...do you think you're...you know?" she asked, waving a finger in the direction of Zee's head.

Was Chernov back?

"It's not..." Zee couldn't really say for sure when she thought about it. Only that it wasn't her head that felt foggy now, just everything outside of it. It was a slippery, distracted feeling. Something shifted at the corner of her eye and Zee jumped in place to stare out the front door.

Grace Harper was marching down the sidewalk with her shoulders hunched and her hair swirling around her face. Was it windy out? Or had she just been looking into the shop?

"Should you head back to the house?" Sam asked, voice softening.

"No." Zee rolled her shoulders and shook her head. Her fingers wrapped around the jar of lotion a little tighter than necessary and she found a smile to reassure Sam. "No, I'm fine. I *am* just out of it."

"Would that have anything to do with watching Luke and Johnny out on the lawn this morning?" Sam said, rolling her eyes to hide the nervous edge of her own smile.

Zee started to snark back and then bit her lip, hurrying over to the shelf to grab the rest of the order Sam had been lecturing her over. It had been a nice view over her coffee cup, watching the two of them on the lawn, shirtless and doing yoga, eyes fixed to one another. She caught herself daydreaming and turned to head back into the workroom and pack up the order when something warm oozed over her shoulders and then slid away.

"Sam."

"Zee."

Their eyes met across the room. Sam was standing at the far corner, one hand pressing at the wall while she cradled a collection of bottles in her other arm.

"I feel it. What is this?" Sam asked.

Zee put her own hand up, reaching over jars to the wall. Heat flashed up the bones of her hand, gripping at her wrist for moment before she tore herself away.

"We need to get-" she started.

"I smell-" Sam said.

There was a bright burst from the work room and a blast of the smell of charcoal and kerosene.

"My test recipes," Sam shouted, dropping the bottles in her arms to the floor and rushing for the back.

The smoke was sudden and overwhelming. Zee was only just pulling away from the wall when long, crackling vines of flame spread out of the doorway from the back room. They ran across the walls of the shop like sparking lightning strikes, all orange and yellow and blue, sucking up the oxygen in the room.

"Sam!"

Zee ran for the doorway as the air around her turned dry, making her gasp feel thin in her chest. Sam dashed through a thin sliver in the doorway before the flames covered the opening. By the time Zee made it to the desk she could barely see Sam flickering through a dense wall of fire.

"Zee!" Sam called her voice nearly drowned out by the roaring.

"Get out!" Zee answered.

"The back door is blocked...I have your phone!"

"I'll call 911," Zee screamed. "Call Luke, or Johnny! Call the boys!"

She thought she heard Sam repeat her name, something like a whimper, but she was pulling the shop phone off the desk and dialing. The front door was barricaded, orange licks of heat cracking and sparking over the floorboards, billowing up ash and smoke.

"911, what's your-"

"Fire at the Lab on Main Street," Zee shouted over the line. Heat was building at her back as she spoke and she shuffled to the center of the room, covering her ear with one hand to try and drown out the thunder of the fire around her. Her skin was scorched and clammy at the same time, sweat breaking out and shivers of fear running down her spine.

Through the inferno at the front door Zee could see faces on the street, staring at the shop with wide eyes and phones pressed to their ears. She tried to take a breath but nothing seemed to gather in her lungs but smoke and she choked out a cough. On the phone the voice at the other end sputtered and then cut off. The line went dead and Zee tossed the hot plastic aside. A crowd was gathering outside, watching the fire in horror. With any luck the fire department was already on its way.

Zee's eyes were running, tears drying on her cheeks before they could travel far enough to make salt tracks. Her mouth tasted like cedar and sulfur. She was kneeling on the floor before she could realize she was falling and her shins and knees rang with shock. Her fingers tried to plant themselves to the floor but everything was burning hot. She crawled over to a display, found a little clean air under the table cloth, but all it did was make her cough. Her eyelids were sweating, drawing more tears out with the sting. She thought even her teeth might be sweating.

Her body drooped to the floor and Zee closed her eyes, trying to find the glow of safe, clean blue light inside of herself. It bubbled in her chest and small raspy coughs spilled out of her mouth. She opened her eyes and winced at the heat. The fire had crawled up the walls and across the ceiling, clinging and dripping from the old wooden beams like a red dragon.

She even thought she could see a face staring down at her. Craggy cheekbones and a jaw like the head of an axe with dark hollows of smoke for eyes. She licked her lips to speak - to curse or cry out - and the taste on her tongue was charcoal.

Your protection charms are very pretty, my dear, whispered the smoke overhead. *But you've closed the gate with me inside.*

There was a crash from the back room and the fire that circled around Zee bloomed, chewing away at the floorboards and making her head spin with the heat. There might have been a shout or it might have been the massive crack in the beams above—the groaning as the wood sagged and rained down heavy sparks like fluffy snowflakes made of fire. Zee dragged herself under the display table, but the sparks bit at the back of her hands.

The smoke spiraled down from breaking beams, curving through the air like seeking hands. *My red flower may never surrender to me...But I have enjoyed the chase. And I will enjoy taking you in her stead.*

Zee thought she would gladly take Nadia's place if it meant keeping Chernov away from her aunt's spirit. From Sam. From Luke and Johnny and the boys and the island. And Chernov was smart too because nothing would hurt Nadia more.

"Zoya!"

"Zee!"

It took a moment before the shouts registered in Zee's head. Everything seemed to be in slow motion; the fire rocking deeper into the room like waves coming in, the slow search of the smoke in the air, the sweat drying on her skin even as it beaded.

"Zee!"

"Johnny," she said but her voice was papery and clumsy, mouth so dry from smoke. Luke too, and worry ran through her. He needed to stay far away from this. From Chernov.

There were voices on the other side of the doorway and through the smoke and the fire Zee thought she could see a wavering shadow, tall and lanky with shoulders that stretched wide and straight. The vision swirled and before her stood a mountain of a man with a haggard face defined by more lines than a map. But he stood over her like rock, skin the color of smoke, one shoulder drooping. His eyes seemed like black hollows.

"Zee!! Where are you?" Johnny was closer and Zee winced, Chernov flickering and then vanishing in front of her. Johnny cut through the apparition, and there were little whorls of flames sticking to his shoulders and arms, like birds settled on a wire.

"Don't be stupid," Zee said, although there wasn't any sound coming from her throat.

But Johnny looked down, a crown of fire hanging over his head and little sparks dying out against his skin after burning holes through his t-shirt.

"Too late for that, pixie," he answered, feet kicking up ash as he ran to her.

Everything was stuttering around her, her sight going in and out. Johnny was kneeling in front of her and his normally scorching hands felt comfortingly cool as he pulled her out from under the table, smoke and fire parting around them.

"'Sides," he said in her ear. "My girlfriend fireproofed me."

Then he scooped her up off the floor and the world spun and went black.

She came to on the pavement behind the shop, sitting at the back of an ambulance with a plastic mask over her face filling her nose and mouth with warm and sharply clean air.

It pinched at her cheeks and she plucked at the elastic straps until a large pair of hands batted at her.

"Leave it." Luke, soot streaking his face, and eyes creased with worry.

Sam was sitting just behind her, leaning against a little metal cabinet with another oxygen mask over her face. Her eyes were red and her hair was speckled with ash.

"Where's Johnny?" Zee asked.

Luke nodded across the pavement to where Johnny stood shirtless and annoyed, gray soot combed into his hair where he'd been running his fingers through. A team of EMTs circled him curiously, checking his skin and flashing little lights into his eyes as he rolled them impatiently. When he caught sight of Zee sitting up from her cot, he pushed through the crowd and rushed across the pavement.

Zee blinked as her eyes watered and blamed her wobbling chin on the oxygen mask.

"Zee." Johnny's voice was hoarse and Zee wasn't sure if it was from smoke or the worry digging lines into his forehead.

He stepped in close and between him and Luke they blocked out the smoldering shop building behind, the gawkers on the sidewalk, the team of firemen and police and EMTs. Zee leaned forward even as Johnny bent and pressed his lips to her forehead. He huffed at the smoke and ash in her hair and she took an unsteady breath.

"You okay?" he asked. His hands reached for hers and Zee hissed behind the mask, both of them leaning back. His thumb was resting against a burn on the back of her hand. "Sorry, pixie. But I know this salve that'll heal you right up."

Zee pressed her face into Johnny's chest before he could see the tears and sucked in breaths as she felt his fingers sorting through her tangles. A shadow joined them at John-ny's side, massive and safe.

"They want to take you all to the hospital," Luke said, body tight with tension. "Eric and Will are going to the house to get you changes of clothes."

"I don't want to," Sam said, mumbled but stubborn from behind her mask. Cameron had arrived too, holding her face in large, gentle hands.

Zee could feel Johnny tense against her forehead and pulled back to say, "I do."

Johnny's fingers carried on with their task and Sam's set shoulders softened. Luke's hand brushed softly over Zee's shoulder, nodding, before stepping away.

"I'll let them know," he said.

The town was visible again as Luke moved away, a cluster of familiar faces standing on tiptoes on the other side of yellow caution tape. Jasper Doyle was with the girl who ran the coffee shop across the street, a little notebook in his hands. It seemed like he was taking his job seriously for once. Maria James stood, staring up at the spiraling smoke, arms crossed over her stomach and hands clutching at her elbows.

And at the very edge of the sidewalk, almost out of sight, Grace Harper stood white-faced and stricken, stunned eyes fixed on Zee's face. She jumped in place, as if she'd been caught, and rushed out of sight.

Chapter 22

Balancing

August 16th 2017

Zee was dozing, the night after the fire somewhere between a witching hour and the first gasp of morning. Johnny was sitting up, her head propped in his lap on pillows. Her skin was greasy with burn salve and her chest stung and ached with the smoke damage, breaths broken and shallow.

The doctors had let Johnny go after running tests, baffled by his lack of any injury despite charging through the fire. And Sam, who had been the first out of the shop (her notebooks in hand) had been released not long after. They'd been less agreeable about letting Zee leave and it had taken words, and possibly magic, from Luke before the papers were finally signed.

The door creaked and Johnny flicked the sheet up over her bare skin.

"Sorry."

Zee tugged on Johnny's fingers linked with hers at the sound of Luke's voice.

"Come in," Johnny said.

"Are you...?"

"Just get in here, okay?" Johnny said, tired and rasping.

Zee heard his feet padding on the floorboards and the bed sink behind her back, Luke extra careful not to drag the sheet against her abused skin.

"I couldn't sleep..." and in the quiet that followed Zee thought she understood the missing words. *Without you.*

"I think it's a little dumb right now for us to all pretend that you don't belong right next to us anyway," Johnny muttered.

Zee took three delicate breaths, hearing the rattle from her chest, and then started to shift and turn onto her back to see Luke.

"Zoya, don't, you should be sleeping."

"But I'm not," she whispered.

Luke smelled clean, dressed in Johnny's pajama bottoms, skin pale and dark hair scattered across his chest and around his belly button. There were lines around his mouth and his eyes were pale as they swept over her, the sheet covering her but not really hiding anything from his view.

"You should've fireproofed you too," Luke mumbled, and a hand reached out to brush her curls away from her forehead.

"I did what I could," she said, thinking of that protective blue light she'd managed that had helped keep the worst of the smoke out of her lungs. "Has Sam gloated about that working yet?"

"Only a little," Johnny said. "Think she's just relieved it worked cause it saved you..."

"Give it time," they said in unison and Zee lifted her head to meet his grin with one of her own.

"I should go," Luke said. "I just wanted to see you."

"You should stay," Zee said, and then she reached up to his shoulder, and when he was too tall for that to work he bent so she could catch him.

She tugged him down, watching his eyes grow huge, flicking to Johnny and then to her mouth. The kiss was barely a brush, her mouth was chapped and felt sunburnt, but Luke hovered there, the two of them exchanging breaths. He pressed in again, achingly slow and careful and Zee's fingers held tight on the back of his neck as his lips sipped and stroked at hers until she made a soft, sweet whimper in her throat.

"Stay," she repeated the word on his open mouth.

He nodded and then Johnny's warm fingertips tapped at her's on Luke's neck. She released him and Luke looked up, guilty and hopeful, as Johnny leaned across her and wrapped his hands around the other man's face, pulling him for a hard and hungry kiss. They both groaned and below them Zee caught a breath, her body clenching in desire. Where Luke had been tender with her he was fierce with Johnny, teeth dragging and tongues thrusting until they were arched above her, hands fisted and chests pushing forward.

Luke's knee slipped on the mattress, bumping against Zee's thigh and she tried to muffle the small sound she made in response behind her hand, but they both froze above her, panting.

"I'm fine," she said, voice almost a squeak. "Keep going."

Johnny grinned, one last teasing nip on Luke's bottom lip, before sinking back down to the bed.

"Maybe later, pixie. When you can do more than watch," Johnny said, lifting the pillow with her head off his lap sliding down onto his side at her back.

Luke mirrored him, leaning in and dropping another light kiss on her lips. "I've had enough dreams to know you'll be worth the wait, Zoya," he said, voice a rumble over her skin. "Now let me help with your breathing."

His fingertips skimmed across her forehead, down her cheek and jaw and throat, slipping under the hem of the sheet to stop at her breast bones. Cool magic prickled at her chest, making her feel as if she were about to cough before spreading out, soothing at the burn in her lungs until it felt numb enough to take a deep breath.

"Knew he'd be good for something," Johnny whispered in her ear, loud enough to leave Luke narrowing his eyes.

She smiled and set her hand over Luke's as his power spread out, chasing away the hovering sting of the burns until drowsiness returned and took her under.

August 17ᵗʰ, 2017

Zee tried to resist the tickle of irritation in her chest, instead listening to the beat of Luke's heart under her ear. It was warm and humid in the backyard and every deep breath she managed almost felt like a drink of water. The small cough escaped her lips and Luke twitched on the chaise lounge beneath her.

"*Stay*," she said, pressing her palm down on his stomach.

Luke huffed and settled. "Staying," he said, amused, hand reaching up to her collar and a cold bite of magic working its way into her lungs.

He'd been suffering a need to *do something* ever since the fire. But the island was warded as well as it could be against Chernov. There was no way to keep the witch from cracking into the residents' consciousness and forcing them to wreak havoc. Still, Luke kept to his research and terrorizing the rest of the house with meditation and spellwork. It was Cameron of all people who'd asked Zee to keep him out of their hair for a few hours and the only way to do that seemed to be by sitting on him.

Gravel stirred under tires on the road past the house and they both twisted in the chaise as a small red sedan pulled in next to Johnny's car.

"Uh oh," Zee whispered.

Luke stiffened as Grace Harper emerged, pausing half-out of her car as she met their gaze.

"Who is she?" he asked, voice dark.

Zee hadn't mentioned her suspicions to the others, but she wasn't surprised to see Grace. Maybe impressed, but not surprised.

"Will you go ask Sam to make some tea?" Zee asked as Grace gathered up her courage and started to the gate.

"Not when-" he started.

"Luke, go inside," Zee said, sitting up and giving his hand a squeeze.

His jaw clenched, but he stood. "I'll be keeping an eye on you from the kitchen."

"Best second boyfriend ever," she said, winking at him.

Luke paused, his lips twitching even as his brow furrowed, amusement battling annoyance. "Can I get that on a mug?" he asked, words dry.

You can get anything on a mug, Zee thought. *And also, He's cute.*

Luke disappeared into the greenhouse, probably heading directly to alert the others as Grace approached her with halting footsteps.

"Do you want to sit?" Zee asked.

Grace chewed at her lip, fingers rolling over the cuffs of a gray hoodie that was too warm for the weather.

"I wouldn't have done it," she said. "I...don't know why I...I don't know how...I wouldn't have done it." Her eyes were pale and bloodshot and Zee watched them for a long moment until they started filling up with tears.

"Yeah," Zee said. "I know you don't like me. But I also know you don't want to kill me. Sit down and I'll explain."

Grace looked up at the sky for a long moment until the tears had vanished and then dragged a wicker chair closer to Zee.

* * *

Johnny brought tea out and then Will came with brownies, both of them dismissed back into the house, Grace looking a little curious about the change in men. Zee had just finished describing the dreams Chernov had sent her.

"That was how it started," Grace said.

"Dreams?" Zee asked.

"Yeah." Grace's gaze went distant focusing on the sunset. "After the festival. They were...I dreamt I was like you."

Zee caught the surprised dribble of tea spilling from her lips just before it fell off her chin.

"Like me?"

Grace turned her face away but Zee thought she could just make out an eye-roll. "Oh you know...all...magical and-"

"Weird," Zee finished for her.

"Magnetic," Grace said and then grimaced as if Zee had dragged it out of her.

Zee tried to put her tea mug down and nearly let it drop to the ground.

"I dreamt I was a witch," Grace said, voice catching. "That this was my island. That you never existed." She eyed Zee fidgeting in her seat and turned back to the sunset. "Haven't wanted that in a long time. And this was just...every night. Every night I was happy, I was...powerful."

"You think that if I-?" Zee started.

"No," Grace snapped. "No, I know that it was just a fantasy. Now at least I know it wasn't even really mine. But it just kept coming." She fussed at the torn knee of her jeans. "And then it was in the daytime too. There was this...other version of me, with me. And she was so angry and so trapped and...It wasn't me. It was him," she said, firm.

"Yes," Zee said. And she she thought that some of that person, that resentment, had been Grace. That was how Chernov must have found her. Bitter eyes on Zee and Johnny at the festival, or around town. It didn't matter. For the first time, in a long time, Zee really felt like it didn't matter if Grace Harper hated her.

"She felt like me," Grace said quietly. "She...taught me things."

"He almost got me to drown myself," Zee said, as if in consolation. She watched the sun sinking for a moment before the words really settled in her own head. "Grace. What did he teach you?"

August 18th 2017

Johnny's breaths had evened out, shifting into those snuffling little snores of deep sleep, and Zee was still laying in bed with her eyes open. She rolled over and there was Luke, staring up at the ceiling, one arm under her neck, the other stretched back on the bed. She nudged his leg with her toes and he turned to smile at her, neck stretching to kiss her. She took the kiss, and then another for good measure, before climbing over him and standing up from the bed.

He sat up and she pushed him back down, whispering, "I'm going to see Sam and Nadia. I'll be back."

He relaxed, gaze following her as she snuck out into the hall.

Cameron was snoring on the bed, but Zee could see Sam's silhouette on the balcony and she joined her there. Nadia was on Sam's other side, more than a blur and shadow for the first time in weeks. Sam's hands were wrapped around the bannister and Nadia, the delicate gray outline of her with stars shimmering through her eyes and cheeks, leaned into her cousin's shoulder.

"The solar eclipse," Sam said.

"I remember," Zee said. "It's only a few days away."

Sam's lips pressed together and Zee couldn't tear her eyes away from Nadia's small smile, trying to translate its shape. Did she have a crinkle in the corners of her eyes? Was it for sympathy or laughter?

"I don't...I can't tell how it turns out yet," Sam said.

You've closed the gate with me inside.

It took Zee a moment, fear spiking up her spine, to realize that Chernov's words were only a memory, not the echo of his power influencing her thoughts.

When he goes, so will I, Nadia said. She curled around Sam's back and then fit herself between them both. Her touch on Zee's elbow was a soft spot of warmth, a little radiant of heat soothing at nerves.

"You're not sacrificing yourself," Zee whispered, pleased with how firm she sounded. She would have gone in Nadia's place. In Sam's place. Again and again, she would have chosen them first. They would too, of course, which seemed to be a family problem.

Not if I don't have to, Nadia said, and Zee read the sly smirk and the equally stubborn star-gaze expression on her aunt's face. It wasn't really an agreement. *But I think...I think he is the end of my story, no matter what. When he is gone, you will both be safe. And you will be loved. That's all I need.*

"That's stupid," Sam said, lips turning white between her teeth before she burst out with, "Who'll watch all the babies Zee's bound to start popping out? Two pesnya dushis? She'll never stop nursing!"

"Shut the fuck up," Zee snapped, as her stomach flipped in surprise. Cameron snorted in the bedroom behind them and then went back to his heavy snores.

She found Sam's hand on the bannister and their fingers tangled together until Zee's knuckles hurt with the grip. But she didn't let go.

Nadia hummed in her head, happy and quiet and seeming peaceful in way that made Zee's brittle heart crack and her shoulders soften with relief.

Eric and Will will do fine as babysitters.

There was, unfortunately, no arguing with that. So instead Zee said to Sam, "Don't you *dare* start prophesying any offspring in the stars or I'll slip fertility potions in every substance that gets within a half-inch of your lips."

"Shhh," Sam hissed. "You'll give Cameron's subconscious ideas."

You've closed the gate...

"I..." Zee stalled, thoughts spinning nervously in her head. "I think I have an idea."

Chapter 23

Union Reunion

August 20ˢᵗ 2017

It started off as a very good day.

She was laying on her side, sandwiched between Johnny and Luke in bed, chewing her lip and blinking up at texture of the ceiling and trying to decide what *exactly* she should do about the two cocks poking her at either side. There were so many options—some of which would have to be tabled for a later date, but plenty left were worth considering. Johnny nestled in closer and Zee lifted her thigh to rest it over Luke's hip, and suddenly they were both thrusting forward, hard lengths meeting between her thighs, brushing against each other through sleep pants.

Luke groaned, mouth falling loose and eyes squeezing shut and then just as he began to pull away, Zee wrapped an arm around his back. His eyes popped open, right in front of hers, brow tangled.

"Fuck," Johnny grunted from her back and she felt him jerking his hips in needy thrusts, Luke's breath catching in time with the movement.

"Please stay for morning sex," she said, bumping her nose to Luke's, pecking at his tightly folded lips.

"Aw, Jesus, *finally*," Johnny pleaded.

Luke's expression relaxed fraction by fraction with the invitation, the begging, until he was smiling. He raised his eyebrows at Zee.

"Sounds like someone needs our attention,' Luke murmured.

Johnny moaned and Zee felt his hard cock tapping between her thighs. She grinned at Luke and nodded and then they both sprung into action. Zee climbed over to Johnny's far side, throwing the sheet back and finding the head of his cock peeking out of the waistband of his pajamas, like he'd already been halfway to freeing it. Luke had Johnny pinned to the mattress in a half-second, fingers fisting through blonde hair, rough stubble scraping against soft lips as Johnny squirmed and whimpered beneath him.

Zee pulled him loose from the pajama pants, ducking down to lick away the pre-cum gathered at the tip. She lapped around the head of him, hands stroking over his thighs, sucking him gently into her mouth until Johnny was one long, taut muscle straining.

"Shit, shit, shit," he panted as Luke sucked noisily along his neck, hand trailing down to join Zee's at the base of Johnny's cock. "Wait. Oh fuck, wait or I'll finish. I wanna watch. I wanna watch you two."

Luke backed away, but Zee continued to play, teasing Johnny's weakest spots until his voice was high and cracking, and he was twitching on her tongue. She leaned back, satisfied with the heave of Johnny's gasping breaths and the way that Luke's eyes were blown black at the sight of her straddled over Johnny's lap. Her nightgown was wadded up high on her hips and she tugged it the rest of the way over her head.

Luke's lids turned heavy as he took her in. "Moon bloom," he said, the words so sweet on his tongue it made her flush.

"Come back here, pixie," Johnny said, patting the bed between him and Luke. "Right here, I wanna watch."

Zee sank back between them on her side, Luke tilting her chin to his as he ducked down, licking at the seam of her lips before stroking his tongue into her mouth. It was a heady kiss, magic like sun in winter glittering through her veins and turning her weak until she was leaning back into his chest, arms circling his neck as he mouthed wetly down her neck. Johnny's hands were covering her breasts, squeezing and rolling and crouching down to suck at her nipples, cock laying heavily on her thigh.

"She's so small," Luke said into her throat. "How do you manage her?"

Zee raised an eyebrow and Johnny grinned, pulling away from her breast with a 'pop'. "Don't let that fool you," he said. "She rides hard."

Zee grinned and moaned as Luke marked her shoulders with scratches of his teeth and soft kisses. She ran her fingertip up and down Johnny's length where it touched her, watching him shiver in response, his hands clenched on the pillow behind his head. Luke's hands covered the tops of her thighs, fingers dipping between her folds, spreading her open and toying with her clit, his hips nestling closer.

"Save riding for another time. I want to hold you," Luke whispered in her ear, and then he was pressing against her back, his cock sliding between her folds against her pussy.

She whined at the touch, the head of him nudging her clit and spread her knees wider apart as he lifted her leg up over Johnny's hip. Johnny's eyes were fixed between her legs watching where they touched one another, and one hand reached down to stroke and squeeze at his own length. Luke's cock nudged at her opening, his chest pushing forward at her back until her breasts were pressed to Johnny's chest, their mouths on her neck, shoulders, cheeks.

"I want to fill you, Zoya, " Luke said, voice tight. "I've been dreaming of it for months."

"You witches and your sex dreams," Johnny teased, gifting them with that sunbeam smile, one hand sliding over Zee's sides to play between her legs, scarred fingertips catching against her clit and making her head drop with a throaty cry. "Now, she's ready," Johnny said over her shoulder.

And Luke pressed in, not quite as thick as Johnny but longer, sliding in deeper until Zee was shaking, mouth opened and breaths coming at a rapid pace. Luke kissed the back of her neck, the both of them sighing, Johnny moaning in front of them, hips circling up to nudge at where they were joined, cock slippery and soft against her clit.

"Oh god, the both of you. Somebody, move," Zee begged, eyes squeezed shut, blood thrumming.

Johnny obeyed with an eagerness she knew by heart, but Luke only wrapped his arms around her, hips nudging softly and *still* making her see stars.

"Tease him for me, Zoya," Luke said, brushing her hair over her shoulder to kiss her opposite cheek. "I want to see you both fall apart."

Zee relaxed, Johnny's neck stretching up to reach her mouth in a sloppy, licking kiss as Luke cuddled close, cock pumping in long, thorough drags, breath puffing on her back. She scratched her nails over Johnny's chest, up and down, teasing further each time until her fingertips were sliding through the hair at the base of his cock. Her hand wrapped around him, bumping against his own hand, twisting and making him bite at her lip.

"Come on, pixie," Johnny mumbled into her cheek. "Make him break."

Zee rocked, every shift rubbing Johnny's fingers against her clit, but rewarded with a new sound of Luke's control unravelling. Luke held her hips in his hands, working her over his length, hips starting to snap with urgency. His mouth wrapped around her shoulder, burying a groan as she squeezed him inside of her.

"Please," she whispered, voice crack. "Please, Luke, Johnny."

They answered her, one of Luke's hands curving around the back of her neck as he leaned back, hips thrusting quicker, making Johnny's touch on her clit rough and frantic. The summer was turning humid in her bedroom alone, none of Luke's magic enough to cool the heat in her veins, the gathering pressure of pleasure skidding through her bones and settling in her center.

Zee felt like her pleasure was at the very tip of a sewing needle, waiting to tip, and then Luke's fingers tangled with her hair, tugging lightly, and Johnny nudged against her clit and she came apart with a muffled scream, body shaking between them. Luke rolled over onto his back, taking her with him, feet bracing on the bed as he readied to race to his finish.

"Wait, wait," Johnny said, scrambling after them. "I want to taste. Taste you both. C'mere pixie."

Zee let him pull her off Luke who groaned and arched, as if to chase her warmth, and then Johnny was crawling between Luke's thighs, tongue lapping up the other man's stiff length, before sucking him between his lips.

"Fuuuuck, Johnny." Luke was gasping up at the ceiling before reaching out to Zee, his other hand diving into Johnny's sun bleached hair. "*Fuck.*"

Zee bit her lip, torn between watching Johnny work a practiced mouth over Luke's cock—she could learn a thing or two from that mouth—and giving Luke some way to occupy his need. She lay down at his side, pulling his face to hers, before he seemed to lose control, clutching her hair in his fist and fucking his tongue into her mouth with the same rhythm of Johnny's bobbing lips.

Luke tore away with a loud groan, "Stop. Together. Johnny get up here."

Johnny didn't wait for another order, climbing over Luke's chest, their cocks bumping against one another until, as if they'd been reading each other's mind, all three of them wrapped their hands around the aching flesh. Johnny and Luke moaned into a shared kiss, Zee mouthing at shoulders and arms and necks as she felt them rutting into their grips. An arm circled her back, squeezing her so close she was almost pressed between them, could feel the echoing push and retreat as they growled and pumped to their shared finish.

Johnny tore away from the kiss first, his teeth latching onto Zee's shoulder with a muffled shout, and she felt him twitching against her palm. And then Luke was hissing through gritted teeth, back bowing off the bed, and they were all one terrible, lovely, sticky heap. Johnny was heavy on top for a moment, before groaning and rolling past Zee, grabbing his pants from the foot of the bed and wiping the majority of the mess away, a dopey, dazed smile curling over his lips.

Luke panted, chest heaving beneath her cheek, and then turned them, curling against her side, and pressing his face to her neck as Johnny fitted close from the other side. They held her there, hands grazing over her skin until they were both soft and almost back to sleep again. Lips made soft passes over the tops of heads and across necks and shoulders.

"The dreams are...understatements," Luke said eventually, his face tucked into her dark curls.

She hummed her agreement and Luke draped an arm over the pair of them.

"We keep this up and you'll both be so charged full of magic, Chernov won't know what hit him," Johnny said, a proud grin stretched across his features.

"I love you," Johnny said in her ear at the coffee maker.

Luke was out on the lawn with the others, draped in a chair like the most relaxed oversized cat. She was feeling a little smug about *how* relaxed he looked, in fact.

"I love you," she answered.

She thought he might crack a jaw with that smile until it quirked and settled and he said, "I thought so."

She snorted and pushed him back, letting their fingers twist together and savoring the fuzzy flutter of happy nerves buzzing through her. Soon this would be all three of them.

"Come to New York with me. I'll buy you and Luke tickets," he said, tugging her back into his side.

"Can't. Sam and I have the insurance people to deal with." Johnny wrinkled his nose at this answer and Zee continued, "Both owners need to be there. And I'm not sure it's a good idea for me to leave right now."

He combed his fingers through his hair and his brow

furrowed. "You know I can tell when you're worried, right? If you're worried then I'm worried, about *you*."

"I didn't mean-"

"I know, but I can cancel."

"It's just one day," Zee said, looping her arms around his waist and resting her chin on his chest. "Luke and Sam and I can handle one day."

"Given this summer, that doesn't make me less nervous," Johnny said, raising his eyebrows.

"I will call if *anything* happens," she said.

Johnny sighed and she knew she'd won. "Still doesn't make me feel better," he said.

"I love you?" she offered.

His smile flickered back and he grimaced around it in happy irritation.

She would pay for that trick later. But he would forgive her too. They had a rhythm going now and Zee finally felt like she had found her footing.

* * *

"I can stay," she said for the fifth time.

Luke was curled up like a black cat on the sun room couch in his t-shirt and ripped jeans, toes peeking out. He looked up as she entered and waited for her to sit next to him before leaning into her side, an arm wrapping over her shoulder. He kissed her temple, fingertips sliding under the collar of her t-shirt.

"No, moon bloom. I want you far from here today," he said.

"It shouldn't be you," Zee said, turning her face until the ends of their noses touched.

"Yes it should. Bit of penance, for all the trouble I

caused earlier," he said, smile crooking in the corner, eyes soaking her up one freckle at a time. "Go to work. Come home. Defeat Chernov. And then we'll start our plans, yes?"

Zee laughed and Luke's gaze took on a rare warmth, green eyes deepening.

"Everything's going to be alright," Zee said, taking Luke's chin between her fingers and stretching up for a kiss.

He licked at her lips, sucked softly on the top, and then the bottom. His arms circled her back, drew her up onto his lap all while teasing her mouth with gentle nips and sips.

"Everything will be fine, Zoya," he said, words gravel in his throat. "Go to work. Come home."

"Defeat Chernov," Zee said with a single nod, and then Luke released her.

* * *

"Luke, we're home," Zee called as she shut the door behind her and Sam. The house was dark and the floor felt uneven under her feet. There was a shadow stretching down the hall from the warm light of the kitchen. "Will and Cameron back yet?"

Luke's footsteps were too heavy on the floor, like the gait of a much larger person.

"No, the storm must be keeping them out on the water," Luke said, voice careful, a haughtiness there that had been missing for days.

Zee conjured a smile for him and nodded to Sam as she passed them on her way to the kitchen. "Alrighty, how's the house?" Zee asked.

Luke paced closer, a smirk sliding onto his lips as he stopped in front of her. "Secure, love" he said, bending his head for a kiss.

Zee raised her hand between them, stopping his lips with a touch.

"Did you think I wouldn't see you?" Zee asked, tone flat and watched him stiffen. "Hiding inside of my own lover? Wearing him like a mask?"

Luke straightened, towering over her tilting his head until the light behind him put his profile in silhouette, the edges of light revealing the way his features didn't quite fit together, something too big stuffed inside the elegant face.

"I admit," Chernov said from Luke's lips. "You have done a great deal of work on him in a small amount of time. But I appreciate his familiarity, and proximity to you, dear. To this house, my little red flower's palace so far out of reach."

"Yeah, I thought you might feel that way," Zee said, heart pounding in her chest. "Sam and Luke thought so too. So this morning we bound him."

Chernov blinked with Luke's narrow green eyes, face shifting into a sharp edged frown. Something feral. But Zee had seen Luke that morning, every inch of his face lined with sweetness and trust and the illusion of Chernov was nothing but a bad trick.

"Feeling...grounded?" Zee asked, raising an eyebrow. "...Trapped?"

Chernov took a heavy step forward, a delicate hand raised in a claw and then stopped abruptly, body heaving in place as if it had taken a hit.

"Or maybe you're just getting predictable," Zee said with a shrug. Chernov snarled at her and Zee pushed off the door. "I just got off the phone with Will and Cameron, by the way. They're on their way back from the docks. Johnny and Eric will have a flight soon. And I'm sure we'll have a few other visitors before too long."

"Where is *she*?" Chernov hissed, voice labored as he pushed Luke against his bindings. He could do no harm inside of Luke. He could go no farther than the bounds of their property. And he could not leave Luke's body. Zee had locked the gate with him inside.

Zee walked up to Luke's side, watched Chernov thrash inside his cage, unable to reach out and inflict whatever harm he was dreaming of. "You won't be seeing her," Zee said against Luke's cheek. "You won't ever be seeing her."

A growl rolled up out of Luke's chest, foreign and deeper, like rockfall.

"We saw you coming in with that storm out on the sea," Zee said. "And he was waiting here to meet you."

"You've martyred him," Chernov said, spit popping from Luke's lips as his shoulders twisted uncomfortably like he was trying to squirm out of his own skin.

Zee swallowed as footsteps came up the front steps and she stepped back. "I hope not," she said.

Maybe they had, she thought. Maybe Chernov would win *again* and take Luke with him and...

Would Johnny forgive them?

Cameron and Will walked into the house and before Chernov could react, Cameron had lifted Luke and thrown him over his shoulder. He was snarling and bucking and roaring as Cam walked him down the hall back to the kitchen.

Will sighed heavily at Zee's side. "You shouldn't have waited to tell us," he said.

"I needed to make sure the binding would hold," Zee said.

"No, I get your reasoning," Will said. "But you shouldn't have waited. Johnny's gonna be mad."

Zee scrubbed her hands over her face. "I know. Sam and I need to go undo our bindings..."

Will blinked. "You bound yourself too?"

"Of course." She shrugged. "We didn't know who he'd choose. Hey, be careful in there. Just because he *should* be contained doesn't mean he's safe."

Will stared down the hall where Luke was still screaming bloody murder from the kitchen. Zee hadn't ever even heard of half the curse words he was using.

"Right," Will said, his shoulders stiffening like he was going into battle.

She bit her lip, wondering if she shouldn't wait, keep an eye on Chernov herself. But she trusted Cameron and Will to keep Luke in line and she trusted Sam to keep *them* in line too. So she headed upstairs to where Nadia was waiting in her bathroom to guide her through unravelling the bindings.

Chapter 24

The Solar Eclipse

⁓) ꓲ ꓒ ● ꓯ ꓒ ꓲ ⁓

August 21ˢᵗ 2017

Johnny and Eric arrived somewhere between the dead of the night and obscenely early. Zee, Cameron, Sam, and Will were propped up around the kitchen listening to a drugged Luke slur between some old Slavic tongue and violent curses. Zee had grown tired of the screaming about an hour in and had force fed her lover a sedative tea with the help of Cam's muscles. Still, no one had given up their vigil of keeping an eye on the only semi-tamed Chernov.

"*...Blood running from the seam of your lips...*" The words devolved into the foreign tongue as the rest of their party stopped in the kitchen doorway.

"He's been spouting nightmare omens at us for hours," Zee said, drooping on the floor against the sink cabinet.

Johnny took one look at her and left the kitchen. Zee let her head thunk back against the wooden door. 'I love you's in the morning. Silent treatment by night. No more than she deserved though.

But he came back a few minutes later with her blanket and pillow and an armload of couch cushions and made her a bed on the kitchen floor. It had a clear sightline of Luke—strapped down to a kitchen chair, head lolling uncomfortably while his lips shuddered with unconscious nastiness.

"It could have been any of us," Zee whispered to Johnny.

"Is that supposed to reassure me?" he asked, head tilted, eyes narrowed.

"No, I just… didn't want you to think I had set up him up," she said.

Johnny's face fell and he dropped his forehead to hers. "I know you better than that. Settle in, pixie," he said, patting the cushions. He kissed her as she tilted her head back and spread the blanket up to her shoulders, sitting down at her knees and slipping her hand into his.

* * *

"Who's the hottie out in the yard suntanning?" Maria James asked, arriving in the early morning with two full coffee carriers and a basket of triple chocolate muffins over her arm, dressed in tidy linen and cotton.

Zee blinked at the other woman. Maria looked like she'd walked off the set of a catalog photo shoot and zee was wearing the same clothes as the day before. Also, her hair was sticking up on one side and the couch cushion impressions might not have faded off her face yet. Maybe she should have showered before the others arrived.

"That's…" Zee trailed off and looked around for someone to save her until Johnny appeared from the hall.

"Our boyfriend," Johnny said, taking a coffee and the basket of muffins.

Zee had asked Johnny to gather up anyone who was likely to take the situation *seriously*. They needed a good number, like nine, and she had come to a complete blank at the thought of who to call. Maria James might not have been on her short list. But who would have?

"You're welcome to go talk to him," Johnny said and Zee whipped her head in his direction. "No coffee though."

"What? Is he... fasting or something?" Maria asked, brow wrinkling.

"Or something," Zee said taking the coffee carriers.

Maria headed out to the backyard.

"I'll go mediate," Johnny said, following Maria out. "But that's the best way to explain the situation to her."

Zee returned to the kitchen with the sense that she was sleepwalking. Brian Grimm was at the counter with Will. *Grace Harper* was on her way. With Cam and Sam, and if Maria James didn't run screaming out of her yard, they would be nine.

Now Zee knew for certain the house had never been so full.

Maria came into the kitchen through the greenhouse, face pale as Johnny trailed behind her. She stopped at the threshold and scanned the room, eyes landing on Zee.

"What the hell is that?" she asked, arm pointing limply back into the yard.

Zee could just see the edge of the chair where Luke was contained. Eric was on the greenhouse steps keeping an eye on him. Cameron had an eyeline from the kitchen table, Sam at his side. But it had been a long night. And none of them were so eager to get close to Chernov's vitriol spitting mouth again.

"That is who was responsible for the scene at the docks

during the festival, and my night of sleepwalking, and the fire at the shop," Zee said.

"Is he ill?" Maria asked, brow furrowing.

"He's possessed," Johnny said.

Grace Harper was coming in from the hall and Zee twisted in place to block Johnny at her back.

"What's she doing here?" he whispered.

Grace cocked her head to the side as she stared back at Zee and then said, "I kind of assumed it'd be you in the chair."

Johnny's hands on her sides twitched but Zee was too tired to take offense. Or maybe she agreed.

Grace had only managed contrition for as long as it took Zee to outline what she and Sam needed her to do. And then Grace had simply been cooperative. And surprisingly helpful. And a little bit terrifying if Zee was being honest. It occurred to her that if Grace hadn't been shocked and appalled by the fire at the Lab, by her part in it, Chernov would have had another dangerously potent ally on his team.

"Sorry to disappoint," Zee said with a half smile and Grace's lips twitched before she wove her way into the room, settling in the pantry doorway by Will.

"Possession," Maria repeated, with a raised eyebrow. But her gaze flicked to the yard. And then to the other occupants of the room. Grace made a little accommodating tilt of the head and Maria looked back to Zee. "Okay."

She didn't sound convinced. But she didn't look ready to argue with her on the topic. Yet.

The front door opened again and Nadia was at Zee's side.

Nine, she said. *They're all here.*

Nine people. Nine people and Luke holding Chernov.

It was a full coven. Three had always been their number. Nadia, Sam and Zee. Three women working together in a harmony born out of family and a wealthy inheritance of power. And now, three times as many. Half of whom she'd barely known before this summer. She'd even considered Grace, *Johnny*, enemies. Well, she wasn't sure what Grace was now. Not a friend, exactly, but something. And Johnny, Will and Eric, they were as good as family.

It was still a few good hours before they had to start. That gave Zee and Sam some time to train Grace and Brian and Maria in the art of ritual.

Everyone was looking at Zee.

"So what exactly are we doing here?" Maria asked.

"Well...That's...that's going to take awhile to explain," Zee said, voice wobbling. Johnny's hand squeezed at her side and Nadia was stirring and shifting. "But first...first I just need you to believe that...that any of this has a basis in reality, I suppose. So I'm going to show you something."

Johnny stepped away and Sam took her place, fingers sliding into Zee's. Zee held out her free hand to Nadia. Maria was standing just a few feet past and she shifted, brow furrowing as she met her gaze as if asking if the hand was some offer to her. But then Nadia's fingers, wispy soft breezes, settled into Zee's grip.

She shivered and leaned into Sam's side as her breath caught. Nadia met her gaze and Zee felt the tug of energy, her skin going clammy. The room took a collective inhale as Nadia's edges hardened and her colors deepened.

"This is our aunt Nadia," Zee said, smiling and pretending that her voice was thin because of the energy transfer and not because it always felt so good to *see* Nadia. She added, for good measure, "She's a ghost."

* * *

There was a stack of cellphones on the kitchen island, shut down with dark screens. Eric was helping Sam pick herbs in the greenhouse while the others were running over Zee's written list of the ritual. Maria was silently practicing a chant, brow twisted skeptically as she tried to wrap her tongue around an old slavic word, unaware as Nadia whispered helpfully in her ear.

Johnny and Cameron came to the kitchen in from hauling out the old wooden bath tub up from the cellar to where Luke was hoarsely caterwauling on the lawn. They met Zee at the cauldron. Johnny had a knot in his forehead that had been there since before he'd left Zee the morning before. His eyes were watching Luke, worry and fear and a little shame mixing together.

"Is this going to work?" Johnny asked.

"Luke will be himself by the end," Zee said. She met Johnny's eyes and spoke with as much firm certainty as she could press into her words, "That's a guarantee."

Johnny's shoulders eased a fraction and he nodded, lowering his eyes.

Zee leaned in and he was there, his arm curving warmly over her shoulder. "I don't know if Chernov will be...gone," she admitted. "Permanently. I don't know what state he's actually in. But if we don't... if this isn't over today I should at least have a better idea of what to do next."

She needed it to be over. Nadia was rallying for her and Sam, but her aunt was fading. Zee wanted to dig her fingers into whatever thin fragments of Nadia were left on this earth and *ground them*. Save them. But as much as she refused to listen to the words, she knew that Nadia's remaining spirit was what tethered Chernov. And Sam and

Zee, their struggle of acceptance and love and having a *home* was what tethered Nadia.

Eric squeezed in between Zee and Cameron, scattering handfuls of herbs into the cauldron and pressing a quick, light kiss to Zee's hair as he left. Cam's hand squeezed briefly at her shoulder before heading out to stand vigil with Sam over Luke. Johnny's arms wrapped loosely around Zee's stomach as she stirred in the additions.

She glanced over her shoulder and watched the crowd in the kitchen weave and work around each other. The sanctuary of the house was suddenly full of new energies that bounced off one another and blended in a noisy, cluttered kind of harmony.

"If you had asked I could have found you another nine people to come here and help," Johnny said in her ear. "Not one of them would ask why."

"Are you telling me I've been wrong about the island this whole time?" Zee asked, but there was no heat in the words.

"I'm telling you..." he hummed for a moment, going over his words. "I guess I'm starting to think that the best way of teaching the island how to accept you is to..."

"Teach them how to exorcise a horrible witch's influence from my lover?" she asked, fighting a smile.

"You know what I mean," Johnny said.

She nodded. "I do."

"I love you," they said.

* * *

It was far too hot out for this kind of work, Zee thought. Luke, trapped to the kitchen chair, was flushed red with the heat and possibly burnt from the sun. His hair was inky with sweat, sticking to his face, clothes tangled in strange directions from all his thrashing. He snarled, teeth snapping in Eric's direction as he helped Will and Cameron drag him inside of the circle. A circle, a coven; of neighbors Zee had never once considered doing any kind of ceremony with before this month. Of even telling them about rituals.

But now Grace Harper was lighting candles around a wide ring of her backyard while Sam was pouring clean seawater into the herbal bath Zee and Eric had made. Maria was standing next to Brian, taking his rough hand firmly in hers and ignoring the slightly dazzled expression he was giving her. Zee looked again and realized that, no, the woman wasn't ignoring it. She was preening—almost so slightly you couldn't see it, with a small lift of her chin and a twist in her lips—under Brian's gaze.

"The longer you trap me in him, the less of your lover remains," Chernov hissed, Luke's voice ragged from most of a day's vocal wrath. Zee didn't answer. There was a shattered scream from Luke's throat as the chair sank into the the wooden bathtub. The water bubbled dangerously for a moment and then swirled restlessly around Luke's legs, the leg of his pants darkening as the moisture soaked in.

"Close the circle," Zee said, urgent as she stepped forward and knelt in front of the bath. Luke's bindings were loosening under Chernov's strain and the banishing influence of the solar eclipse layered with the new moon. The timing was too precise for the ritual and it made her heart thump nervously.

"You think you can hex me into oblivion, little witch? I will take him with me. I will find my sweet red flower here, I can smell her on you," Chernov ranted and then stopped abruptly as Sam and Will joined hands.

Zee felt it in her chest as the circle closed, as if the

world had been sideways for so many years and suddenly settled itself back to flat again. She glanced around her in surprise. It was an odd collection of people, some of whom she barely knew and yet...the circle was balanced.

"That was-" Maria's eyes were bright, excited.

"Start the chant," Will said.

"We bind our circle with the strength of the earth,
We bind our circle with the beat of our breathing,
We bind our circle with the heat of the flame,
We bind our circle with the crash of the waves."

It was clumsy at first, with Zee and Sam carrying the words for the others. But in bits and pieces it came together until the chorus of voices drowned out the cursing from Luke's lips. Zee could pick up the threads from every person. Eric's curious breeze versus Sam's gathering wind. Cameron's heavy tide and Brian's fathomless well. Johnny's blaze burning across from Grace's simmering coals. Will's burrowing roots and Maria's immoveable mountain.

It was as much a surprise as a confirmation of the people she had known *of* but not *known* for most of her life.

Meanwhile Chernov was settling in front of her even as the water in the tub swirled faster around Luke's legs. There was a tangle of anger in the man's eyes that was so strong it made Zee want to crawl away. But his body was sagging in the seat and his head was starting to loll.

Zee's hands slammed down over the hemp ropes that bound Luke's arms to the chair.

"You're not taking him," Zee said, pressing power into the words, drawing more from the circle around her as they chanted.

Chernov had flooded Luke's body. Zee searched for the icy lick of magic she loved but there was no trace left. Chernov was squatting in Luke and in his mind, corrupting him with that sticky red residue of power. There was a flicker, a curl of slippery and snagging sensation at Zee's wrist and she yanked herself away before Chernov could get a grip on her.

The words died and settled around the circle as the sky shifted above them, the faintest gray-green tinge spreading in the sky.

"It's starting," Will said just as Chernov shuddered in the chair and the water sloshed in the bath as if the whole thing had been kicked.

"Keep going," Zee said.

"We call upon air for swift endings,

We call upon fire, to burn away darkness,

We call upon water, to wash away cruelty,

We call upon earth, to hold and bury."

Luke groaned and his eyes fluttered, rolling eerily beneath his lids. The circle around them was creating a thin bubble of power, something that wavered in the air like steam. It was enough to settle a weight over Chernov, over Luke by extension, but Zee could see the way it might only amount to pressure and pain for him. And not a resolution. She glanced at Johnny and found him watching her. Whatever he read in her face made the knot of concentration on his forehead deepen into a scowl. But he nodded. Not in permission, since that wasn't something Zee was about *ask* for, but in acceptance.

"You're not taking him," Zee repeated in a hiss, leaning in close to Luke's face. Green eyes, slitted and bloodshot with the heat, sparked against Zee's gaze.

"Careful, ved'mitchka, or you'll kill us both," Chernov rattled out, barely lifting Luke's chin.

"You're seriously underestimating him," Zee whispered. Then her fingers caught at the knots in the rope, Chernov jerking under her touch. Weak nibbles of irritated and caged power nipped at her fingers as she worked and Brian and Maria's voices stumbled as she dragged Luke's body out of the chair, letting it sag into the bath of spelled purification water.

Luke screeched and thrashed like a cat until Zee tossed the chair out of the water and pushed his body back down into the water, climbing in after him. Chernov's scream turned into a cackle as the water surged as if it had the weight of an ocean behind it, grasping at her waist with that iron band arm she'd dreamt of in the beginning of the summer.

"We'll all go together," he growled.

"Then I deserve to see your face," Zee said. And then with every synapse in her brain and cell in her body and every bit of focus she had struggled to tame growing up under Nadia's gentle tutelage and all the strength Luke demanded of her, she *pressed in*.

It was like a beam of light running up against the densest smoke. There was no illumination cutting through the darkness, only the sudden absorption of clarity into black fog. She was in the middle of the circle, a wall of strength building around her, and then she was lost. Chernov was a black hole and Zee had thrown herself in, had sacrificed Luke to be erased by this. Never mind Johnny, would she ever forgive *herself* for this?

There was a sense of gravity, of falling through emptiness. Or maybe the feeling of something being dragged over her, not sinking into the hole, but of the hole rising up around to contain her. She was soaking in an ink so black it would transform all her shape and color into nothing. She had come here to vanish.

Which was...

Not right.

She had come here to...to *see him*. To see Chernov, see what was really left of him, this giant of a man who had haunted Nadia, had scratched and scrambled through time and space to torture what was left of her on this Earth.

Luke.

She had come here to save Luke. Just like he'd agreed to this plan to save her.

And Chernov had let her in. Either too confident to see her as a threat, or too weak to stop her.

So Zee relaxed, locating the terror in her thoughts and untangling it into thin threads and then brushing them away. She found the panic in her muscles and uncoiled it until the sensation of falling settled and passed. The roar in her ears hushed into the whisper of quiet and the deep gasp of unsteady breaths. The black faded to gray and the gray began to take on shape around her.

The room was smokey, clogged up with incense and candle wicks snapping and spitting heat into the cramped space. It reminded Zee of a cellar, or a mausoleum, with arched walls of stone and floors that seemed more dirt than floorboard. There were two narrow windows covered in grease and soot across from Zee that let in a dim but scarlet light. There were three figures kneeling on the floor, supplicants or statues—it was hard to tell for how still they held themselves. Their hands were braced on the frame of a low platform. For a moment Zee thought they were praying to a crumpled pile of rags.

And then the rags gasped and Zee saw the impression of a body, a map of brittle bones draped in a patchwork of fabrics.

"She...is...here," a voice like a creaking door said from the bed.

Zee braced herself, waiting for a strike. From the frail creature on the bed that simmered and boiled with magic. From the three people who fed the turmoil of power with a blank focus. She moved closer, up to the shoulder of an old man on the floor who seemed almost near sleeping except for the subtle twitch of his head as she stopped behind him.

Chernov was on the bed.

Just an old man, he growled in her head. It was the voice of the man from seventy years ago. Not the broken note of the body on the bed.

He looked like a deconstructed man. Something made out of wax. A thin covering over the skeleton form of a body unbuilt.

He had turned Luke near mad, pulled birds from the sky and slithered into Zee's and Grace's dreams. He was the most powerful thing Zee had ever seen. But he *was* just a frail old man. She had wondered how he could be anything else, and wondered how someone who *must* be withering away could do so much awful.

"Do you expect me to feel bad for you?" Zee asked.

She imagined the rattle that sounded around her was laughter, but it could just as easily have been a warning bell.

Do you expect me to give up and die? He asked.

Oh, how nice that would be, Zee thought.

Did you gather your novices and expect them to measure up against my best pupils?

"I expected them to keep Luke safe," Zee said.

The cavernous face on the bed rolled toward her, eyes sunken in and shining wet and red in her direction, blue gray skin turned violet in the sinking sunlight. *Then you expect to best me yourself.*

"I came to make a deal."

The air rattled again, and this time she was sure it was

with satisfaction. There was an accompanying wheeze from the bed.

Giving up the dead for the living.

"Do you believe in it, the *pesnya dushi?*" There was a long pause so Zee added. "Do you believe that it destines you to be with her? Nadia."

Yesssss, hissed the voice in her head.

"She's already dead," Zee said.

Chernov's body coughed, or maybe scoffed, from the bed. *Our souls will entwine in the afterlife. You know this. You have found your partners.*

Zee felt a warm bud of love for Johnny. "I chose them," she said and the old man coughed again so she repeated it, "I chose them. Johnny was always going to shape my life. As you shaped Nadia's. But *I* chose him. Just like I chose to give Luke a chance to be who he deserved to be, away from you. Do you think I'm wrong?"

I think you're naive...and hopeful.

"I think I'm right," Zee said. "But I understand that you *are* a very old man. So you'll assume you know better. Would you like to find out?" He was quiet and this time Zee waited.

Does she know?

"She's there, watching," Zee said.

And she trusts your scheme? Believes she will be free of me?

"Honestly, I'm not sure that matters to her," Zee said, a horrible burning ache in her chest. "She wants us safe. But I trust my scheme, or I wouldn't be here giving you this choice. Give up this..." she hesitated over the word, "Life? Release Luke. Nadia is ready to pass on."

Chernov sighed on the bed, a wisp of breath, and the three kneeling men held their position. They looked almost as old as their master and Zee wondered how they would get up from the floor without any help. Were there others waiting? Did Chernov generate this semblance of life with shifts of people pumping magic into him day and night?

"Leave...us..." The words came with pauses so long between them that they felt almost unrelated. But first one man on the floor stirred, and then another. Slowly, carefully, with what Zee imagined were bitten off groans of discomfort, the men rose from the floor and turned their haggard faces to the space behind Zee, passing around and almost through her until the room was empty.

She was over the bed and there were milky white and bloodshot eyes rolling in their sockets, searching for her.

Hurry, your soul song is fading.

Zee plunged forward with her thoughts, gripping at the strings and flickers of life left in Chernov and then dragged them both out of the vision, leaving a wasted, empty body behind on the bed, lifeless.

She sat up in the water of the bath, gasping. Luke was kicking in her hands and there was a hurricane of water around them. The color of the sky had turned stranger overhead, bright and dim all at once, some cross between the yellow of after a storm and the gray of dawn and the crimson of sunset. Outside of the torrent the wavering figures of the circle stood tall, their shapes twisted and magnified by the gate of wild water.

"Zoya!" Luke twisted in her hands, eyes wide and startled, face blurred by the super imposed smear of Chernov that trailed his movements like a delayed image tracing after. There was a glimmer of a face like rock with sharp eyes, and then another slower glimpse of the withered body from the bed on the other side of the world.

"Where is she?" Chernov asked, sneering at the shield around them.

"You're still bound," Zee said, almost having to shout over the whooshing roar.

"Where is she?" He repeated.

Zee tightened her grip on Luke's arm with one hand and raised the other, running her fingers through the water around them like a knife. It rained down into the bath with a loud splash and the voices of the circle stuttered as they reappeared, soaked and ruffled. Johnny stepped forward and then was pulled back again by Cameron and Sam. Nadia stood at the side of the bath and Luke went still in Zee's hand for a long moment. Then he roared and surged up and Zee heaved herself forward, tackling his body back into the water.

Chernov stretched at his bonds and Maria gasped as he seemed about to pull free of the cage of Luke's skin, like some kind of immaterial alien bursting forth. Zee shook at Luke's shoulders and he settled into place again.

Nadia was clear as crystal, somehow vanishing in the eerie light of the growing eclipse and somehow sharpening at the edges. Zee could almost have imagined making an outline of the space she occupied in the yard, could almost pretend that her aunt was casting a shadow on the grass.

"You wasted your life hiding from me," Chernov spat up at her.

I wasted nothing. You wasted your life searching for me, Nadia said.

"There is no hell. No heaven," Chernov said, Luke's teeth snapping with the words. "We are going to the same place at the end of today."

Maybe.

"Nadia," Zee whispered, heart thumping too heavy in her chest.

Nadia's sheer gaze landed on her, smile faint but full. *Maybe*, she repeated and a breeze of air brushed at Zee's cheek, smelling sweet from the garden and salty from the sea.

"Your time has passed Kazimir Chernov of Olensk," Sam said, voice low and heavy with authority.

Chernov yanked at Zee's grip on Luke's arms, but Zee held on.

"Ya izgonyayu tebya," Zee and Cameron said together. "Move on."

Chernov tried to growl, but Luke's mouth twisted and then pressed shut, trapping the sound. The water in the tub began to steam and sting at Zee's skin.

"Your time has passed Kazimir Chernov of Olensk," the circle said in unison. "My izgonyayem vas. Move on."

"Enough!" Chernov managed to shout through Luke's lips before he made a strangling sound, sagging against Zee and whimpering. "Please," he begged. "Please stop."

"Your time has passed Kazimir Chernov of Olensk," Zee whispered in her cousin's ear as the chant built up around them. "My izgonyayem vas. Move on."

"Stop!" Luke bellowed, wrestling for control in Zee's tight embrace. Their legs slipped in the water, knees sliding out and water splashing into their faces. "Stop it!" screamed Luke as the bath bubbled, a horrible heat building in the stirring current.

"Your time has passed Kazimir Chernov of Olensk," said the circle.

"It's almost over, it's almost over," Zee promised. Her hands slipped over Luke's back and where their cheeks pressed together felt warm enough to start a fire.

My izgonyayem vas. Move on. Nadia's words made the air rush around them.

"She's coming with me!" Chernov snarled. Luke's legs wrapped around Zee's body and threw them to the side. Zee's elbow and the back of her head smacked against the frame of the too tight tub and then Luke's hands were trying force her down into the water.

"Zee!" Johnny shouted from the circle.

"Your time has passed Kazimir Chernov of Olensk," Zee said, spitting water as she spoke, the taste of rosemary and sagebrush and juniper burning and bitter on her tongue.

"My izgonyayem vas. Move on," the circle continued and Johnny stayed in line.

"She's coming with me," Chernov said, his borrowed hands around Zee's throat.

"Maybe," Zee said, voice tight. She stared up at the strange and brilliant light of the shadowed sun overhead. "Maybe not."

Chernov stretched his shape inside of Luke again and the hands at Zee's throat loosened. His face twisted away from Luke's and he made a soundless scream up at the sun, face tearing into a deep wince at what he saw.

Unbind him, Nadia said as the circle carried the chant. *It's time.*

Zee reached up for Luke's wrists, felt the little knot of power over his pulse and loosened them. Luke started to pull away and there were phantom hands that remained, large and gray and knotted with age. Zee repeated the same at Luke's neck, at the top of his head, at the base of his spine, until Luke was leaning away, panting against the side of the tub. The ghost of Chernov remained, pinning Zee to the floor of the tub, his edges ragged as the light of the eclipse overhead shone through him.

"Your time has passed Kazimir Chernov of Olensk," Luke whispered, voice raw and panting for breath.

You have not saved her, Chernov rumbled in Zee's head.

"You were never going to follow the deal," Zee said. There was no pressure on her throat now, but she could feel his grip in her chest, making breath come thin and short.

He grinned above her, or snarled, or opened his jaws wide to swallow her whole, but the distorted sun tore through the open maw and widened the brilliant gash of light.

Zee took a gasping breath and Luke took her hands in a tight grip. The moon layered over the sun and the island shuddered beneath them and an enormous wave of power ran in a spiral around the circle. It was power made of the light above them, and the sea surrounding them, and a strange kind of safety Zee had never imagined finding with the group of people that stood guard over her family. It kicked up the air and leaves and grass around them and she could see it pass over every face in the circle. The feeling, the *knowing*, of magic. The race in the heart and the drumming beat in the blood and the spinning in the head. The feeling of running down the hill, your feet too fast to command beneath you. The wondering if the rush would ever slow.

It happened so gradually she almost didn't catch the change at first. Chernov vanished first in shades, and then in the bitter smell like a blown fuse passing out of the air.

The water in the bath settled and cooled against Zee's raw skin and she released a relieved little moan, sinking back against the wall of the tub, chin bobbing in the water.

"Zee?" Johnny said.

"He's dead. He's gone," Luke said, his own head dropping backwards over the wooden edge.

Zee's skin ached like a burn and Luke's knee was pressing sharply against her spine, but she was certain she wouldn't be moving in the next few minutes.

"I'm okay," Zee said, answering Johnny's actual question. "Settle in. We need to stay here until the eclipse is over."

Everyone held still for too long and Zee scanned their faces. Half of them were pale and shocked and the others looked hungry with curiosity. Johnny and Sam looked like they were itching, mad with wanting to break the circle.

"Sit," Zee said, uncertain if she felt amused or irritated or absurdly touched. Luke snorted.

One by one they sat. Nadia too, kneeling at the side of the tub. She reached a gossamer hand into the water and Zee sighed as it turned pleasantly cool against her feverish skin. The other hand reached back to Sam in the circle.

"Don't go," Sam whispered to Nadia.

"You don't have to," Zee said. "He's gone. You're safe."

You're safe, Nadia echoed gently. *It's time for me to go.*

"You're safe," Zee said, flinching at the tears gathering in her eyes. "So stay."

Only until the moon passes, Nadia said.

"Please," breathed Sam.

Ghosts have unfinished business ved'mitchka, and now I have none.

Zee could see Grace Harper through Nadia, eyes lowered to the ground, hands held loosely by Maria and Eric wearing smooth and sympathetic expressions.

You have something here, Nadia said, *and it is more than I could have dreamed of for you. Let it fill up the corners of this house. Of the island. The greatest part of me will always remain with you.*

Zee couldn't speak, her chest and throat and tongue glued shut by emotion, by the exposure of their audience, and being overwhelmed with the day. But she refused to close her eyes and lose any remaining time with her aunt. So she soaked in the bath, Luke settling into her side so he could hold her, and she let the tears spill.

Nadia passed on in silence, sunlight cutting through the red of her hair, her smile lasting until the end.

* * *

Johnny and Luke found her sitting on her bed in front of her window, rubbing burn cream into the pink and sore skin of her legs.

"We can ask the others to leave," Luke said from the doorway. He looked worse off than she did, although better than he had while Chernov had rented his body for the day.

Zee reached her arm out behind her and she sighed as they came up to the bed and settled against her back. Downstairs, Maria was exclaiming *loudly* how full of shit she thought they all were when she'd arrived that morning.

"They need this," Zee said. "You've got to unwind after a ritual and this was...a doozy. Is Sam working?"

"I can't tell if she's baking or brewing potions but whatever it is Cameron is nearly tripping her while trying to help," Johnny said. His arms were circling cautiously around her and Zee eased the way by snuggling in tighter, drawing Luke to her chest and starting to apply the cream to his skin.

"She needs this too," Zee said.

"But if you need them to clear out..." Luke continued.

He'd been the focus of some awkward attention from Maria and Grace after the circle had broken up and Zee honestly wasn't sure if it was because he had been possessed, or because he was the third in her and Johnny's love story.

"It's not that, I just..." she wasn't sure what exactly.

Johnny kissed down the side of her face, gentle and soft. "You need processing time."

She bristled for a moment. Johnny didn't tense this time and when she twisted in his hold she found him smiling, something small and mischievous like he was waiting for her correction.

She *did* need processing time. "You think you know me that well now, huh?" she asked, raising an eyebrow.

He grinned. "I dunno. Do I?"

She tried to bury her smile, but he was looking pleased with himself so she was probably failing. "I love you," she said, just to throw him off a little.

Sure enough his eyes grew big and his grin bubbled into something giddy and loose. And the feeling echoed in her heart.

"Love you too, pixie," he said. "You want me to go get you a brownie?"

"N- yes, please," she said, and she lifted her cheek for his kiss as he left Luke and her in bed.

Luke lay against her, legs hanging off the edge of the bed, content and lazy for a long time. She breathed him in, hunting for that deep woods smell beneath all the herbal stink of the bath they had both taken.

"Are you alright?" she asked finally.

"I told you, Zoya," he said, mild, voice a little shredded from the day. "You're more powerful than you realize. He should have feared you."

Zee huffed in annoyance. "Power doesn't change

anything. I'm still just the island witch. I'm still going to run the Lab with Sam and-"

"I know," Luke said, turning over her, pressing her down into the mattress, smile brilliant and full. "I *know*. I've seen those dreams too. I know what we will be. Here, together, with Johnny. I love you, Zoya Lane."

Oh. She sighed, and when she couldn't stop herself, smiled back. "I love you, too, Lucas Wolfe."

"Where should we hide until our burn mark gets back?" Luke asked, lifting an eyebrow.

"The tub," Zee said. She nipped at his smile with her lips and teeth and said, "I want to see if it fits three."

Epilogue

October 5th, 2017

Maria James passed Zee the other end of a string of fairy lights and together they hung them in front of the dark patterned curtains that made the Fortune Teller's tent. Behind them the activity in Odd Fellow's hall reached a crescendo as all of the animatronic 'hauntings' went off at the same time while Eric cackled like a mad scientist behind the control panel. Will and Sam, both victims of the robotic werewolves they had been setting up, flipped him off in unison.

Faith Ryan, the local elementary principal, approached Zee's tent like a skittish cat, jumping as she caught Zee's eye and then hurrying forward.

"I really appreciate you and your cousin putting so much work into our fundraiser," Faith said.

Sam was at the other side of the hall, arranging a station for kids to make herbal bath teas or Dark(chocolate) Magic Brownies with their parents. Zee had a feeling she knew which would be more popular.

"We're happy to help," Zee said.

Which was mostly true. They had been happy to help once Grace and Sarah and Maria had all made it clear that it wasn't really up to them.

"About the...readings you'll be doing," Faith Ryan said after clearing her throat nervously a few times.

Maria paused in her meticulous arranging of a set of crystals around the tea table. Zee watched her lips purse and her eyes narrow on the school principal.

"I have a special set of cards," Zee said before Faith could dig herself a hole or Maria could start one for her. "They're simplified, and very friendly."

"Perfect!" Faith said, overly bright. "That's perfect! Great. Okay."

Maria sighed, heavily, and Faith Ryan found a reason to be somewhere else.

"This island," Maria said with a roll of her eyes.

"I don't mind if I make them a *little* nervous," Zee admitted and the other woman laughed.

"We have a present for you."

Zee spun and found Johnny and Luke at the curtained entrance of her tent. Johnny was carrying a box wrapped in red and gold paper under his arm, while Luke fought a smug smile. Behind them Brian was walking in, watched by an avid Maria.

"Hang up this lantern for me," Maria said, passing Brian a decorative lamp that she could have easily hung herself.

"What's the occasion?" Zee asked, taking the box from Johnny, the weight of it surprising her.

"Us being the best boyfriends ever," Johnny said, grinning.

"And very, very clever," Luke added, darting forward to kiss her cheek.

Sarah had hooked Luke up with the property for his bookstore the week before, and Zee was fairly certain he'd worked a decent amount of magic to get his visa approved to stay in the country. But it was official. He was staying. They were a *thing* and it was an entirely new scandal for the island to gossip about. Zee had bought them a set of best boyfriend mugs but hadn't gifted them yet.

"Hmm," she answered, wrinkling her nose. But she ripped through the paper all the same and opened the white box inside. Her reflection, warped across the sphere, stared back at her.

"It's a crystal ball," Johnny said as Zee lifted it free.

There was a simple wooden stand still inside the box carved and darkly stained, but Zee set that aside to admire the globe in her hands. It was heavy and perfectly round with an almost unnoticeable glimmer of color running through it. It felt warm in her hands, and then suddenly icy cold, and it seemed to carry some kind emotional residue of...love.

"It's beautiful," Zee said, blinking. "You made it."

"Uhh we did, yeah. Will it work? If not, is it...is a decorative crystal ball kosher?" Johnny said, shifting in step at her side, his hands drifting from elbows to pockets to the back of his neck.

"Of course it will work," Luke snapped, grabbing one of the straying hands and locking it tight in his own.

Zee stepped forward, and they surrounded her. "It will work," she said, feeling stunned by their efforts, Luke teaching Johnny the ability to charge this glass with their feelings for her, the magic that flashed in her palms.

"You could use it tomorrow night at the fair, if you want," Luke said, returning her closeness, wrapping an arm around her.

"No, this should be personal," Zee said. "It's too...it means too much." She looked up and found them blushing. "I love it."

"Okay. Good." Johnny was nodding, softening with relief, grin growing.

"It's a full moon tonight," she said and his grin widened. "I'll charge it in the window."

"How soon can we leave?" Luke asked, and Brian snorted behind them.

* * *

Maria took over finishing Zee's booth with Brian. (Zee was pretty sure that they were dating and the only person who hadn't realized yet was Brian.) Johnny left his car behind for Eric and Will to drive and together the three of them walked back to the house by the island park trails. Zee stopped at each of the handblown witch balls they had made—innocently decorating the island's perimeter—so she and Luke could check the wards and renew the protective energy.

Nothing was interrupted. The island was safe again. But it felt good to check.

Johnny and Luke watched Zee crawl up her bed to set the crystal ball on its stand in her windowsill.

"This means a lot. You know that, right?" Zee asked.

They had made *magic* for her, Johnny was barely a beginner but she could feel his own flickering strength in the glass. She could feel ice spinning around the surface from Luke. It kissed at her fingertips and made her bedroom feel charged and safe.

"That was the idea," Luke said and she looked back to

see him tucking his smile away and shucking his shoes to the floor.

Johnny was tugging his shirt off the back of his neck. "Have I mentioned how much I like full moons?"

Zee smiled and folded her legs underneath her, reaching up to undo the buttons on her blouse. "I had noticed," she said.

"You tired?" Johnny asked. "Want a bath?"

She shook her head. "Maybe later. I'm just a little worn down. Got ideas for that?"

Luke hummed, shucking off his t-shirt with a shrug and then coming to join her on the bed. He leaned in, pushing gently at her shoulders until she was laying back. Johnny wasn't far behind, stumbling out of the legs of his pants and jumping in at her side. It was too early in the evening for moonlight, but Zee thought she might like the sunset fire colors burning over their skin even better. Johnny's hair was lit up orange like the first moment she had seen him and she reached up to run her fingers through the strands. Luke's dark hair looked like bright coals as he ducked down, peppering kisses on her shoulder.

"Relax, moon bloom," Luke whispered as she shivered at their touch.

"Let us take care of you, pixie," Johnny said, fingers loosening buttons as his mouth set small, damp fires lighting down her neck and across her chest.

"I will," she murmured, voice trailing off with an excited sigh.

Also by Kathryn Moon

Acknowledgments

I have the most amazing and enormous support team and I genuinely consider myself the luckiest person to know each and every one of these people.

My parents who have supported me in every possible way through this journey. Also Lindsay, who is essentially family in every way that matters.

My Moongazers for sticking to my side.

Incredible betas guiding me closer to the best possible version of this book- Alicia, Kristina, Cassna, Chloe, Emily, Meri!

Editor and friend, Sara Box for keeping me clean and readable and also sane.

Incredible cover artist Covers by Combs who brought Johnny, Zee, and Luke to life in this new cover!

My writing crews, a network that has grown and developed so much recently and left me feeling buoyed and hopeful about all of our futures.

Also I just need to give a special shout out to Lana for making my book trailer and Emma for listening to all my whines. You are both incredibly responsible for keeping me focused on the future and the joy of writing.

I really appreciate you all!

About the Author

Kathryn Moon is a country mouse who has been trying to write reverse harem since The Backstreet Boys had their first album. When her hands aren't busy typing they're probably knitting sweaters or crimping pie crust. She definitely believes in magic.

You can reach her on Facebook, hang out in Kathryn's Moongazers, and contact her at ohkathrynmoon@gmail.com!

 facebook.com/kathryn.moon.9022

 instagram.com/ohkathrynmoon

www.ingramcontent.com/pod-product-compliance
Lightning Source LLC
Chambersburg PA
CBHW061300190726
48288CB00002B/292